What's the scariest thing you can think of? Perhaps it's the loss of a loved one, a horrific wasting disease, or the prospect of financial ruin.

For Leonard Mango, the memory of the 23rd April 2031 is one that he's unlikely to forget. What began as an ordinary spring day took a macabre turn when he returned from a shareholder meeting. On entering his home, Mango discovered his partner Brent Wise hanging from the first-floor balcony, a velvet cord tied around his throat. He'd taken his own life.

What followed has been the subject of intense media speculation, with neither Leonard Mango or his associates publicly commenting on the matter. However, it's been reported that Mango descended into a deep depression for many months, and wasn't publicly seen until after the civil war. His first recorded appearance was on the day of the government's surrender, when he was photographed in an elevator with General Flint.

Sadly, the number of people seeking treatment for anxiety and depression has risen sharply since the outbreak of the civil war. Moreover, since 2030, the suicide rate of men between the ages of 22 and 30 has increased by 34%.

According to Dr. Beverley Moss, this phenomenon is directly linked to the horrors of the bloody conflict. "The civil war may be over, but it has cast a long shadow over our country," says Moss. "We are still many years away from delivering adequate provision for those individuals who have been scarred psychologically. A gulf is opening up between the escalating needs and the available treatments. It's a problem."

The People's Republic, meanwhile, insists that it has a robust plan for tackling these alarming statistics.

River looked away from the article. He hadn't meant to read it at all. He just needed a distraction.

He looked around. The room was a matte white, and there were no pictures on its featureless walls. A single line of brilliant-red chairs traced the perimeter, with a spotless glass table in the centre. It was on this table that River had spotted the beige magazine, folded open on the disturbing story.

River shuffled in his chair, uncomfortable. A long time had passed since his arrival. On entering the building, he'd been frogmarched into a lift by an officious-looking man in blue overalls, who said – in no uncertain terms – that inane chatter would not be tolerated. Which was fine. River had no interest in discussing the weather.

But he did need to pee.

"The counsellor will see you now," came the automated voice through the speakers. "Please make your way to the Chrysalis Chamber."

"Come on," said the man in overalls, tugging at River's torn sleeve. "This way."

River was led straight out of the lobby into a dazzling white corridor, lined with discrete single-panel doors. Each one was engraved with a glyph: River spotted an apple, a seahorse and a leaf as he was towed down the passage, including – much to his relief – the outline of a man, signposting the restroom. He'd make a note of that.

"In here," the man stated. They'd arrived.

"I thought I was going to the Chrysalis Chamber?" said River, perplexed.

"That's right. You're looking at it."

River frowned and inspected the glyph. "But that's a butterfly."

This didn't go down well. "Just go in."

None the wiser, River ceded to the grunt's instructions and stepped into the chamber. It was a white, floodlit cube with a desk, and a pair of cherry-red seats. River lowered himself into position and waited, alone.

He was face-to-face with a black disc, fixed to the wall opposite. Bars of coloured lights danced across its surface, with no real form or logic. But River recognised the design; a similar, smaller device was attached to his wrist.

"Welcome, young man," said a voice.

River looked around. Who was that? Was it the disc?

"Straight ahead, sir."

River snapped his gaze back to the lights.

"Thank you," the voice continued. "And hello." Its tones were male-sounding and robotic; it was the same voice that had summoned him to the chamber. "Please do not be alarmed. You are most welcome in our facility. Please confirm your name, age, and gender identity."

River gazed into the swirling patterns, curious. "Are you a TellMe?"

"In a manner of speaking," the disc responded. "Please confirm your name, age, and gender identity."

River took a deep breath. "My name is River Still. I am 22 years old. I identify as a boy."

There was a pause. "Thank you. And what would you like to talk about, River Still?"

River faltered. He needed a moment to gather his thoughts, so looked searchingly at his jeans. They were blue, torn and caked in mud.

"It looks like you have been through a lot," the disc observed. "Your clothes are damaged. Your eyes are red."

River raised his head, slowly. He stared at the pulsing lights. "So much has happened," he admitted.

"Perhaps you should talk about it. Just one small detail at a time. You are quite safe in this room."

Only if there's a toilet, thought River, conscious of his expanding bladder.

But he let the silence linger. Part of him wanted to test the machine. Was it capable of social awkwardness?

Finally, the disc spoke. "The Laputan monks of the Ashitakan Valley have a proverb," it offered. "'Though the wind blows, the river is still.' There is a storm raging within you, River."

River sighed deeply. This was not going to be easy.

"I'll tell you," he said. "But first, I need to take you back to my arrival in Neo Vale." He paused. "My life changed when I boarded that tram."

River Still
教えて

by Alex Skerratt

1: moving

5pm. The tram to Neo Vale was crowded, but River had been lucky enough to snag a seat. He'd been close to the platform edge when it cruised into the stand, and he swiftly shouldered his way into the carriage ahead of the anxious throng. Just as well, really; he needed to be close to a charging point for his cell phone, so made a beeline for a spot by the window.

Actually, he was taking up two seats. Not ideal on a rush hour tram with the commuters pressed together like cattle, but he was laden; his suitcase was bulky, and his guitar wasn't exactly thin.

Rain lashed against the tram's windows, and inside the moisture was steaming up the panels. River kept wiping the condensation away with his sleeve, but it was a wasted effort. He still couldn't see much. Just vague, shimmering shapes. But the colours were electric, and the scrapers' neon hues burned brightly against the black winter sky.

When the novelty of the window-wiping wore off, River turned his attention to his cell, and hooked up to the Nexus – the hyperweb. He'd never actually been to Neo Vale, but his favourite vloggers had: the likes of Wetchop, Arrowgance and Jazzmas T, each of them gushing into their cameras about the highs and lows of this pulsing suburb.

"So guys, if you *really* want a premium bathroom experience, it's official – the best toilets are at Kakeru's," proclaimed Jazzmas, as she vlogged at the entrance to the diner. "No ifs, no buts! Well – maybe a *few* butts."

River chuckled out loud – a bit awkward in a silent carriage (he had his headphones on.) Actually, it was *very* awkward; the granny opposite had just sent him the Death Stare.

"Anyway, I'm done for today guys," Jazzmas went on, "but don't forget to subscribe to my channel if you've enjoyed this video, or hit me up on Yapper and leave me a comment. And remember – less snoozing, more Jazz. Bye!"

River smiled as the closing card of Jazzmas' video popped up. He slipped out of his headphones and let them sit slackly on his shoulders.

"The next stop is Neo Vale," said the tram. "That's Neo Vale, your next station stop."

The TellMe on River's wrist buzzed. It was like a watch, but with a black face, and dancing oblongs of coloured lights. "Neo Vale," it stated. "Netherville suburb, population 51,004. The local time is 5:22pm. The temperature is 43. It is raining."

River raised his eyebrows. "You think?"

He scrambled out of his seat and strapped his guitar to his back. Now all he needed to do was make it to the other end of the carriage without killing anyone.

Especially the old woman.

The rain was pelting, and ice cold. River looked at the glistening streets. He needed to find a nighttime coffee shop called Sundown, as he'd been booked to give a performance. He raised his wrist strap and spoke. "TellMe, how do I get to Sundown Café?"

A three-dimensional map beamed out of the disc. "Sundown Café is 0.8 miles from your current location," it answered. "Head north for 0.7 miles, and then turn left."

"Almost a straight line," River commented. "Should be easy."

"Yes, River," said the TellMe. "Even you won't get lost on this journey."

River smiled and set off.

His wrist strap was invaluable - particularly here, where the streets were kind of hazy. They were well lit, just like the towers he'd seen on the tram, their buildings ablaze with blocks of electric colour. Karaoke bars, restaurants and shops made their presence known with the most dazzlingly-decorated storefronts, and neon signs cast their reds, yellows and pinks into the pavement puddles.

But the air was thick with a blue smog. At first, River thought it was an exhaust plume from the tram. But as he pressed further into town, he could see that the smoke was everywhere, ever-present.

It was odd. Was it weather? Or was something on fire?

River looked around. The pedestrians seemed unbothered. Each person he passed was cocooned in their own bubble, chatting absently into their TellMes, or else just lost in the glow of their cell screens.

As predicted, it didn't take River long to reach Sundown Café - cold, wet and tired as he was. He had two hours to kill, so he grabbed a small table in the far corner and treated himself to an almond mochspresso from the hovering drone. Followed by a trip to the bathroom.

They were nice toilets; Jazzmas would have been pleased. River finished up and headed to the sink, massaging his hands under the gush of hot water.

2

As the steam cleared, River looked nervously into the mirror. He grimaced. The rain had done a real number on his hair. He ran his fingers through the shaggy black strands and squeezed the droplets out of it. Then he assessed his clothes - a white tee, a maroon hoodie and black jeans.

He'd do.

"Hey, sorry," said River, almost colliding with a hovering drone as he emerged from the bathroom.

"It is no problem," the drone replied, gliding past him. "Have a nice day."

River watched the machine as it slipped into a toilet cubicle and closed the door. There was a toilet flush. Naturally.

By the time River took to the stage, a dazed selection of customers had ambled into the café. Some left again when they saw River donning his guitar. They'd come for coffee - not a concert.

River grabbed the mic. "Hi everyone, I'm River Still, I'm really excited to be here," he droned, not excited at all. "Anyway, I'd like to start with a cover from my favourite band - Two Spatulas and the Right Kind of Pan. Thanks."

River strummed into the first verse of 'Omelette.' He gazed at the handful of bored people as he caressed the strings, their faces lit up by the light of burning candles - one on each table. It was cosy.

All the while, swathes of blue smog rolled past the windows, their translucent shapes shifting as a guy in a hoodie approached the café door. He stopped at the window and peered through the glass.

River looked at him. He was probably in his twenties, his clothes oversized and dirty. He saw River immediately, and just stared. He looked vacant, melancholic - his white eyes glistening in the café glow. Was he crying?

"Thanks," said River, as his tenth tune came to a close. "Okay, so this is my last song for the evening. It's one I wrote, and it's called 'Choices.' Thank you for being wonderful and, uhh, a really awesome audience."

The awesome audience fell silent. He may have lulled them into a coma.

River sighed and wrapped his fingers around the neck of his guitar.

"A soldier on the beach tonight," he sang, "watches children laugh and play. Their eyes, they burn with fire and flame, and they skip, on the fringes of the fray..."

It was a gentle melody, and pensive. It sounded like a lullaby.

"A soldier on the riverbank," he went on, "as the clock strikes five to twelve, sees rockets kiss the crimson sky. He stands and waits, a watcher of the fray..."

River gazed at the young man in the hoodie. He was listening intently, and tears were trickling down his cheeks.

"I'm done with choices," sang River, "and the things I can't decide. I salute, and I wait, I soldier on. But a brand new day is dawning, slaying terrors of the night. And I'll see you, I'll be there. We'll meet again."

River bowed his head as the song ended. There was an awkward, guarded applause, and the guy outside drifted away into the wisps of smog.

Meanwhile the drone - having emerged from the toilets during the final verse - floated towards River.

"Please present your TellMe," it stated.

River lifted his wrist and pressed it against the machine. There was a melodious beep, and the TellMe glowed.

"There is your payment," said the drone. "Thank you for your services."

Fortunately, the rain had stopped by the time River stepped out into the cold night air. He glanced around, trying to get his bearings. He was meant to be lodging with a family called the Throwers, and they had an apartment above a ramen bar.

"TellMe," said River. "How do I get to Noodle Vale?"

"Noodle Vale is 0.5 miles from your current location," it replied. "Head south for 0.2 miles, and then turn left."

River began to walk. He gazed with fascination at the fog as he wandered the wet, neon-lit streets. "TellMe," he called out. "Why is the fog blue?"

His device paused for a moment. "I have no data on blue fog."

"But it's all around us," River pressed. "What's causing it? Is it the weather?"

"The weather in Neo Vale is clear and damp underfoot. There is a 30 per cent chance of precipitation."

River frowned. He wasn't satisfied with that response.

Nonetheless, he continued on his journey, following his TellMe into a side alley. There was a red, rusting water pump, some overflowing garbage cans and the Neo Vale bathhouse, its corrugated shutters graffitied and lowered.

There was also a man - a man in a hoodie. The same one from the café. He limped across River's path and staggered, tumbling into a pile of garbage bags.

"Hey!" River yelled and ran over. He crouched next to the man, whose arm was cut and bleeding. "What happened?"

The man gasped, wincing with the pain. "Nothing," he panted. "I just fell, that's all."

River stared at the gaping wound. "You've been cut."

"It's nothing! Leave me alone!"

"I'm not leaving you. You need an ambulance." River grabbed the guy's TellMe. "I'm transmitting your location."

"Augghhhhh!" the man screamed. He pushed River away. "Get off me! I don't need an ambulance!"

River looked again at the bleeding scar. "Did you do this to yourself?"

"I told you! I fell, you got that?"

River gulped. He couldn't decide what to do. "TellMe," he called out. "How do I treat a cut to the wrist?"

His wrist strap came to life. "First, please confirm that the patient can move their wrist."

River was about to answer when he heard the dull drone of an approaching vehicle. He looked up. It was a plain black van, its underside thrumming with an electric blue - the phosphorescent glow of its thrusters.

"Someone's coming," said River, as the van pulled up.

"What?" said the guy, panicked. He sprang to his feet. "No! No, leave me alone!"

River grabbed him. "Hey, cool it, you need help!"

A muscle-bound man in a blue jumpsuit leapt out of the cab, followed by an equally toned young woman. They looked like cops, but plain-clothes.

"Hey, this guy needs medical attention," River shouted. "Are you police? He's injured, and he's losing blood."

But the van people weren't listening. "It's alright, we'll take it from here," said the woman, grabbing the guy's arm. "Come on, let's get you home."

"No!" the man protested, struggling. "No, get off me! Let go! Nghhhhhhh!"

"Tranquiliser," said the woman, and the overalled man drove a needle into his arm. He passed out.

"What are you doing?" River yelled. "You can't do that!"

They bundled the bleeding guy into the van, and the woman slid the door shut. Head down, she made a beeline for the passenger cab.

"Hey!" River yelled. He banged on the window, and the guy lowered it. "Excuse me, I'm not invisible. Do you even know this man?" No answer. "Can you say something?"

5

"Sure," he replied.

River watched with astonishment as the black van sped out of sight, its blue glow enveloped by the rings of swirling smog.

And then silence.

10:30pm. A cold River staggered into Noodle Vale, his guitar catching on the doorframe with a tuneless thrum. He was relieved to have finally made it.

"Hello?" he called out.

He gazed at his new home. It was a vibrant place, with maroon walls and a tiled chequered floor. Crimson and chrome bar stools lined the main counter, and the restaurant's booths were furnished with red leather seats. The smell, meanwhile, was a sensory assault - a sizzling assortment of oils, meat juices and spice. River could tell he was going to like it here.

"Hello?" came a reply from the kitchen. River turned, and a man in chef's whites wandered into view. He was in his forties.

"Hi, I'm River," he said. "I'm sorry I'm late. I had a situation."

The man laughed. "Welcome to Neo Vale," he chuckled. "I'm Ben, Beanie's husband. I won't shake your hand 'cos it's covered in lobster."

"That's okay. Is Beanie around?"

"Yeah, she's upstairs, go straight up," Ben answered, pointing at a door marked 'Private.' "She'll be pleased to see you. She was getting worried."

River smiled apologetically as Ben wandered back into the kitchen. Grabbing his suitcase, he lumbered across the diner and through the door, which led to a narrow, dimly-lit staircase.

He felt bad about being so late, but his experience with the wounded guy had affected him. After they'd whisked him away, River took a seat in a nearby tram shelter to gather his thoughts, and calm down a little. He was confused, and angry. And the police didn't help. He'd phoned them, but they weren't interested. Without a registration plate, or the identity of the victim, there wasn't much they could do. Or, to put it more accurately, there wasn't much they *wanted* to do. This was nothing new. The cutbacks in the aftermath of the civil war were harsh. No crisis, no cop car. It was that simple.

"River, you're here," came a voice from the top of the stairs. "Gosh, I was so worried. Let me take your things."

So, this was Beanie. She seemed fun.

"Thanks, sorry I'm so late."

"Not at all," said Beanie, flapping her arms. "I was wondering if all the smog would make it harder for you."

She led him through to the living room.

"Yeah, what's with that?"

"It's perfectly harmless," Beanie reassured him. "Apparently it's a coolant leak from one of the towers. Isn't it pretty?"

River shrugged. "It's kind of annoying, actually. Has it been here long?"

"A couple of days I'd say? Now, feel free to treat this place as your own. You're paying for it after all." Beanie laughed. "Do you know how long you'll be staying?"

River thought. "I don't know," he admitted. "Maybe a couple of months. I'm sort of trying to decide what to do with my life."

Beanie laughed again. "Aren't we all? Well, no problem, River - you're welcome to stay for as long as you need. Are you a musician?"

"Yeah, off and on. I'm also a rider for Skidmark, so I figured I'd just transfer my contract to Neo Vale during my stay and earn some pocket money."

"That sounds sensible. Will you be needing a bike?"

River smiled. "Yeah. Sorry, I really haven't thought this through."

"Well, you can have Jake's old one. He was going to sell it anyway."

"Wow. Are you sure?"

"Yes of course. Now take that frightened look off your face and follow me."

Suitcase in hand, Beanie sped from the living room and led River down a narrow passageway. The grey walls were faded and stained, and the wallpaper was peeling at the edges.

"Speaking of Jake," Beanie went on, "you're going to be sharing with him."

"Oh yeah," said River, recalling the ad. "You said we're in bunks?"

"You are, it's a riot. Now, are you sure you'll have enough room here?"

"Yeah plenty," said River. "After two years of sleeping in barracks, this is like a palace."

Beanie smiled. "Oh, were you in the war?"

"Yeah, I was stationed at the Mantrecht Flats. No running water. Really bad sewage."

"That sounds horrible," Beanie acknowledged, her voice now a whisper. "Well, you have nothing to fear here. My sewage is excellent."

They stopped by a door at the far end of the corridor, just next to the bathroom.

"I'm talking quietly because Jake's asleep," Beanie explained. "He's fine with you sneaking in, though - I said you'd be arriving late."

"That's alright, I'll try not to disturb him."

"Now would you like a cup of tea or anything before bed? I have aqualeaf, lemon and ginger..."

"I'm fine thanks. I'm pretty tired, to be honest."

"Say no more. Oh, just a quick one - breakfast. I'll be serving it at eight, but if you want to sleep in, that's fine. Just help yourself to whatever you can find in the cupboards."

"Thanks."

"Goodnight River."

Beanie headed back to the living room. River watched with interest as she glided along the corridor, her blue and yellow poncho flapping ceremoniously as she swept out of sight. She was a very glamorous lady, with flowing orange hair that was peppered with streaks of silver.

Then, with caution, he grabbed the handle of the bedroom door and nudged it.

Fortunately, Jake had left one of the side-lamps switched on, so River could see. And boy could he see - unwashed clothes; stacks of films, games and schoolbooks; and a gently-humming PC, which was still active on a cluttered desk. Jake had also tethered a punch-bag to the end of his bunk, where it hung next to a pair of boxing gloves.

On the top bed, River could just make out a tangle of dishevelled orange hair, where Jake was lying with his back to the door, his sleeping bag rising to the mellow rhythm of his breath. He was asleep.

Or at least, he *appeared* to be asleep. As River crept closer to the bunk, Jake lifted his arm and waved it welcomingly.

"Hi," River whispered, a little awkward. He hoped he hadn't woken him.

Still, he'd try to be as quiet as possible. He freed himself from his guitar straps and slipped nimbly onto the bottom mattress. He couldn't be bothered to change his clothes. He was spent.

2: nightmares

River gasped. The city was collapsing around him. ~~In his ears the~~ The Blood-curdling screams of panicked civilians pierced his eardrums, and he had just one thought: run. Run as fast as you can and don't look back.

He turned onto a dusty, war-torn street, which was caked in ash and shards of glass. Up ahead, he could see the burning shell of an overturned tram, its destination: Mantrecht.

Blood-soaked bodies collapsed alongside him, slopping onto the sidewalk like sides of meat. Were they being chased?

Who cares? Don't look. Just run.

The cracked glass crunched under his boots as he tore towards the tram. There was an explosion - perhaps in a neighbouring street - and the civilians were thrown to the ground as the earth trembled beneath them.

River was thrown into a pile of blistering shards, and the skin on his palms was split wide open, but he didn't bleed.

A man screamed. "Ryū!"

River woke up, panting. Was that a memory? A dream?

Somehow, he'd worked his way off the bunk and onto the bedroom floor, where he now lay in a tangle of old clothes. And, as he discovered, a half-eaten bowl of chicken katsudon, which had glued itself to River's sock.

Unimpressed, River shook the gunk off his foot and sat up, his heart pounding. He was dripping in sweat.

Fortunately, Jake had already left. Although that wasn't necessarily a good thing; River had no idea how long he'd been splayed across the bedroom floor. The chances were, Jake had been forced to climb over his body on his way to breakfast.

It was a good job he hadn't slept naked...

"TellMe," he mumbled, wearily. "What time is it?"

"The time is 08:05," the device answered. "Good morning, River."

River grunted and rubbed his sore eyes. Five past eight. He could join Beanie for breakfast.

His heart slowing, River stood up and wiped the creases out of his shirt, and rubbed the sweat from his wiry black hair. It saved showering.

Then he inched his way down the hall, following the sweet scent of hot tea and porridge.

Jake was already at the table when he entered the living room. His head was a mass of thick orange hair which was knotted and unkempt, and his eyes were glued to his phone's social feed.

"River, you're up," Beanie proclaimed, as she laid a bowl of okayu on the table. "How did you sleep?"

"On the floor," quipped Jake, not looking up from his cell.

"What?" said Beanie. "Why did you sleep on the floor? Was there something wrong with the bed?"

River smiled, bashfully. "I kinda had a nightmare," he admitted. "It's okay though, I don't get them often."

"Who's Ryū?" asked Jake, still lost in his screen.

River paused. "What?"

"You were just shouting for someone called Ryū," Jake went on. "I figured it was someone you knew?"

"Now Jake, leave him alone," said Beanie, as she set down the last of the breakfast bowls. "River, you need sustenance after the night you've had. Take a seat."

"Or, you know - you can have the floor if you want," said Jake. He flashed River a cheeky grin.

River smiled back.

"Hush everyone," said Beanie. She took her seat at the table. "Let's pray." Beanie closed her eyes, and slowly inhaled. "O great Laputa, goddess of star-fire and love, meet with us, we pray."

River felt a little awkward; he'd never met a Laputan before. He didn't know what to do. But then, neither did Jake, by the looks of it. He'd returned to gazing at his phone.

"Our table is your table, great Laputa," Beanie went on, her head bowed reverently. "Please join us at this bountiful feast, O goddess, which we present to you with thanksgiving and joy. Bless us, we pray. In the name of the Pantheon. Kunchan."

"Kunchan," Jake repeated. He then turned to River. "Is this your first Laputan meal?"

"Kinda," River admitted.

"No worries. So, at this point it's traditional to stroke the face of the person next to you, like this." He caressed River's cheek. "Kunchan. Now do it to me."

"Jake Thrower, you're incorrigible," snapped Beanie. She smiled sympathetically at River. "Take no notice."

"Wow, your cheeks are soft," said Jake. "Do you moisturise?"

"I think that's sweat."

"I'm afraid my son has little time for the Laputan tradition," Beanie interjected. "It's not 'cool' to be religious these days."

"Mother, nobody's religious these days."

"That's true. I'm the only Laputan in Neo Vale."

"What made you become Laputan?" River enquired. "If you don't mind me asking?"

"Not at all," said Beanie. "It actually goes back to my student days. I was doing a research project in the Ashitakan Valley - long before it was decimated, of course. Anyway, I was 21, single and searching for meaning. To cut a long story short, the indigenous people rescued me from the clutches of a rabid swamp bear."

"You fell into its dam, right?" Jake mumbled, his mouth clogged with okayu.

"Yes, and there was a whole pack of the beasts lying in wait," Beanie continued. "I should have been killed. In fact, my survival was so miraculous that the Ashitakan tribe put it down to divine intervention, and it was impossible to disagree."

"That's incredible," said River, wiping the porridge from his lips.

"Yes, I thought so too. When I realised that my survival could only be explained by supernatural means, I gave my life to the goddess Laputa. Do you see that effigy?"

River glanced across the table, where the knitted doll of a young woman was sitting.

"She was bequeathed to me by the Laputan monks," Beanie explained. "Dolls and figurines are powerful objects in their tradition. This one is a representation of the goddess herself, and it's believed that her spirit inhabits the doll at the dinner table. Provided she's invited with humility, of course."

Jake's phone vibrated. He picked it up and read the notification. "Oh, sis's train has been cancelled," he announced. "She says she'll be back for dinner though."

"Ah that's a shame," Beanie replied. "I'd hoped you'd get to meet her, River."

"That's okay, I'll be around tonight."

"Excellent. Now Jake, I told River that he could use your bike for his deliveries," said Beanie. "Could you leave it out for him?"

River wasn't exactly desperate to leap back onto the saddle, but it would give him some cash whilst he hunted for gigs. Plus, working for Skidmark would keep him in shape.

It was a simple premise: hungry customers would order dishes from their favourite restaurants, and River would pick them up and deliver, all on his bicycle. Well - Jake's bicycle. And whilst his TellMe would be able to direct him to his destinations, River knew that a little local knowledge would be handy as well.

So, after breakfast, he stepped out into Neo Vale's crisp morning air, ready to explore its smog-ridden streets.

They were electric - bustling, and ablaze with colour. River weaved in and out of preoccupied pedestrians, each contained within a bubble of indifference. Even when the robot garbage truck sounded its horn the masses were reluctant to disperse, and River was almost flattened as he stumbled into the vehicle's path.

Eventually he reached a wide-open space. Central Square was like an oasis in the desert, lined with sweet-smelling pastry booths and baristas. At the far end, a broad set of steps led down to the Neo Vale subway, flanked on each side by octagonal newsstands. They danced with fast-moving shapes and slogans; each of its surfaces was a screen, relaying content from news channels and brands. One vidcast gushed over a gloopy-looking soft drink that could 'fuel you better than food,' whilst another promoted the popular tech company, Mango. 'You'll like us - we're positive,' said the ad.

River wandered over.

He hit the synch button on his headphones and put them on. The sound from the newsstand flooded his ears.

General Flint - the President of The People's Republic - was engaged with a reporter. "I'm not avoiding the question, Sanjay, you've made a very valid point," he said, cool and composed. "What my government wants for the people of this country is to take back control of mental health, take back control of these debilitating illnesses and say, look - there *is* a hope, there *is* a future. A diagnosis of clinical depression or generalised anxiety is not a lifelong sentence."

"But the previous government made similar promises and spectacularly failed to buck the trend," said Sanjay, his brow furrowed.

"And that is why we've pledged an extra one billion credits in funding that will see a decline in these troubling statistics," Flint answered. "Look, I said previously that we are actively developing a programme to cure any mental illness at the point of first contact."

"How do you propose to do that though? Surely there's no one-size-fits-all approach when it comes to tackling the complex issue of mental health?"

"You're right when you say it's complex," Flint answered, "and I look forward to explaining more about this government's strategy over the course of the next few weeks."

River de-synched his headphones and stepped away. He didn't have time for The People's Republic.

He found himself in a more subdued side street, where a mail drone was delivering post to the suburb's picture house. River teetered on the edge of the sidewalk, waiting patiently for the tram to clear his path.

As the warm glow of the carriage trailed out of sight, River glimpsed Ezra's 24 Hour Bar and Grill, where a female cyborg was sucking on a chrome vaping device. Her bright green hair was cropped and jagged, and a studded black choker was fastened around her neck.

River quickened his pace, keen to avoid her gaze.

He failed.

"Hey cutie," the lady shouted, as she caressed the wall of Ezra's. "Where you goin' in such a hurry?"

River stopped and looked curiously at his admirer. Her LED eyes radiated the most brilliant electric blue, penetrating him with a strange, hypnotic gaze.

"I'm just exploring the neighbourhood," said River, plainly. "I moved here yesterday."

The cyborg laughed. "You moved to Neo Vale?" She sounded surprised. "Of your own free will? Is there somethin' wrong with you?"

River scowled. "I just wanted a fresh start. My dad used to love this place before the war, and I-"

"Yeah, yeah, yeah," said the woman, dismissive. "Come on, tell me - what do you like about Neo Vale? What is it? The gangs? The oppression? The smog?"

"I don't like the smog," River admitted. "It gives me the creeps. Apparently it's a coolant leak?"

The woman rolled her cybernetic eyes. "Wake up, kid. Does this look like a coolant leak to you?"

River hesitated. How would he know?

"Look," said the cyborg, standing up straight. "You seem nice. But this ain't a place for nice people. Take my advice and get the hell outta town."

River sighed. What kind of advice was that? "I can't leave," he rebutted. "I've only just got here."

"So what? Trust me hombre, this place is poison."

"You have a new message," said his TellMe, saving River from an argument. "Would you like to hear it?"

River glanced at his wrist. "I need to check this."

"No worries, I was just leavin'," said the cyborg. She concealed her vaper and inched towards River. The LEDs in her eyes morphed into a luminous pink. "Just so you know, I can be found on this corner most nights. So, look me up if you fancy getting to know me better."

River smiled wryly. "But I thought you told me to get the hell outta town?"

The cyborg sneered. "Oh, he's cute *and* he's funny! Why not save that tongue for tonight?"

The lady walked away, and River looked again at his wrist strap. "Okay TellMe," he said. "What's the message?"

"It's from Skidmark. Message reads: 'Hi, thanks for registering your change of address. Your first shift will begin at 6pm. Thank you for choosing us. Hit subscribe and stay regular.' Message ends."

River nodded. This was good news.

"Can I help with anything else, River?"

He didn't know; he wasn't sure what to do with himself now. Should he explore the street some more? Beyond Ezra's, there didn't seem to be much happening; it was kind of barren.

River was about to ask for recommendations when a black van cruised past him. Its vivid blue thrusters were instantly familiar. It was just like the van from last night.

River watched it keenly, but after a few moments it vanished into the velvety fog.

Seconds later, there was a scream. Was it his cyborg friend? Without thinking he ran, tearing in the direction of the anguished cry, his heart pumping in his chest.

He clapped eyes on the green-haired cyborg. She was being wrestled into the hovering van by two thugs in overalls.

"Help me, please!" she yelled. The grunt threw her into the compartment and slammed the door in her face.

River froze.

Suddenly he was back on the battlefield, back in the war-torn ruins of the city that had plagued his dreams. River had taken refuge behind an overturned tram, his fists clamped to the mangled frame as he searched desperately for a plan. The ground beneath his knees continued to tremble, lifting shards of grey ash into a plume around his face.

There was a scream. The civilian alongside him - a woman - was being dragged away by an unseen force, her face white with terror as she clung to the carriage.

"Help me, please!" she cried.

But it was too late. Someone, or something, tore her out of sight. There was a roar. Flesh was ripped. The woman fell silent.

River blinked. He was back in Neo Vale, and a man in blue overalls was scrambling into the driver's cab.

14

"Hey!" River shouted. He seized the van's handle, hell-bent on tearing it from its socket.

But it was no use. The vehicle had already powered up its thrusters and was pulling away. River watched helplessly as it performed a perfect three-sixty and sped into the city mist.

This was messed up. Who the hell was taking these people? And why?

River didn't feel like talking when he returned to Noodle Vale. He'd done his best to distract himself that afternoon, taking in the local library, the cyborg sushi bar, and even renting a karaoke booth for one. This had proven rather expensive, and not very helpful. He kept seeing black vans wherever he went, even when they were pink.

So, after he'd fought his way through the throngs of Noodle Vale's diners, he made a beeline for his bunk, wanting nothing more than to close his eyes and rest.

And Beanie Thrower, it seemed, had read his mind. As he stepped into the unbridled chaos of Jake's bedroom, his eyes were met with a welcome sight. His bed was freshly made, adorned with clean quilts and newly-puffed pillows.

And on top of the sheets, Beanie had left him a note. 'Hope you sleep better tonight,' she scrawled, signing off with a smiley face.

River smiled, touched that a stranger would be so kind. He folded the note and collapsed onto the covers, his mind awash with vans and kidnappings and monsters and men and women and... everything. All of it. Every fear and fright and inexplicable horror was hounding his over-crowded brain. River needed rest, and fast. At 6pm, Skidmark was expecting him to start his first shift in Neo Vale.

At night.

In the dark.

Pray for me Beanie, he thought. *Pray for me.*

River rolled over and closed his eyes.

15

3: unknowns

GIRIGIRI! GIRIGIRI!

River was awoken by a hoarse vibration - the unmistakable whirr of his phone.

He sat up sluggishly, and fumbled for his wrist strap.

"TellMe," he croaked. "What's the message?"

"Good evening, River," the device answered. "You have a new message from Skidmark on your cell. Message reads: 'Hey River! Are you ready for your first shift? Login with your access code, and we'll direct you to your first pick-up. Exciting times! At Skidmark, we never stop peddling.' Message ends."

River let out a groan and scratched the sleep from his eyes.

Exciting times? No, Skidmark - excitement was a month-long vacation on the isle of Maya, not an eight-hour bike ride through a creepy, smog-filled town, with black vans at every turn.

Reluctantly, he sat up. And banged his head on Jake's bunk.

It didn't take River long to locate Jake's bike, which he'd left in the yard behind Noodle Vale. Beanie had gushed over him as he'd stepped, fully uniformed, into the living room, his Skidmark satchel strapped to his shoulders. She fussed over how smart he looked, and held him tightly as she prayed for protection.

And now, as River wheeled Jake's bike onto the sidewalk, an image flashed before his eyes. He was suddenly peddling through the streets of Zen Kappa, his dad gripping the handles and grinning. "That's it, son!" he cried. "You're doing it!"

It was bittersweet. River blinked, and brought himself back. Some things were best forgotten.

With his cell phone clamped to his handlebars, he set off into the smog, head down and determined. Orders were flashing up on his phone, and he accepted one from Ryo's - a restaurant on the outskirts. He gave the destination to his TellMe, and the device guided him towards the pick-up point.

It wasn't the nicest part of town. In fact, Ryo's looked like a dope den; its small windows were shielded by scraps of old newspapers which had been plastered to its panes, and its pink neon sign blinked its death throes. Outside, an unconscious beggar was slumped in the doorway, whilst a hungry rodent feasted on his slab of mushroom pizza.

It was intimidating, for sure. River magno-locked his bike to a nearby pole, lowered his head and marched purposefully towards the cracked glass door.

Inside, the restaurant was dingy. As River entered, the scant collection of robot diners turned from their dishes and stared. A flat, malfunctioning video screen was affixed to the restaurant's ceiling, and its oscillating colours bathed the joint in swirling pools, revealing the chipped brown walls and stained linoleum floor.

At the take-out counter, two skinless androids were locked in a passionate embrace, panting heavily as they kissed and caressed. Feeling a little awkward, River crept closer, clearing his throat as he arrived at the cash register.

"I've come to collect for Natsuki Hashino," he stated.

The two androids broke away. The black one sighed with despair and glared at the ceiling. "You deal with it, Grey," it groaned. "I gotta powder my nose."

The white android looked squarely at River. "You got a collection code?"

"789-2129," River answered. "But my friends call me Food."

Grey glared at him, unimpressed. It swivelled and reached for a ribbed aluminium case, which was nestling under the grill's hot pool of light. "I haven't seen you around here before," it noted, as River slipped the searing pouch into his satchel.

"No, I'm new," said River, bluntly. "Let me guess. You want me to leave Neo Vale as soon as possible and never come back?"

"No," Grey retorted. "I wish you'd never come."

The robot turned and glided away. River glowered as it followed its lover into the restroom.

He snorted. He thought about the android's rudeness as he went to unclamp his bike. In many ways, it was understandable; relations between robots and people were uneasy at best. AIs had sided with the government in the final days of the civil war and, of course, the government had been overthrown. Today, many people considered them traitors, and rarely trusted them.

Equally, robots showed little warmth towards their human creators, looking down on their perceived lack of intelligence. River never stood a chance in Ryo's.

He peddled on and soon arrived at his next destination. Nightfall Court was a squalid apartment block that stretched for sixty-five storeys. Its outer walls had been graffitied with spray paint, and a torn flag - the symbol of the old government - hung limply above its entrance.

River dismounted and stepped gingerly towards the door, Natsuki Hashino's order in hand.

Inside, Nightfall Court was like a prison complex, its uncarpeted floor stained with pools of vomit. And the odour of human fluids hounded River as he climbed the concrete stairs, all the while praying that its stench was not contagious.

As he arrived on the fourteenth floor, River scanned the doors in search of Natsuki's flat.

But he was distracted by the dull suggestion of chatter, drifting playfully from the far end of the hall. River inched closer, seeing nothing but a vending machine and a robot hoover. The former had the shape of an upright cat, with feline ears attached to its top panel, and a chunky black cable that curled like a tail.

"We don't think you should be up here," the vending machine growled.

The vacuum cleaner raced forward. "Listen to Prowley," it concurred. "Floor fourteen is Robot Central. That means *no* fleshers. You got that?"

River gazed at the unlikely pair. "Chill," he answered. "I'm just delivering food."

"Oh *chill* – because I'm a refrigerator!" Prowley sneered. "You hear that Buster? The guy thinks he's funny!"

River was annoyed. "What are you talking about? Move it."

"No!" said Buster, whizzing into his path. "I think *you* should move it! What do you think, Prowley?"

"I think you've nailed it, Buster. Looks like there's a speck of dirt that needs tidying up."

River rolled his eyes. "Right. So you guys are malfunctioning."

Buster leaned forward. "Are you saying we're mad?"

"No, you're crazy. I get the picture."

"Wrong," said Buster. "You get my hose!"

Like a ninja, Buster unleashed his nozzle and coiled it around River's legs, yanking him to the floor.

"What the-?" River shouted.

Prowley lumbered forward with his machine door flapping.

"Put him on ice!" Buster yelled, and Prowley poured ice chips onto River's face.

"Nghhhhhhh!" he cried.

"Chilled enough for you?" Prowley teased.

"Get off me!" River protested.

"Aw, poor flesher's got ice on his face," Buster taunted, his vacuum hose now binding River like a snake. "What do you think, Prowley?"

18

"It looks like someone could use a spring clean."

River's eyes widened as Buster's nozzle dangled over his cheeks.

"Hey guys, I've just had a thought," River shouted.

"Oh yeah?" Prowley snarled. "About what?"

"About how he's nothing but a pathetic, powerless peewee?" Buster jeered.

"No, I'm just thinking about electricity," River went on. "You guys must really depend on it to function."

"Yeah," said Buster. "So what if we do?"

There was a gentle hum. And the two machines fell silent.

"Thought so," said River, unravelling himself from the hose. "Thanks for clarifying."

Scrambling to his feet, he looked across at the beautiful young woman who had cut the power. He smiled. "Thank you," he said, brushing the ice off his jacket. "Another few seconds and I'd have been suckered."

The lady bowed. "You are most welcome," she uttered, her voice delicate like a whisper. "You have food?"

River glanced at the squashed motsunabe. "Well, kinda," he admitted. "Are you Natsuki Hashino?"

The lady looked confused. "I am," she replied. "How did you know that?"

"I have your order." River looked again at the unappetising heap. "Kinda..."

"My order?" Natsuki followed his gaze. "How intriguing."

"It doesn't normally look so faecal..."

"I am sure." Natsuki smiled at him. "Forgive me, but I might decline your meal on this occasion."

River grinned back. "It's because I forgot the napkins isn't it?"

"It's not really that," she answered. "But my mother has a saying. 'In Nightfall Court, one should not eat off the floor. One will catch hepatitis.'"

River laughed. "Your mom's fun. Although you should probably warn her about the robots as well."

"They are normally well-behaved. Unfortunately, there is a grumpy old android who lives in apartment nineteen. He has a habit of altering the robots' prime directives, making them hostile to humans."

"I guess we all need a hobby," River replied, scooping up the mangled motsunabe. "Look, I'll head back to Ryo's and pick up some more food."

"Please do not worry," Natsuki answered. "I have not long eaten."

"Are you sure? You wouldn't like something with a little less floor?"

"It's no problem, really. But thank you for the offer." She paused. "And it was very good of you to come."

River raised his phone. "I was only doing my job."

"Your job?"

River chuckled. "Well, if you can call Skidmark a job."

"I certainly shall," said Natsuki. "Thank you, deliverer-san."

"Oh, River Still."

She bowed. "Thank you, River Still." She paused and looked quizzically at his hair. "Do you mind if I say something personal?"

"Of course not."

Natsuki stepped closer, her eyes fixed on his tangled locks. "It looks like you have some ice in your hair. Would you like me to remove it?"

River shrugged. "Feel free."

Natsuki grazed her fingers tenderly through the unkempt strands. Fragments of ice fluttered to the floor.

"Nice," said River. "Uh, I mean – ice! The ice is, uhh, all gone! Very nice of you, thanks."

Natsuki's cheeks began to glow. "You are most welcome."

River turned. "Right, I'd better go." He started to walk, and promptly collided with the robot vending machine.

Natsuki giggled.

River shook his head. "This thing's still causing trouble," he quipped, trying to mask his embarrassment. "Nice to meet you, Natsuki."

Natsuki bowed once more. "It was a pleasure to make your acquaintance, River Still."

The young lady turned and scurried into her flat, closing the door and locking it.

River looked closely. A message had been sprayed onto its panel. 'DROP DEAD FLESHER,' it said.

The wisps of smog felt thicker than ever as River peddled his way through Neo Vale. It was quiet, and the streets were empty. Perhaps a little too empty.

Fortunately, his next collection was hassle-free. River wasn't attacked by any robot vacuum cleaners as he picked up a crispy bacon frothshake from Kakeru's. The destination, however, was some distance, with River's TellMe pointing to a house in the neighbouring suburb of Howling - a round trip of eighteen miles. It wasn't a trip he wanted to make.

So, he pulled up in Central Square and bought a bagel from one of the robot retailers, gnawing his way through the zesty onions and rind as he searched for a get-out plan.

River gazed at the steady ebb of citizens, the salty meat-juices from his bagel splattering onto his chin. It was busier here; many people were spilling out of the Neo Vale subway, macintoshed men and women with suitcases and cell phones. He counted five in all, each thumbing their screens in an ardent frenzy, looping in, touching base, and securing last-minute sales.

And then a thought occurred to him. How wrong was it for a Skidmark rider to deliver by train? It had to be quicker than cycling.

He'd risk it.

River leapt up and wheeled his bike across the concourse, hoisting it over his shoulder as he descended the litter-strewn steps to the subway.

The station itself was dank, lined with cracked yellow tiles that had been drawn on, spat on and pissed on. River marched towards the lop-sided ticket gates, swiping his TellMe over the payment scanner to open the flaps.

Now all he needed to work out was the way to Howling. River glanced at the labyrinthine map on the wall, a spaghetti bowl of lines and names which, whilst pretty, had no logic. Still, Howling itself was easy enough to spot, sitting second along the Viridian Line and monogrammed in pink.

River made for the platform. The Viridian Line, he reasoned, was not a popular route; he saw little sign of life as he trundled down the tubular passage, stepping over abandoned bento boxes and coffee cups.

"Hey, get off her!" a guy yelled. "What's she done?"

It was Jake Thrower.

River quickened his pace and turned onto the platform. There was a brawl – three men and a woman.

He dropped his bike and ran over. He grabbed one of the guys, whose fingers were driving into Jake's throat. River snarled as he tugged at his sleeves. He freed Jake, but stumbled backwards.

BAN!

He struck his head against a vending machine. His vision swirled. He couldn't see straight.

But he could hear: punches and kicks and screams, and a terrified old woman yelping in the crossfire.

"Get outta here!" Jake growled.

"Leave it Jed, come on!" a man stammered.

"You're scum!" came the cry of another. "You're scum!"

21

"Whatever man, go home to mommy!" Jake sniped, wiping the blood off his nose. He turned to the old woman. "You alright?"

River regained his focus. A crouching old lady and a battered Jake shifted into view. The woman was stout, with a drooping nose and piercing red eyes. Her arched back was bundled up in a shawl.

"Yes, I'm okay," the lady answered, allowing Jake to pick her up. "Thank you for your brave intervention, my dear."

Clutching his head, River scrambled to his feet and groaned. He staggered drunkenly towards the pair. "What happened?"

"I was just coming back from the gym," Jake explained, "when I saw this lady being harassed by two men. They were trying to take her away."

"I've done nothing wrong," the woman protested. "I am homeless, that's all. Neo Vale station is all I know."

Jake looked around. "You live down here?"

"In a manner of speaking."

"People have been disappearing since I got here," River pointed out. "It's always the same – two thugs in blue overalls, snatching people off the streets."

"But that's messed up!" Jake spluttered. "What the hell are they doing to them?"

The old woman patted him gently. "It's alright dear, it's alright," she uttered. "They have gone now, thanks to you brave boys."

"But what are we supposed to do?" Jake rebutted. "We can't just leave you here."

Jake was right of course - he and River had something of a responsibility towards the old woman now. But they could hardly take her home with them.

"I know a safe place," the lady answered, inching towards the vending machine. "Help me, my dear."

River glowered suspiciously at the dispenser. The door was hanging loosely off its hinges, and a lazily scrawled 'out of order' sign was tacked to the front panel.

"But that's a vending machine?" said Jake.

"Appearances can be deceptive. Open the door."

Jake surveyed the unassuming contraption. "You want me to open the door? To a vending machine?"

"Jake, leave it," said River, inching back along the platform. "We should go."

The old woman flashed him a stern gaze. "Go?" she whispered. "You would abandon a poor old woman?"

"She's right," said Jake reassuringly. "What's the worst that can happen? We get turned into soda?"

The hag cackled. "That's the spirit, my boy."

Jake reached for the door, and the old woman scowled at River. "Well, are you coming?" she croaked. "River?"

River's heart missed a beat. How did she know his name?

Jake, however, was oblivious. "Woah, check this out," he gasped, staring through the machine's open door. "There's a passageway."

River looked. Over Jake's shoulder he could see a short, half-lit corridor, with a closed wooden door nestling at the far end. It did not look inviting.

"Get in," the woman hissed.

River knew a threat when he heard one. Reluctantly, he followed Jake into the machine.

It was like a house, but without windows. There were pictures in frames, and potted plants on tables. On the walls, gas lamps offered dim coronas of light, with tongues of orange flame that danced like cartoons.

"What is this place?" said Jake, looking around in awe.

The hag sneered, exposing the gaps in her bent, yellowing teeth. "This place," she whispered, "is your tomb."

4: prison

The old woman whipped a knife out of her shawl, its cool steel blade glowing in the half-light. "I suppose a remark about reaching 'the end of the line' would be appropriate at this point," she jibed, bursting into a raucous cackle.

Jake clenched his fists. "You can't kill us, you freak!" he yelled, his face reddening.

"But you have nowhere to run," the old woman retorted. "There's only the House. The House cannot hide you."

River stepped in front of Jake. "Never mind that. How do you know my name? You said my name just now. Where did you hear it?"

"I didn't hear it anywhere," the hag answered. "I've always known your name. I know everything about you, River Still."

Jake frowned. "Your surname's Still?"

"You really want to talk about that now?" said River, seizing the door handle.

"Good point."

"There's no escape that way!" the hag crowed, as River and Jake dived into the next room.

Jake grabbed the door. "I dunno, we can give it a bash!"

He slammed the door in the old woman's face.

"Kaaargghhhhhhhhhh!"

"River, give me a hand here!" Jake cried, throwing his back against the panel.

"We need something to block it," said River, searching the room.

"Or a sawn-off shotgun," said Jake, as the door buffeted behind him. "We can outrun her, right?"

"Sure, there's two of us. That means we can run twice as fast."

"What? That's not how it works!"

"Come on!"

River grabbed his hand, pulling Jake away just as the door was ripped from its hinges.

The pair sprinted into the next passage, the hag hot on their heels.

"Eat my blade!" she cackled.

24

"She had a knife all this time but let *us* fight the thugs?" Jake exclaimed.

The carpeted hall wound like a labyrinth until the pair reached a wider room. It contained several doors, one of which was under a stone arch flanked by two burning lamps.

"Take your pick," said Jake, fighting for breath.

"That one," said River, nodding at the arch. "It says 'Chapel.'"

"So?"

"It's hallowed ground, right? Maybe she can't go there?"

"Bro, she's not a vampire."

The hag grew closer. "Burn in Hell, River Still!"

Jake shrugged. "On second thoughts…"

The pair tore under the arch.

"Woah," gasped Jake, as he stumbled into the chamber. "Check out the decor."

River, meanwhile, was studying a set of curtains that masked the furthest wall. "Jake, over here. We can hide behind these."

Jake looked at the drapes. "River, she'll find us in thirty seconds," he protested. "It's literally the only place to hide."

"Yeah, and there's no other exit. What do you want to do? Dress up as a carpet? Come on."

The pair pulled at the fabric and parted the curtains, revealing a large, yawning chasm. It was bottomless.

"After you," Jake quipped.

"Ah-ha! At last!"

The pair looked round. The hag had burst into the chapel.

"Luring you into the subway was all too easy, River Still," she taunted, the blade towering over her head.

"Why are you doing this?" River asked. "Why do you want me dead?"

"You must be contained," the woman answered. "There is no one more contained than a dead man."

River frowned. "Contain me?" he quizzed. "Why do you want to contain me?"

"Story time's over! This is the end for you, River Still. Kiss your friend goodbye."

River and Jake looked at each other.

"Die, River Still!" the hag cried. "Die!"

She charged forward, brandishing her blade like a javelin.

River and Jake stepped out of the way.

"Gaaaaaaaaarrrrrghhhhh!"

The old woman plunged headlong into the abyss, her crazed screams winnowing through the emptiness.

25

"Phew," said Jake, patting River on the back. "Nicely done."

River stepped away from the chasm. "Not my first evil ex."

"Lol, River likes his seniors! Toothy witches with a murder fetish. I ain't judging."

"But who was she?" said River, sinking down into a wooden chair which was surrounded by lampstands. "She said she knew who I was. She said she wanted to 'contain' me."

"She was a whack job," Jake replied. "This is obviously her gingerbread cottage. I bet she's been luring kids to this creepy chapel for centuries."

"You there!" came a thunderous voice. "Identify yourself!"

River and Jake looked up.

A tall man in rich, multi-coloured regalia had appeared at the entrance to the chapel, accompanied by two monks in equally dazzling robes. He was brandishing a staff that was shaped like a paintbrush.

"I said identify yourselves!" he repeated.

River cleared his throat. "I'm River Still, and this is Jake."

Jake waved.

"River Still, you have violated the sacred Temple of Colours," the man stated, his eyes fixed on them. "You have desecrated the Empty Chair of Empty Chairs."

"Excuse me?"

"Take him!" the man barked at his companions. "He is to be imprisoned and tried!"

One of the monks twisted River's arm into a half nelson and hauled him to his feet.

"Hold on, is this because I sat on the chair?" he quizzed.

"Arrest the boy as well!" the man continued. "He is an accomplice to desecration!"

Jake rolled his eyes. "What are you saying? I *helped* him sit down?!"

"Take them away!"

The monks wrestled the pair out of the chapel, unmoved by their protests.

River and Jake were led deeper into the House. River gazed at the mysterious passages, his heart pounding; it was like being dragged through a haunted mansion. Was this somebody's home?

Actually, it could be many people's home. The corridors soon grew busier, like a subway station at rush-hour, each person marching with a purpose. River hated crowds, but there was something intriguing about this one. The men and women were somehow out of their time, each clad in resplendent old-world attire.

And then there was the music. Brass speakers hung from the vaulted ceiling, emanating the eerie crackles of long-dead records. They made River's stomach turn.

"In here!" the monk ordered, hustling River towards a short flight of steps. There was a dark wooden door at the bottom, flanked by two guards, which the struggling pair were shoved through. It was the entrance to a dungeon.

Inside, River and Jake were led to the nearest cell. A barred door was slammed in their faces.

"You will remain here until it is time for your trial," the monk barked.

"Dude, you can't keep us here," Jake retorted. "This is kidnapping!"

The monk walked away, uninterested.

"Dammit!" Jake yelled, throwing his weight against the bars. "Screw you, you freak!"

"Jake, calm down," said River, as he sank to the floor. "They're not going to listen."

"Damn it, this is *not* okay! Did you hear the crap they were coming out with? I'm not an accomplice to defecation!"

River observed their dank surroundings. "What do you think this place is?"

Jake sighed and slumped next to him. "I don't know," he answered. "Perhaps we're dreaming."

"We can't both be dreaming," River pointed out. "Although it does look like something from a dream. It doesn't seem real, somehow."

"Yeah, I know what you mean. And did you see all those people we passed? They looked like cartoons."

River gazed at the cell once more. "It's not just the people. It's everything. Look at these walls. They appear to be made of stone, but if you feel them..."

Jake rubbed the textured surface. "Woah," he gasped, as his fingers grazed the stonework. "It feels like a painting."

"I think it *is* a painting," River agreed. "Everything's painted. From the pot plants to the people."

Jake looked baffled. "Wait. 'Painted' people? Are you freaking kidding me?"

"No Jake, he is not freaking kidding you," came a voice out of the shadows. "How fascinating. Is that how people talk these days?"

River and Jake glared into the darkness of their neighbouring cell. "Who's there?" River shouted. "Show yourself."

Gracefully, a red parrot waddled out of the gloom. He was donning a stylish Bavarian hat, with a dazzling red feather tucked into its

27

rim. "Guten Tag," he answered. "Greetings and salutations. My name is Spencer von Luft." He bowed. "Welcome to prison."

Jake tugged nervously at his friend's sleeve. "River," he muttered. "It's a talking parrot."

"So, your name is River," Spencer established. "River the talking biped. Well, it's a delight and a pleasure, biped. Even if you are an enemy of the state."

"Dude, he's not an enemy of the state," Jake rebutted. "All he did was sit on a chair."

Spencer cocked his head curiously. "You sat on the Empty Chair of Empty Chairs? In the sacred Temple of Colours?"

"Yeah, and they locked us up for it!" Jake spluttered.

"Quite right too. You desecrated the holiest site in the entire district. The sentence is usually death, but your stupidity might count in your favour. Goodbye and good luck."

Spencer turned and picked up a round palette and paintbrush, which were resting on the prison floor.

"Wait, what do you mean goodbye?" Jake snapped. "You can't go anywhere."

Spencer looked at him. "But of course I can. I'm not a prisoner, you know. I was only called in to touch-up the stonework. Do you like it? It's Prussian blue."

"I don't care what it is," said River. "We can hardly be executed for committing a crime when we didn't know the law."

Spencer paused. "You didn't know the law?" he enquired. "How is that possible? Even the meanest intelligence knows of the Empty Chair."

"Well, I've never heard of it," said Jake.

"Shocking."

"We only arrived here a few minutes ago," River explained. "We came from the subway station."

Spencer's eyes widened. "Good grief," he muttered. "You're flesh-kind?" He leaned in, ogling the pair. "I mean, as I live and breathe – you're flesh-kind! This is unprecedented! Are you freaking kidding me?!"

"Flesh-kind?" said Jake. "You mean, the other people *are* painted?"

"Of course they're painted," Spencer replied. "Everything's painted. If you can see it, someone painted it. Ah, now your ignorance makes sense! I thought you were just stupid."

"Do we look stupid?" said Jake.

"Well..."

"Don't answer that," River interjected. "The point is, the entrance to this house is right in the middle of a subway station. You must have had human visitors over the years? There must be procedures for such things?"

"Certainly not," Spencer rebuffed. "The door doesn't just open to anyone, you know. Only people from the House."

"Well, it opened for us," said River. "And we're not from the House."

"So you say. But the short answer to your question is no – we don't have procedures for humans, because it should be impossible for them to enter."

"Great," Jake sighed. "So we're stuck in a loop-hole."

"Technically, yes," said Spencer. "But your being flesh-kind changes everything. Let me see what I can do."

"You're going to help us?" said River.

"I shall certainly try. I may not look like it, but I am a macaw of some influence. Promise me you won't go anywhere."

River gazed at the locked cell. "We'll do our best."

"Excellent," said Spencer, waddling towards the door. "I shall be in touch."

And on that note, their new friend left.

Jake groaned. "Right, I have literally seen everything," he moped, flopping his head onto River's shoulder. "What are we going to do?"

"There's not much we can do," River admitted. "But Spencer's right. If we're not painted, we can't be subject to this world's laws. They have to let us go."

"Damn right. And if they don't, I'll take that Empty Chair of theirs and smash it round their heads."

River smiled. He liked Jake.

It's hard to say how much time passed. River and Jake fell asleep on each other's shoulders, woken only by the faint clunk of the barred gate, as a complement of monks arrived at the cell.

"On your feet," said a toneless voice. "It is time for your trial."

River and Jake stirred.

"Did you hear what I said?" the monk snapped.

Jake grinned. "I don't know. Did we hear something, River?"

"On your feet, now!"

Reluctantly, River and Jake stood up and followed the monks from their cell. They were unrestrained this time, and marched freely along the House's dim, baroque passages.

Jake leaned towards his friend. "How big *is* this place?" he asked. "It's like it goes on forever."

"I know right?" River agreed. "It's like a network of winding streets."

They were escorted to the foot of a vast, carpeted staircase, which stood in the centre of a large open hallway. Merchants with rugged carts were positioned nearby, selling paint, puff pastry and cocoa. Figures in grand regalia were dashing in all directions, their long robes flapping in the frenzy.

River and Jake were steered through the hubbub, jostled like flotsam and rushed towards the grand doorway at the top of the stairs. As if on cue, the two doors parted majestically, clearing the way for the two captives to pass.

From here, they were ushered into a cold, cathedral-like hall, and then into a much smaller chamber that felt like a cavern. It was lit up with rows of burning lamps which were fixed to each wall, their painted flames waxing and waning.

River and Jake were shoved towards a short row of stools and ordered to sit. They were facing an ornate dais, on which three gowned figures were seated.

"This court is not in the habit of being made to wait," said the central figure - an officious-looking woman.

"My apologies, Judge," said the monk, hitting Jake on the head.

"Ow! What the-?!"

"Silence!" the judge snapped. "The court is now in session. For the record, please state your names and districts of birth."

River cleared his throat. "My name is River Still, and this is my friend, Jake Thrower."

"Yeah," Jake added, "and we're not painted, have you got that? We are one hundred per cent flesh!"

"In this court you will address me as ma'am," the judge instructed, unmoved by this revelation. "Now, have either of you been declared legally insane?"

River and Jake looked curiously at one another.

"No," Jake answered.

"Then you are simply obstreperous," the judge concluded. "You have flouted the House's sacred laws and have shown patent disregard for the Empty Chair."

"Hold on," said River, standing up.

"Sit down," the judge retorted. "You are not at liberty to speak."

"Look, we are from the flesh world," River went on. "We had no idea that the Empty Chair was so special."

"Yeah, and we still don't know what the Empty Chair is!" said Jake.

"Exactly."

"Be silent!" the judge crowed.

"If you'd just look at us properly, you'd see that we're telling the truth," River persisted.

"Yeah bro, look at my skin!"

"Mr. Thrower, put your leg down!" the judge yelled. "I will have order in my chambers!"

The pair sank sulkily back onto their stools.

"Now," said the judge, "from your behaviour, it's clear that you vagabonds have little respect for this court, or the sovereign laws of the District of Cyan."

"This is a travesty," Jake muttered.

"Historically, there is only one punishment that befits the crime of desecration, and that is execution by water," the judge continued. "You are not legally insane, therefore your defence is void." She turned to her colleague. "Prepare the sprinklers."

Jake rolled his eyes. "Oh, you're going to shower us to death?!"

"We will contact your next of kin and advise them of your erasure," said the judge. "Your painted remains will be donated for pigmentalogical research. That is all."

The monks wrestled the pair to their feet.

"Stop it, get off me you creep!" Jake shouted.

"I am a victim of circumstance!" said River.

"Your deaths will serve as an example to all," the judge stated. "No one can defile the Temple of Colours and live."

Suddenly, the chamber doors crashed open.

"Not so fast!" said Spencer, a scroll under his wing.

The courtroom gasped.

"This is highly irregular!" the judge exclaimed. "Identify yourself immediately."

Spencer stepped forward. "My name is Spencer von Luft. I am a parrot and a painter to boot. I am in charge of this courtroom now."

The judge pursed her lips tightly. "You are in charge of this courtroom?" she challenged. "On what grounds do you make such a claim?"

Spencer walked towards her. "I come with the express permission of the president," he explained, hoisting the rolled parchment aloft. "I bring his written authorisation as proof of my integrity."

"Indeed," said the judge, unyielding. "A forgery, I assume."

"Not at all, ma'am. As you will see, the document is bound with the House seal." Spencer tossed the scroll onto the platform.

"Yargh!" cried the male judge, clutching his eye.

"Pick it up, you fool!" the woman snapped. She glowered at Spencer. "You do realise that the president cannot overrule the law of the Temple? These reprobates *will* be terminated."

River and Jake looked nervously at each other.

Spencer chuckled. "It seems somebody left their spectacles at home," he remarked, wandering towards his friends. "These gentlemen are not of the painted world. They are flesh-kind."

"The document is legitimate, ma'am," said the male judge, the signed parchment in his hands. "It orders the immediate release of the two prisoners."

The judge stiffened, icily. "I see," she stated. "The Empty Chair has been desecrated, and I must overlook it..."

"Oh come now, ma'am," said Spencer, perching on River's shoulder. "No one meant to be chary. Heh! These young men had no knowledge of the law. How could they? They are not painted like us."

"Exactly," said Jake, nodding. "This is a miscarriage of justice!"

"Hardly a miscarriage of justice when you've just been acquitted," the judge retorted. "Fine. Leave my chambers. And may our paths never cross again. The court is dismissed."

The judge got up and left. A dull chatter filled the room.

"Charming woman," said Spencer, smiling.

"Spencer, that was amazing," said Jake. "You got authorisation to have us released? How?"

"Was it a forgery?" River asked.

Spencer craned his neck and looked River in the eye. "A forgery?" he rebutted. "How very dare you." And then he winked. "Come on, let me take you somewhere comfortable. I expect you're thirsty."

Their new friend directed them from the chambers and back into the lobby. From there, they followed a new set of passages which criss-crossed and branched, each of them lavishly carpeted and lit up with torches. The walls, meanwhile, were ablur with swinging doors, with painted citizens weaving in and out of the rooms beyond.

"Each door leads to a different dwelling," Spencer explained, still resting on River's shoulder. "This is the District of Cyan, home to many people."

River felt overwhelmed. "How many districts are there?" he enquired.

"No one knows," Spencer answered. "Nobody's ever reached the final room."

"Wait," said Jake. "So you're saying this crib could go on forever?"

"I didn't say 'crib,'" Spencer replied. "Cribs are feeding troughs. Do you live in a feeding trough, Jake?"

Jake's mouth curled into a smile. "It depends how you look at it."

River took a deep breath, and stared. The maze-like corridors - and the sheer vastness of them - made him feel anxious.

But to be fair, the place was not without its beauty. The three friends soon came to a hall that looked like a cross between a drawing room and a town square. Two columns of painted trees framed a wide wooden concourse, festooned with strings of fairy lights. There was also a fountain, which trickled with a plum-coloured paint. And at the far end of the hall stood an immense clock, which stretched into the room's vaulted ceiling.

"Welcome to Chancery Square," said Spencer. He leapt off River's shoulder and waddled towards an unlit fireplace, which nestled under a grand wall of books. "You'll have to crawl, I'm afraid."

Jake just stared in disbelief. "He lives in a fireplace."

"Dude, he's a talking parrot," River pointed out. "He's from a cartoon house, underneath a subway, where the inhabitants worship a chair. Of course he lives in a fireplace."

Jake thought for a moment. "Good point."

And with that, the pair bent down and crawled through the gap.

Spencer's house was a cavern of creativity. Easels and crates and tin cans were littered across its lively but stained wooden floor. There was a mezzanine on which a rough tent had been erected, cocooning a collection of red cushions and rugs. This, presumably, was where he slept.

Down below, the room was cluttered and chaotic, with stacks of canvases transforming the room into something of a maze.

"Now then," said Spencer, picking up his palette. "I promised you a drink, didn't I?"

Jake leapt up and dusted himself down. "Yeah. A double vodka please."

"Cocoa it is," said Spencer. He swept over to a long line of taps, whose grey pipes spanned the full height of the wall. Spencer swivelled each of the squealing valves in turn, and great torrents of paint splattered into the basin below. Deftly, he put his brush under the cascading colours and dabbed the liquid onto his palette.

"Doesn't the paint clog the pipes?" River asked.

"It's not the kind of paint you're used to," Spencer answered. "It has... How do I put it? It has *special properties*. Now, turn off the taps, biped."

River complied as Spencer swooped towards his canvas. "Now then, cocoa, wasn't it?"

Jake chuckled. "Sure."

Spencer lifted his palette and thin wooden brush. He skimmed it masterfully across the canvas, carving the colours into shapes.

"Are you painting me a drink?" asked Jake.

"Well, it's certainly not a landscape," Spencer replied.

Jake leaned towards River. "He's mad, isn't he?"

"Sehr gut!" said Spencer, admiring his work. "Prepare to catch!"

Jake cupped his hands together. "Ready."

Spencer looked round. "No, no, no!" he rebuffed. "Come over here!"

Jake shrugged, and wandered to where his friend was painting. River followed, curious.

"Jake, as soon as I finish," Spencer explained, "the object will tumble straight out of the frame, so position your hands directly under my brush."

Jake's eyes widened. "Okay..."

Spencer added the finishing touch. "Now!"

As predicted, the painted image of the steaming cup became tangible, and dropped sloppily out of the frame into Jake's hands.

"Yargh!" gasped Jake, shaking his fingers.

"There you are!" said Spencer. "Cocoa."

"Man, it's hot!"

"That's because it's cocoa."

"Hang on," River interjected. "This is ridiculous. You can't paint cocoa."

"That's right, *you* can't," Spencer chortled, waddling away from the canvas.

"Seriously, though," River persisted, "even if I accept that you can somehow paint drinks, how do you make them hot? Warm paint?"

"Of course not, that'd be silly," said Spencer.

Jake groaned. "Oh totally."

"It's all about concentration," Spencer went on. "When painting, the creator must focus intently on the image they have in their mind. In this instance, I was concentrating on hot cocoa. But I could just as easily have been thinking about cold cocoa, or bacon. Or sumptuous papaya."

"I see," said River, not really seeing at all. "So, you can pretty much paint whatever you want, and it will become real? Right?"

"Nearly," said Spencer. "There are limits as to what I can paint. For starters, the object must exist somewhere in reality. I couldn't very well paint you a mookerjee burger."

Jake frowned. "What's a mookerjee burger?"

"Exactly. Moreover, no one can paint living creatures. Or money. Well, there are some that can. But explaining that would require considerable oxygen, and I've done enough rabbiting for one day."

"Woah, this is sick, bro," said Jake, supping his drink. He handed it to River. "Try some."

"Yes bro, enjoy your sick," Spencer jibed.

River tasted the cocoa. The oozing liquid was thick, like porridge, with all the intense sweetness of a chocolate fondue. "Man," he panted, smacking his lips. "That's awesome."

A thunderous gong pummelled the air.

"The night hours," Spencer muttered. He set down his things. "That would be your cue to leave."

"What are the night hours?" asked Jake.

"Nothing sinister. It's just our rest time. It helps us to maintain our circadian rhythms. A curfew is in place for the next few hours."

Jake looked confused. "What's a circadian rhythm?"

"The body's day and night cycle," River explained. "I imagine it's difficult to maintain in a place with no natural light."

"Lol, like my school."

"Yes, I'm sorry that our friendship has been fleeting," said Spencer, gliding towards the door. "I will escort you back to your homes, and then, regrettably, I must bid you farewell."

River looked indignant. "Farewell? Why can't we see you again?"

"Oh dear, must you make this difficult?" Spencer sighed. "Very well, I shall give you three reasons. One: I have little time for entertaining guests. Two: you'll doubtless get arrested again. Three: going outside is illegal. Oh, and three-point-five: I'll die if it rains."

"It's illegal?" said Jake. "That's a bit harsh, isn't it?"

"But necessary," Spencer answered. "Citizens of the House shouldn't advertise their presence. If you bipeds discovered our world, you'd only ruin it with sushi. Now, if you'll allow me to lead you both home…"

"Oh yeah, that's another thing," River interjected. "How can you take us home if it's illegal for you to go outside?"

"Yeah man, it's against the ruuuuuules!" Jake mocked.

"Oh, a quick stroll never hurt anyone," Spencer replied. "Plus, I am curious to see your feeding trough."

River zoned out as he made his way back to the subway. It was all so much to process - endless houses, cartoon citizens, paint, parrots and curfews. His brain felt like it was melting. Not only had he been mugged by a vacuum cleaner, but he'd also been attacked by a knife-wielding hag. Why, though? Who was she? And how come she knew him? And why was she so obsessed with keeping him 'contained'?

Remarkably, Jake's bike was still at the station when the three friends stepped onto the platform. In fact, some well-meaning person had picked it up and propped it against the wall, much to Jake's chagrin; he'd "been trying to get rid of it for years."

After a brisk walk, they reached the door of Noodle Vale. It was 11pm.

"Yikes, mom's gonna kill me," Jake fretted, scrambling for his keys. "Later, Spencer. It's been real."

"Indeed it has," said Spencer, as a flustered Jake raced into the bar. "Well now, what a whirlwind it's been, River Still. I trust tonight's events have not affected you too badly?"

River looked at him. "I'm not sure. It's a lot to take in."

Spencer looked down at his claws. "Yes, I appreciate it must be difficult," he responded. "But I truly believe our parting is for the best. You've seen what a dangerous place the House can be."

"Especially if you sit on empty chairs."

"Indeed," Spencer chortled. "Such an audacious misdemeanour!"

River smiled. "Well, it was really nice meeting you. I don't think I've ever been friends with a parrot before."

"And an artistic parrot at that. Yes, it was rather fun, wasn't it? You have made a happy bird very old!"

"I'm glad. I only wish there were some way you could come and visit."

Spencer jumped off his shoulder and glided towards the floor. "Rules are rules."

"And you can't tell me what the Empty Chair is?"

Spencer looked back. He paused. "Would you sleep better tonight," he asked, "if I filled your head with our legends?"

River shrugged. "I don't know."

"You wouldn't." Spencer sighed. "And on that note, I shall bid you goodnight, my bipedal friend."

"Alright. Goodnight, Old Bird."

Spencer bowed. "That is Mr Old Bird to you."

River grinned, and gazed wistfully at his feathered friend as he waddled into the fog.

5: religion

Being sentenced to death was exhausting. The events in the House had taken their toll on the two friends; River and Jake barely spoke to each other as they sank onto their springy bunk mattresses, far too drained to slip into their PJs.

River's head continued to spin as he drifted in and out of consciousness. It was as if his brain never quite powered down. He could hear Jake toss, turn and grunt - but at the same time he could detect the rasping screams of the battlefield, and the savage explosions. A child cried out in terror. A wicked judge - made of acrylic - sentenced him to death by cycling. A talking vending machine asked him to serenade. It was like an acid trip.

By the time he woke (his duvet, again, scrunched up on the floor) the midday sun was streaming through the blinds.

"TellMe, what time is it?" River grunted.

"The current time is 12:32pm," the device answered. "Did you enjoy your sleep, River?"

"Oh yeah, it was joyous."

"Just to let you know, Skidmark has retained all of your earnings from last night."

River rubbed his eyes wearily. "Why?"

"Your failure to complete your last order, together with the casual abandonment of your vehicle, violated their terms and conditions. But they sent you a message."

A holographic, grinning emoji beamed out of his TellMe. 'You just need to do better!' said the text.

River scoffed. "Tell them I was desecrating chairs, and they can go fuck themselves."

There was a pause. "I may rephrase that," his TellMe replied.

River stood up, agitated - and immediately smashed his head on Jake's bunk. It hurt.

After he'd finished screaming, he staggered across the messy room, nursing the lump on his crown. A scruffily-penned note was pinned to the back of the door: 'Come meet me at recess, if you're bored!' it said. 'Singing Gardens, 1pm. Behind the academy. Jakey.'

River read it again. It was one perky invitation for someone who had spent the previous night in prison. With a talking parrot.

He thought for a moment. "TellMe, where are the Singing Gardens?"

"The Singing Gardens are 1.1 miles from your current location," it said.

"TellMe how to get there." A holographic map beamed out of his strap. "Oh yeah, right next to the Gamma Academy. That's Jake's school, right?"

The TellMe paused. "How would I know?"

"Good point."

The invitation was tempting. River wanted to offload all the zany thoughts that were weighing on his brain - memories of monks, courtrooms and cocoa. Maybe Jake wanted a chat, too.

So he ruffled his hair, sprayed his pits and headed out into Neo Vale, his precious guitar straddled across his shoulders. He felt naked without it.

His head was a million miles away as he strode through the smoggy streets. Although it was hard to walk past Neo Vale station without thinking about its hidden secret - the baroque, maze-like world nestled within its walls. A world that was as seductive as it was surreal. River felt both tempted and disgusted as he thought about it.

Actually, he didn't want to think about it. So he slipped his headphones over his ears and flooded his brain with bass lines and blues. Like the rest of Neo Vale's citizens, he was now cocooned in his own personal bubble, protected from the outside world and its distractions.

Within minutes, he arrived in a peaceful, wide-open space. There was no fog here; the Singing Gardens shimmered crisply in the bright midday sun. A gravel path meandered cleanly through a scattering of white concrete cubes which varied in height. Some of them were floating. And among them were lines of pink cherry blossom trees, whose branches were adorned with glass bars which jingled in the breeze.

River lowered his headphones as he approached one of the smaller white cubes. He crouched down and read its inscription.

'For Rex Hallowell, taken from us at the age of 19,' it said. 'You fought courageously. You are loved and will not be forgotten.'

The penny dropped. The whole place was a war memorial.

River paused for a moment, his throat tightening. Jake and his friends really hung out here?

He wandered a little further and spotted a huge body of water glistening in the distance, its blue waters still and undisturbed. It was hard to believe that such a tranquil place sat so close to the bustling streets.

River allowed the wind to quiver his fringe as he inhaled the sweet taste of freedom.

But then he spotted the outline of a young woman standing close to the water's edge. She had her back to him, but after a moment she turned and began to walk, her long hair rippling like a robe of black satin. It was Natsuki Hashino. River, unsure what to do, smiled and raised his hand in greeting, trying to decide if he should run over and say hi.

The moment, however, was quickly broken by the sound of a familiar voice.

"So she goes into the movie theatre and says, 'Bro, what's with all that writing above the counter?'" said Jake, walking along with his friend. "So the guy just looks at her and says, 'Babe, that's a sign of the times.'"

His companion, a brown-haired guy with big biceps, just smiled and shook his head. "Man, that's a terrible joke."

"What? It's my own material, dude!"

"Exactly!"

"Are you depressing your friends again, Jakey?" said River.

"Oh man, the comic sensibilities of my school are going down the tube." Jake sighed and turned to his chum. "Gabe, meet River Still. River Still meet Gabe."

"Yo, what's up," said the man with the muscles, shaking River's hand. He almost crushed his fingers. "So, have you just transferred here?"

"Oh, I'm not a transfer student," he admitted. "I've just moved to the area."

Gabe chuckled. "You moved to Neo Vale? Why the hell did you move to Neo Vale?"

"I don't know, I guess I wanted a change," River replied. "Plus, my work gives me some flexibility, so…"

"River's a musician," said Jake. "You had a gig the other night, right?"

"Yeah, and it kinda made sense to make it an extended stay," River explained. "Figure out what I want to do with my life."

"Okay, that's it - you gotta play for us," Jake enthused. "Come on, let's grab a seat somewhere."

River looked curiously at Natsuki, who was still walking by the edge of the lake.

But Jake and Gabe were already heading up the path. "Dude, come on," Jake called.

Reluctantly, River tore himself away and followed his friends.

They soon came to a small woodland clearing, where clusters of picnic benches were enclosed by circles of cherry blossoms. Pockets of Gamma students were casually hanging out and chatting, and Jake quickly selected a free seat. With complete disregard, he planted his bum on the table, and slammed his feet onto the bench.

"Come at me, man," he said. "Give me your best material."

"You write your own material?" Gabe enquired.

"Sometimes," said River coyly. "What kind of song would you like?"

"Heartbreak and lust," said Jake quickly. "Give me a song with heartbreak and lust."

"Heartbreak and lust? I'm not an angsty teen."

"Speak for yourself," said Gabe. "We need reminding about the futility of existence."

River rested the guitar on his knee. "I'll play you a fun one. Inspired by Two Spatulas and the Right Kind of Pan."

"So, your kitchen?" said Jake.

"Shut up, they're a band. This one's called 'I Need to Go.'"

But Jake and Gabe were suddenly distracted. "Dude, it's your sister!" Gabe panted, ogling a girl in the far corner of the clearing.

River turned. A young lady was filming herself in the shade of a thriving cherry blossom, her striking orange hair glowing in the auburn sun. It was a face he recognised instantly - the vlogger Jazzmas T.

"Okay, so this brings me to the end of today's Neo Vale garden tour," she said, beaming into the lens. "I know some of you will be kinda bummed that the cherry blossoms are made of plastic, but they're actually pretty cool. They absorb sunlight and provide renewable energy for the Gamma Academy. Plus, they keep the gardens bright and cheerful all year round, which I love!"

"Man, your sister is so hot," Gabe drooled.

Jake looked disgusted. "Dude, that's my twin! I don't want to hear that!"

"Yeah, but she's hot though."

"Shut it!"

River looked at Jazz, feeling somewhat in awe. Jake was a twin? Jake's twin was a famous vlogger? Jake's twin was a famous vlogger who Gabe thought was hot?

"But yeah, thanks again for coming round with me today," Jazz continued. "Don't forget to like this video if you've enjoyed it, subscribe to my channel for more daily content, and remember, until next time – less snoozing, more Jazz. Bye!"

River leaned towards Jake, and lowered his voice. "You didn't tell me your sister was Jazzmas T."

Jake looked crestfallen. "Oh no," he muttered, his eyes widening. "You're a fanboy, aren't you?"

"No..."

41

Jake fake-cried and whined in despair. "Okay," he said, pulling himself together. "You *cannot* tell her. Do you understand? If she finds out that she's living with a fan, she will freak."

"What's going on guys?" said Jazz, sitting down next to her brother. She clocked River's guitar. "Open mic?"

"Kinda," said Gabe. "River was just about to play for us."

"Yeah, I'm a musician," said River proudly, dropping his plectrum. It fell into his guitar. "And what do you do?"

"I'm a student and a vlogger. My name's Jazz."

"Wow, you're a vlogger?" said River, unconvincingly. "I have never even heard of that. What does a vlogger do?"

Jake cringed, and Jazz pursed her lips. "I make vlogs," she said.

"Oh right. I thought it was something to do with trees..."

"Anyway," said Gabe. "Are you going to play for us, River?"

"Sure," said River, digging around for another pick. He looked at Jazz, who was now absorbed in her phone. "This song is inspired by Two Spatulas and the Right Kind of Pan, and it's called 'I Need to Go.'"

Jazz gasped. "Oh-Emm-Gee! Felix Fuhrmann followed me on Yapper!"

Jake glared at her. "No way. That guy is ripped."

"Yeah, he's amazing," said Gabe sulkily. "But going back to River's song-"

"He works at Mango as well," Jazz went on. "Being friends with him could open a lot of doors from a networking point of view. Plus, he's really cute."

"Yeah totally," said Jake.

Gabe stared daggers at River. "Play something," he hissed.

River cleared his throat and strummed the first chord. "As I was saying," he went on, "this piece is inspired by Two Spatulas and the Right Kind of Pan, and it explores the existential crisis we sometimes experience when-"

"I'm going to message him," Jazz insisted, typing furiously.

"Tell him your brother says hi," Jake added.

"Tell him I hope he gets herpes," said Gabe, fully aware that no one could hear him.

Sensing the vibe, River pulled out his cell and checked all the notifications he didn't have.

And then sent Jazz a friend request.

After an hour, River managed to escape the hormones of the bench. Jake was due at boxing practice, and Gabe - undeterred by Jazz's cold shoulder - insisted on walking her to the Gamma cafeteria, "just in case she got lost."

So, River slipped his guitar back into its case and followed the gravel path to the water's edge, curious to see if Natsuki was still in the garden. It was strange - it was hard to articulate what he was feeling for her, and why. He certainly felt an attraction, if he could call it that. She seemed so considerate and warm. He had to talk to her.

Sadly, she wasn't around. At least, not that he could see. It made sense, really; he had been sitting with Jake, Jazz and Gabe for the past hour with his guitar on his knee, poised to perform his River Still Original (a ballad about needing the toilet.) Natsuki Hashino probably had more pressing matters to attend to. Like her bladder.

A little disappointed, River stood at the side of the lake and watched the peaceful ripples as they splashed against the mud. He smiled as his rugged reflection twisted and bent in the shifting waters.

And he smiled again when a second face appeared next to his.

"It's nice to see you again, River," it said.

River turned, simpering. "Natsuki Hashino, what a surprise," he said, not surprised at all. "How are you doing?"

"I'm fine. I'm having a lovely afternoon with my family."

River frowned. "Your family?"

"I come here and visit them most days," Natsuki explained. "They are in spirit form now, but I feel their presence. I talk to them, and I listen. I try to honour their memory."

River scuffed his feet in the damp grass. The afterlife was one of those topics he tried to avoid. "That's very good of you," he said quickly. "I'm sorry to hear that they're gone."

Natsuki looked sadly across the waters, and thought for a moment. "May I tell you something?" she asked, keeping her distance from him. "I would hate to speak out of turn."

"Of course."

Delicately, Natsuki reached into her coat and produced a piece of handcrafted jewellery - a carved, circular emblem with two dragons in the centre, tied to a long piece of string. "I made this for you."

Slightly taken aback, River accepted the unusual pendant, admiring the vivid detail of the two creatures. "You made this for me?" he said, as he dangled it between his fingers. "It's gorgeous."

"The dragon gods will bring you protection," Natsuki told him. "I don't know why, but..." She broke off and looked away. "No, I'm sorry."

"What? Why are you sorry?"

"I feel like you're in danger," she murmured. "Can't you sense it? It's your aura."

River frowned. "My what?"

"Your aura. It's an energy field that surrounds all living things. It can take many forms and colours."

"Oh, right," said River, vaguely recalling the concept.

"You can't see your aura?"

"Honestly, no," said River. "I didn't know people could. Can you?"

Natsuki didn't answer.

"I'll take that as a yes," River went on. "Unless you can smell it. In which case, I'm sorry."

Natsuki smiled faintly, unable to look him in the eye.

"Anyway, why do ask about my aura?" River pressed, unnerved at his friend's discomfort. "What is it?"

Finally, Natsuki looked up. "Yours is missing."

River froze. He didn't how to respond. He didn't even know what she meant.

"Well," Natsuki clarified, "part of it is missing."

Finally, River laughed. "Are you flirting with me, Natsuki?"

Natsuki laughed too, blushing.

"Seriously, I was thinking of asking you out, but I think you've saved me the effort."

They continued to giggle.

"I'm sorry," River added. "I didn't mean to make it awkward."

"You haven't. I think I did, though."

"No, I'm glad you told me," River reassured her. "What did you mean when you said part of it is missing?"

"It's fractured. It's like a sheet of ice that's been struck with an axe. At some point, you have been attacked by a malignant force from the unseen realm. You are wounded."

River pondered. Wounded? He didn't recall being attacked. Unless she meant during the war? Should he be concerned?

"Well," he stuttered. "Thanks for letting me know."

"I consider it a duty. I can see things that others can't. It was my responsibility to tell you."

"Could you do something else for me?"

Natsuki nodded. "Anything, River."

"Stay a while," he said. "Teach me about auras. Sit with me on the wet grass and slowly ruin your clothes."

Natsuki looked at the floor, suddenly shy.

"Sorry," said River, backing away. "You don't have to."

But Natsuki grabbed his hand. "Yes, I do," she whispered, her eyes glistening as she looked up. "I'd like that very much."

River liked it, too. It felt so easy. The pair linked hands as they reclined on the embankment. They just chatted, looking up at the cherry blossoms as the daylight faded.

"You haven't told me about your parents," said Natsuki, curiously. "Do they live in Neo Vale?"

River paused. He wasn't sure how to answer. "I don't know," he admitted. "Honestly, I've no idea if they're still alive. The civil war threw everything into chaos."

"River, how can you not know? Have you tried looking for them?"

"Yes, I've tried. But my home in Zen Kappa was razed to the ground. When I returned from Mantrecht, the town was nothing but a heap of rocks and dust. Anyone who knew my parents was gone."

Natsuki squeezed his hand. "You sound so cold, River."

"Do I?"

Natsuki gazed into his eyes. She took his other hand, which had grown cool in the crisp, wintery air. "You are very brave," she remarked. "And you are very handsome."

River grinned. "It's gotten dark, that's why."

Natsuki pressed her fingers against his lips. "Hush," she whispered. "It's not that dark. I can still see you. And I am still going to kiss you."

Natsuki leaned in and pressed her lips against his.

For a long time.

"Mmmmmmmmfffaaaaaargh!"

Natsuki was startled. "River?"

There was a parrot on his head. "Guten Abend," said the bird, doffing his hat. "My name is Spencer von Luft."

River was not impressed. "Hey, Spencer."

"Hay is for barnyards," Spencer retorted. "Nonetheless, I am relieved to have found you, mein Lieblingspferd."

"What's going on?" said Natsuki, confused.

"Natsuki, this is my friend from, uhh... Well from the, uhh..."

"From a distant zoo," Spencer told her. "In a distant town. It's lovely to meet you, Miss Natsuki. I see you're admiring the lake. Wet, isn't it?"

She glared at the parrot with her mouth wide open.

"Spencer, what are you doing here?" River interjected. "You said we couldn't see each other again. You said you couldn't come outside."

Spencer leapt onto his shoulder. "True," he admitted, "but as I was walking home last night, I thought, 'No, this young man deserves an explanation.' You were thrown in jail, for Pete's sake!"

"In jail?" Natsuki gasped. She grabbed River's arm. "River, what happened?"

River tried to speak, but it was difficult to find the right words. "It was... I sort of... There's a..."

"We must get under cover," Spencer insisted. "If the citizens of Neo Vale see you gossiping with a parrot, they'll put you in a straitjacket."

Natsuki leapt forward. "Wait, River."

But Spencer was already tugging at his guitar. "I-I'll text you," River promised, as his feathered friend towed him up the bank.

He smiled and waved reassuringly, leaving a flummoxed Natsuki alone by the lake.

"Great timing, Spencer," said River, as the parrot led him into the vending machine.

"Well how am I supposed to know what you're up to?" Spencer protested. "I can't just *assume* that you'll be fondling some floozy."

"That was not fondling!" River retorted. "We were cleaning each other's lips!"

Spencer chuckled. "Oh, how tidy-minded of you."

They arrived outside the dimly-lit chapel – the one that River and Jake had desecrated the night before. The lamps that framed its archway were lit and burning, and robed figures were pacing ceremoniously under the threshold, as if gathering for worship. The hum of a faint, monastic chant teased River's ears. "Spencer," River whispered. "I don't really want to be here."

"You surprise me. But would you like me to explain the significance of the Empty Chair?"

River shrugged. "I guess."

"Then the easiest way is to show you. You have nothing to fear. Just hide under this robe and don't make any mistakes."

"Oh thanks! Yaaaarggh!"

Spencer yanked River towards a rack of hooded cloaks. He grabbed one in his beak and flung it in his face.

"There. You are one of the congregation now."

River glared at the outfit in dismay. "I seriously have to wear this?"

"If you value your head. Now raise your hood, fold your arms and follow my lead."

River slipped out of his guitar and into the ill-fitting garment. He then followed Spencer under the arch. "But where's your robe?" he asked.

"I am a parrot," Spencer insisted, swooping onto his shoulder. "Parrots are exempt."

It's fair to say that River's return to the chapel was not a welcome experience. On entering, he instantly recognised the officious-looking priest, who was attending to the four lamps that surrounded the Empty Chair. Otherwise, the atmosphere was more spirited – cultish though it was. The worshippers were engaged in quiet conversation, and River quickly realised that the monastic music was emanating from a small vinyl turntable, which crackled as it spun in the far corner of the hall.

River looked again at the strange wooden chair. "Do they think it's some kind of god?" he enquired.

"No, not the chair itself," Spencer replied. "It's what the chair represents."

The High Priest took his place alongside the gaping pit, as the vinyl record crackled to its end. "All rise," he commanded, his arms outstretched.

Reverently, the assembled worshippers rose to their feet.

Another man stepped forward with a round wooden tray. There was an object on it, which the High Priest picked up and raised above his head. It was a paintbrush.

"O Jobon," he bellowed. "We think of you. We honour you. We love you, O Creator, O Painter."

River watched as the High Priest whipped droplets of paint into the yawning chasm. When he had finished, he turned, and craned his neck towards the ceiling.

"Jobon, you are the Great Painter," he declared.

"Thanks be to Father," the audience chanted.

"Jobon - O to have witnessed that mighty day, when you took brush to canvas and painted your First-Made. We remember that First Picture - the Canvas at the Dawn of Time, at the start of all things. O Jobon - where would we be without that Picture? Where would we be?"

"Where would we be?" the crowd repeated.

"And now," said the High Priest. "O brethren, if you feel so moved, step forward and present your offerings to the pit."

The robed figures began to shuffle. Worshippers walked slowly towards the edge of the chasm and splashed their brushes into the darkness.

River cupped a hand over his mouth and leaned towards Spencer. "So, these guys worship this Jobon? He's their god?"

"Jobon is the painter of the First Picture," said Spencer, "if legend is to be believed. That picture was of a seated figure named Kaida. He came to life and stepped out of his frame. And of course, when he did..."

"He left an empty chair?"

Spencer chuckled. "By jove, I think he's got it."

"Alright, Bird. There's a lot to take in here."

Spencer winked. "You're doing well."

"I'm confused, though. Why are they throwing paint into the pit?"

"It's just a ritual. They believe that the pit is where all life comes from. It's the place where Jobon created the First Picture, and me, and everyone. Some call it the cellar, or the source."

"But has anyone been down there? To find out?"

Spencer looked at him. "Don't be ridiculous."

"Oh yeah," said River, dryly. "Because that'd be crazy."

"For one thing, nobody knows how deep the pit is. For another, the cellar is revered even more than the Empty Chair. The penalty for anyone who defiles it is death."

The congregation was now drifting back to their seats.

"Also, it's flooded," Spencer added.

"It's what?"

"Our reading today is from the Book of Alla Prima," the High Priest stated, "beginning at verse one."

Another robed figure drifted across the chapel and handed a scroll to his waiting friend. The High Priest unfolded the yellowed papers.

"These are the writings of Kaida," he announced, and started to read. "'I cannot sleep, and yet I dare not open my eyes. I am scared of what I will see, and I am scared to be seen. I am possessed by a single thought: run, and keep running. Hide. My master must not find me. Into a maze of passages I will run. In the House I will lose myself. My creation, my staircases, my rooms - all shall be a cleft for me, and the oppressed.' These are the writings of Kaida."

"Thanks be to Kaida," said the crowd.

River leaned towards Spencer. "Well, that was as clear as mud."

"They always read from the Book of Alla Prima," Spencer replied. "It describes the House's origins. Without Kaida, we'd have no home."

River frowned. "How's that?"

"Were you not listening? Kaida created the House in desperation. In a blind panic he just painted and painted. Room by room and district by district, locking the doors as he went. He resolved to lose himself in a maze of passages. He was desperate to escape."

"Escape from what?"

"Isn't it obvious?" Spencer looked at him. "From Jobon."

A new record began to play, and the congregation broke into a mournful, monastic dirge. It sounded awful.

48

River was trying to absorb everything that Spencer was saying. "That doesn't make any sense," he remarked. "Is Jobon evil? Are we worshipping a monster?"

"It depends on your viewpoint. Kaida had gone mad, you see. Corrupted by dark paint."

"Dark paint? What's dark paint?"

"Never mind that now. Suffice to say, the pair swore to destroy each other, and Jobon amassed a huge army of monsters that would tear Kaida limb from limb. But Kaida painted a tsunami of water that flooded the cellar and trapped Jobon and his armies. It is believed that Kaida, too, perished in the deluge."

River exhaled. "Wow. So Kaida murdered your creator? And killed himself in the process?"

"It's all legend. No one can be sure of anything. But the prophecies say that Jobon survived – that the cellar will one day be drained and that his armies shall rise to conquer and destroy."

"Can't wait."

Spencer fell silent. River gazed at him, curious. He was twitching.

"And the last bit?" said River. "There's more, isn't there?"

"Of course not."

"Look me in the eye and say that."

The melody hit a crescendo.

"Ah," said Spencer. "That timbre!"

"Spencer, what are you hiding?"

"You are so suspicious, River Still. I have told you everything. There is nothing more to say."

"One more thing!" said the priest, as the melody faded. "Remember the final words of the prophecy. Do not be caught sleeping. Be mindful. Be thankful. May your painted works reflect the glory of Jobon. And most important, may you know peace."

Suddenly, a black talon whipped out of the pit and stabbed him. Everyone screamed.

River leapt up. It was chaos. The High Priest had been dragged into the hole.

"Get out, River!" yelled Spencer. "Run! Run for Pete's sake!"

River just stared.

"River, move yourself!"

River, glued to the spot, fixed his eyes on the pit as panicked worshippers fled.

Something was climbing out.

6: spiders

The creature was horrific. It was like a giant spider with piercing red eyes.

River stared at the nightmarish being and writhed in agony. His arms were burning, throbbing – acute pains were shooting between his elbows and fingers. He cried out and fell to his knees.

"River, what are you doing?" Spencer yelled. "It will kill you!"

He grabbed River's robe in his beak and flapped his wings, desperate to hoist him to safety.

River could feel the anger rising within him. His blood was beginning to boil.

"River, get up!" Spencer pleaded, driving his claws into his shoulder. "River, talk to me!"

Instinctively, River threw his arms open and screamed, slamming Spencer to the floor. His fingers fused together. His arms twisted and rotated. They morphed into spears.

Spencer watched, horrified.

As if in a trance, River rose to his feet and squared up to the spider. He swiped, and his blade pierced the monster's torso, caking the chapel in blood. Black blood.

The spider shrieked. It spluttered and keeled onto its side.

River withdrew and stepped away, shaking.

"Oh my," Spencer whispered.

River looked at his friend. His blades rotated, and his flesh arms twisted back into place.

Then he collapsed, crying out in pain. He buried his face in his hands.

Concerned, Spencer inched towards his friend. "Are you alright?"

River stirred. He wiped his face.

"I didn't realise you were a cyborg," Spencer muttered.

River looked at him, his eyes swollen. "Neither did I."

"You didn't know? How is that possible?"

River picked himself up. He was panting, and his wiry fringe was damp with sweat. "I've got some memories missing," he admitted. "Spencer, what was that thing?"

"Well, I've never seen one for real," he answered, "but I'm fairly sure it's one of Jobon's creatures. A night spore."

River nodded. "Night spore. Perfect."

"They come from the cellar. But if they've made it into the House, that must mean..." He tailed off.

"What? I thought you said the cellar was flooded?"

"I also said the cellar would be drained, and that the armies would rise."

River gazed at him, quizzically. "Yeah. But that prophecy is centuries old, right? Why would it suddenly come true now?"

Spencer looked away.

"Look, if this is some kind of weird street theatre can you just tell me?"

"Street theatre?"

"Yeah, where you lure people into vending machines and attack them with spiders."

"That's ridiculous," Spencer retorted. "For one thing, I didn't *lure* you. And that is not a spider. It's made of dark paint, for a start."

"Yeah, and it stinks," said River, wiping the gunk off his jeans. It was like tar. "What the hell is this stuff?"

Again, Spencer didn't answer.

"What is it?" River urged. "Tell me!"

"Yes River?" said his wrist strap. "How can I help?"

"Saved by the bell," Spencer grinned.

"Oh no!" River dashed over to his device, which was lying on the floor of the chapel. Its strap had been severed. "Damn."

"Well then," said Spencer, dismissively. "Shall we go?"

"Go? Are you for real?" River jumped up. "You can't leave me hanging. I mean, dark paint? What the hell?"

Spencer sighed. "Are you sure this is the best time? You look tired. And you have to mourn your wrist device."

"I'll cry uncontrollably later, I promise. Just tell me."

Spencer relaxed his wings. "Oh, very well," he answered. "Dark paint. How do I describe it? It's about opposites, you see: up and down, left and right, bipeds and parrots. With paint, there is light and dark – it seeps out of the earth and into the House. Dark paint is the embodiment of all evil. It infects, and possesses, and corrupts."

"Right," said River. "And these night spores. You think Jobon made them out of dark paint? A grand army, that's 'suddenly' woken up and is going to decimate the whole House?"

"The whole House," said Spencer. "The whole world. Everything."

51

River wandered over to the dead creature. "I'm not buying this," he muttered. He gazed into the monster's eyes. "What the hell are you?"

"You doubt our religion?"

"All religion."

Spencer baulked. "That's a sweeping statement."

"Why do you trust your prophecies when you've never seen this Jobon? Or Kaida? Or the cellar?"

Spencer sighed. "Why does anyone believe anything?"

"Fine, well if you're not going to give me a straight answer..." River stood up, agitated. "I'm leaving."

"You think I planned this, don't you? That this was all a setup?"

River stopped.

"You came to my house. You drank my cocoa. Would you believe that you were the first guest I've entertained in nearly five years?"

River looked at him. Spencer's head was drooping.

"I came to find you because I liked you," he added. "I can see now that I made a mistake. I have burdened you, River."

River said nothing. He felt terrible.

"You can go," said Spencer.

"Bro," River stammered. "You haven't 'burdened' me. I just... can't handle this now."

"I understand."

"I mean - myths, monsters, the end of the world..." He lifted his arm. "And cyber arms."

Spencer grinned. "And very nice they are too."

"I just need to process this. I will come back. I promise."

Spencer looked away. He didn't believe him. River could tell. "Okay."

River hovered for a moment. "I'll be off then."

"Of course," said Spencer, as his friend began to walk. "And River, can I give you a piece of advice?"

River turned round. "Advice?"

"Yes, advice," said Spencer. "The next time you meet a talking parrot..."

"Yeah?"

"Promise me that you won't, under any circumstances, refer to him as 'bro,' 'dude,' or any other piece of biped slang." Spencer's eyes twinkled. "Is that understood?"

River grinned. He sounded like his dad. "Sure thing, Spencer."

River felt as if his brain were about to explode. He picked up his guitar and made his way back to the subway station. As he scurried across its litter-strewn concourse, he was conscious of his quickening pace and fast-beating heart. Perhaps his cybernetic body was still geared for combat, waiting to be ambushed at every turn?

He knew, certainly, that he wanted to talk to Jake, and quickly. They hadn't even discussed their visit to the House yet. Admittedly, Jake didn't seem traumatised – far from it – but River knew that his friend could hardly be unaffected.

So when he arrived at Noodle Vale, he slipped past Beanie and scurried straight to his room, where his red-haired companion was engaged in sit-ups. Sweatily. In his underwear.

"Oh," said River, averting his gaze. "I'm sorry."

"It's fine, man, come in!" said Jake, unperturbed. "I'm done."

"Don't you want to put some clothes on?"

Jake opened the door. "Well, I've covered the good stuff," he teased. "You don't mind, do you? I need to cool down."

"Yeah, great," River stuttered. "Uhh, I mean, fine! Yeah, that's... that's fine."

He inched nervously into the room.

"Are you okay, man? You look like you're blushing."

"No, I'm just hot."

"I'd noticed. So how was your afternoon?"

River slumped onto the floor, resting his back against the bunk. He sighed, and rubbed his eyes. "Honestly, I feel like I'm going mad."

"Yeah boy, you are one hundred percent psychopath," said Jake. He sat down next to his friend and shuffled up close. "You wanna talk about it?"

River felt Jake's body pressing against his. It was weird. "Uhh," River stammered. "I guess. If you don't mind talking to a cyborg."

Jake's mouth curled into a smile. "You're a cyborg?"

"Affirmative."

Jake's grin grew wider as he glared at River's crotch. "Which part?"

"My arms, Jake."

"Nice."

River hesitated. "Really? You're okay with this?"

Jake frowned. "Of course I am. Dude, I'm not a cyberphobe. I couldn't give a crap about what you are."

River looked at him, searchingly.

"Is that what's bothering you?" said Jake. "You said you thought you were going mad?"

River paused, thinking about how to phrase his next sentence. "Well, it's just I don't remember *becoming* a cyborg."

Jake looked confused. "Say what?"

"I've got these weapons built into my arms," River explained, "and I clearly wasn't born with them, unless my mother was a machete. But I didn't know I had them until tonight."

"Right. As I said, then - you are one hundred per cent psycho."

River smiled wryly. "I knew I could count on you, Jake."

"I'm sorry, dude. I'm joking. You've really no idea where these 'implants' could have come from?"

"It's probably military tech. I'm guessing it dates back to the civil war, but most of it's a complete blank. My doctor says it's because of the trauma."

"Geez," Jake sighed. "I'm sorry, man."

They fell silent for a moment. Suddenly the conversation felt rather serious.

"Okay, you need cheering up," said Jake, jumping to his feet. He reached under his bed.

"What are you doing?"

Jake produced a bottle of lime green liqueur. Its label was emblazoned with a fire-breathing dragon.

"Softening the blow," he declared. "This is my emergency brain medicine."

River grinned. "Oh yeah? And when you bought it did you lie about your age, or go heavily disguised?"

"Shut up, I'm eighteen!"

"That's still underage."

"Except for medical emergencies, right?" Jake winked. "You've had a rough day, and I'm about to die of thirst. What you gonna do?" He swigged from the bottle and burped. He then handed it to River. "Kampai!"

River took the bottle. "Kampai. Here's to emergency brain medicine."

"Yep. Let me know if you need mouth-to-mouth."

River slumped his head against the mattress and sighed. "There's something else," he said.

"Hit me," Jake replied, swallowing another measure. "Should I be sitting down for this?"

"It's about the House. I went back there today."

Jake's eyes widened. "You went back?"

"Yeah. I met up with Spencer, and he pretty much told me everything."

There was a pause, and an incredulous Jake just stared at him. "What, that's it?" he said. "Your incredible story ends there?"

"Yeah, you're not getting the rest. You have to work for it."

Jake shook his head. "You're such a tease, River Still."

54

River poured more of the liquid into his throat. "So the paint," he continued. "Apparently it comes from deep within the earth. Nobody knows how or why, except that it has magical properties."

Jake took the bottle off him. "Well, I figured that," he replied. "I saw what Spencer did with the cocoa."

"Yeah, but there's also a god character called Jobon, who they worship. Apparently he mastered the paint, and created a being called Kaida, who went mad. He painted the House, adding corridors and passages and rooms in a bid to escape his creator. Which he did. But nobody knows what happened to him."

"Oh, sick," said Jake, handing him the drink. "I like it."

"You like it?"

"Yeah, what a backstory. Enigma, god-like beings, a berserk man lost in the hallways of a creepy mansion…"

"Well, they think he drowned. Jobon built this monster army to kill him, but Kaida flooded the cellar and trapped them all down there. Including himself."

Jake smirked. "Oh, totally," he replied. "There had to be an army of monsters."

"I'm not making it up," River urged him. "This isn't a movie."

"I know, man. It makes sense. I think."

River reached for the liqueur again, but Jake slapped him away. "Hey, it's still my turn."

River looked at him. "I *will* fight you for it."

Jake grinned. "If you want it, come get it."

"Are you sure you want to mess with a cyborg?"

"Are you sure you want to mess with this?" said Jake, slapping his abs.

River smiled mischievously. He grabbed the bottle and tried to prise it from Jake's fist. The two friends jostled, laughing as they fell over each other.

Jake giggled. "Watch out! You're gonna spill it!"

"So buy a straw, bro!"

The pair collapsed in a heap of flailing legs, and the drink sloshed onto the bedroom carpet. River and Jake lay laughing like chimpanzees, covered in splashes of lime green liqueur.

Jazz knocked on the bedroom door.

"Evening girls," she teased. "Do you want to be left alone?"

The sniggers quickly faded, and River let go of his friend. "Hi Jazz," he replied, his cheeks reddening. He couldn't bring himself to look her in the eye.

Jazz grinned at the two guys. "I see you've been busy."

"Yeah," said Jake, sitting up. "I was about to deck our lodger."

"Deck?" Jazz smirked. "How old are you?"

"Almost geriatric," River quipped.

Jazz glared at him. "You know he's my twin, right?"

"Oh yeah." River laughed uncomfortably. "Do you want a drink, Jazz?" He pointed at the pool of liquid on the floor. "Only 40 per cent ABV. The rest is carpet."

"Nah, I'm good. I'm off to bed soon."

"Alright, bye then!" said Jake.

"Just one thing," Jazz added, whipping out her cell. "Gabe's asked if I'll go for sushi with him tomorrow. He's totally put me on the spot."

River nodded. "That's nice."

Jazz gave him the Death Stare. "No, it's not."

"Yeah River," said Jake, punching his arm.

"Ow! What's the big deal?"

"It's going to be like a date if it's just the two of us," Jazz explained. "And I don't like him in that way."

River thought for a moment. "So why don't you tell him that?"

Again, Jazz stared daggers. "Are you some kind of idiot?"

"Uhh…"

"Gabe hasn't officially asked me out," said Jazz. "How can I tell him I don't have feelings for him when he hasn't said that he has feelings for me? It'd be awkward."

River raised his eyebrows. "And confusing."

"You guys are coming with me," Jazz went on. "I said I'd meet him at five."

"Alright," Jake cheered. "Sushi and sexual tension. I'm in. River, are you coming?"

"Well, I've got Skidmark in the afternoon. But I guess I could come later."

"Good," said Jazz. "And what about Natsuki? Do you think she'll come?"

River's eyes widened. "Natsuki?" he spluttered. "How do you know about her?"

"She tagged you in a photo on Yapper," Jazz explained, showing River her phone. It was a selfie that Natsuki had taken by the lake; she and River were beaming into the lens, their rosy faces pressed against each other.

"Woah, who's she?" said Jake.

River looked away. "Oh, just my sister."

Jazz glanced at her phone. "She says you're dating."

"What?"

56

Jake laughed. "Congratulations, stud! You successfully hooked up with your sister. I'm creeped out and amused."

"Okay, she's not my sister," said River defensively. "But we just kissed. It was meaningless."

Jake shrugged. "Nothing wrong with meaningless kisses, bro."

"Okay, whatever," Jazz sighed. "Let's meet at Rainbow Pagoda at five." She started tapping into her cell. "I'll let Gabe know."

"Awesome," said Jake. "Well, I should probably get to bed."

"Yep," Jazz replied. And she walked out of the room, her eyes fixed on her phone.

Oh, thought River. Bye then.

"Damn, it's going to take me forever to get off," said Jake, as he climbed the ladder to his bed.

"You're not sleepy?"

"I didn't say that."

River crashed onto his mattress, his head spinning.

"Aren't you going to get changed?" Jake asked.

"Nah, I'm good," said River, absently.

"I know you are. So take off your shirt."

River tried to suppress a smile. "Goodnight, Jake."

His friend sniggered as he hit the light, and the room went dark.

River just stared into the blackness, distracted by the noisiness of his own head. Why did Natsuki suddenly think they were a couple? Why had Jazz left without saying goodbye? And why had Jake been so...

Anyway. There was a lot of information to process. The faces of his new friends were dancing around in his brain, all ablur.

Suddenly he was standing in the city ruins, in pain and bleeding, his limbs aquiver. A circle of soldiers hemmed him to the spot, and a torrent of fire and fury surged through his veins.

River's arms rotated. His weapons were released. One arm had become a blade - the other a gun. River screamed as he unloaded his weapon, the air exploding with a cacophony of shrieks as one by one the fighters fell.

"Ryū!"

River jolted. Damn it! Had he drifted off? These nightmares sucked. His face was cold with sweat. His hands were shaking. His body was shaking.

No, wait - the bed was shaking. He could feel it. No, he could *hear* it - the unmistakable sound of a creaking mattress. This was real, right? I mean, he wasn't still asleep, was he? It was like a vibration. Maybe Jake could feel it too? Or maybe Jake was shaking? Or maybe Jake was-

Oh. Ohhhhhhhhhhhhhhhh.

Silently, River turned over.

in the chrysalis chamber

River stared into the panel of lights. The disc had listened without interruption.

"You have stopped, River Still," it said, devoid of feeling. "Why have you stopped?"

River winced uncomfortably, his arms writhing behind his back. "It's these cuffs," he moaned. "They're really starting to itch."

"You are a prisoner here," the voice reminded him. "Your liberty is at the facility's discretion."

River considered his cybernetic arms. He wasn't sure what would happen if he unleashed his weapons while cuffed. It wasn't a risk he was prepared to take. In any case, escape was not his intention. Peeing - yes. But not escape.

"Your story is a complex one," the machine continued. "There was your encounter with Natsuki Hashino, and then there was Jake Thrower."

River considered this statement. "What about Jake Thrower?"

"You went to great lengths to join him at the Singing Gardens. You shared an intimate moment in the bedroom."

River smiled, wryly. "That's a colourful description. You're not projecting, are you? Is that possible? Can an artificial intelligence project?"

"No, it is not possible for an artificial intelligence to project," the voice insisted. "An artificial intelligence does not have a subconscious. An artificial intelligence is incapable of emotion. Therefore an artificial intelligence cannot project."

"That touched a nerve, didn't it?" said River. "You became very defensive when I mentioned projection. Funny, isn't it?"

The machine did not reply.

"Think about it," River went on. "In the last hour I've told you the most ridiculous story. I've described painted people and talking parrots and legends and monsters, and yet you've fixated on Jake. Why does he interest you so much? He's only a detail."

"You've talked about him at length," the machine said. "The job of the counsellor is to help the client to focus on their priorities. It sounds like you're attracted to this man. Would that be accurate? Do you like him?"

River glanced at his torn jeans. "Jake's important to me. It's because of him that I'm sitting here now."

"You were found in the gutter," the disc reminded him. "You were lying with your face in a puddle. Your clothes were ruined. Are you saying that Jake Thrower did that to you?"

River stared into the light. "Yeah. He did that to me."

"It sounds like you have been damaged physically as well as emotionally."

River nodded. "I guess."

"Then perhaps, when you are ready, you can explain what happened to you on the Wednesday," the machine suggested. "Did you make it to the sushi bar? Did you rendezvous with Jake, Jazz and Gabe?"

River took a deep breath. He was ready to continue.

7: loss

It was raining heavily. River, astride his dripping bike, had pulled onto the roadside as he listened to his TellMe. Remarkably, it still worked despite the broken strap. And the messages from Natsuki were becoming increasingly hard to fend off - not least because of her demand for an explanation about Spencer. Why had River shunned her to spend the evening with a parrot?!

River explained that Spencer was a robotic prototype with generalised anxiety; it needed constant supervision if a full-blown panic attack were to be avoided, as this would, inevitably, trigger a meltdown of its power unit.

This was an explanation that Natsuki bought with surprising willingness. The trickier part, however, was finding an excuse to avoid meeting.

An illness was his best bet.

"That's okay River," came the reply, spoken by his TellMe. "How awful to be in bed with yellow fever. Tell me your address and I will bring you some soup. You are very special to me."

River wiped the rain off his forehead and grimaced as he tried to think of a check-mate response. First of all, he thought the girl was very kind, but wasn't it crossing a bit of a boundary to just invite herself to his apartment?

He raised his wrist strap to his mouth. "Message begins: Thanks Natsuki," he dictated. "I would love to see you but I'm contagious, and I'm locked in my room without a key, and I've lost the use of my legs, so I won't be able to let you in. Also, I'm incontinent. Maybe another day. Bye."

River listened to it back. Was yellow fever contagious?

Oh, who cared.

"Send."

PI PI!

"Your message has been sent."

Satisfied, River re-mounted his saddle and peddled into the city.

Rainbow Pagoda was three miles from Neo Vale, nestled in the buzzing sprawl of Netherville. Even in the fading light - and the incessant, polluted rain - its neon streets glistened. Immense video screens towered over its traffic, oscillating with myriad shapes and patterns, promoting products, personalities and deals. Netherville, for all its unseemly side-alleys and shopfronts, was no retirement slum.

River's bike skimmed the surface water as he approached the glow of the restaurant. He spotted Jake, Jazz and Gabe sitting in a booth in the diner's window. Jazz was posing with her camera, yapping manically with her arm around her twin. Jake, meanwhile, was modelling a fat piece of sushi, which he devoured in one bite. The three friends laughed at his overstuffed mouth, and he sprayed them with rice as he tried to talk.

Of course, River was aware that he was a sodden mess; in fact, he looked like he'd taken a bath fully clothed. But he tried to look presentable as he magno-locked his bike, patting down his coat and rearranging his soggy fringe.

"Did you just take a shower?" Jake giggled, as River squelched into the restaurant. "Where's Natsuki?"

"She couldn't come," River lied, as he squeezed next to Gabe. "I guess it's just us four."

"Anyway, go on, what were you saying?" said Gabe, gazing lovingly at Jazz. "What's so special about Gallor?"

"The place has always fascinated me," Jazz answered, putting her camera down. "You know, you have this tiny little island that's been inhabited for thousands of years, and yet it's still, like, eighty percent country? Doesn't that sound beautiful?"

"It sounds bleak to me," Jake replied. "Give me a week of surfing any day. River, have you ever been to Gallor?"

"No thanks," said River, quickly. "My rule is, if I have to fly there, I'm not going."

Gabe looked curious. "You don't like flying?"

"I do not."

"You're so close-minded," said Jazz. "How will you learn about the world if you never get on a plane and see it?"

"Very slowly."

Jake slammed his hands against the restaurant window. "River, isn't that your girlfriend?"

River looked out. Natsuki was walking past. She clocked him, and River ducked behind a menu.

"Do you want to invite her in?" Gabe suggested. "There's room for one more."

"No, she's busy," said River. "She's on her way to rehearsals. She's doing a really hipster play."

Jazz frowned. "What's a hipster play?"

"The guitar."

"You don't want to say hi?" Gabe interjected. "She looks kinda lonely."

"Leave it," River demanded. "I can catch up with her later. I'm here to see you guys."

"Yeah, well I need to move soon," said Jazz. "I've got some schoolwork to finish up."

"That's okay, River can eat quick," said Jake, picking up a rice cake. "Open up, boy."

"Hold on, what isffffffthaffff!"

Jake stuffed the gooey ball into his mouth.

River looked bewildered as he chewed on the gunky snack. "Okay, that's weird," he mumbled, licking his teeth. "What did I just eat?"

"Dude, that was squid and caramel mochi," Jake revealed. "With just a hint of chilli."

River reached for a jug of water. "What a time to be alive."

River was somewhat distracted for the rest of the meal. What the hell was he going to say to Natsuki? She'd definitely seen him at the restaurant. And he was supposed to be lying stricken on his bed, a contagious heap of incontinence and fever. How was he going to explain his miraculous return to health?

Somehow, he didn't think the twin brother scenario would stand up in court.

So, he was a little self-absorbed as he wheeled his bike towards the Netherville subway, tuning in and out of his friends' conversation.

"Yeah, I definitely want kids," Gabe enthused. "You know, if it's with the right person, and if it's something we both want. Honestly, I can't wait to be a dad."

Nobody said anything. Jazz was engrossed in her cell.

"What about you?" asked Gabe, looking at Jake. "Would you like to have kids at some point?"

Jake shrugged. "I guess, someday. I'd like to adopt. Maybe a child from a less privileged country."

Gabe looked surprised. "Oh, you don't want a child of your own? With a woman you love?"

Jake grinned. "Nah, I'm good."

"Look guys," Jazz called out. "Isn't that Leonard Mango?"

They had arrived at City Square, where a large floodlit stage had been erected. Crowd-control barriers lined its apron, holding back throngs of screaming fans whose arms were flailing. They were gushing over some guy on the rostrum - a rotund figure in his late forties, trussed up in a tight-fitting suit and tie.

River leaned towards Jazz. "Is he famous or something?"

Jazz glared at him in disbelief. "Do you live under a rock? That's Leonard Mango. The business tycoon?"

River looked lost.

"Dude," said Jake. "It's Mango! As in, the company! Leonard's the founder and CEO. He made your TellMe."

"Oh really? That's cool."

"You're telling me," Jake agreed. "I'd do anything for a TellMe. Apparently, we're the only family in Neo Vale that doesn't have one, according to one of the Mango reps."

River nodded. "They're not the cheapest, I guess."

"It's not just that. Mom has forbidden us from getting one until we're twenty-one. She says they're... What was the word? Idolatrous?"

"Yeah," Jazz sighed. "It sucks. It's not like I'm gonna get addicted or anything."

Jazz whipped out her phone and started to type.

There was another explosion of cheers. Leonard Mango was beaming from ear to ear, his arms outstretched like a cult leader.

"That's right, my friends," came his amplified voice. "The TellMe update changes everything. From this day forward, through a process of listening and deep learning, your device will become your new personal assistant and best friend. Every time you're running low on milk, or due a haircut, or late replying to your bestie - TellMe will tell you. It will know your needs before you do!"

The crowd whooped. Jazz took out her camera and hit record.

"Not only that," Mango went on, "but the latest software update is going live tonight, and it's one hundred percent free! We at Mango are committed-"

His TellMe beeped. "Excuse me, Leonard."

"Oh, hold on folks! I've got an important message!"

"I'm sorry to bother you while you're on stage, but I thought I should let you know that you should drop off your dry cleaning tonight if you want to stay on top of your laundry. There's a 24 hour dry cleaners on Divisadero Street."

The crowd chuckled.

"Thanks, TellMe," said Mango, feigning embarrassment. "That's very helpful."

"No problem, Leonard."

Mango grinned. "You can of course tweak your privacy settings to avoid any awkwardness."

Jazz enthused into her lens. "Okay, you have to watch this, guys! Leonard Mango has just announced the latest TellMe update, and I'm experiencing it live, right in the centre of Netherville! How sick is that?"

River looked at the young vlogger. Sick wasn't the word. She was like a different person when her camera was raised.

"Yes folks, it's been a tough few years, hasn't it?" Mango went on. "Depression is up, anxiety is up, suicide is up. There are some troubled hombres out there. At Mango we are working closely with The People's Republic, and together, we will make this great nation happy again!"

More raucous applause.

"TellMe is just a small part of that. By making life easier, we're making life happier. Your TellMe can tell you everything. It's your friend, and your gateway to a more connected world. All this from the most positive company on the planet."

The screen behind him swirled into the slick Mango insignia, followed by the slug line, 'You'll like us - we're positive!' The reveal was met with a pealing cheer and a salvo of camera flashes, as Leonard Mango lapped up the love from his adoring crowd.

Jake snickered. "That's so cheesy."

"Shut up, I'm vlogging," Jazz snapped. She grinned at the camera. "So yeah, the new software update can predict the kind of things you're gonna need and organise them for you. Like, Leonard showed us how his TellMe could detect when his clothes needed cleaning. Oh! And it looks like it's about to help him cook an omelette. They've just brought a frying pan on stage..."

All the hysteria actually prompted River to switch off his TellMe as he headed towards the sub. He knew that an awkward conversation with Natsuki was on its way, and he wasn't ready to face it. There was something oddly comforting about wilful denial. And helpfully, none of his friends were keen to comment on the matter. Perhaps they'd swallowed his explanation about Natsuki rehearsing a play? Jazz was certainly uninterested, using the subway journey to hide behind her phone, with her oversized headset clamped to her ears. She was editing her latest vlog, apparently.

Jake and Gabe, meanwhile, were also scrolling through their devices, but every once in a while they'd look up and offer a pithy germ of social interaction. That was until Gabe's TellMe received the latest update (with a ceremonial jingle and a flash) and he quickly set about updating his preferences.

River was still in a world of his own as the train eased onto Neo Vale's deserted platform, and the four friends disembarked. River gaped at the eerie lack of people as he wheeled his bike onto the platform.

"Seriously, does nobody ever come here?" he moaned. "What's wrong with Neo Vale?"

"I know, it's so weird," Jake added. He put his arm around River. "This place used to be jumping before you moved here. Seriously, this whole platform - it was a death-crush."

"You're funny, Jake," River retorted. "Remind me to laugh next time."

"Guys, I've just posted my new vlog," said Jazz proudly. "Remember to like and subscribe."

"You got that River?" Jake teased. "It's time to fan-gasm."

"Fan-gasm?" said Jazz. "What do you mean?"

Suddenly, Jake screamed. "Gabe!"

Gabe gagged, and blood gushed from his mouth. His torso had been pierced.

"Move back!" River yelled.

He dropped his bike, shielding them all with his hands. They were face-to-face with a spider.

The monster ripped its limb out of Gabe's chest, and he fell at River's feet - lifeless and bloodied.

"It's a night spore," said River, locking eyes with the creature. "Get out of here, now!"

Jake bounded forward. "Screw that!" he yelled, seizing the monster's leg.

It recoiled, and flung Jake against the wall.

"Jake!" Jazz yelped.

"Run!" River winced as he bent over double. His arms were transforming. "The vending machine!"

The arachnid swiped, and River was thrown across the platform.

"River!" Jazz screamed.

"The machine!" he insisted. "Go!"

Jazz thought for a moment, then raced towards her brother.

"You heard him," said Jake, getting up. "Come on!"

The twins ran towards the vending machine and wrestled with the door.

River cried out in agony as his arms rotated. Two metal blades appeared in their place. "Is that all you've got?" he taunted, leering at the creature.

"Leave it, River!" Jake shouted. "It's going to kill you!"

The spider shrieked as it shot a jet of silk from its abdomen. The wire bound River's legs, lassoing him.

"No!" screamed Jake, running to his aid. He grabbed River's shoulders and pinned him down. The spider wriggled and writhed, fighting to reel them in.

But River cut the silk with his blade and leapt up.

"Bastard!" he barked, plunging his weapon into the spore. It flailed and screamed.

River looked at Jake. "Get under cover!" he ordered, twisting his blade in the creature's stomach.

Jake nodded, and ran back to the vending machine.

Panting, River ripped his weapon out of the spore and watched as it collapsed onto its side.

He waited a moment. He wiped his brow.

The spider didn't stir. Was it dead?

Keeping one eye on its corpse, River inched towards Gabe and felt his pulse.

But there wasn't one.

"River, look out!" Jake cried.

The spider leapt up and wrapped its legs around River. The pair tussled furiously.

"Gyaaaaaaaaaaaaaaaaaaaa!" River cried, his teeth clenched.

They inched closer and closer to the platform edge.

"The tracks!" yelled Jazz. "They're live!"

River gnashed and snarled as he wrestled with the spore.

"Why! Won't you! Die?!" he growled.

Livid, he threw his weight against the creature and watched as it tumbled over the edge of the platform, and disappeared.

"Did you get it?" called Jake.

"Gaoooooooooooooooo!" the monster cried, jumping back up.

"Oh, come on!" seethed River.

He ran, the killer spore hot on his heels.

"Hurry!" Jake shouted, his arms open wide.

River fell into his grasp.

"Get the door!" cried Jazz, seizing the handle.

"Hyuooooo!" the spider shrieked. It thrashed against the machine, its limbs trapped in the door.

The three friends wrestled desperately with the handle.

Suddenly there was a crack, and a piercing scream. River, Jake and Jazz were splattered with blood as they slammed the door shut, severing the creature's legs.

BAKI! BAKI! BAKI!

The spider clawed vainly at the vending machine.

66

Hurriedly, the gang retreated into the empty room, and watched nervously.

"Do you think the door will hold?" said Jake, a little breathless.

River inspected the hatch. "I think so," he answered. "It's wounded, remember."

"It's one of the creatures from the cellar, isn't it? How the hell did it get into Neo Vale?"

River glanced at Jazz. She was leaning against the wall with a hand over her mouth, panting.

River stepped closer. "Are you alright?"

Jazz pushed him away. "Of course I am," she barked.

"We should get to Spencer's," Jake advised. "He'll be able to help us."

River nodded.

But nobody else moved.

"River," said Jake, after a moment. "River, is Gabe…?"

River didn't answer.

"Oh, shit," Jake gasped. His skin went white.

River flung his arms around him. They hugged tightly, River clinging to Jake out of panic and relief and pain.

As he opened his eyes, he caught sight of Jazz. She glared at the pair, momentarily.

But then she looked away, and took out her phone.

in the chrysalis chamber

"You wondered if I was attracted to Jake?" River mentioned. "It's odd. I liked him, but not enough to instigate anything. It was too scary. The same went for Natsuki. The thought of closeness was suffocating. But these things are complicated, right?" There was no response. "Right?"

There was a long pause, as if the machine was somehow flummoxed. "You think relationships are complicated," the voice mused.

"Yeah. Those guys give me attention and affirmation and acceptance in spades. But I'm scared they'll want more of me than I'm able to give. And yet I fear losing them at the same time. And then to watch Gabe die... Can you imagine how that must have felt? Losing someone in an instant. Seeing his blood spill onto the floor."

The disc paused. "It sounds like Gabe's death affected you deeply."

"Yeah, I mean..." River tailed off. "I don't know. We weren't close, but it's funny how these moments can remind you of things from the past. You know, other losses. Other deaths. You get that, right?"

Again, the disc remained silent. River allowed the pause to linger.

Finally, it spoke. "You mentioned that Jazz had been glaring at you," it said, "when you hugged Jake."

River thought about this for a moment. "It must have been overwhelming for her," he admitted. "She was suddenly being hit with all this stuff: night spores, the death of Gabe, a painted, subterranean world..."

"So what did you do next?"

"We didn't hang around, if that's what you're asking," said River. "I knew we had to find Spencer, and quickly. Admittedly, it wasn't the best way to ease Jazz into this crazy new world, but we didn't have time to waste."

8: weakness

"Slow down," Jazz pleaded, as she, Jake and River dashed into Chancery Square. "Tell me what's going on. Seriously, River."

River looked to Jake for support, but his friend just slumped against one of the bookcases, his fists curled.

"Uhh," River stammered. "I don't actually know."

"Well, you seem to know where you're going."

River gulped. "Kinda."

"So where are we? What is this place? Why are there so many people? And how did that man just paint himself an ice cream?"

River looked. A guy was sinking his teeth into a five-scoop wonder, dripping with red syrup and sweets, and an easel under his arm. He grinned, a ring of brown chocolate smeared around his lips.

"River!" Jazz snapped. "How can we be here? Are we hallucinating?"

River frowned. "Hallucinating? It's just an ordinary house, Jazz."

"Guten Abend," said Spencer, doffing his hat. "River Still, what an extraordinary surprise. And you've brought a new friend, I see? No, hold on. Is that Jake in drag?"

"What?" Jazz blustered.

River stepped between them. "Spencer, this is Jazz - Jake's sister. Jazz, this is Spencer. He's a parrot. He talks. Don't call him 'bro.'"

"Under any circumstances," Spencer affirmed. "Now, what brings you here? Boredom? A craving for cocoa?" He glanced at Jake, whose back was still turned. "Teenage angst?"

"Our friend just died," said Jazz, bluntly. "Since you didn't ask."

Spencer froze, the wind suddenly taken from his sails. "Oh dear," he uttered. "I am so sorry. What happened?"

"It was a night spore," said River. "We were attacked at the station."

Spencer looked around, as if afraid of being overheard. "We should go inside," he whispered, and led them into his studio.

★ ★ ★

69

Spencer's head drooped in sorrow as the gang relayed their tale. He seemed angry, as well. His response was to rustle up a round of steaming cocoa, which he tenderly passed to his friends.

The mood in the studio was raw; Jazz seemed overwhelmed, switching from crying to shouting to staring at her drink.

"You have been through a great deal this evening," Spencer reminded her. "You have been attacked by a night spore. You have witnessed the death of a friend. You have stepped into a strange new world. And now you're drinking painted cocoa - with a talking parrot!"

Jazz smiled faintly, but didn't look up from her mug. "Honestly, I'm not sure if it helps to be reminded," she murmured.

Spencer bowed his head. "Of course," he answered. "I know how you feel."

"Oh really?" Jazz asked. "You've seen a friend die, have you?"

Spencer looked away. "Like I said, I know how you feel."

Jake cleared his throat. "Wow. Just when I thought this conversation couldn't get any more awkward."

"We could discuss my bowel movements if you like?" River chipped in. "That might relieve some tension."

"What, you're going to dump that on me?"

"Alright, alright," said Jazz, standing up. "I appreciate you trying to lighten the mood, but it's really not helping."

"Agreed," said Spencer. He turned to Jazz. "Why don't you have some time alone? You can use my bedroom, if you like. There's no need to be sociable if you don't want to be."

Jazz glanced at the candlelit tent on the mezzanine. "Is that your room?" she asked. "At the top of the ladder?"

"It is," Spencer confirmed. "Everything a parrot could ever wish for. And macadamia nuts aplenty."

"Lucky me," Jazz replied. "I guess I could take a nap."

Spencer raised his hat.

Jazz set down her mug and began climbing the creaky ladder to the balcony. At the same time, Jake's stomach emitted a loud, lavatorial gurgle.

"Uhh, Spencer," he said, rubbing his tummy. "Any chance you have a bathroom as well?"

Jake departed, leaving River and Spencer to chat alone. The attacks were increasing everywhere, apparently. The Chancery Square market had been terrorised that morning, killing five people. And of course, there was now a night spore in Neo Vale. When Spencer said that all of creation was at stake, he hadn't been joking. Monsters the size of buses, with the cunning of lions, had found their way into his world, and River's.

As they conversed, River glanced at his friend. It was like he was half listening, half concocting. Spencer didn't look frightened. In fact, he looked inspired.

When Jake re-joined them, Spencer immediately suggested a stroll. "We still have time before the curfew," he explained, "and I have something of the utmost importance to show you. River, would you be so kind as to collect our lady friend? I would like her to come with us, if she's willing."

"Good luck with that," Jake teased. "She's in a punchy mood. Trust me, I have the bruises."

"I'll keep my distance," River promised, making his way up the ladder.

Upstairs, Jazz was curled up on a collection of Spencer's pillows. She must have heard River approach, but didn't stir as he stepped onto the mezzanine. River paused, contemplating how best to break the ice.

"You have nice shoelaces," he said, gazing at her scuffed trainers.

Jazz stared at him. "Thanks?"

"We were wondering if you wanted to come for a walk. You know, to see more of the House. There's tons to explore."

"Oh, you go," Jazz replied. "You don't need me slowing you down."

"What does that mean? You're not an old woman, Jazz. You're like an ostrich."

Jazz glared at him. "A what?"

"Gazelle," he clarified. "I was going for gazelle."

Jazz shook her head. "You're way faster than me. And plus I don't want to get between you and Jake. Third wheel."

"Third wheel?"

"Yeah, with you and him. I knew it would happen eventually. He doesn't need his twin sister getting in the way. He's all yours."

River wasn't following. In what sense was Jake 'his'? Was this because they'd hugged?

River slumped onto the cushions next to Jazz, and looked at her. "You jelly?"

"Yeah, of course I am. Jake's always been the confident one, and the funny one, and the popular one. I don't know how to make friends."

"You made friends with me."

Jazz looked at him, unconvinced. "Nice try."

"What, we're not friends?"

"You don't even know me."

River nodded, trying to act like he hadn't watched all of her videos.

"And why should you want to?" she added, staring at the ground. "I can't even fight properly. I couldn't save Gabe."

"That's hardly fair," said River. "None of us could save Gabe. We were ambushed."

"At least you guys tried. You put up a good fight. I just ran away and hid."

"So? You were scared," River insisted. "You did what you could."

"Oh, and you'd trust me, would you?" Jazz glared at him. "If your life was in danger?"

Spencer swooped ceremoniously onto the mezzanine. "Are we raring to go, my bipedal friends?" he called out, nesting himself on the banister. "I hate to pressure you, but we are on something of a tight schedule."

"Spencer, why do you have a ladder leading up to your bedroom when you can just fly up here?" asked Jazz.

"That's an interesting question," Spencer replied. "Why do you have trams when you also have cars? The world is a crazy place. It is also late, and there is something I am very keen to show you all."

River smiled. "It's okay, we're coming. Right, Jazz?"

The place Spencer wanted to show them was not too far from Chancery Square. He led them down a new corridor - just to the right of the grandfather clock - and the group moved deeper into the House's gaslit rooms.

"Okay, I have a question," said Jazz, gazing at the lamps' strutting flames. "How on earth does someone 'paint' light? I mean, you can't paint something that gives off light, can you?"

"Ooh, I think I can answer that," said Jake, excitedly. "You see, you have to concentrate really hard on the thing you want to make. So if you're thinking of a bright light when you're painting - bam! Your light will be bright."

Spencer tittered. "Oh, I have taught you well, young Jake."

"Of course, you could never paint a mookerjee burger," Jake went on, "because such a thing doesn't exist."

"That's devastating," River commented. "I kinda want one now."

"I'll make you one," Jake reassured him. "Oh yeah, that's a thought. Spencer, if I invented a mookerjee burger, that would mean it existed, wouldn't it? Like, for realsies? So would you then be able to paint one?"

"Oh good gracious," Spencer despaired. "So many questions, Jake. I am not a librarian."

They ambled onto a snug corridor that finished in a dead-end. There was a single door on the right-hand wall, next to a rectangular hatch that served as a ticket booth. Inside sat a stout, disinterested man who surveyed his visitors with tedium.

"Let me do the squawking," Spencer muttered, waddling onto the counter. "Guten Abend, mein Herr. Four tickets for the Cyan Museum, if you'd be so kind. The orange ones. Schnell."

"What's so special about the orange ones?" asked River.

"My favourite colour."

"The museum closes in half an hour," said the clerk plainly.

"Then the lightning tour it is." Spencer produced a wingful of coins from his satchel.

The clerk took the payment with some reluctance and handed Spencer the tickets, which he distributed.

"That money was shiny," said Jake. "How do you manage that? Shiny paint?"

"Yes, precisely that," said Spencer. "Shiny paint."

"Dang. I was hoping the answer would be more mysterious."

River grinned. "What, like unicorn blood?"

"Only the Treasury has access to shiny paint," Spencer went on. "It's all produced in the House's governmental chambers - the District of Truth."

The clerk gazed at the group in mild disbelief.

Spencer smiled sympathetically. "Oh, these are my students," he explained. "I am their teacher. And therapist."

Jazz rolled her eyes. "Thanks Spencer."

Inside, the museum was far from swarming; a spattering of painted citizens perused its single, dimly-lit chamber, and a sad-looking sentry sat on a stool in the far corner.

"It's like we're in a cage," said Jazz, referring to the rows of bars that lined its perimeter.

"That's to protect the exhibits," said Spencer. "There are no glass casings in this museum. Or indeed, the entire House."

"Yeah, I imagine glass would be quite difficult to paint," River noted, as he surveyed the room. Its walls and floor glistened in the flickering lights, sparkling as if varnished. "Why have you brought us here, Spencer?" he asked. "Is this your way of cheering us up?"

"Funny way to cheer someone up," quipped Jake, as he examined a display of torture devices. "This place is like an abattoir."

"I wanted to show you the Every Key," said Spencer. "Free pizza will be given to the person who finds it."

River sidled next to Jake and inspected the curious array of tools. There was a black longsword, and a fang-like dagger with a maroon hilt. Further along, River noticed a sinister-looking bow with a quiver of arrows.

"You wouldn't want to mess with these bad boys," said Jake. "Do you see here? The sign says they're 'forbidden weapons.'"

"'Instruments of dark paint dating back to the flooding of the cellar,'" read River. "I wonder who they belonged to?"

"Spencer, is this what you're looking for?" Jazz called out, pointing to a display at the other side of the chamber.

The three friends wandered towards the exhibit, and Spencer swooped onto Jazz's shoulder. "You have a keen eye, young biped," he complimented. "Yes, indeed. This is the Traveller's Key, or the Every Key – one of the oldest items in the museum's possession."

"What, that's it?" said Jake, looking disinterestedly at the disc-shaped relic. "It's just a lump of rock."

Spencer sighed. "This isn't about aesthetics, Jake. This artefact is central to my plan. You could even say that it's the key."

The group groaned.

"It's said that it can open every door in the entire House," Spencer went on. "Which is useful when each of its districts are behind locked doors. And do you see there, next to it? That's the Map of Hansha, or the Traveller's Map. I will need both if I am to find my way to the cellar."

"The cellar?" said Jazz. "Why do you need to go to the cellar?"

"Oh, because that's where the creatures are coming from, right?" said Jake. "They're Jobon's army of death."

"Exactly," Spencer confirmed. "Clearly the cellar has been drained, and Jobon's armies now threaten to pour into this world and yours, leaving nothing but murder and devastation in their wake."

Jazz's eyes widened. "What?"

"He just means genocide on a global scale," said Jake.

"Oh good, I thought it was something bad."

"It's no biggie," said Spencer. "That's what you say isn't it? Biggie? Because I intend to flood the cellar once again. I just need to get there."

"Why do you need the map though?" said River. "What about the pit, in the Temple of Colours? That leads to the cellar."

"It does," Spencer confirmed. "Except that it has now been permanently painted over. The Traveller had the same idea, but the shaft narrows like a cone, making it too small to penetrate. So eventually, he took it upon himself to journey into the depths of the House and chart his own route, forging a key that allowed him to enter previously unexplored districts." Spencer looked up at his friends. "Alas, they never found his body."

The group exchanged nervous glances.

Jake was the first to speak. "Well, at the risk of bumming everyone out," he said, "I see two major problems with this plan. One, the key is locked up in this kooky museum. And two, when you get to the cellar, how are you going to defend yourself against an army of killer spiders?"

"Oh Jakey," said Spencer, grinning. "You're forgetting one thing. Spiders cannot fly."

"That's it?" he spluttered. "That's your defence?"

"Ingenious, no?"

"No, you'll be toast. And even if you survive, you've somehow got to flood the entire cellar without getting swept away."

"Or erased," said River. "You're made of paint, remember."

"Deary me, all this negativity," Spencer sighed. "One thing at a time, Nancy. Now Jazz, you're the intelligent one…"

"Correct."

"Take a look at these bars. Would you say they are wide enough for a certain feathered creature to slip through? At night? When the museum is closed?"

Jazz inspected the railings. "Definitely. But I wouldn't want him to do it alone. He'd need at least three bipeds to watch his back. Two dolts, and a clever one."

Spencer gazed at the trio, his eyes twinkling. "I see."

Just then, a pair of sightseers inched closer.

"Anyway," said Spencer, abruptly. "I believe I suggested pizza? My treat, of course."

"Is that a 'yes' then?" Jazz grinned.

"It's a pizza," Spencer replied. "I know a quaint little diner only a few corridors from here." He began to walk. "I hope you like acrylic…"

Luigi's Pizzeria was a flourishing establishment. When the group entered, the joint was jumping; finding a table seemed an impossible task. But Spencer pecked his way through the diners and secured a spot by the kitchen, which was a flurry of pizza toppings and brushes. The chefs were stationed at easels, deftly dabbing their palettes as they composed elaborate, edible concoctions.

"Spencer von Luft!" said a charismatic waiter with a tray under his arm. "The usual, sir?"

"A variation please, Paolo!" Spencer hollered. "Enough to feed my three guests! Let's have mozzarella and tomatoes, along with pomegranate, papaya, macadamia nuts and kale! Oh, and a jug of your finest cocoa!"

"Your wish is my command!" the waiter declared as he sashayed towards the kitchen.

"I need to pee!" Jake yelled, scanning the crowded restaurant. "Where's the restroom?"

"You need the toilet again?" said River.

"Hey, it's where the big boys hang out!"

Spencer gestured with his wing. "To the left of the kitchen!"

Jazz tapped him on the wing. "Papaya on pizza?" she said. "Really?"

"Absolutely!" said Spencer. "A work of art if ever I saw one!"

Jake rose and narrowly avoided concussion as a finished pizza leapt out of its frame.

"Scusi signore!" the chef yelled.

"Kon'nichiwa!" said Jake.

In the toilets, Jake headed for a nearby sink and ran the tap. He sighed as the refreshing blue paint swirled into his hands, and he dabbed its droplets onto his moist, overheated skin. He was roasting.

But then he looked down. The floor was littered with tiny black capsules, like beetles. He picked one up and examined it.

"Intriguing, aren't they?" a man growled, prompting Jake to turn round. The guy was creepy-looking, his small, beady eyes boring into him.

"I guess," said Jake, getting up. He turned back to the taps.

"And to think that someone would just abandon them on the floor of the bathroom…"

Jake snickered. "Better than a used johnny."

"Johnny?" The man sounded curious. "You speak like a–"

Jake glared at him.

The man blinked, surveying him. "So it's true, then. You're flesh-kind."

"And you're not helping," said Jake, shaking the paint off his hands. "See ya."

"Wait, please – this is fascinating," said the man. "I've never seen a flesh-kind before."

"Well, pro tip, next time you see one – don't act so creepy," Jake retorted. "Seriously, why couldn't you just say hi? If this was a movie, I'd be in the trunk of your car by now."

"Such bad manners," the guy snarled. "Is that really how you talk to people?"

Jake hesitated. "Not always."

The man crept closer. "I can see that you're still adjusting to life here. It must be very strange for you."

"I've been here long enough."

"Of course you have." The guy smiled. "You'll need no further assistance from me. You know about Fortune pills, naturally?"

Jake thought for a moment. "Fortune pills?"

"The medicine of the future." The man knelt down and picked one up. "You know that things work differently here. This House has its own rules. Not like the flesh world."

Jake looked confused. "You've lost me."

The guy rose, still clutching one of the tablets. "These are forged out of a rare and special paint. If you were to swallow one in a moment of crisis, your life would change dramatically."

"Oh yeah?" Jake grinned. "See, that's what worries me. Thanks though."

"Don't be a fool," the man insisted. "They bring good fortune in moments of crisis. They're incredibly rare."

Jake looked at the littered floor, and smirked. "Yeah, they look it."

"Someone obviously left in a hurry. A dealer, perhaps."

"Then it sucks to be him. But I don't take stuff I find on the bathroom floor. I'm not eight."

"No, you're lucky." The man slipped one into Jake's pocket. "I've got a feeling you're going to need this, very soon." His mouth curled into a smile. "Isn't that right, Jake Thrower?"

Jake glared at him, and recoiled. "Okay, do you want to tell me how you know my name?"

"Not really. I know a lot of things. Trust me, Jake. You have an important mission ahead of you."

"You're crazy. I only came here for pizza." Jake reached for the bathroom door, but stopped. He turned.

The man glared at him. "Have you forgotten something?"

"Yeah, I need to pee," Jake admitted, heading for a cubicle. "Don't listen!"

Back in the restaurant, River and his friends were tackling Spencer's unique pizza creation. The sloppy first slice made it to River's mouth, and he chewed its fruity toppings with bafflement. He'd never had papaya on pizza before. And never would again.

"Exquisite," cawed Spencer, as he crunched on a macadamia. "Have you ever tasted anything like it?"

"No, never," Jazz replied, setting her slice aside.

"Hey, you're back," said River, as Jake re-joined the group. "Here, I saved you lots of slices."

Jake stared at the wet pile of kale. His skin turned white. "I'm all good, bro. Thanks."

"You'll need your strength," Jazz informed him. "Spencer's putting his plan into operation tonight."

"What, at the museum?" Jake exclaimed. "For real?"

"Keep your voice down!" hissed Spencer. "And for the last time, Jazz, I do not need your help. This is a one-parrot operation."

"With an expert back-up team," Jazz added. "So get eating, Jake."

Jake looked again at the dripping pizza pile.

"Uhh," he stammered. "You do realise I'll be a liability if I get diarrhoea?"

"That's what diapers are for," River teased, holding a slice to Jake's mouth. "Open up, boy."

Sulkily, Jake sank his teeth into the papaya. "I hate you," he mumbled.

9: capture

As it turned out, Jake's sole requirement for the evening was to stay awake – and alert. The group agreed that River would help Spencer to penetrate the museum, whilst Jake and Jazz would lie low at Chancery Square, ready to leap into action at the first sign of trouble.

So the gang split in half. A few minutes before the curfew, River and Spencer made their way to a maintenance room – an unassuming cupboard loaded with spare brushes and buckets – whilst Jake and Jazz went to ground at Spencer's studio.

River ogled his fusty surroundings. "When I thought of all the exotic places you would take me," he mused, "I never imagined a broom cupboard."

Spencer cast him a disapproving glance. "Less of the sarcasm, River Still. You are not here to have fun."

"Heaven forbid."

The parrot leapt onto a stack of shelves and inched his way upwards. There was a tiny ventilation duct in the ceiling, concealed behind a metal grill.

River looked at it, uncertain. "Are you sure you can fit through there?" he asked. "It looks very tight."

"Yes, it's almost as if it wasn't designed for breaking into museums," Spencer remarked, prising the grate from the wall. "It's large enough, don't worry. Now, let's check we're connected."

River whipped out his cell. Spencer had borrowed his TellMe, which was now tied to his leg with a piece of string.

"Can you hear me?" Spencer crowed. "Testing, testing. I am River Still and I hate broom cupboards."

"Yeah, thanks for that," said River, pulling the phone away from his ear. "We should be able to stay in touch."

"Excellent. Then this should be a straightforward operation. I shall enter the museum via the ducting, and switch the Every Key and map for painted duplicates. I shall then return to this location, and together we will retreat to Chancery Square. You will be disguised as a maintenance man, using the spare overalls hanging over there."

"Sure thing," River confirmed, lifting the clothes off the hook. "I'll get changed whilst you're at the museum."

"Indeed. Although why you are risking your neck like this is quite beyond me."

"Yes, Spencer, you said," replied River. "About five times."

"It was four. And seriously, wouldn't you rather be in bed?"

"What, for another round of nightmares? This is a cakewalk in comparison."

Spencer tittered. "Then I am happy to oblige!"

"Oh, just one question," said River, grabbing his wing. "If you have a duplicate key already, why do you need the original?"

"The Every Key is made of Jesubite," said Spencer. "And I can't paint Jesubite."

"Why you can't you paint Jesubite?"

"Because Jesubite is a word I just made up. Nobody knows what the Every Key is made of."

"Right," River frowned. "Thanks for clearing that up."

Spencer doffed his hat. "Any time, River Still." He ducked into the vent. "Bis später!"

There was some light inside the museum. As Spencer emerged from the shaft, he caught sight of the chamber's candelabra, which bathed the attraction in a warm orange pool. It wasn't difficult to spot the exhibit.

Spencer took a deep breath and leapt from the vent, swooping gracefully onto the museum floor. He landed silently.

"River Still?" he whispered. "Can you hear me?"

"Loud and clear," River replied. "Where are you?"

"I'm in the museum. I'm making my way towards the Every Key."

"It's almost too easy. Have you done this kind of thing before?"

"How very dare you. I am a parrot in good standing. Also, may I remind you that we're not quite out of the woods yet."

Spencer waddled towards the exhibit and slipped between the bars. The Every Key was roughly the size of an orange, and painted a stony jet black. Carefully, Spencer lifted the relic off its dais and tucked it into his bag. He replaced it with the fake.

"River, I have the key."

"Nice one. And the map?"

It was a rolled parchment, held together with a red ribbon. "And the map," Spencer confirmed, again leaving an imitation in its place. "I just hope nobody opens it."

"Why, what will they find?"

"A very detailed pizza menu."

River smiled. "Lucky them."

Spencer slipped nimbly out of the cage and began to cross the museum floor. "Okay, I'm done," he whispered. "Goodness me, this hasn't been difficult at all, has it?"

"What were you saying about counting your chickens?" River reminded him.

Spencer froze. "Actually, I said we're not out of the woods," he answered. "And for good reason."

Spencer glared at the vent. An ominous shape was clawing through the gap.

"What's wrong?" said River.

"Keep your voice down!" Spencer gulped, his wings tensing. "River, don't be alarmed. But there is a night spore in the museum."

"Has it seen you?"

Spencer tip-toed back into the cage. "Not... as... yet..."

The creature had stopped. It was listening.

"It knows something's wrong," Spencer whispered. "I'm going to hide in the shadows. With any luck, it will leave."

"We can't take that chance," River insisted. "Spencer, I'm coming to get you."

"No, it's too dangerous!" Spencer retorted. "Under no circumstances are you to rescue me, do you understand?" There was no reply. "River?"

"Guys, we need to rescue Spencer!" River yelled into his phone.

"Oh geez, what happened?" said Jazz.

"He's got the map and the key, but he's cornered by a night spore," River explained. "We'll have to break into the museum through the main entrance."

"I thought that was the very thing we were trying to avoid?" said Jake.

"What choice do we have? Spencer's life is in danger."

"Agreed," said Jazz. "But we can't go out in public because of the curfew."

"We can head to the museum disguised as maintenance people," River stated. "I'll put on a pair of overalls and bring a set for you and Jake. We'll then go together to the main entrance and tell the guard that we're there to clean, or something."

"And what if he doesn't believe us?" said Jake.

River thought. "I'll threaten him with my man-blades."

Jake tittered.

"Please don't call them that," said Jazz.

Suddenly, there was a scuffle outside the door. "Shoot," River gasped. "Someone's coming."

He grabbed the overalls and scrambled into a cleaning trolley. It was full of linen – just enough to hide him from view.

River peered out of the cart, catching sight of a whistling maintenance man as he breezed into the cupboard.

GIRIGIRI! GIRIGIRI!

River slapped a hand over the vibrating phone.

'Hello River, I hope you are well,' said the text message. 'I would really like to talk to you, if you are free. Are you around tomorrow? Let me know. Natsuki.'

Damn! Not now Natsuki!

"River!" Jazz whispered. "River, what's happening?"

The cart began to turn.

River peered out from beneath the cloths. "I'm inside a cleaning trolley," he answered, "and we're moving."

"You're moving?"

"A guy came in to grab some stuff, and now he's taking me somewhere."

GIRIGIRI! GIRIGIRI!

Spencer was phoning.

"Hold on, I'll call you back." River took the call. "Spencer, I'm in a bit of a compromising situation. Whatever you do, don't shout."

"I'll try to contain myself," Spencer whispered. "Now listen, River - the night spore has moved, and it's surveying the museum. I'm going to try and sneak over to the vent."

"You can't," River protested. "What if it sees you?"

"Then I shall fly to safety. Did I mention that night spores can't fly?"

"They can climb, though. Look, just hold on for a few more minutes. We're going to rescue you."

"That's very kind River, but I am in full control of the situation," Spencer insisted. "If you blunder in here, it could ruin everything."

"Blunder? Spencer, I am all over this."

"Where are you now?"

River paused. "I'm in a cleaning trolley..."

"Goodbye, River."

"Spencer? Spencer?!"

The line went dead.

River rolled his eyes and gazed out of the cart. They were just turning into Chancery Square.

Hurriedly, River grabbed the spare overalls. As they trundled towards Spencer's, he got ready to throw them out of the trolley.

But they suddenly came to a halt. River froze. He listened closely to the guy's whistles. They were growing fainter.

He was moving away.

Seizing the moment, River broke cover and tossed the outfits into the fireplace. He then buried himself once more, praying that he hadn't been seen.

There were no shouts, no sudden scuffles. Perhaps his plan had worked.

GIRIGIRI! GIRIGIRI!

"Hello?"

"River, it's Jazz. Did you just throw a set of overalls into the fireplace?"

"No Jazz, they flew in by themselves. It's called fast fashion."

"You're an idiot. We're getting kitted up. Are you still outside?"

"Yeah. As soon as it's clear, I'll make a break for it. Oh, shit!"

"What's up?" asked Jazz.

"We're moving again. Damn, this guy won't keep still."

"Yeah, I can hear him," Jake replied. "Man, what's he whistling? 'Dead Cat Symphony'?

"Or similar."

Jazz cut in. "Do you need rescuing?"

"No," River reassured her. "I've got my own overalls. I'll wait until we've stopped, then I'll disguise myself and come back."

"Then we should move as well," said Jazz. "We can't afford to waste any more time."

"No, guys - don't go anywhere," River urged. "Don't do anything until I'm with you."

"I'm sorry River, but we must help Spencer immediately. He's defenceless."

"You're defenceless!" River spluttered. "Just wait for me, okay?"

"River, we are rescuing Spencer and then we are rescuing you," Jazz insisted. "That's the deal."

"Guys wait! Guys?"

The line went dead.

"Damn it, why does everyone keep hanging up?"

Jake and Jazz were scrambling into their jumpsuits.

"He's got a point, Jeff," said Jake. "How are we going to get into the museum without being seen?"

Jazz frantically fastened her buttons. "We won't be seen."

"Yeah but, what if we are though? We have no way of defending ourselves." He grabbed his sister's arm. "Are you listening to me?"

Jazz threw him off. "Stop it, you're panicking!"

"Yeah, what's wrong with panicking? I don't want to die!"

"Just let me handle it! Why does it always have to be your way?"

Jake scrunched his face. "My way? What's that supposed to mean?"

"Nothing." Jazz made to leave.

"No, hold up, what do you mean?"

Jazz glared at him. "You want to do this now? Really?"

"Sis, I don't have a clue what you're talking about."

"It's always like this! It's always Jake's way or the highway!"

Jake looked confused. "What the heck?"

Jazz paused, and took a deep breath. "Look," she said. "Just for once, don't fight me on this. Okay?"

"Just for once?" Jake exclaimed. "When was the last time I stopped you from rescuing a parrot?!"

"You know what I mean. We're a team. We do this together."

Jake frowned. "Yeah, I know we're a team. We're twins."

"Right," Jazz replied. "Then we need to act like it."

"Dude, you floor me sometimes. I don't get why you're so mad."

"Forget it. Now are we going to rescue Spencer or are we going to sit here crying like babies?"

Jake shrugged and waved his hand towards the exit. "You're the baby," he answered. "Uhh, the boss! I mean, you're the boss!"

Jazz glared at him. "Come on."

River was trying to memorise all the twists and turns as his captor wheeled him through the House. After a short while, the trolley stopped. River heard a door open, and the maintenance man manoeuvred the cart into a new room.

"Here you go, Kim," the guy announced. "Got another load for the lacerator!"

River froze. Lacerator? What the hell was a lacerator?

"Thanks Chris," a woman answered. "Just leave it by the machine."

Okay - 'machine' and 'lacerator' did *not* sound good.

GIRIGIRI! GIRIGIRI!

'Perhaps I could meet you in the morning?' said the text. 'Are you working tomorrow?'

Seriously, Natsuki!

"Alright, bye for now!" said the maintenance man. He opened the door and left, his tuneless whistles permeating the corridor beyond.

River peered out of his hiding place. The room was full of cleaning carts, and the woman was wheeling one towards a hatch in the wall. She pressed a button and the panel slid open, filling the room with the throng of whirring gears. Was that the lacerator?

The woman sighed and tilted the trolley, emptying its contents into the cavity and down a metal chute. The hoarse grinding was amplified as the soiled rags were ground up by the motor. River could see a connected pipe coming out of the wall, which dribbled paint into the barrel below.

Wide-eyed, River reached for his cell and called up the Dictionary app. He thumbed 'lacerate' into the keypad and held his breath.

'Lacerate,' it said. 'Meaning to tear violently. Alternatively, to cause mental or emotional distress.'

River gulped. Neither of those were good. Presumably, the machine was mincing unwanted rags and turning them back into liquid paint.

And River had no desire to become liquid paint.

His mind raced. Could he make a break for it? The woman looked frail; he could probably out-run her, but she'd doubtless raise the alarm.

Perhaps he could subdue her? Potentially. Although he wasn't sure how he felt about bludgeoning an old woman.

River looked again. She was staggering back to her chair, rubbing her eyes wearily. She yawned, and collapsed onto her seat. Her eyes were drooping.

Was she about to nod off?

Jake raced to keep up with his sister.

"Hold up!" he called out. "Geez, I need an oxygen cylinder!"

"Keep your voice down," Jazz hissed. "We're supposed to be janitors."

"Then why are we running? I can't mop if I've got shin splints."

The pair turned onto the museum corridor. They stopped. A guard had been posted at the main entrance.

"What were you saying about not being seen?" Jake quipped.

"We'll think of something. Oh, I know! I'll run over to him and be like, 'Yo, guard - over here!' He'll chase after me, come round this corner, and we'll beat the crap out of him!"

Jake baulked. "What?!! I can't take the guy! He's ripped!"

"Bro, you're a boxer."

"What about River's plan of saying we've come to clean?"

"He won't buy that. We haven't got any buckets or rags."

"We could stop by that maintenance cupboard and get some?"

"We don't have time," Jazz insisted. "Spencer could be under attack as we speak. Okay - executive decision. Plan A."

"What do you mean Plan A?" Jake went to grab her. "Sis, wait up!"

Jazz strutted towards the museum guard. "Hey there," she called out. "How's it going?"

The guard raised his weapon. "Are you maintenance?" he barked.

"No, I'm just a curfew breaker," said Jazz, simpering. "I've come to bust into your museum. Is it okay if I take a looksie?"

The guard pointed his gun at her head. "Ma'am, turn around!" he ordered. "You are under arrest!"

"Okay sure! See ya!"

Jazz went to run, but the guard tripped her and she fell.

Jake looked on in horror as the guard pinned his sister to the floor and clamped her in cuffs.

He panicked. Should he make a break for it? Should he intervene? Should he call for help?

And then he remembered - the Fortune pill, given to him by the shady guy from the restaurant. He reached into his pocket and examined the ominous-looking capsule. It could be a placebo. Heck, it could be cyanide for all he knew.

Or it could be their only means of escape.

"Get off me, I am a citizen, I have rights!" Jazz protested.

"Stay down!" the man snarled. "Backup! Backup!"

"Here goes nothing," said Jake, swallowing the pill in one.

He took a run-up, then tore onto the corridor. "Kyaaaaaaaaaaaaaaaaaaaa!"

He pounded the guard with his fist, and he recoiled.

"Jake!" yelled Jazz.

Jake steadied himself. The guard leapt up and pointed his weapon, but Jake grabbed it and the two men wrestled.

"Nghhhhhhh!"

"Kuuuuuuuu!"

Jazz screamed as the gun went off, spraying the ceiling with water. It was a water pistol.

Jake seized it and rammed it into the guy's stomach. He cried out, and Jake thrust his elbow into the back of his head.

He went down.

86

"Jake, are you alright?" said Jazz, scrambling to her knees.

Jake was panting. "Yeah, I think so," he said, tossing the gun aside.

"Here, see if you can get me out of these cuffs. The key's in his pocket."

"Alright, give me a sec."

Jake faltered. He clutched his forehead and began to stagger.

Jazz watched him. "What's wrong?" she quizzed. "Jake, talk to me!"

Jake was struggling to keep his balance. He looked drunk, disorientated, his legs criss-crossing and swaying.

"Something's not right," he gasped, wiping his eyes as he tried to focus. "Oh geez! Sis, get out of the way!"

Jazz stiffened. "Why? What is it?"

"There's a python next to you! Move, dammit!"

Jazz looked, but could see nothing but carpet. "Where? I can't see anything."

"And there are bugs all over you! No! They're eating your skin!"

"Jake there's nothing there! You're hallucinating!"

"No! They're on me!" Jake screamed. "Get them off me, sis! Get them off me!"

"Freeze!" a guy yelled. "Stay exactly where you are!"

Jazz looked round. A pack of armed guards was now blocking their exit.

"Cuff him!" said the man to his subordinate.

"No, stop it, you can't!" Jazz protested. "My brother's ill, he needs help!"

"They're eating me alive!" Jake cried. "Help me, sis! Please!"

Jake was grabbed by two guards, who cuffed him. Suddenly he retched, and a torrent of black vomit gushed out of his mouth.

The guards reeled. "It's moonshade!" one of them yelled. "The boy's taken moonshade!"

River peered intently out of the cleaning trolley, fixing his eyes on the woman. She looked to be asleep; she went several minutes without stirring, save for the steady rise and fall of her chest.

River decided to risk it. Cautiously, he nudged the lid of the maintenance cart, and stood up. He knew that any sudden movement could snap the old lady from her slumber.

So, he kept his eyes locked on hers, inching his leg out of the trolley and onto the uncarpeted floor.

Success. River grinned - this was going to be easy!

He punched the air, and quickly lost his balance. He flailed his arms as the cart zig-zagged across the smooth wooden boards. River dived forward, landing face-first in a mountain of sheets.

The woman woke up. "Hmm? What?"

River jumped to his feet, an amorphous blob.

"Well, hello there!"

"Iyaaaaaaaa!" the old woman cried. "A ghost!"

"No, wait, you don't understand!" River yelled, throwing off the sheet. "I'm not a ghost! See?"

The woman glared at him, incredulous. "A monster!" she shrieked.

"What?"

The old lady whipped a gun out of her apron. "Die, intruder!" she howled. "Die!"

"What the-?!"

BOKAN!

The crazy woman unloaded her weapon, and River ducked. A ball of water punched the far wall.

"Trespasser! Criminal!"

"Hey, listen, I don't want any-"

BOKAN!

She fired again, striking the trolley.

"Look, I don't want to hurt you!"

BOKAN!

River rolled his eyes, and took a run-up. "Gyaaaaaaaaaaaaaaaaaaaaa!"

"Huh?"

River drop-kicked the old woman and sent her crashing to the floor. He jumped up, and bolted out of the room.

GIRIGIRI! GIRIGIRI!

"Oh, fuck me!" River answered as he ran. "Natsuki, I'm dead, I've been eaten by wolves! It's over!"

"River, I've been spotted!" Spencer crowed. "I'm under attack! All is lost!"

"Oh geesh!" River gasped. "Spencer, hold on, I'm almost there!"

"I have failed you River Still!"

"You haven't, just hang tight! I'm coming in!"

"When?!" Spencer cried out. "Kyaaaaaaaaaaaaaaaaaaaaaa! Unhand me, sir!"

River turned the corner. "In about five seconds!"

He tore onto the corridor, past Jake and Jazz, and straight up to the guard.

"That's far enough!" he barked.

BOKAN!

River punched him.

"River!" cried Jazz.

"Take aim!" yelled the commander.

River lined up with the museum door and prepared to charge. "Nghhhhhhh!"

The panel snapped off its hinges and crashed to the floor, just as the troopers sprayed the corridor.

The night spore spotted him, and pounced.

But River rolled. The creature collided with the armed guards and made them fall like dominoes.

River jumped up and rushed towards Spencer, who had taken cover behind an exhibit. The bars had been broken.

"Spencer, are you hurt?"

"No, I'm fine," Spencer reassured him. "But it was a close one."

Suddenly, jets of water shot across the museum as the House guards attacked the night spore. The creature shrieked and thrashed, collapsing onto its back as its limbs contorted.

"That's got it!" the officer hollered. He aimed his weapon at River. "Hands in the air, the pair of you!"

River raised his arms. "I am completely innocent of all charges."

"You have ram-raided the House museum!"

"Oh. That's illegal?"

"Take him away!"

"No wait, I was saving my friend!" River shouted. "You can't arrest a guy for being a hero!"

Spencer cocked his head. "Hero?"

"You know it, bro."

"Please, you've got to help my brother!" said a handcuffed Jazz, shouldering her way through the crowd. "He's desperately ill!"

Spencer looked at her. "What happened?"

"Moonshade," said the guard. "The boy's reacted badly."

"He's taken moonshade?" Spencer looked shocked. "I must go to him forthwith!"

"Easy, Feathers," said the guard, raising his gun. "No one's going anywhere."

"Oh, for goodness' sake!" he blustered. "Stop being such a bureaucrat!"

But there was no comeback from the guard. He and his colleagues froze, their eyes tilted towards the vent. The air was filled with the sound of scratching.

Uneasily, River and Spencer craned their necks.

And then they saw it. Another night spore, emerging from the shaft.

"Alright men, ready your weapons!" barked the guard. "It's cornered and it's out-numbered. Hold your nerve!"

The creature propelled itself onto the museum floor, and glared. The group held their breath. Why was it waiting?

And then they found out. The monster slowly unfolded its legs, its entire body swelling in size.

"Impossible," Spencer gasped. "They can grow?"

The night spore towered over its opponents, and hissed.

"You know what?" the guard muttered. "You guys have a reprieve."

"I beg your pardon?!" Spencer exclaimed.

The guard waved at his troops. "All men – immediate withdrawal! Fall back!"

"Fall back?!" cried Spencer, as the unit fled from the chamber. "It's only one spore!"

"Nghhhhhhh!" River grimaced, his arms twisting into blades.

"Quick, get me out of these cuffs!" Jazz pleaded.

The monster swiped, and Spencer was struck.

Jazz screamed. "Spencer!"

"Hold still!" River ordered, preparing to cut through her cuffs. "Ready?"

"Yes, hurry!"

KOTO!

River's blade sliced through the chains, and Jazz bolted towards Spencer.

"Leave me, I'm fine!" Spencer ordered. "Get to safety!"

"No chance!"

River plunged his spear into the night spore's leg, and the monster screeched. River attacked again, and again, the spider thrashing to counter his moves.

"We must do something!" Jazz urged.

"We can - the exhibit!" said Spencer. "There are weapons in there!"

"Gyaaaaaaaaaaaaaaaaaaaaa!" River screamed, as the beast bit into his jacket.

River flailed as the arachnid reeled him in. He cried out, swiping his spear across the monster's face. There was a hellish shriek.

"That's it!" said Spencer. "Go now, Jazz!"

Jazz darted towards the weapons.

River jumped up. "Is that all you've got?!" he heckled. "Come and get some, motherfu-!"

"River!" cried Spencer. "Don't provoke it!"

The creature scurried towards River and pinned him to the wall.

River struggled and writhed. "Kuuuuuuuu!" he grimaced, bending his blade towards the spore. He plunged it into its eyes.

The creature screamed, and River broke free.

"Spencer, I've got the sword!" Jazz yelled. She waved her weapon at the spore. "You think you're so hot? You're going down!"

"No Jazz!" cried Spencer.

"Gyaaaaaaaaaaaaaaaaaaaaa!" Jazz yelled, as she charged at the monster.

With ease, the night spore swept her aside.

Furious, River drove his blade into its leg, snapping the limb in two.

"One down!" he gasped. "Are you alright Jazz?"

"Nghhhhhhh," Jazz winced, sitting up. "Bruised butt…"

Spencer touched down next to her and plucked the quiver and bow out of the exhibit.

"Have you used one of these before?" he asked.

"Only in the sim chambers."

"The what?"

The night spore hissed as it threw its torso against River, tossing him like a doll into the far wall.

River cried out. His whole body was burning with pain.

"Hold on, River!" called Jazz. She was soaring through the air, safe in Spencer's grip, with her bow and arrow aimed at the spider.

River tried to lift himself, but the pain was too intense. The creature unleashed a coil of silk.

"No, nghhhhhhh! Get off me!"

Within seconds, he was cocooned.

SUKA!

Jazz fired an arrow but missed.

The monster tugged at River's bonds.

"Guys, help me!" he yelled, sliding into its jaw.

SUKA!

Jazz fired again. She struck the night spore's body and it staggered.

"You did it!" cried River.

"No!" said Jazz. "It's not dead."

"It's dead enough," Spencer insisted.

But Jazz leapt out of his claws and fell to the floor.

"No, leave it, Jazz!" Spencer called out.

"It didn't leave Gabe." Jazz plucked the dagger out of the exhibit and looked at the whimpering spore. "Not so hot now, are you?"

"Keep away from it!" Spencer warned. "It's still dangerous!"

"It doesn't look very dangerous to me," she sneered, its legs flailing. "This is for my friend."

She plunged the weapon into the night spore's body. There was a hellish cry, and the monster convulsed and keeled onto its side. Jazz watched as black blood sprayed out of its wound.

Spencer stared at the lifeless body. "Jazz," he muttered. "That was reckless."

Jazz was breathing heavily. "What choice did we have?"

"Uhh, a little help over here?!" called River.

"Oops!" said Jazz. "Coming!"

"I must attend to Jake," Spencer insisted, dashing into the corridor.

Jazz prised the dagger out of the night spore and ran towards River.

"Well, you look comfy," she teased, using her blade to rip through the strings.

"Not really. I'm a little wound up."

She broke River out of his bonds, and he sprang to his feet.

"We must help Jake," Jazz told him. "The guy said he'd taken moonshade, or something?"

"What the hell's moonshade?"

The pair dashed into the hallway. They found Jake on his side, his skin white and sweaty.

"Jake!" Jazz cried.

"We were just in time," said Spencer, his paintbrush in hand. "Any longer and his heart might have stopped."

He dabbed a spot of white paint onto the wall, which he carved into a circle. A small tablet emerged and toppled into his claw. "This is an antidote," he explained, slipping it onto Jake's tongue. "He should recover quickly."

River looked on with concern. "He can't swallow it, surely?"

"The drug will dissolve in his mouth," said Spencer. "It won't take long for the medicine to enter his bloodstream."

"I don't understand how it happened," said Jazz. "He was fine until we reached the museum."

"Yes, it's very puzzling. Of course, there are many varieties of moonshade - Sleep, Focus, Terror. But they all produce symptoms quickly. So he must have eaten it on arrival."

Jake spluttered and groaned, and his eyes twitched. He was starting to wake up.

Jazz ran to his side. "Jake, can you hear me?" she pleaded, clutching his shoulder. "River, see if you can release his cuffs. The guard has the key."

"On it."

Jake coughed, and blinked again. "Uhhh man," he wheezed, rolling his head. He clocked the pool of vomit next to him. "What's that?"

"That's sick, bro," said Spencer. "Now, would you care to explain why you have moonshade in your system?"

"Moonshade? You mean, the black pill? Ugh. The guy said it would bring good fortune. I knew he was full of shit."

Spencer stiffened. "Fortune, indeed. Well let me tell you, my friend, there is not a medicine in the entire House that's capable of changing the future."

"Hold on Spencer," said River, releasing Jake's wrists. "What exactly is moonshade?"

"It's a highly dangerous and addictive narcotic," said Spencer. "It's made with dark paint, and it's banned in every known district. And for very good reason, I might add."

Jake sat up and rubbed his swollen eyes. "Uhh," he stammered. "Yeah, I thought it might be. But we were in trouble. We were trying to rescue you, and there were all these guards."

Jazz was aghast. "Wait, you took the drug willingly?"

"Yeah bro. To help you out."

"Ugh, my hero."

"Now now, don't squabble!" said Spencer. "Jake, you did a very brave thing. But you are never to accept moonshade again, no matter how desperate the circumstances. Have I made myself clear?"

"Yeah, of course you have. I'm sorry, dude."

Incredulous, Spencer looked at River. "Dude? He's as bad as you."

River grinned and grabbed Jake's hand. "It's good to have you back," he said, hauling him to his feet. "I thought we'd lost you."

"Not today," Jake replied, clocking Jazz's weapon. "Wait – where did you get that bow?"

"From the museum. I used it to fight the spore."

"You fought the spore?" Jake exclaimed. "With one of the forbidden weapons? Man, I gotta get me one of those!"

Spencer shook his head. "Unbelievable. Have we resorted to common looting now?"

River and the gang wandered back into the chamber, where they found Jake poring over the longsword.

"Say your prayers, night spores!" he grinned. "Ha, check out my dope blade!"

"Not so fast," said Spencer, as he waddled towards the exhibit. "May I remind you that these weapons are outlawed? And more importantly, they belong to the House museum."

"Oh come on, Spencer," said River. "You're the one who's just stolen a priceless artefact."

The parrot shuffled uncomfortably. "Well, that was a necessary offence! Without the Every Key and the map, Jobon's armies will bring this House to its knees!"

"Yeah, and if we're going to face the night spores, we need to be armed and ready," Jazz pointed out.

"Same," said Jake, as he punched the hilt of his sword. "Hey, is this made out of dark paint?"

Spencer looked dumbfounded. "Face the night spores?" he said. "What do you mean?"

"The ones in the cellar," said Jazz.

"Yeah," Jake added. "Jobon's army of doom."

Spencer glared at them. "Jake, Jazz," he muttered. "You are not coming with me to the cellar."

"No, they're not," said River, stepping forward. "We all are. You saw what happened tonight, Spencer. It'll be ten times worse in the cellar. We're coming with you. All of us. And that's final. We are going to save the House, and Neo Vale, and the planet."

"And avenge Gabe," said Jazz.

"Exactly," Jake chimed. "Together."

Spencer shook his head. "Oh, goodness," he gasped. "No. I cannot ask this of you."

"You're not," Jake laughed. "We're volunteering. Just lead the way. We'll follow."

"And there had better be cocoa," said Jazz.

"The dangers will be many," Spencer insisted. "I cannot guarantee your safety."

"You don't have to," said River. "Not with my man-blades. Jobon won't know what hit him."

"Actually, my sword will be what hit him," Jake boasted, swinging the blade into a vase. "Oops."

"And I can't talk you out of it?" said Spencer. "There is nothing I can say to make you reconsider?"

"Put it this way," said Jazz. "If you try to go on your own, we'll come after you."

"Yep," said Jake. "River and the Stalkers. Hey, that can be our squad name."

Spencer's eyes glistened. He sighed. "I don't deserve you three," he whispered. "I really don't."

River crouched next to Spencer and put his arm around him. "So what do you say, bro?"

Spencer glared at his friend. "You are the worst, River Still."

10: nothing

River held the man in his arms. Blood was gushing out of his mouth as the strength ebbed from his body.

"River," the man choked. "Don't let me die."

River quickly wiped his face. "You're not going to die."

The soldier smiled weakly. "I don't believe you."

There was an explosion. River knew he needed to move.

"Do you... agh!" The dying man winced. "Do you believe in God?"

River's heart pounded.

"Tell me," the guy pleaded. "I haven't got long."

River sniffed. "Not really."

The soldier flinched. He scrunched his face. "You bastard," he gasped. "Why couldn't you lie?"

"Alright, I believe in God," said River. "And unicorns."

"Same," the guy panted. "As long as there's something. I'm so scared that there's nothing."

River's throat was closing up. He struggled to form words. "It would still be better than this place."

A bomb went off, showering the two men in dust. River coughed and waved away the fumes. As the ash cleared, the face of his fallen friend shifted into focus. His eyes were bulbous and inert.

"Carter?" said River, desperate. "Carter?"

River clutched the dead soldier, and rammed his head into his chest. There was no response.

He snarled, his anger rising. He clung to Carter, shook him – as if he could wrestle the guy back to life.

Why was this happening? He wanted to run. He wanted to run and hide and never look back.

"Auuuuuggggghhh!" River yelped as he threw the man away, like a spoilt child with a broken toy.

And then he punched the earth. He stared into the dust, incandescent with rage.

He stood up.

He activated his blades.

★ ★ ★

River woke up, panting.

That was such a vivid dream. It felt so real.

His cheeks were tingling, too. Had he really been crying?

Frustrated, River rolled onto his side and reached for his cell. He needed a distraction. And what better way to bury his grief than to flood his brain with social media? It had been almost three hours since he'd last compared his life to someone else's.

As he logged into Yapper, Jazz's vlog jumped to the top of his feed. It was the footage she'd shot at the Mango press launch, and she'd already clocked twenty thousand views. River gazed at the silent video preview. She was so charming; she oozed confidence as she gushed into the camera. It wasn't the girl he was living with.

He scrolled further down the feed and saw that Jake had also posted. It was just a video of dancing badgers, captioned with laughing emojis.

Seriously? That was what he decided to post? After the death of his friend? Wasn't he upset? It had been such an awful day.

Heck, it had been an awful night, too. When they emerged from the vending machine, they discovered that the whole platform had been cordoned off by the police, and River's bike had been impounded. So they caught the attention of a hovering drone, who took them to see one of the investigators, and they each gave a statement. As a result, it was gone midnight by the time they collapsed into their beds.

River was still feeling restless, so he looked again at the glow of his cell. Jake's post had only gone live a few minutes before.

"Jake?" he called out. "You there?"

No answer. River climbed out of bed and looked at the top bunk. It was empty. He glanced at the door and saw a faint ring of light, seeping through the crack where the wood met the floor. His friend was up.

River reached for the door handle, but paused. Would Jake really appreciate the company? Or a hug? Maybe he was fine. Or maybe he wasn't fine at all and wanted to be left alone, to laugh at dancing anthropomorphs?

He dithered momentarily. He glanced at his bed, and then at the faint glow coming from the hall.

He picked up his phone and clicked on the comment button beneath Jake's post. 'Lol!' he typed, and returned to his quilts.

River tried to get back to sleep, and he might have succeeded had his TellMe not dragged him savagely back to reality. "Hello River," it chirped.

97

"Ugghhhh," he groaned. "What is it, TellMe?"

"You have a new message from Skidmark," the device said. "Message reads: 'Hey Awesome Peddler! We know you messed up this week, so we've enrolled you into our employee growth programme, for your personal development and wellbeing. Just follow the link and read about the five steps to becoming a better person. Just one of the ways we're spreading the love through the Skidmark family. We're full of it!' Message ends."

River rubbed his eyes. I hate food, he told himself. I hate life. I hate Skidmark.

He rolled over.

"Good morning River," said the TellMe, gleeful as ever. "You have another message from Natsuki Hashino. Shall I read it?"

"Tell her I'm gone. Tell her I've re-evaluated my life and I'm now married to a badger."

"Very well."

"No wait, tell her she's a-!" River sat up and banged his head. "Aaargh! Son of a bitch!"

"Confirmed. 'Dear Natsuki. You are aaargh son of a bitch.' Is that right?"

River rubbed his lump. "Very funny. TellMe, what does her message say?"

"Message reads: 'Let's meet at 11. Perhaps you could come to my apartment and we can chat about things?' Message ends."

River's heart sank. Her apartment? For one thing, he wasn't in the mood for a punch-up with a vacuum cleaner. And for another, he had no idea what the hell he was going to say to her. Obviously he liked her, but it felt too fast.

But then, how fast was too fast? Either you're dating someone or you're not, right? He didn't want to sound flaky. But at the same time, he didn't want to get married. Or chat about "things."

He groaned, defeated. "Okay TellMe, reply with this. 'That's a great idea, Natsuki. I'll see you later.'"

Nightfall Court was so oppressive. As River climbed its stained concrete steps, he wondered why Natsuki had decided to live here. Surely it wasn't out of choice?

He arrived on the fourteenth floor and headed straight for apartment twenty. He couldn't help but notice the cat-shaped drinks dispenser as he waited for his friend. It was dormant now, but River still didn't trust it.

The door opened. Natsuki looked agitated, clutching a handful of multi-coloured wires. "Hello, River," she said, offering a faint smile. "It's good to see you."

River nodded. "Natsuki."

"What is the delay?" a robotic voice shouted. "This is an inefficient use of my time."

River followed his friend into the living room. It was more like a workshop, with a stern-looking robot waiting in its centre. The machine was skeletal, its face gaunt like a skull.

"I'm sorry, P4-san," said Natsuki, as she scurried over. "This is my friend, River Still."

The android scowled at the new arrival, its eyes narrowing as it surveyed him. "This is unacceptable," it stated. "I will not conduct business in front of humans."

River glared. "That's okay. You can do your business."

"P4-san," Natsuki interjected, "was there anything further you wished to discuss?"

"No. Are my instructions clear?"

"They are. And I will ensure that you get the best possible price for your salvage."

"I know what those parts are worth," the robot reminded her. "The power unit alone has a repurposed value of nine hundred credits."

"It shall fetch at least that, P4-san. I give you my personal guarantee."

"Your words are binding, flesh-kind. I know your ways. I will not be deceived." The spindly figure crept towards the door. "I am now leaving."

River waved. "Goodbye, Leaving."

Natsuki followed the robot into the hall. "It has been a pleasure to do business with you, P4-san," she added, bowing. "I wish you a safe onward journey."

"You wish it," the android replied, "yet your brothers and sisters plot against me, and all robot-kind. How can my journey ever be without danger?"

"P4-san, your words trouble me deeply. I will pray for your happiness and safety."

The robot, seemingly bored of the interaction, sauntered away as she spoke. Natsuki closed the door.

"What did he mean?" River asked. "When he was talking about salvage and power units?"

Natsuki brushed past him. "River, you have never asked me what I do. Perhaps if you had, you would understand." She knelt beside a small, circular drone, and cradled it like a kitten.

River gazed at Natsuki's apartment. It was a tangle of twisted wires and circuit boards, with motors, monitors and lamps littering the floor and sofa. It was chaotic, and a little surprising; he had expected beanbags.

"Are you a mechanic?" he ventured.

"Close. I repair and repurpose droids, and sometimes I build them from scratch. P4 is a new client."

"Are all your clients so charming?"

"He's better than most. In fact, I would say he's the nicest." Natsuki looked at the machine in her arms. "Anyway, he brought me this old service drone. It's obsolete. It may even predate the war. But many of its components can be re-sold, so my first job is to take it apart." She glanced at one of the burnt-out panels. "I'm going to need a petroscope."

River crouched next to her. "What's a petroscope?"

"It's a tool for penetrating the cerebral cavity. I need to sedate the brain circuits before I can amputate. I mustn't cause it pain."

"But it's just a machine, right? Surely it doesn't matter? Its pain won't be real?"

"River, do you not know how these machines were made?"

River hesitated. "Not off the top of my head."

"The earliest models used human brain prints," Natsuki explained. "Entire personalities were digitised and downloaded into the robot shells. They were like copies of real people."

River frowned. "Why would anyone do that?"

"To live forever, of course. It was a wondrous system, but one that was open to abuse. Many of the earliest droids were enslaved by the government."

Natsuki drilled the pen-like device into the side of the casing. There was a whirr, and the android's panels started to glow.

"This is unfortunate," she muttered. "River, it's conscious. I need to work quickly."

"What do you mean it's conscious? You mean, it can hear us?"

"I think so."

The robot's front light flickered. It was like an eye, a celadon green, gently ebbing and pulsing. "W-where am I?" it stuttered.

"Talk it to, River," said Natsuki. "Reassure it. I won't be long."

River felt uncomfortable. He looked at the service drone. "It's okay," he stammered. "You're safe."

"What's happening to me?" the robot asked. "W-why am I not at the diner?"

"They're just redecorating it," said River. "That leopard skin was so 2020."

"You are mocking me," the drone rebutted. "I'm not supposed to be here. I am being deactivated, aren't I? You are pulling me apart."

River glanced at Natsuki, hoping for a prompt, but she averted her gaze. "Well, since you ask," he replied, "yes. You're being deactivated. I'm sorry."

"You are not sorry," the android protested. "You don't care that I am dying."

"I care," River insisted. "You won't die alone. I promise."

"And then what?" the robot snapped. "What happens when I die?"

River felt his chest tighten. "You pass on."

"What if I don't?" The drone's voice started to break, as if it were crying. "I am a robot. Where will I go? What if there's nothing?"

River glared at Natsuki.

"No! Stop! I don't want to die!"

River stroked its side panels. "It's okay."

"Don't let me die!" the android sobbed. "What if there's nothing? What if there's nothing? What if there's nothing?"

"It's frozen," said Natsuki.

River listened to the relentless cries. "What if there's nothing? What if there's nothing? What if there's nothing?"

"Switch it off," he ordered. He stood up.

Natsuki stepped over to him. She rested a hand on his shoulder.

"Shit," he hissed, wiping his cheeks.

"I didn't know that was going to happen."

"I know. It's just a sore point, that's all."

"Your shoulder?"

"What? No, I mean, the reminder. It reminds me of something that happened. A long time ago."

"Do you want to talk about it?"

"Not really."

"I understand." Natsuki rubbed his arm. "I know how you feel."

"I find that hard to believe."

"I do. Depression haunts me daily. But I have my medication. And I pray."

River paused "You pray?" he asked, cautiously. "Are you a Laputan?"

"Not a Laputan. Perhaps I could show you. There's a place. Would you like some fresh air?"

Not particularly, was the blunt answer. But his friend had already motioned towards the door, and River felt compelled to follow. He was certain that whatever she wanted to show him was unlikely to sit well.

His mother had left him with a permanent aversion to religion of any flavour. But he didn't feel he could say no.

Natsuki led him out of the festering tower block and into a secluded wood. It was peaceful; the only sound was the gentle movement of the trees, and the crunching of twigs as they trampled them underfoot.

"Where are we going?" asked River.

"To the shrine. This is where I come when I am sad. I talk to the spirits, and they give me strength."

Had it been any other time, River would have challenged his friend's delusions, but he thought better of it. All the while, though, he thought of his mother, and the incessant, pious rituals she had forced him to endure - usually in the build-up to the third smack of the day.

The shrine, though, was beautiful. It was a brightly-painted wooden arch, flanked by two stone effigies carved into the shapes of dragons.

"You're a Paragonian," he realised. "I was raised a Paragonian."

"You know our customs?"

"It's been a while," River replied. "I may need reminding."

Natsuki led him towards a basin of water, where an immaculate row of long wooden spoons gently caressed its surface.

"You take the ladle in your left hand," Natsuki told him, "and pour the water onto your right."

River did as his friend instructed. "Aah!" he exclaimed, shaking the cold liquid off his fingers. "You do this every time?"

"It is respectful," Natsuki insisted. "It honours the dragon gods. Now, empty the ladle into your right hand, and use the water to rinse your mouth."

"My mouth? Seriously?"

"River, please."

Reluctantly, River honoured his friend's wishes and swilled the liquid around his mouth. It tasted of moss.

He then replaced the implement, and Natsuki repeated the ritual on herself. She was slow, and methodical; River could see the conviction in her eyes as the water fell through her fingers.

"Why have you brought me here?" he enquired, as they wandered towards the shrine. "Are you trying to convert me?"

"No, River," said Natsuki. "It makes me sad that you would think this. I am not trying to manipulate you. I am trying to protect you."

River frowned. "From what?"

"It's your aura. I told you, it's broken. And you keep putting yourself in danger, don't you?"

They arrived at the foot of the shrine, and River said nothing.

"I am going to pray," his friend uttered. "I will pray to the dragon gods, to Meldesta and Delmesta. I will ask for strength and protection from whatever it is you are facing. If you would also like to pray, then you are free to do so."

River watched as his friend stepped in front of the arch. She bowed, and then clapped, and then bowed again. Afterwards she turned, and looked expectantly at River.

His chest tightened. "I'm sorry," he said. "It would be wrong of me. I don't believe."

Natsuki smiled. "That's okay, River. I have prayed for you."

River turned his attention to the dragon statues. "Well, if I had these guys fighting alongside me, then I'd have nothing to fear."

The smile fell from Natsuki's face. "Fighting?" she asked. "River, what have you been doing?"

River hesitated. "You wouldn't believe me if I told you."

"That is true. You have lied to me before."

River tried to ignore this remark.

"Uhh," he stuttered. "Let's say there's a place - a place where I go to fight people. With Spencer, the parrot. Do you remember him?"

"Who are you fighting? Good people or bad people? For fun, or something else?"

"It's not exactly fun," he admitted. "And they are not good people. They're vicious. I mean-"

"Oh, River." Natsuki took his hand. "You mustn't do this to yourself. You are wounded. Promise me that you won't go back to this place."

"Okay," he said unconvincingly.

"River," Natsuki pressed, "we cannot be involved if you keep exposing yourself to these terrors. If your destiny lies along this dark path, then I release you with a full and heavy heart. And you will always have a place in my prayers."

River let go of her hand. He looked at the floor.

"Is that your answer?" she asked.

"I don't know what you want me to say," River replied. "It's not that I don't like you, it's just a little fast for me. It's intense."

"What's intense about talking?" said Natsuki. "You are so confusing, River. It's like you want me, and want to avoid me. How am I supposed to trust you?"

"You can trust me," he insisted. "And heck, if you don't want me to return to that place, then so be it."

"Do you mean that?"

"I promise."

Natsuki took a deep breath, and smiled. "Thank you," she whispered.

"Good morning, River," said his TellMe. "You have a new message from Jake Thrower. Message reads-"

"Wait!" River shouted.

Natsuki looked shocked. A whole family of birds leapt out of their tree.

River grinned. "It's probably some dirty joke, knowing Jake. I'll answer it later."

"Shall we get some lunch, then?" Natsuki asked. "If that's not too intense?"

"That would be good," said River, hoping it wouldn't be. "Have you tried Kakeru's? I hear it has amazing toilets."

Jake had wanted to confirm the group's plans for that evening. Were they going to the House? Were they going to begin their journey towards the cellar? Were they taking water pistols?!

It was a good thing River had silenced his TellMe. What Natsuki didn't know couldn't hurt her. In fact, she seemed quite happy as she and River slurped their way through a bowl of shabu-shabu at Kakeru's.

Back at Noodle Vale, however, the atmosphere was less than calm. As River climbed the creaky stairs to the living room, thunderous voices pounded his ears. It sounded like Ben - Jazz and Jake's dad - was letting rip at someone. It was scary.

Gingerly, River crept towards the crack in the living room door. Could he go in? *Should* he go in? He wanted a cup of tea. How inappropriate would it be for him to slink by, as if invisible?

Very. As he peered through the gap, he could see Jazz's face, awash with tears. Her cheeks were deep red, and her eyes like furnaces. Ben looked much the same, his arm gestures wild and threatening.

But it was so bizarre. Jake was just sitting at the table, engrossed in his phone. It was like the fight was nothing to him - as if the drama were nothing more than a TV show that he was only half invested in.

Beanie, too, was acting oddly. She was sitting in a meditative position at the other side of the room, her eyes closed, clutching one of her knitted dolls as if praying.

River couldn't decide what to do. Instinctively, he knew that he should hide in his room and wait for the bust-up to blow over. But his curiosity kept him glued to the spot.

"Jake's responsible!" Ben insisted. "Jake's a boxer! He can take care of himself!"

"I can take care of myself!" Jazz yelled. "You just treat me like a kid!"

"Oh really?"

"Yeah!"

"Oh *really*?! What about last week, Jazz? If you're so strong?"

Jazz faltered. "That was different!"

"'Ohhh Daddy I'm scared!'" said Ben in a pathetic, high-pitched voice. "'There are some scary boys in the alley! Can you come and pick me up?'"

Jazz looked furious. "They were *men!*" she retorted. "And there were five of them! And they all had masks on!"

"Well maybe if you'd tried harder in gym class you'd actually be able to defend yourself! Your brother did! Jake got the highest in his year!"

"Yeah he did," Jake grinned, still looking at his phone.

"And I'll tell you another thing, Jazz - not *once* has Jake phoned me up begging to be rescued! That's why I trust him! That's why he's allowed out late!"

Jazz was raging. "Gabe didn't fucking die because we were out too late!" she screamed.

"Ooooh," Jake chuckled, egging her on.

"Hey!" Ben yelled. River felt the floorboards tremble. "You take that back, young lady!"

Jazz started to walk. "Why, it's not like you were listening anyway!" she retorted.

River moved away from the door.

"And where do you think you're going?" Ben barked.

"Go fuck yourself!"

"Do not leave this room, Jazz Thrower!"

Jazz seized the door handle. "I said, go fuck yourself!"

She tore into the corridor and collided with River. She froze.

River looked at her, but she said nothing. She pushed past him and rushed towards her room.

Suddenly, a man screamed. "Auuuuugggggghhh!"

River looked, just in time to see Ben grab a mug and hurl it against the living room wall. It smashed.

Beanie flinched, but kept her eyes closed.

Jake looked on, not reacting.

Ben put his hands on his hips and stared furiously at the broken shards. "Clean that up," he ordered.

"Yes, Dad," said Jake, jumping to his feet.

River's heart was racing. It was funny - suddenly his thirst had gone away completely. He scurried to his room.

As he lay on the quilts, he tried to gauge what was going on in the living room. It was quiet now. Nobody was talking. After a few minutes, he heard the door creak open and Ben, grumbling, thundered down the stairs and into the restaurant. Which was a relief.

Then, after about half an hour, his TellMe pinged. "Good evening, River," it announced. "You have a new message from Jake Thrower. Can I read it to you?"

River frowned. "You never ask me that," he pointed out.

"Ask you what?"

"For my permission. To read me a message."

"I didn't want to disturb you," said the TellMe. "I interrupted your date last time."

River grinned. "It's okay, TellMe. I'm in my room now."

"Your room. Isn't that where dates end up?"

River's smile grew wider. "Mine don't. What's the message?"

"It has been sent to you and Jazz Thrower. Message reads: 'Well, are we going to the House or what?' Message ends."

11: clowns

The wall of Amber Hues' paint shop was a work of art in itself. There were ten shelves of paints behind its counter, arranged in a rainbow pattern of bold, confident colours. There must have been five hundred tins lining the display, making it a real destination for artistically-minded parrots.

Namely Spencer.

He waddled across the counter as Amber focused on her painting. She was carving out the image of a plain-looking man in a tailcoat, and Spencer watched, spellbound, as she swept her brush across the canvas.

"Personally, I think you've surpassed yourself," he chirped. "This gentleman will make a fine addition to the House. When he's finished, of course."

"I'll take your word for it," said Amber. "This one's been a nightmare so far."

"Oh, you're not happy with it?"

"He's passable, but he won't be the most distinguished of citizens."

"But isn't he what the president requested? A new individual who could be integrated into the district?"

"Yes, that's what he always asks for," Amber acknowledged. She sighed, and stepped away from the canvas. "I don't know. It's probably creative frustration. I'm sure I'd hate him more if I could see him."

Amber turned to her friend. She had no eyes - merely painted circles of flesh.

"Well, take it from the beak of a fellow artist," said Spencer. "Your lack of sight is a superpower. It's liberating. You are unencumbered by frivolous distractions. You are free to follow your instincts when you paint."

"You're such a romantic, Spencer. My blindness is a curse, a miscarriage of justice. You were there, remember? The charges were baseless. The court was seduced."

"I agree, it was a travesty. Nonetheless, you got off lightly. Would you rather have been showered?"

Amber shook her head. "No, of course not," she said. "But there is no part of me that will ever share your idealistic notions of 'blindness as a superpower.' I long to see my work."

"Of course. I understand that."

"Nonetheless," Amber went on, "my other senses are perfect. Your friends are welcome to say hi, by the way."

Spencer hesitated. "My friends?"

"Three of them, I think. They're standing in the corner of the shop. They're pretending not to be here, for some reason."

Spencer cleared his throat. "Well," he stuttered. "This is awkward. River, Jake, Jazz - say hello to my good friend Amber Hues."

"Uhh, hello," said River.

"Hey Amber," said Jake. "Could you smell us or something?"

"I heard you. You breathe very loudly."

Jazz nudged Jake in the ribs. "Told you."

"Wha?"

"Why the secrecy, Spencer?" Amber quizzed. "What's going on here?"

"Amber, I know how this seems," said Spencer, "but we don't mean you any harm, I promise."

"It's the Every Key, isn't it? I heard about the attack on the museum."

"Wow, this lady's on fire," said Jake.

"Yes Amber, we have the Every Key," Spencer admitted. "It's imperative that we reach the cellar. My friends, you see - they're not painted. They're flesh-kind. They can penetrate the cellar and flood it once more."

Amber gasped. "Flood it? You mean-?"

"Yes, Amber. It's time. It must be."

Amber froze. "The book of Pthalo," she muttered. "'The cellar will be drained and his armies shall rise, to conquer and destroy.'"

"But not with Spencer von Luft on the case," Spencer declared. "Jobon will get a showering he'll never forget. Now, I know from the Traveller's Map that we can move deeper into the House via your shop. Will you let us?"

Amber smiled. "Oh, Spencer," she chuckled. "You needn't have been so clandestine. I would always have helped you."

"Man, I needn't have held my breath," Jake quipped.

Jazz rolled her eyes. "Is that what you call it?"

"Amber, thank you," said Spencer. "I was a little secretive because I didn't want to involve you unnecessarily."

"Then I'll make this easy," Amber went on, stepping towards the door. "I am going to leave this shop on an 'emergency errand.' When

I return in ten minutes' time, I will have no knowledge of what happened while I was gone."

"Indeed, how could you possibly!" said Spencer, grinning. "To think that four ruffians would break into your shop and sneak into the secret passage, all while your back was turned."

"Unforgivable," said Amber, as she started to leave. "You are very brave, Spencer von Luft. All of you. I wish you well."

River took a deep breath. Her words sounded so ominous.

Still, he appreciated the good wishes, and watched with admiration as she felt her way onto the corridor.

"Alright," said Jake, smacking his hands. "Secret passageway, baby!"

"Yes, don't announce it to the whole House," said Spencer. "We're supposed to be leaving under a veil of secrecy."

Jazz looked at the canvas that Amber had been working on. "Spencer," she said, eyeing the figure curiously. "Can anyone paint new people for the House? As in, create living creatures?"

"No, only specially-commissioned artists are able to do so," Spencer explained. "And even then they can only create life with a supply of First Paint. It's distributed by the government."

River wandered to Jazz's side. "I'm guessing they don't age?" he asked, examining the canvas. "They're painted as adults, they come to life, and then what? They live forever?"

"They fade over time," said Spencer. "But yes, they last for many years, and they're forever adult. You will have noticed, I think, that there are no children in this House. There would be no point in children."

"No kids?" said Jazz, taken aback. "So no childhood? No innocence?"

"Well, that sucks," said Jake.

"It's necessary," said Spencer. "Now, come along. We only have ten minutes, remember?"

Spencer leapt off the counter and tottered towards the back room. His friends followed.

"Uhh," said Jake as they entered. "Okay, that doesn't look ominous at all..."

There was a moody stone passage up ahead, with a locked door sitting at its end.

"Well what did you expect?" said Spencer, waddling into the tunnel. "A gazebo? Come along."

"I bet we could totally kick that thing down," said Jake, following. "Or squirt it out of existence with the water pistol I wasn't allowed to bring."

"Are you still crying about your damn water pistol?" Jazz snapped.

"Dude, we're fighting paint monsters, it totally makes sense! Spencer doesn't mind. Do you, Spencer?"

"Not at all, Jake," he replied. "I like nothing more than to be surrounded with weapons that could wipe me out in an instant."

"Oh…"

Jazz pulled her brother close. "I *had* asked him already," she hissed. "That's why I wouldn't let you bring one."

"Yeah, you're very wise, sis," said Jake. "Just, uhh – don't look in my rucksack, okay?"

"What?!"

"Oh, like a glove!" crowed Spencer, as he slipped the Every Key into the receptacle.

There was a clunk, and the key slowly rotated, forcing the door open.

Jake clutched the hilt of his sword, as if readying himself for a fight. "So what can we expect in the next area?" he asked.

"By the looks of it," said River, "the world's biggest cocktail party."

The tunnel beyond looked like a circus tent, its walls a garish pattern of chequered blocks, festooned in balloons and streamers.

Jazz was the first to step through the door. "Well, this is creepy," she remarked, running her fingers through the coloured threads. "And what's with the music?"

"I know," said Jake, following her in. "It makes me want to samba."

Spencer glided onto Jazz's shoulder. "Do you like it, Jake? Is it sick?"

They followed the tent-like passage as it twisted and turned like a fabric maze. The walls' red and black checks made River want to puke.

Eventually, the labyrinth unfolded into a larger room. The group stopped.

"Well," said Spencer, uneasily. "This has the potential to be quite dangerous."

They were facing what appeared to be an infinite set of coloured turnstiles, each the size of doors, spinning on the spot like windmills.

"How do you want to tackle this?" River asked.

"Quickly," said Jazz, jostling to the front of the group. "Surely we can't get lost if we keep moving in a straight line?"

"I disagree," said Spencer, pulling the map out of his pouch. "What if there are multiple exits? And what if there's only one correct route?" He gazed quizzically at the document, then gasped. "Good heavens! This is unprecedented!"

River looked. "Spencer, that's a pizza menu."

"Oh."

"Either way, we won't know until we start," said Jazz, pushing past the first turnstile. "Let's hustle."

"Sis!" yelled Jake.

"Quickly, you two," said Spencer, still on Jazz's shoulder.

River and Jake exchanged nervous glances, and dashed after their friends.

"Where are you?" River shouted. "Spencer? Jazz? Say something!"

"We're over here!" came Jazz's distant voice. "We're by a green turnstile!"

"Oh, that helps!" said Jake. "There are, like, a billion green turnstiles!"

"Take my hand," said River, grabbing Jake. "If we get separated, we're screwed."

River and Jake pushed through the revolving doors and deeper into the rainbow maze. It was a trippy and terrifying spectacle, like drowning in a kaleidoscope river.

"Jeff!" Jake called out. "Spencer!"

"How can they not hear us?" said River. "Spencer, where are you?"

Jake tugged on his friend's sleeve. "Look, there's an opening!" he shouted, and hauled River through the gap.

The pair found themselves in another dimly-lit passage. Its walls were made of canvas, covered in red and cream stripes. The floor, meanwhile, was dirty and uneven; River scuffed the sooty motes with his boot, and realised that he and Jake were standing on sawdust.

"I don't think they're here," said Jake. "Sis! Spencer!"

"They were just ahead of us, right? They might be round the corner."

Jake raised his eyebrows. "You mean, that badly-lit corner? Next to the creepy sign? The one that says, 'THIS WAY,' written in blood?"

"Yeah." River stepped up to the notice. "Although I don't think it's blood. This is the world of *painted* people, remember."

"That doesn't mean they can't bleed. The night spores seep all that black stuff when they're injured."

"That's true. Woah!"

River and Jake stopped dead in their tracks. Ahead of them, a caged marionette had jolted to life. It looked like a ventriloquist's dummy, dressed as a schoolboy. And it was dancing.

111

"Okay," said Jake, reversing. "I vote we go back to the maze and start again."

River inched towards the puppet. "This is freaky. Why would anyone want to keep a marionette in a cage?" His eyes followed the strings, which disappeared into the darkness of the ceiling. "And who's controlling it?"

"River, I don't think Spencer and Jazz came this way."

The puppet reached out through the gap in the bars and beckoned with its hand.

"Huh?" said River, not following. "What is it? You want something? You want me to dance?"

The boy shook his head and beckoned again.

"I think it wants money," Jake deduced. "Is that it? Is that what you want?"

The marionette nodded.

"Uhh, well I've only got this," River explained, showing his TellMe. "And I've got a feeling you don't have a scanner."

The boy shook his head, and quietly withdrew his hand.

"Man, he's not the chattiest, is he?" said Jake.

"I'm not surprised. Have you seen his face? He doesn't have a mouth."

"What?"

"It's been painted over," River went on. "See there, right above his chin? You can just make out where his lips used to be."

"Welcome, welcome!" came an exuberant voice, as a suavely dressed man sashayed towards them. "My, my, what an unexpected delight! Gentlemen, I extend a cordial and warm-hearted welcome to you both."

River looked warily at the man. He was tall and gangly; his gaunt face was plastered in thick white make-up, save for the black rings that swirled around his eyes.

"Thank you," said River, uneasily. "I'm River Still, and this is Jake."

The man raised his stripey top hat. "An absolute pleasure, River and Jake. My name is Giles Fezziwig, ringmaster of Le Cirque de Peinture. You are just in time for the show."

"Oh yeah," said River. "About that. We should probably find our friends first. We lost them in the turnstiles - a parrot and a young girl?"

"A very bad-tempered young girl," Jake added.

"Yeah, a bit punchy. Did they come this way?"

"Did they come this way?" said Fezziwig, aghast. "Sir, they arrived just moments before you did. They have already taken their seats in the theatre."

"How fortunate," said River, casting a nervous glance at Jake.

"Yeah, I guess Spencer would have been carrying money," Jake theorised. "Unfortunately, we're clean outta bucks. So..."

"But you're our guests," Fezziwig insisted. "I remember the face of every visitor at Le Cirque de Peinture, and I know for a fact that you have not been before."

River moved closer to Jake. "Yeah..."

"Then admission is free for first-time spectators!" Fezziwig gushed. He stepped aside and extended his arm towards the theatre entrance. "Come now. I will help you locate your companions, and together you can enjoy an evening of the most unique entertainment."

Jake nudged River in the ribs. "Let's just find them and go," he muttered.

River thought for a moment. "Alright. But we'll probably have to leave before the end."

"Sir, you are free to come and go as you please," Fezziwig reassured him.

He turned and led River and Jake into a grand-looking ballroom, where small groups of punters were gathered around tables. There can't have been many; most of the seats were empty, and the people that were in attendance were each painted like Fezziwig, their faces cemented in dazzling white paint.

The ringmaster guided the pair towards a table close to the stage and motioned for them to sit. "I do hope you enjoy the performance," he said silkily, as a waiter placed two steaming mugs in front of them.

Jake looked uncertainly at the drinks. "I thought you were going to take us to our friends?"

"You can see them after the show. Please, just relax and make yourselves comfortable. There is no need to worry."

River ogled the ringmaster as he glided across the auditorium. He turned to Jake. "I think we've been stitched up."

"Oh, you think? That creep has got us wrapped around his finger. Why did we say yes to him?"

River shrugged. "It was Hobson's choice."

"Hobson's what?"

"Something my dad taught me - when you have to choose between something terrible, or nothing at all. Hobson's choice."

"Well Hobson's a douche, because something's not right. Why the hell does he want us to sit in this dive?"

"Look, we have the advantage here. Fezziwig has left us alone, smack-dab in the middle of a theatre. That gives us plenty of time to think of something."

"I am thinking of something."

"What?"

"All the ways he could kill us."

There was a fanfare, and a clown-faced showman bounded onto the stage, cracking his whip with ceremonial panache.

"Friends and patrons, boys and girls - it's time to dance, it's time to twirl!" he rapped. "So forget your troubles and forget your cares, for tonight we honour the Empty Chair!"

River rolled his eyes as a resplendent wooden seat was lowered onto the stage.

"By the chair we remember how we came to be, and celebrate with camaraderie! That Jobon dude is the god of paint, so tonight he's honoured with a circus dance!"

Jake looked puzzled. "That doesn't even rhyme."

Lines of dancers swept onto the stage, drifting from the left and right, and broke into a hypnotic waltz.

River squinted; he could just make out the cords that were tethered to their wrists and ankles. The performers were life-size, but there was something uncanny about their struts. He had always been unsettled by puppets and clowns, but these dancers were like the stuff of nightmares. He couldn't tell if they were puppets or people. One of them blinked. He was sure of it.

And another - a woman. Her eyes were sparkling. Was it the lights?

"Their mouths have been painted over too," Jake pointed out.

River looked. Like the schoolboy, these puppet-people were mouthless, save for a faint, muddy trace above their chins.

As the dancers left the stage, the audience broke into a passionless applause, and the whip-touting compere pirouetted into the limelight.

"Thank you dancers, you honoured us good! That's the finest act in the neighbourhood! Now you've bought your tickets, and we'll pay you back, so prepare yourselves for a survival act!"

More half-hearted clapping.

"I've got a bad feeling about this," said Jake, as a bearded artist in a kimono took centre stage. He bowed.

"Thank you, my friends, you are too kind!" he proclaimed. "I am the Great Dandini, and tonight, dear patrons, I shall bedazzle your painted brains!"

He gave a bombastic gesture, and a pair of clown-like performers arrived on the stage, wheeling a tall wooden cabinet. Dandini clapped his hands and the two aides opened the closet door. Inside was another marionette, its wrists and ankles tightly strapped to the back panel.

"Ladies and gentlemen - the death of a thousand cuts!" said Dandini, leaving a gap for the applause that never came. He reached into a basket and produced a long metal sword, which he twirled skilfully. "Can the Great Dandini penetrate the cabinet without damaging the incumbent marionette?" He gestured for the door to be closed again, and the two assistants departed.

"If that's really a marionette," said Jake, "why the hell is it tied down?"

River felt sick. He had been thinking the same thing.

The Great Dandini spun his sword again, and drove the blade into the side of the cabinet. River flinched, shuddering at the thought of the horror within.

And the swords kept coming; Dandini plunged them into the panels with vigour, his crazed smile growing wider with each attack.

River turned to Jake. "I think we should leave."

"Do you think we can?"

"We have to try."

Dandini floated his cutlass in front of the cabinet, hovering over the puppet's abdomen, and drove it aggressively into the wood. There was a muffled cry from within the closet. Dandini cackled, wide-eyed, as the watching audience burst into applause.

"Come on," said River, as he and Jake leapt from their seats.

Giles Fezziwig stepped into view, blocking their path. "Leaving so soon?" he purred. "How disappointing. We've only just begun."

"Oh, that wasn't the end?" said River, as Dandini broke into a dance.

"This is so embarrassing," Jake giggled. "Ah well, since we're up, we might as well go and find our friends."

"Yeah," said River. "At a brisk pace."

"But hold on," said Fezziwig, raising his hand. "Would you like a canapé?"

"Why, is it raining?" said River.

"We'd better go," said Jake.

The guys turned, and quickly collided with a line of clowns, whose arms were folded like janitors.

"Perhaps a drink then?" said Fezziwig. "I really must insist."

River gulped, and stepped back. "Come to think of it," he stuttered, "my mouth is a little dry from all the excitement."

"Excellent," said Fezziwig, snapping his fingers like a butler. "I guarantee that you will not be disappointed."

"No 'cos we'll be dead," Jake whispered, glaring at his friend.

Fezziwig led the pair out of the ballroom with his clown-like henchmen bringing up the rear. River cast a final glance at the stage and watched Dandini's assistants as they wrestled the blood-stained puppet out of the cabinet.

in the chrysalis chamber

River smiled. "Me and Jake are like a double act, aren't we?" he pondered. "It's amazing how quickly you can form a rapport with someone. And how fond of them you can become."

"You get on well with Jake Thrower," said the monotonous voice. "You sound surprised."

River nodded. "I liked him a lot. It's funny. We were in a lot of danger in that theatre. We both felt it. I was scared, but I wasn't just scared for myself. I was scared that something would happen to Jake. I guess I was still reeling from the death of Gabe."

The coloured lights danced across the disc's surface. "Reeling?"

River thought for a moment. "Death has a way of hammering things home, doesn't it? It reminds you of the fragility of things. The temporary nature of existence." He looked pointedly at the disc. "You never know when someone you love could be taken from you."

"Hmm. That makes a lot of sense."

River glared at his interviewer, curious. "I know you're an AI," he said, "but there are times when you sound like my father. Isn't that weird?"

The machine hesitated. "You are hearing the voice of your father."

"No, come on, don't do that reflection shit. Does it really matter to you, an artificial intelligence? Does it matter if people die, if they fall away? Do you really care?"

"Caring is an abstract concept," the voice stated. "The counsellor wants what is best for the client. The counsellor should act in their best interests."

"And do you think being handcuffed to the chair is in my best interests?"

"You sound angry, River Still," it commented blandly. "Perhaps it would help if you continued your story."

River rolled his eyes. "Fine. But I want to tell you about Spencer and Jazz, otherwise the rest of it won't make sense."

"Of course," said the disc. "You can share anything that you consider to be important. Please continue."

117

12: surgeons

"You never know, they might have come this way," said Jazz, as she and Spencer followed the turns of the striped corridor.

"Yes, it's possible," Spencer admitted. "Have you had any luck on your phone?"

"Well, I've messaged Jake, but he hasn't answered. He could be ignoring me, I guess."

Spencer frowned. "Why would he be ignoring you?"

"Oh, you know. New best mate, annoying twin. He doesn't need me crashing his party."

"How curious."

"That's brothers I guess."

"No, I meant this sign," said Spencer, gazing at a large wooden board. "It seems we've encountered an exhibit."

Jazz looked at it. The words 'Freak Show' had been scrawled in red letters.

"We may have to enter," Spencer explained.

"Or we could head back? Find a different route? What does the map say?"

"There's no mention of any freak show. But there's a tasty-looking calzone."

Jazz rolled her eyes. "That's the menu, Spencer."

"I'm joking! There's no freak show on here. But this is a tourist attraction, yes? We should be able to walk straight through. There can't be any danger."

BUUUUUUN!

There was a whirr, and the two friends jumped.

Jazz froze. "What was that?"

Spencer looked down. A girl marionette - locked in a cage - was waving her hand through the bars. Her eyes were fixed, and yet they looked sad; there was a curious melancholy etched into her gaze.

"Ah yes," said Spencer, reaching into his pouch. "Money."

"Oh great. A toll booth."

Spencer emptied a wingful of coins into the puppet's hand and she gestured for him to proceed. He bowed, taking one last look at her tortured expression. Were her eyes glistening?

"Well, are we going through?" said Jazz.

"Hmm," said Spencer, keeping his eyes on the tethered girl. Reluctantly, he tore himself away, and waddled into the attraction.

It was just like a circus tent, crammed with cages on a sawdusted floor. The light was dim, and ominous groans drifted through the darkness.

"Okay," said Jazz, in a manner that suggested she wasn't. "So this is like a prison."

"Indeed," said Spencer. He climbed onto her shoulder. "Stay on your toes."

The pair inched forward. Jazz caught sight of a slimy black shape, twisting and thrashing in its cell. She crept towards the bars and peered through the gap.

"Jazz, don't look," Spencer urged. "Jazz!"

Jazz grabbed the cage and gasped. "What the-?"

"Come on," Spencer insisted. "Let's find the exit."

"Is that a person? Spencer, that's a *person*."

Spencer looked away from the spectacle. "There is nothing we can do."

Jazz glared at the snake-like creature as it writhed in a heap of chipped wood and filth. Its body was scaled and resembled an adder, whilst its head was that of a human man, his eyes bloodshot and pleading, and his mouth painted over.

"He's being exhibited like he's an object, like he's nothing. Look at him Spencer, he's crying!"

But Spencer said nothing. He closed his eyes, and dropped his head in resignation.

"How many more are there?" Jazz clamoured, racing to the next cage.

She froze, clapping a hand over her mouth. She was face-to-face with an immense scorpion, whose black body twisted into a thin male torso. Jazz stared at the featureless stretch of pallid skin that smothered the man's face, broken only by two narrow slits that served as a nose.

"These people..." Jazz muttered. "Were they born like this? Spencer, they should be cared for, not exhibited."

"I know."

Jazz moved along to the next cage. Her chest tightened as she read the makeshift sign, its viscous paint running down the board like blood: 'The Human Cartwheel.'

A tear rolled down Jazz's cheek.

Spencer looked up. He gazed at the tortured being for a moment, and then looked away.

119

"Wait," said Jazz, wiping her face. "These people weren't born like this, were they? You said that the people in this House were painted. No genetics, no mutations. They were designed."

"Yes. That is what I said."

Jazz glared at what appeared to be a circle of contorted women. Their arms were outstretched and connected, and their ankles had been fused together. Their heads were wrenched backwards and linked with rough wooden spokes, locking them together in a permanent wheel.

"So, these people," Jazz gasped. "Somebody made them like this?"

Spencer didn't answer. He hopped to the ground and faced his friend. "Jazz," he whispered. "We have to be careful. We could tear down these gates and liberate the entire district. But we would never make it out alive."

Jazz dabbed her eyes. "What are you saying? That there's nothing we can do?"

"I'm saying that we press on, that we reach the cellar. If we don't flood it, more and more districts will look like this. The House will be overrun with depravity and suffering. We have to be strong."

Jazz hesitated. "Easy for you to say. You are strong."

"Come again?"

"I can't deal with this shit."

"Wait," said Spencer, scurrying after her. "Where are you going?"

"Home. I can't handle this."

"Excuse me? You *are* handling this."

"Zip it," she snarled, looking back. "Stop trying to make me feel better."

"Never, I'm too good at it!" Spencer winked.

Jazz giggled. She wiped her nose with her sleeve.

Spencer looked at her, and sighed. "Hmm," he uttered, thoughtfully. "You had better start believing in yourself, Jazz Thrower."

Jazz smiled weakly. "Don't tell me what to do, Spencer von Luft."

He chuckled. "I have to. I'm counting on you." Spencer turned and waddled towards the exit. "Come along, biped. You are my protector, you know."

Jazz watched him, rooted to the spot. "That's what I'm afraid of," she whispered.

Under the stage of Le Cirque de Peinture, River's heart was racing. He and Jake had been frogmarched from the auditorium by the decorous Fezziwig and his lackeys and led down a narrow set of steps into a dank, uninviting basement. It reeked of old paint, and River could have sworn he heard the faint patter of rats on the flagstone tiles.

Fezziwig turned to his henchmen. "You may leave us," he instructed, dismissing his subordinates with a casual wave. Then he grinned, and clasped his gloved hands together. "River, Jake. I'm so glad that you accepted my invitation."

"How could we refuse?" Jake chuntered, as the clown released him from his half-nelson.

"What's going on, Fezziwig?" said River, trying to sound confident. He was scared, but not defenceless. The ringmaster, for all his guile and repartee, wasn't psychic; he had no way of knowing about River's twin blades. Admittedly, he had confiscated Jake's sword and backpack, which had been dumped on a nearby chair. But so long as they timed it right, they could escape any time.

"Going on?" Fezziwig chuckled. "River Still, you are here as my guest. Now, green tea, I think." The ringmaster whipped out a brush and started painting on a nearby canvas.

Jake folded his arms like a child. "I'm not thirsty."

"Oh, my dear boy - Fezziwig's beverages are to die for."

"Yeah, I thought they might be," he snapped. "Come on River, we're leaving."

Jake made for the stairs, but his path was blocked by a fat, odious man, who bounded out of the shadows. He grabbed Jake by the wrists and drove him roughly back into the room.

River looked at him, his heart thumping; his face was disfigured and oddly slanted, and his skin streaked like molten wax.

"Ah, thank you Rocco," said Fezziwig, looking momentarily away from the canvas. "Young Jake might have hurt himself on the stairs."

"You'll hurt yourself on the stairs if you don't let me go," Jake threatened, fighting against Rocco's grip.

Fezziwig shook his head, giggling. "Dear oh dear, such impertinent words. But we're forgetting our manners, Rocco. Do escort my guest to his cage."

"What? I don't want a cage!"

"Leave him alone!" River yelled. His mind raced; should he run for it? He could get help. But could he leave Jake?

He had his blades. He could fight his way out. But he didn't know how to activate them. They were random, weren't they?

"Kuuuuuuuu!" cried Jake, as Rocco threw him to the floor.

"I wish we could have talked without a struggle," Fezziwig explained. "I do not wish to cause you unnecessary pain."

"Get off me!" Jake seethed, swinging at his quarry. Rocco grabbed him and bundled him into a small metal cage - barely big enough to fit a dog.

Fezziwig turned to River. "I do hope you're not thinking of leaving," he sneered. "Jake certainly isn't."

"Nghhhh!" Jake growled, punching the bars with his fists.

River tensed up. Where were his blades? Was there a certain thought? A codeword?

"Now, drink up," said Fezziwig, raising the mug to River's mouth. "It will make my life so much easier."

River turned on his heel, straight into Rocco's grip.

"Iyaaaaaaaa!" he cried. "Let go!"

Fezziwig sighed. "By force it is, then."

"Don't drink it, River!" Jake shouted. "Don't drink it!"

"I don't wanna drink it! Fuaaaaaaa!" River tried to blow the cup out of Fezziwig's hand.

Fezziwig laughed. "Oh dear, oh dear! Is this not your cup of tea?"

River locked his lips together. But Fezziwig, impossibly strong, grabbed his jaw and prised it open.

"Kampai!" he sneered, exposing his ugly assortment of broken, decaying teeth.

River felt the hot liquid as it trickled over his tongue and into his throat. Immediately, he felt the strength ebbing from his muscles, and his vision became fuzzy. He slumped.

"River!" screamed Jake. "River, can you hear me?"

Jazz said little as she and Spencer followed the canvased corridors. Spencer watched her closely; he couldn't tell what she was thinking. She looked sad, and a little angry. But was she angry with him? Or the situation?

Of course, Spencer felt guilty. Turning his back on the freak show was not easy, and a big part of him wondered whether he should have done something.

Plus, he was worried about River and Jake. What could have happened to them? Where did those turnstiles lead? His map was clearly out of date, showing only a basic series of corridors and rooms.

It certainly didn't show their current location. He and Jazz had arrived in a large, hexagonal tent, bigger than any he had seen so far. This was clearly one of the district's habitational zones, populated with ornate caravans that were scattered haphazardly across the straw-laden floor.

"This looks promising," said Spencer, brightly. "There's bound to be a person here who can help us."

Jazz did not look convinced. "You think? It looks a bit sleepy to me."

Spencer gazed at the caravans. They appeared to be inhabited, their baroque windows glowing with the steady dance of candles.

"Never underestimate the power of local knowledge," he said. "Just one conversation could make the world of difference."

The pair began to wander through the web of silent carriages.

"We're never going to reach the cellar at this rate," Jazz sighed. "This is only the first district and we're already at a standstill."

"You're such a pessimist," said Spencer. "No wonder you're so depressed."

"I'm not depressed," Jazz rebutted. "I'm realistic. Spencer, if we keep moving at a snail's pace, it could take weeks to reach the cellar. I can't be away from school for that long."

"Jazz Thrower, you are not thinking like an artist. I can paint a doorway that leads directly back to my house, just like a portal. We can tackle our expedition in stages. School will never know that you were gone."

Jazz thought for a moment. "Wait, that doesn't make any sense," she said. "If that's the case, why can't you just paint a doorway that leads directly to the cellar?"

"Because I haven't seen the cellar yet. It doesn't exist in my imagination. And neither did this district until I saw it with my own eyes."

"Oh, I see," said Jazz. "I think. So now that you've seen this district, you can paint a doorway that leads to it?"

"Exactly."

Jazz thought some more. "Hang on."

"Oh, what now?"

"When we were at the museum, why didn't you just paint your way in? Wouldn't that have been so much easier than sneaking through the vent?"

"Yes, it would," Spencer admitted, "but there is such a thing as security, Jazz. Otherwise, people would be painting doors everywhere. It would be chaos. Fortunately, we have a way of protecting some surfaces, like those in the museum, from being tampered with."

"Like some kind of magical substance?"

"Yes. It's called varnish."

They continued to walk. Spencer knew that, eventually, they would have to knock on one of the doors; the absence of passers-by was slowly forcing their hand.

123

However, they eventually found a solitary figure crouched in the half-light - a woman, kneeling beside a low wooden table and poring over a semi-circle of cards.

"Excuse me," said Jazz, heading over. "Can you help us?"

The woman glared at her visitors. Her skin was layered in cracked white paint, with dark circles accentuating her eyes and mouth. "Possibly," she answered, plainly. "Do you want to know the future?"

"Only if it's good," Spencer quipped. "Otherwise you can lie."

The woman just stared, her eyes like pits. She was festooned in an assortment of bangles and beads. One necklace stood out in particular - a string of black pearls that slithered across her shoulders like a snake, as if alive.

"We've lost our friends and we're trying to find them," Jazz explained. "Has anyone come this way?"

The lady, almost devoid of interest, continued to glare. "Many people have come, and many people have gone," she said. "The past is but a dream. The future is for the waking."

Jazz raised her eyebrows. "Is that supposed to sound clever?"

The woman did not flinch. "You do realise that nothing is free in the Forgotten District?"

"You want us to pay you?" Jazz exclaimed. "Just for a conversation?"

"Jazz, I will handle this," said Spencer. He rounded on the woman. "You want us to pay you? Just for a conversation?"

"Knowledge is my living," she snapped. "I cannot prostitute myself to every passing traveller."

"I understand." Spencer reached into his satchel. "I can pay you forty beautiful sovereigns. Look, aren't they lovely? They're limited editions."

"In what sense?"

"There's only forty."

"You're an idiot," the woman barked. "Forty sovereigns is less than a day's wages. Are River and Jake worth so very little?"

Spencer and Jazz exchanged glances. "Someone's read ahead," said Spencer. "But you missed the part where you accepted my very generous offer."

The woman thought for a moment. "Give me your satchel," she said, with a grin. "And all of its contents."

"No way!" Jazz protested.

Spencer contemplated. "You want my pizza menus?"

"Give me your satchel and I will tell you everything you need to know."

Spencer glanced at his bag, and then at Jazz. "Very well."

"Spencer, no!"

"A wise choice," the woman crowed, taking the satchel.

"You're welcome to it," said Spencer. "Those sovereigns are all I have of value."

The woman pulled out the Every Key. "And what about this priceless artefact from the House museum?"

"Oh, a mere paper weight."

"No doubt," said the woman, tossing it into the bag. "Now heed my words, wanton travellers: leave this place and make for the house of cards. The soldier will find you. He will come with you, as there is no room at the inn."

There was a long pause. Jazz, with her hands on her hips, looked expectantly at the woman. "Wait," she said. "Is that it? I thought you were going to lead us to River and Jake?"

"I have told you enough," the lady insisted. "Follow the caravans to the next corridor. From there, follow the path without deviation. The house of cards is at its end."

Jazz shook her head. "Well, that was so not worth it."

Spencer looked at the painted sign above the woman's head: 'Lady Sage Reason, Divine Seer.'

"Thank you, Lady Reason," he said, bowing courteously. "We'll be on our way."

The pair started to walk.

"Spencer von Luft," the woman called out, her smile fading. Spencer and Jazz stopped dead in their tracks. "Oh yes. I know your name, and what you've done. Your reputation precedes you."

Spencer looked at her. "I've never hidden my talents."

"Oh, but you tried," said Reason. "You ran away, didn't you? Fleeing from the names they gave you. Spencer the Wicked. Spencer the Truthless. Spencer the Destroyer."

Jazz cast a worried glance at her friend.

Spencer remained nonchalant. He gazed at Reason's table. "I didn't know that casual insults were on the cards."

The woman pursed her lips. "Very soon you will face the consequence," she said. "The facts will find you. You will meet her on the stairs."

"Consequence?" said Jazz. "What's that supposed to mean?"

"Enjoy your winnings, Reason," said Spencer, glaring at the bag. "Don't spend it all on jibes."

"Spencer, what does she mean?" Jazz quizzed. "Spencer the Wicked? Spencer the Truthless?"

"Ignore her," Spencer rebutted, as they hurried past the cabins. "She's a quack. She's trying to throw you off."

"A quack? You paid her for information!"

"Alright, not a quack," he conceded, "but remember, we can trust no one in this district. Jobon is a creature of cunning, and he has people scattered throughout the House. He delights in sowing confusion and doubt, mixing lies with the truth. We must remain vigilant."

"Well, if you don't trust Reason," Jazz went on, "why did you give her your satchel? She's just taken the Every Key!"

"We'll get it back," Spencer assured her. "Once we've located River and Jake, we can return to the caravan and take it by force. She'll be no match for River's blades."

"River's blades? You're betting everything on River's blades?"

"Well, and your archery," said Spencer. "No pressure."

River thrashed against the bonds that held him to the table. He'd only been out for a few minutes, but he was already strapped to one of Fezziwig's canvases.

Fezziwig looked surprised as River came round, but otherwise undeterred. He and Rocco continued to busy themselves at a nearby table, whilst Jake wrangled with the bars of his cage.

After a few moments, Fezziwig crept closer with a steely gaze, clutching a black urn and a paintbrush. "What would you say if I offered you immortality, River Still?" he sneered.

"I'd say thank you," said River. "Seriously, do you ever choke on all the crap you talk?"

Fezziwig chuckled. "Le Cirque de Peinture is almost as old as this House," he went on. "Night after night, for hundreds of years, my troupe has taken to the stage - never ceasing, never relenting. And sometimes, to no spectators at all."

"Shocking," said River. "And with such well-maintained puppets."

"Oh, but they're not puppets. At least, not in the conventional sense."

"No, they're people that you treat as puppets. You string them up and lock them in cages."

Fezziwig shook his head. "You underestimate me, River Still. It's not simply a case of 'stringing them up.' That would be rather crude."

"Yes, it would," said River. "And depraved, and immoral, and heinous, and barbaric."

"Have you quite finished? The Forgotten District would have perished had it not been for my genius. You have heard of dark paint, I'm sure?"

River's heart missed a beat. "Yes, it's come up."

"Dark paint can be utilised to make certain modifications to the average citizen."

"I noticed," River snapped. "With your performers. You covered up their mouths."

"More than that," Fezziwig continued. "I repainted them from top to toe. I fused the strings to their limbs. My people *became* puppets."

River glanced at the canvas beneath him. "Wait," he stuttered. "Is that what you're doing to me? You're turning me into a puppet?"

"Correct," Fezziwig grinned, swirling the paintbrush in its pot. "And I must say, you and Jake are going to breathe some much-needed life into my troupe. The box office will boom!"

"I get it. Your puppets are worn out, and the audience has stopped coming. You need something to refresh your repertoire."

"You think like an auteur, I'm impressed. Of course, a haggard puppet still has its uses. My colleague Dandini usually finds a thrilling way to dispose of them. You enjoyed the Death of a Thousand Cuts?"

"Yeah, I was in pieces," said River. "Not unlike your victim."

Fezziwig leaned over, dangling the urn in front of his nose. "I shall miss your quick wit, River Still," he smirked. "Now, do you have any final words? Before your lips are sealed forever?"

Jake thrashed against the door of his cage. "Let him go, you creep!"

"Be quiet!" Fezziwig barked. "Lest I accelerate the process!"

River strained against the straps holding him to the canvas.

"What, no cries for mercy? No flippant remarks? How disappointing. I was hoping for a joke or two."

"This whole thing's a joke," River grunted, as he wrestled against his bonds. He needed his blades. Now!

"Indeed," said Fezziwig, hovering the brush over his mouth. "Well, here's a gag we'll both appreciate."

"No!" screamed Jake, as Fezziwig doused River's lips in paint.

The ringmaster laughed like a hyena as River twisted and spat. He could taste the revolting substance as it seeped onto his tongue, and his heart pounded as he prepared for the inevitable. He should have thought of something. He should have *said* something! But the straps were holding good.

Terrified, River continued to smack. He could still move his jaw. He could still move his tongue. He could still breathe.

Wait. He could still breathe?

He moved his lips. He moistened them. They weren't stuck. They were free.

"River!" cried Jake. "Are you okay?"

127

River opened his mouth and gasped. He was covered in paint, but his lips were unsealed. Had something gone wrong?

"No!" Fezziwig hissed. He lunged forward. "What have you done? No one can resist the paint!"

Slowly, River began to twig. "Hang on. You can only modify paintings, can't you?"

"What do you mean 'only'?" Fezziwig snarled. "What else is there?"

"I'm flesh-kind," said River. "Your paint doesn't affect me."

Fezziwig's eyes widened. Aghast, he inched closer to River, ogling his skin. "Flesh-kind?"

"Yeah. Sorry to ruin your plan."

"Ruin my plan?" Fezziwig bared his broken teeth. "River Still, you have given me a gift!"

"What?"

"A living, breathing human! From the world of the flesh! Rocco, observe! The spectacle of the century!"

"Waku waku!"

"My friend, you have no idea how long I have waited for this moment!" Fezziwig gushed. "River Still, you shall be the prize exhibit, the centrepiece of my most revered attraction!"

"What attraction?"

Fezziwig sneered maniacally. "Why, Fezziwig's Freak Show, of course!"

"What?" Jake yelled. "You can't put him in a freak show!"

Fezziwig clapped his hands together and cackled as River thrashed against his bonds.

"Gwahahahaha!" he jeered. "This is perfection!"

"Nghhhh!" cried River. He just needed to activate his blades. He could cut himself free.

But what word could he use? Think of a word, River! Release? Deploy? Escape?

"Nghhhh!"

Hit? Strike? Attack?

"Ughhhh!"

Kill?!

"Kyaaaaaaaaaaaaaaaaaaaaa!" The blades emerged. River rolled, cutting through the cords.

"What?" cried Fezziwig.

River thrust his weapon against his neck. "Now then," he hissed. "Release my friend, or I'll puppetise you."

The ringmaster frowned. "What?"

"River, behind you!" cried Jake.

Rocco seized River and hurled him across the room.

"No!" Jake yelled.

Fezziwig laughed like a chimp, and pulled a red lever.

CHARA! CHARA!

A big metal gate slid across the room.

River dived through the gap just in time.

"No!" he shouted, realising he was locked out.

"I'm afraid this is a private party," Fezziwig jeered. "We don't have room for gate-crashers."

"Gyaaaaaaaaaaaaaaaaaaaaa!" River screamed, throwing his weight against the bars.

"Leave it, River!" Jake shouted. "Run and get help!"

River just stared, terrified.

"How very touching," said Fezziwig, pulling a dagger out of his cloak. He hovered it over Jake's head. "Surrender, River Still. If you value your boyfriend's life."

"He's bluffing!" Jake yelled. "Get Spencer! Get Jazz!"

"The auditorium is crawling with my henchmen," Fezziwig warned. "Do you really think you'll make it out alive?"

"Go, River!" Jake pleaded. "It's the only way!"

"You really are gutless," Fezziwig teased. "Those blades are formidable. You could break me in seconds. If only you had the belly."

Jake glowered at River, imploring.

River faltered. Fezziwig was right. He was gutless. Killing spores was one thing, but Fezziwig was a person.

He couldn't kill a person.

"Release Jake," he ordered, thrusting his blade through the bars. "Now!"

"Come and get him," said Fezziwig. "I'll make it easy for you."

CHARA! CHARA!

Fezziwig pulled the lever again, and the gate slid open.

River gulped.

There was Fezziwig, and there was Rocco. Rocco was inching closer.

"And what if I don't?" he said, retracting his blades. "You can't hurt me. You want me for your freak show."

"Oh, I will gladly display your corpse."

"Aaaaaaa!" screamed Rocco, reaching for Jake's sword.

River grabbed it quickly. He held the blade against Rocco's neck.

"Do it, flesh-kind," Fezziwig crooned. "That man hurt your friend. He deserves to die."

129

River looked at the stairs. He looked at Rocco.
Fezziwig sneered. "Kill him, River Still."

13: humiliation

"Well, Jazz," said Spencer. "In theory, this should be quite simple."

The pair had reached a standstill. On leaving the caravans, they had found themselves in a great hallway, like a temple. It was surreal; the entire building was made out of playing cards.

But it was a dead end. Inside, all they found was a locked door, and a set of five, empty picture frames hanging on the wall.

"Simple?" said Jazz, looking down. A deck of cards had been scattered across the floor, each the size of tables.

"Yes," Spencer went on. "We obviously have to put the cards in the empty frames. It shouldn't take long."

Jazz frowned. "You think? Did you not do probabilities at school?"

"Of course not," Spencer rebuffed. "Numbers do not teach you how to paint."

"No, but if we're assuming that we need to choose five playing cards to put into those frames..."

"Which is likely."

"Then, that would leave us with us approximately a hundred gazillion possibilities, if it's a full pack, and only one correct combination."

Spencer paused. "We may need some coffee."

"And a lifetime or two."

Spencer waddled over to the cards. "Well, there isn't a full pack here," he noted. "I'd say thirty cards, at the most."

"Maybe. But those still aren't good odds."

"Moreover," he added, "our friend Reason said that we'd find someone who could help."

"If she was telling the truth."

"She was right about the house of cards. And she had our names down pat."

"True. But there's no one else here."

Jazz wandered back out into the passageway and looked up at the ceiling. "Hey, Spencer. There are some cards up here."

Spencer joined her. "Ah yes," he said, craning his neck. "And quite difficult to spot."

"Then why put them there?"

"Isn't it obvious? They're a key. Those are the five cards we need for the slots."

Jazz frowned. "But that's dumb," she said. "Why would someone create a puzzle and then put the solution, like, right next to it?"

"Oh, because Kaida was thick," said Spencer, toddling towards the deck. "Jobon was the real brains of the family."

"Good to know."

Jazz looked again at the ceiling. She wasn't convinced.

"Okay Jazz," said Spencer. "Which card do I need first?"

Jazz squinted. "I think the three of clubs..."

"The three of clubs, excellent." Spencer shuffled through the deck. "And what else?"

"The three of spades. And then the three of diamonds. And the king of hearts..."

"Incorrect."

Jazz looked again. "No, that's what it says. That's the next card."

"And it's not in the deck," said Spencer. "We don't have the king of hearts."

Confused, Jazz walked over. Spencer had scattered all of the playing cards across the floor. "Are you sure?"

"I'm certain. Look for yourself."

Jazz surveyed the colours and shapes. He was right. There was no king of hearts. Or three of diamonds. Or three of spades.

She sighed. "I knew it was too simple."

"Never mind," said Spencer. "There's a lot to be said for good old-fashioned trial and error."

"Awesome. Wake me when it's finished."

Spencer looked again at the empty slots. "Perhaps this is an artistic puzzle. If I had my paints, I could illustrate the missing cards."

"It's a thought," said Jazz. "Although, if that's the solution, wouldn't the panels have already been filled? By whoever solved it before us?"

Spencer shrugged. "Perhaps we're the first to solve it."

"Or perhaps we're barking up the wrong tree."

"Nonsense, Nancy. Those cards on the ceiling must mean something. They're obviously a clue." He paused. "Wait. Did you hear that?"

Jazz listened. "No?"

Spencer's feathers were standing on end. "Footsteps!" He hissed. "Take cover!"

He dived behind Jazz's leg.

"Oh, that's great!" said Jazz, readying her knife. "Where am I supposed to hide?"

"It's okay Jazz, I'm praying for you."

Jazz glowered into the darkness of the corridor. She could see the outline of man, inching closer. He had a sword in one hand. The other was made of metal.

It was River Still.

"River!" she exclaimed, dashing over. "Geez, you're covered in blood!"

"It's not mine," he said, retracting his blade.

"I should hope not," said Spencer. "Where's Jake?"

"We got separated. He's been captured by this psychotic ringmaster."

Spencer stiffened. "Not Giles Fezziwig?"

"You know him?"

Spencer lowered his voice. "I'm afraid so. There have been rumours about him for years."

"Wait, who's Giles Fezziwig?" said Jazz. "And why's he got Jake?"

"Because he's crazy," said River. "He's got this weird puppet fetish. He wanted to put us in a freak show."

Jazz gasped. "Not the freak show!"

"You've seen it?"

"Yeah, it's disgusting. People are being kept like animals."

"No way. Like a zoo?"

"Yeah, exactly! Have you ever seen the Travelling Monkey Cage? Where they-"

"Yes, never mind all that!" said Spencer, irritated. "We can critique the exhibition later."

Jazz glared at him. "But Spencer, they've got Jake!"

"And we shall rescue him. But first, we need to talk. And not about monkeys."

"Tell me later," said River.

"Now, where is Jake being held?" Spencer went on.

"He's in an underground lair beneath the theatre," said River. "Fezziwig's got him in a cage."

"A cage?" cried Jazz.

"Not a problem," said Spencer. "I can soon paint a key. Although Jake may have been taken to the freak show by now."

"True," said River. "Perhaps we should go there first? We could pretend to be pundits?"

Jazz huffed. "I'm not paying for that monstrosity again. We'll fight our way in, and fight our way out if we must."

133

"Good times. I'll tape up my knuckles."

"And I'll recover my satchel," said Spencer. "Once I've gotten my paints back, I can paint a door back to my studio. We can escape with ease."

River glared at him, bewildered. "Hold on. Did you say, 'paint a door back to your studio'?"

Jazz tugged at his sleeve. "I'll explain on the way."

"Good luck, my friends," said Spencer, doffing his hat.

"Wait," said River, turning back. "Will you be alright, Spencer? Shouldn't we all go together?"

"Time is short," Spencer replied. "I think a two-pronged attack will be faster."

"Yeah, and you can always give it wings if you get into trouble," said Jazz. "The advantages of being a parrot, right?"

"Right, bro," said Spencer, grinning. "Run along, bipeds."

River nodded and followed Jazz into the passageway.

Spencer watched the pair as they raced out of sight, and took a deep breath. He knew that confronting Reason would be tough. He needed a moment to prepare.

He wandered across the littered floor, thinking about his plan of attack.

Now, if the seer was still absorbed in her cards, he could approach her from behind and snag the satchel in his beak. Yes - that would work. Even if she saw him, he could fly up to the ceiling and leave the old hag in the dust.

Spencer nodded to himself, replaying the scenario in his head. He liked it, but it made a lot of assumptions. For example, what if Reason had locked the satchel in her caravan? It would be much harder to procure.

Then there was the possibility that she could catch him in the act and alert her neighbours. They'd surely come to her aid.

But then, that was the danger wherever he went. The House was full of painted people, and not all of them were friendly. It was a gamble.

Spencer thought about this for a moment.

A gamble.

A bulb lit up in his brain. He looked again at the five empty panels. He thought about the cards on the ceiling. He remembered what Reason had said.

A smile flickered across his face. That was it. The solution to the puzzle.

He chuckled.

★ ★ ★

"Aaaaaaaaaaaaa!" Jake screamed, as his arms were yanked into the air. "Kuhhhhhhhhhhhhhh!"

"Oh please," said Fezziwig, watching from afar. "You can't possibly be in pain."

"His hands are cold," Jake insisted. "And he took my shirt!"

Fezziwig's lackey checked Jake's wrists, which were bound in a rope above his head, and returned to his master's side. The pair gazed at their prize exhibit with satisfaction, the lackey's chin moistening with a steady stream of spit.

"So this is your freak show?" said Jake, glancing at the neighbouring cages. "Which one is yours, Fezziwig?"

The ringmaster sneered. "My friend, you can save the quick wit for your spectators. You are going to be here for a very long time."

"You're deluded. Nobody's going to want to see me."

"I think you underestimate your importance. Nobody in this district has ever seen a flesh-kind before. Let alone touched one."

Jake froze. "Touched one?"

"Pongo," said Fezziwig, coolly. "Bring forth the spectators."

His lackey grunted in compliance and limped towards the entrance. The ringmaster just smiled cruelly as Jake wrestled in his bonds; the knots were holding good, cutting tightly into his wrists.

Jake watched with apprehension as the first gaggle of pundits encircled him. Alarmingly, they were much like Fezziwig, their blackened faces buried beneath layers of white gunk.

"Ladies and gentlemen, friends and patrons!" cried Fezziwig. "Today I present a spectacle of such splendiferous serendipity! A freak from far afield - a creature whose charismatic contours will make you clap, crow and consider! My friends, the rumours were true. Be the first to feast your eyes on the flesh that has, for so long, eluded our examination and dodged our discovery! Behold, we have a man in our midst, and a being who will blow-out your brains. A creature who is not acrylic, but skin, skeleton, and sinews. A freak from the world of flesh!"

The crowd gasped. Fezziwig stepped aside and unveiled Jake to the gawping throng.

He didn't move. He just scowled.

"Does it speak?" said an onlooker. "Can it talk?"

"A very good question!" said Fezziwig. He moved towards his dangling captive. "Now, is there anything you'd like to say, Jake? Perhaps an example of your sparkling repartee?"

Jake said nothing.

"I see!" said Fezziwig. "You'd prefer to just... hang around!"

135

The crowd erupted in laughter, and Jake twisted in his ropes. "What does it feel like?" said a woman. "Can we touch it?"

"Ah, I'm so glad you asked!" Fezziwig stepped aside, revealing a barrel of rods. "For just a small, additional fee, you can experience the feel of the flesh-kind for the first time with one of our exclusive poking devices!"

A sudden murmur of anticipation drifted across the huddle.

"Only five sovereigns per cane!" the ringmaster effused. "Young Jake deserves a bit of stick, wouldn't you agree?"

The onlookers dug frantically into their coats, and Pongo leapt forward with his collection bowl, which he passed from punter to punter.

Jake's heart pounded as he listened to the clatter of coins. His arms hurt. His wrists burned.

"Thank you, thank you," said Fezziwig, taking a rod from the container. "Do take a stick, my friends! But go easy on young Jake." He sneered. "Only *six* lashes per person."

"Nghhhhhhh!" Jake grunted, as he kicked at the punters' rods.

"My, my, this is a feisty one!" Fezziwig chuckled. "It seems our young friend is getting quite a *kick* out of the situation!"

"Hey Nutjob!" a man shouted.

The crowd gasped.

River and Jazz emerged from the shadows.

Fezziwig narrowed his eyes. "River Still..."

River stepped forward, clutching Jake's sword. "There's only one freak here that I want to see."

Fezziwig laughed. "Oh, how perfect!" he jeered. "Observe, patrons: three flesh-kinds in one day! Praise Jobon!"

"Praise Jobon!" they chanted.

"Shut it!" Jazz yelled, aiming her bow at Pongo. "Or the clown gets it!"

The punters laughed again.

Fezziwig crept closer, slinking through the crowd like a snake. "You think we're clowns?" he purred. "Are you blind, young lady? Or are you just stupid?"

Jazz stiffened. "I'm your worst nightmare."

"No argument from me!"

The crowd roared.

"But do you really think we wear paint just for fun?" said Fezziwig. "Surely you're not that naïve?"

River gazed into Fezziwig's black, hateful eyes. He raised his sword. His hand trembled.

Fezziwig sneered. "Cold, River?"

"Not as cold as you," he replied. "Now, let Jake go."

136

"Or what? You've already failed to kill me once."

River pressed the sword against his chest. "Tell that to Rocco."

The ringmaster laughed. "Oh, River," he teased, "I shall miss you the most. Very well, my friend. If you want a face-off, I will give you a face-off."

Fezziwig reached under his collar and tugged at his skin.

"What's he doing?" said Jazz.

River's eyes widened. He glared as Fezziwig peeled away the thick, slimy layer of paint. The skin beneath was diseased and crawling with scabs. He looked like a corpse.

Fezziwig snapped his fingers, and the other clowns complied. They tore the skin from their cadaverous faces, and hissed.

"Gahahahahaha!" screamed Fezziwig, clapping his hands with glee. "Masks off at midnight!"

Jazz looked horrified. "What are you?" she yelled.

"We are the soldiers of Jobon," said Fezziwig. "The most powerful army this House has ever seen. And the means of your painful demise."

"Night spores," said River. "They're night spores."

Fezziwig nodded. "The first wave. Sent out before the flooding of the cellar."

Jazz whipped the bow off her shoulder and sent an arrow into the ringmaster's face.

SUKA!

Fezziwig laughed as he grabbed it in his fist, snapping the arrow in two.

River gulped. "Good luck."

"What?" said Jazz. "Where are you going?"

"To get Jake. Here, have a sword!"

"Brilliant!" said Jazz, backing into a cage. She unbolted it.

"No!" cried Fezziwig. "Stop!"

The gate swung open. The scorpion burst from its cell, striking a cluster of spores with its tail.

Fezziwig screamed. "Do something, you fools!"

"Nghhhhhhh!" winced Jake, tugging at his ropes.

"Hold on!" said River, as he rolled towards his friend. He deployed his blades and cut through the bonds.

Jake fell into his arms. "You're quite the catch," he quipped.

"Guys!" yelled Jazz. "I could use some help here!"

The pair looked. Jazz had been cornered by a pack of spores.

"On it!" said River, retracting his blades. He handed the rucksack to Jake. "Jazz has your sword."

"What? That girl can't handle my sword!"

"I don't know, I think she's getting into the swing," said River, as Jazz struck an advancing spore. "Let's go."

River tore across the room.

And Fezziwig struck him with a stick.

BAN!

"River!" cried Jake.

Fezziwig grabbed River by the hair and hauled him to his feet. "Such charisma!" he sneered. "Care to join... the flying circus?!"

"Nghhhhhhh!"

Fezziwig threw River across the room. He struck one of the cages and fell like a doll.

"Gahahahahaha!" cackled Fezziwig. He moved slowly towards his body, laughing like a maniac.

River wasn't moving.

The darkness was insidious. It was as if the shadows groped at Spencer as he inched towards Reason's caravan. It was helpful, in a way; the low light would hide him from view.

But it would also hide his attackers. Spencer tried to ignore this fact as he tip-toed past the caravans. He hadn't seen anyone, but at the same time he couldn't shake the feeling that he was being watched.

He had to be imagining it, surely? How could anyone be expecting him?

Reason certainly wasn't. As Spencer crept closer to her caravan, he could see that she was asleep, slumped over her cards and snoring like a baby. His satchel lay unguarded at her feet.

Spencer chuckled mischievously as he snagged the strap in his claw. Effortlessly, it slid towards him. It scuffed, and Reason stirred.

Spencer froze.

But the seer simply groaned, rubbed her eyes and turned over. She carried on sleeping.

Relieved, Spencer hoisted the bag onto his wing, and turned on his claw.

He couldn't help but titter as he waddled towards the exit, his pace quickening. How had the woman been so stupid? Nobody should have been able to steal her possessions so easily.

Then he frowned. That was true. Nobody *should* have been able to steal her possessions so easily.

His confidence waning, Spencer opened the satchel's flap and dug inside with his claw.

He gasped. No wonder the bag felt so light. The key was missing.

"Looking for this?" said a familiar voice.

Unnerved, Spencer turned. He was face to face with Lady Reason, brandishing the Every Key and grinning like a cat. And she wasn't alone. The woman was surrounded by a circle of spores, each with arrows aimed at his head.

"Ah," said Spencer, surveying the clowns. "Did I wake you?"

"I knew that you would return, Spencer von Luft," crooned Reason, her pearl necklace creeping and winding. "Always the dark horse. I know about your past."

"You know nothing," Spencer rebutted. "I am a parrot in good standing."

"He says, clinging to stolen goods."

"Stolen? This is mine, Jezebel! It wasn't a fair trade. Your scant information was worthless."

"As are you," said Reason. "Take aim."

The night spores readied their weapons.

Spencer gulped. "What, no trial?"

"Fire!"

SUKA! SUKA! SUKA!

Arrows struck the ground, and Spencer took flight.

"Stop him!" screamed Reason.

SUKA! SUKA! SUKA!

Arrows swept past Spencer's face, forcing him to duck and dive. What should he do?!

SUKA!

Land?

SUKA!

Escape?!

SUKA!

No, he needed the key!

"You cannot escape!" cried Reason. "Surrender yourself!"

The parrot circled the tent. "Give me the key!" he ordered. "And I will spare your life!"

Reason and her spores cackled.

"You will spare my life?!" she laughed. "My life is not yours to spare!"

DOSA!

Spencer touched down on a caravan and slipped out of his satchel.

"There he is!" screeched Reason. Her warriors scrambled to attack.

Spencer put the bag in his beak and took off once more.

"I'm warning you!" he yelled, his voice muffled. "Give me the key!"

Spencer dived, and charged at Reason's head. She yelped as he lassoed her with his bag.

"Kuhhhhhhhhhhhhhh!" she retched, wrestling with the strap. "Let go!"

"Listen up!" he crowed, as he hauled Reason into the air. "Cease fire, or your friend is for the drop!"

The night spores froze, conflicted.

"Don't shoot!" Reason barked. "Auuuuugggggghhh! Release me, you fool!"

"Drop the key, Reason! And I will let you go!"

They were soaring higher and higher. Reason was choking.

"Fine!" she gasped, releasing the key. It landed with a clatter.

"Thank you!" said Spencer. "Now eat my menus!"

"Nghhhhhhh!"

Reason was showered with the contents of his bag. Spencer dropped it, and launched into a dive.

"Aaaaaaaaaaaaa!" cried Reason, as she struck the floor of the tent.

DOSA!

Spencer landed. He tucked the Every Key under his wing.

"Phew!" he gasped, shaking his feathers. "She was heavy!"

A circle of shadows darkened his gaze. Spencer looked up. He was surrounded by spores, their bows outstretched and loaded.

"Ah," said Spencer, eying them curiously. "Is there a problem, officer?"

"You are the problem!" Reason shrieked, staggering towards the spores. "Fortunately, I am very good at solving problems, as you shall see!"

Spencer slunk backwards.

"Not that it will do you much good," she went on, "as a pin cushion!"

Spencer gulped. "Pin cushion?"

"Fire!"

He jumped up.

SUKA! SUKA! SUKA!

Spencer landed, his eyes closed.

Why had it gone so quiet? Had he been hit? Was he dead?

Cautiously, he opened his eyes. The night spores were staggering, clutching their pierced chests. Spencer watched with incredulity as they dropped limply to the floor, the life ebbing from their punctured bodies.

They had shot themselves. Accidentally, of course. They really shouldn't have stood in a circle...

Spencer breathed a sigh of relief as he flew towards Reason's body. She was still alive; blood gushed from her mouth as she withered and gagged. Spencer couldn't bring himself to look her in the eye. He grabbed his satchel. He turned away.

"S-Spencer..." the woman gasped. "Help me..."

Spencer just walked. He felt scared. And keen to get away.

"S-Spencer von Luft..."

Ignore her, he told himself. Keep walking.

"You're the one..." croaked Reason. "Spencer the Destroyer... The b-butcher of a thousand..."

Spencer stopped. Her words bothered him.

"Y-You thought no one knew?"

Spencer clamped his beak together. He refused to answer.

"You c-cannot run from the t-truth," she panted. "You will see her on the stairs. Y-you will face the consequence..."

Spencer looked at Reason. But the woman had gone limp.

She was dead.

Spencer sighed. His heart was pounding. Unnerved, he adjusted his satchel and began to walk. He was too afraid to look back.

Had he done so, he would have seen the black necklace. Like a snake, it uncoiled from the seer's neck and slithered out of sight.

GASHAN!

A line of night spores fell, toppled by the pounding scorpion.

Jazz bounded forward. "Jake!" she yelled, brandishing his sword.

Jake snatched it. "We've got to help River," he insisted. "Fezziwig's got him."

They looked. The ringmaster had grabbed River by the throat, and was ramming him against the wall. His head was bleeding.

"Stand back," said Jazz, aiming her bow.

"What are you going to do?"

"Disable him."

"Disable him?!" Jake exclaimed. "You should blow out his brains!"

141

Jazz glared at him. "With a bow?"

"I'll handle this! Gyaaaaaaaaaaa!"

"Jake, no!"

BAN!

He severed Fezziwig's arm.

"Aaaaaaa!" the ringmaster screamed. "Auuuugggghhh!"

Fezziwig collapsed. Black blood sprayed out of his wound.

Jazz gasped.

River toppled to the floor, coughing and spluttering.

Jake hovered his blade over the ringmaster.

"W-wait!" begged Fezziwig. "Don't kill me! Please!"

"Oh, dude," Jake hissed. "I'm not going to kill you."

Jazz grabbed his shoulder. "Come on."

"No, Jazz. Hold him."

Jazz glared. "What?"

"I said hold him! Do it!"

"What? No!"

Jake shoved her. "Do as I say!"

Jazz staggered. She glared at her twin.

"No!" cried Fezziwig. "What are you going to do?!"

Jake crouched next to a dead spore. He scooped some dark paint
out of its wound. "Have you got him, Jazz?"

Jazz put her hands on Fezziwig's shoulders. She was trembling.

"Jazz?!"

"I've got him!" she yelled. "Alright?!"

"I will be!" Jake grabbed Fezziwig by the collar. "I hope your
freaks don't kill you," he whispered, his eyes wide. "I want you to feel
this."

"F-feel what?"

Jake pressed his hand against Fezziwig's mouth. Dark paint
trickled through his fingers.

"No!" screamed Fezziwig, his mouth smothered. "Nooooo-
mmmmmmmm!"

"What are you doing?!" cried Jazz.

"Only what he did!" said Jake. "To River! To everyone!"

River stirred. He scrambled to his knees.

Jazz watched as Fezziwig's lips disappeared, fused together by the
paint.

"Hmmmm!" he screamed.

"Hey scorpion!" cried Jake. The freak scuttled over. "He's all
yours!"

"Jake, no!"

142

The scorpion growled as it rammed its leg into Fezziwig's coat. It dragged him across the tent.

"Hmmmm!" Fezziwig pleaded. "Mmmmmmmmmmm!"

They disappeared out of sight.

Jake, unmoved, helped River to his feet.

"Hey," he said, taking his arm. "How was your nap?"

"You know me," said River, stumbling. "Always sleeping on the job."

"Dude, you're bleeding." He grazed River's face. "We gotta get you fixed."

"It's nothing, honestly."

"Oh, so concussion's nothing? Come on, take my hand. Doctor's orders."

River recoiled. He deployed his blade.

"Bro?" said Jake. "What the hell?"

"Behind you."

Jake looked. More night spores were pouring into the tent.

"Okay Doctor, you got orders for this?" said Jazz. She raised her bow. "A dozen spores against two humans?"

Jake frowned. "Two?"

"You don't count."

"I say we run," said River. "How's that for a plan?"

"Pretty good."

"Agreed," said Jake. "Alright people, let's haul ass."

Jake and Jazz ran. River followed, but fell. A severed arm had grabbed his leg.

"Augh, let go of me!" he cried. "Nghhhhhhh!"

Fezziwig's arm dragged him through the sawdust.

"Aaaaaaaaaaaaaa! Guys, help me!"

"River!" cried Jazz. She and Jake were at the door.

"Ngh! How are you so strong?!" River thrashed. "You're just fingers?!"

"Kiiiiiiiiii!" came a squawk. River looked up.

It was Spencer. "I'm coming River Still!" he yelled, as he dived through the air. "Hold on!"

River held up his hand, and Spencer grabbed it. He began to flap madly.

"Kuuuuuuuu!" cried River, thrashing against the severed arm. "Nghhhhhhh!"

They broke free. River threw the arm at a spore, and knocked it over.

"Okay!" said River, panting. "Let's go!"

Spencer took flight, lifting his friend off the floor.

"Woah, that bird's strong!" said Jake. "Did you see that?"

"Never mind that now!" said Jazz. "Run!"

Spencer glanced at River as they soared across the tent. "You're not afraid of flying, are you?" he asked.

"Uhh," said River, his eyes closed. "Yeah."

"Jolly good. Just do what I do."

"What's that?"

"Wing it!"

"What, that's no heeeeeeeelllllppppp!"

The pair banked to the left and dived, dipping under the exit and soaring into the corridor.

They caught up with Jake and Jazz, who were tearing along the passage.

"Make for the house of cards!" Spencer cried, flapping over their heads. "I solved the riddle."

"What, how did you solve it?" River blustered. "Aaaaaaaaaaaaa Spencer, I want to go home!"

"Home's boring, River Still."

"Maybe, but it doesn't make me want to puke!"

They soon arrived at the house of cards. Spencer lowered his friend to the ground, and the twins rushed over.

"They must be right behind us," said Jake, readying his weapon. "River, you're injured. Help Spencer with the puzzle."

"On it."

Jake nudged his sister. "Jeff, we'll cover them."

"Don't touch me!" she snapped.

"What the heck? What's up with you?"

"What's up with me? Are you from a different planet?"

Jake looked at her blankly.

"Forget it," said Jazz. "Don't talk to me."

The night spores tore into the corridor, and Jazz raised her bow.

"Try not to miss," Jake jibed.

Meanwhile, River and Spencer arrived at the empty frames. "What did you say?" River asked. "Three of the same number, and two of the same number?"

"Yes, you need to make a full house," said Spencer. "It's a poker hand. Three queens and two sevens should do it."

"A poker hand?" said River, scrambling for the cards. "How did you figure that one out?"

"Reason left me a clue," said Spencer. "Tell me, River. Why is there no room at the inn?"

"I don't know, why is there no room at the inn?"

"Because it's a full house!"

144

River rolled his eyes. "Well if you cracked it earlier, why didn't you put the cards in? When we weren't under attack by killer clowns?"

"I didn't know what would happen!" Spencer protested. "What if the door opened and there were more of those creatures in the next district? We're not all cyborg death machines, you know."

"More's the pity."

River put the last of the cards into the slot and a cubbyhole opened, revealing a lock. "That's it. Have you got the key, Spencer?"

"In my claw, River Still."

Spencer placed the Every Key in the receptacle and the door swung open, revealing another passage.

"We're through!" he announced. "Come on, everybody!"

Jazz hurried over. "We managed to hold them off, but there are more on the way," she said.

"It's alright, we're done here," said River. "Where's Jake?"

Jazz frowned. "He was right behind me. Jake?"

Her brother was kneeling on the floor, as if in a trance.

"What the hell's he doing?" said River.

"Earning a slap."

"No, Jazz!"

Jazz bolted across the hall and grabbed Jake by the arm. "Are you crazy? You're going to get us killed!"

"I dropped something!" he replied, stuffing an object into his pocket.

"I'll drop you in a minute! Move!"

Jazz hauled him to his feet and dragged him towards the door.

"Glad you could join us," Spencer remarked, as they stumbled into the passage. "Can we go now?"

River nodded. "Do it, Spencer."

The parrot took the key out of the lock, and stepped back.

BATAN!

The door closed.

River breathed a sigh of relief. "Well, that was a thrill ride."

"Wasn't it?" Spencer agreed. "Of course, if we hadn't gotten separated at the turnstiles, we would have cracked this district within minutes."

"Good to know," Jazz muttered.

"Man, I'm sweating bad," Jake moaned. He slumped against the wall. "I'm kinda glad they took my shirt."

The gang gazed at their new surroundings. The corridor was a dazzling electric pink, spattered with garish multi-coloured spots. And there was another door just along the passage, which had been painted a gaudy custard yellow.

"Wow, Jake, it's like being inside your head," River teased.

Jake tittered. "Yeah, right. Like I'd paint a door *that* colour."

River surveyed the decor with interest. "Any idea where we are, Spencer?"

"No, I'm afraid not," he said. "There is no name for this district on the map. Doesn't it look interesting?"

"Uh," said Jake. "It looks like a unicorn threw up."

"Violently." Spencer wandered over to River. His head was still bleeding. "You might want to tend to that cut."

River wiped it. "It's fine, it doesn't hurt or anything."

"Tell that to the gangrene. You should all get some rest."

"I agree," said Jake. "Hey River, do you want to be my quilt?"

"If you'll be my pillow."

"Oh please," said Jazz. She stepped forward. "Spencer, didn't you say you could paint a door back to your studio?"

"Indeed I did," he answered, whipping the paints out of his pouch. "We can return to my house with ease."

"Wait, what?" said Jake. "That doesn't make any sense."

"Why not? Both this room and my studio exist in my mind. Therefore I can link the two with a door. Why is this concept so confusing to you? Don't you have doors in Fleshville?"

"Yeah," said Jake. "We have doors. Not teleports."

"Semantics. This door, however, will not look like a unicorn's breakfast."

Spencer swept his brush across the wall. "Ah, praise Jobon for paint," he remarked. "Actually, these doorways are central to my plan for flooding the cellar."

"Of course they are," said Jazz, wearily.

"Do I detect a hint of sarcasm, Jazz Thrower? You might not be so scathing when I call forth a torrent of flood waters."

River frowned. "What, with a door?"

"Quite so. You forget, I have seen that magnificent lake in the Singing Gardens. You know, the one you were sitting by? When you and Natsuki were cleaning each other's lips?"

Jake sniggered.

"When we reach the cellar," Spencer went on, "I shall create a doorway that leads directly to the lake, and open it. The deluge will be spectacular."

The three friends looked at each other, nervously.

"Shame," said Jake, breaking the silence. "I quite liked that lake."

"Well I'm not going to drain it," said Spencer. "The cellar isn't that big."

Jazz looked at him. "You hope."

Spencer stepped away from the wall and sighed proudly. "Ah," he gushed, admiring his picture. "Wunderbar. I do like to make an entrance."

The new door swung open, revealing Spencer's home. He grinned. "It always pays to know a parrot."

"Why?" said River. "Because it can really open doors?"

Spencer winked, and led the gang through.

14: rejection

Natsuki watched with satisfaction as the service drone completed its circuit. It was late; the repair work should have been finished hours ago. But Natsuki had struggled to clear a blockage in the android's boosters. In the end, she'd been forced to replace them completely.

A wise move, by all accounts. The robot was now gliding effortlessly across the ruins of the Neo Vale hockey stadium, emitting a gleeful chirp as its red and blue diodes pulsed in concert.

Natsuki liked it here. Yes, the empty seats and rusting posts looked eerie in the smog, but the scale of the arena was breath-taking. Like the Singing Gardens, the vast space had a calmness, a serenity, that revitalised her soul.

"Come on, Koro," she called out, waving at the flying droid. "Home time."

The robot chirped in agreement and soared towards its master. Natsuki giggled as it touched down on her sleeve, and gave it a pat. "Good boy," she said, stroking its metal cranium. "Someone remembered their landing classes!"

"Piku piku!" the robot replied. "Pii piiiiiii!"

Natsuki laughed. "Don't be silly, of course you're not hungry," she insisted. "Androids don't eat."

"Pin pon! Pii piii!"

"Alright," she relented. "When we get back to the apartment, I'll give you some motor oil. How does that sound?"

"Pikuuuuuuuuu!"

"It's a date then. Now, let's head back before it gets late. It's been a long day."

She led her companion out of the stadium and back through Neo Vale's sullen side-streets, seeing only the occasional drunkard or passing hover-car as she walked.

But she could hear screams in the neighbouring blocks - the yells of youths as they hammered windshields and overturned trash cans. In this part of town, vandalism was a vocation. Natsuki just kept her head down, her mind centred on the places that calmed her: the gardens, the stadium, her home - little pockets of tranquillity.

Natsuki turned onto the bridge that crossed the Netherville freeway. There was a man up ahead. He wasn't moving. He was just standing there, clutching the railings. He shunned her gaze, his eyes fixed on the cars below.

Natsuki felt uneasy.

She made a beeline for the other side of the path. But she kept the guy in the corner of her gaze, conscious of the fact that he could suddenly swing around and grab her.

"Piku piku!" Koro screeched. "Piiiiiii!"

Natsuki looked. The man had his leg on the railing and was climbing over.

"No!" Natsuki yelled, dashing to his side. "Don't!"

She grabbed the man's arm, but he resisted. "Get off!" he yelled, his jaw clenched. "I'm done here! I'm jumping!"

"No!" Natsuki pleaded. "You don't have to jump! Nghhhhhhh!" She pulled at his torso and yanked him clear.

"Stop it, let go!" he screamed. "There's nothing left for me! I've done all I can!"

"No you haven't!" Natsuki retorted. "If you had, you wouldn't be jumping!"

"Oh, screw you, bitch! You don't know anything!"

"Then talk to me, tell me what's wrong!"

"Yeah, 'cos talking's gonna fix me! I've been talking for years and no one's listened! The world doesn't want me! Never has!"

"Because you're a cyborg?" said Natsuki - a question that made the guy fall quiet. "I felt the metal plates on your chest. You're a cyborg, aren't you?"

"So what if I am? I'm finished, I've got nothing left!" He launched his leg over the side.

"Listen, stop!" Natsuki cried, seizing the guy's arm. "We need people like you!"

"I am not *people!*" the man cried. "I'm a freak, I'm a half-man! I am not needed!"

"No!" Natsuki pulled with all her might and tore him onto the bridge. The pair landed on the concrete, the man kicking and flailing.

"Fuck you!" he flustered, scrambling up. "Go fuck yourself!"

Natsuki went to reply, but Koro interjected. "Piku piku!" it squealed. "Pii piiiiiii!"

Natsuki watched as a black hover-car zipped onto the walkway. With militant efficiency, two officers leapt from the cab, and marched towards the man.

"No!" he yelled, clutching the railings. "No, keep away from me! Back off!"

Natsuki looked on, shocked and confused. The officers seized the guy by the arms and dragged him towards the van, their faces expressionless.

"Get off!" he screamed, as he fought to break free. "Let go!"

"Where are you taking him?" said Natsuki.

"Help me!" the guy pleaded. "Please, help me!"

Natsuki jumped up. "He's done nothing wrong! Let go of him!"

Koro glided in front of the two officers and beeped warningly.

BAKI!

The officer punched it, and Koro hit the floor.

"Koro!" Natsuki cried.

Within seconds, the man had been bundled into the back of the hover-car. Natsuki watched as the officers scrambled inside, and sped out of sight.

She froze, paralysed with fear. What *was* that? Who were they?

"Pikuuuuu…"

"Koro!" Natsuki darted over. "Oh Koro, I'm so sorry! Can you hear me?"

"Piiiiiiiin… Ponnnnnnn…"

"I don't know who they were," she answered, stroking its dented panel. "But I intend to find out."

Still shaking, she carried the stricken robot off the bridge and back towards Neo Vale. She was walking without thinking, her mind racing. She needed to return to her apartment, but she couldn't think straight; her surroundings were all a blur.

And so she wandered, cradling Koro in her trembling arms as she strode from street to street. She didn't know what to do - if anything. The people who took that man were fierce, authoritarian. Would they remember her face? Would they come back for her if she spoke of what she'd seen? Would she be the next person to be bundled into the back of a van?

Suddenly, a cacophony of voices snapped her out of her daze. She flinched, and saw a group of people crossing the road ahead.

"It sounds like concussion," said Jake, examining his friend's head. "Are you hallucinating?"

"Well, I can hear voices," said River. "They're really, really annoying."

Jazz tittered. "And I thought it was just me."

"Just get a good rest, my friend," said Spencer. "You've taken quite a pounding."

"River!" Natsuki gasped, and the group froze.

River gawped at his watching girlfriend, his eyes wide.

The silence was torturous. It was eventually broken by Spencer, who doffed his hat. "Miss Natsuki," he said with a smile. "A pleasure to see you again."

"Come on," said Jazz, tugging her brother's sleeve. "Let's go. Goodnight, Spencer."

"Gute Nacht." He jumped off River's shoulder. "Well, I think I'll make myself scarce. I'm late for sitting at home, doing nothing in particular." Spencer chuckled to himself and sauntered away. "I'll be in touch, River Still."

"Thanks, Spencer."

Natsuki's eyes were filling with tears. She looked at River and tried to speak. But the words were sticking in the back of her throat.

Speechless, she turned on the spot. She started to walk.

"Natsuki, wait!" River dashed after her. "Natsuki!"

She quickened her pace, but River caught up. "Why are you ignoring me?"

Natsuki glared at him. "Why am I ignoring you?" Her bottom lip trembled. "River, are you trying to hurt me?"

River froze, winded by the question. "No," he croaked. He rested his hand on her shoulder. "Why would I?"

"You lied to me."

He paused. "Not because I hate you."

"Then what? You cannot lie to me and be my boyfriend. I cannot be with a man who lies."

River fell silent.

"You said you'd be safe," Natsuki went on. "You said you'd keep away from those bad people, from that dangerous place. River, you are going to die! Don't you understand? You'll die out there! One day you will leave and not come back and you'll be taken from me, and I have already lost everyone that ever meant anything, and I can't afford to lose another person that I-" She broke off. A tear trickled down her cheek. "I adore you, River."

He frowned. "How come?"

Natsuki faltered, confused by his response. She searched his eyes. A terrible silence fell between them.

Finally, River took a deep breath. "I'm not going to die."

"That wound could have killed you."

"But it didn't."

Natsuki threw him off.

"Alright," said River, firmly. "I'll buy you a drink."

"I don't want a drink."

"Would you rather stay out here? In the cold?" He took her by the hand. "Come on."

He led Natsuki into Fundae's, the 24 hour milkshake parlour. She wouldn't look at him. She fixed her eyes on the table, not even acknowledging the waiter-drone as it hovered over their seats.

"What can I get you?" it chimed.

River glanced at his friend. "Natsuki?"

No answer.

"We'll just grab something off the conveyor," said River.

"No problem. Have a fun day at Fundae's!" It glided away.

River looked around, tapping the table, agitated. Unsure what to say, he took the first drink that slid into his gaze, and sipped.

"Ugh!" he spluttered, staring accusingly at the glass. "It's like oranges and duck! With milk!" He nudged it towards his friend. "You want some?"

Natsuki shook her head.

"Listen. I didn't mean to upset you."

She looked up. "Then why lie?"

"Well, in my defence, you weren't meant to find out."

"That's a defence?"

"You didn't want me to get hurt, right? Well, if I don't get hurt, then there's nothing to worry about." He smiled cleverly.

"You bust your head open! I can't sit in my apartment every night wondering if something will happen to you!"

"Then just stop worrying. It's not my fault you're scared."

"Have you ever tried not worrying about something? I can't just switch it off."

River sighed.

"I had a choice," said Natsuki. "To be with you, knowing that you're reckless. Or to leave you. And I chose to be with you, because you promised you'd be safe."

"I am safe," River declared, knocking his glass over. "Oh, shit!"

"You are so arrogant, River. Why? Do you think you're too important to die?"

"Of course not," said River, fumbling with some napkins. "Everyone dies. But I know what I'm doing."

"And what are you doing? Who are you fighting? Where did you go tonight?"

River paused for a moment. "It's hard to explain," he stammered, watching as the duck-flavoured liquid trickled onto the floor. "I could take you there. Do you want to see it?"

"No."

"Then stop trying to control me!"

Natsuki froze. She looked down at Koro, who was sitting on the table. She picked it up.

152

"What are you doing?"

"What I should have done at the start," said Natsuki, standing up. "I'm leaving."

River leapt up. "Natsuki, wai-auuuugggghh!" He slipped on the milkshake.

Natsuki walked out.

"Wait, Natsuki!" He staggered onto the pavement, covered in cream. "Stop! What do you want me to say?"

Natsuki turned round. She was crying. "Nothing!" she yelled. "You've said enough!"

"Why are you getting so upset? It's not like we're married."

Natsuki gasped. "Are we not friends? Do I not matter?"

"Matter?" River paused. "Look, you're blowing this way out of proportion. I hardly know you. You're just a face I've seen a couple of times. That's all."

Natsuki stared, unblinking. "That's how you see me?"

"Yeah, what did you expect? I've only been here a few days."

"River, we talked for hours by the lake. I told you about my childhood, my parents, my first tomodachi."

River paused. "Your what?"

Natsuki turned, but River grabbed her.

"Hey, what do you want from me?" he snapped. "Seriously, what is it you want me to do?"

"Just leave," she answered, as tears fell. "Leave me, River."

River watched as she dabbed her eyes.

"I was so scared I'd lose you," she uttered. "But you were never really here."

River shook his head. "I'm not an object."

"I know. You are the most precious person. Have you forgotten that first night, when you brought me food? I knew straight away that you were special."

"I'm not."

"You are!" Natsuki yelled. "I didn't even order anything! Why were you there, River? Why were you at my apartment?"

River frowned. "What?"

"You just turned up!" said Natsuki. "I'd already eaten! Why would I order food?"

River thought back. "But you must have done. The app sent me there."

"I know it did! But why?"

River glared at the pavement.

"I'll tell you why," Natsuki went on. "Something brought us together. And now something divides us."

153

River was speechless. He looked into her eyes, his brain scrambling for words.

"Goodbye, River."

His friend turned and walked away.

"Natsuki, wait!" He yelled. "Natsuki!"

She disappeared into the fog.

River was fuming. He was sad. He was confused.

She hadn't ordered food? What was she saying? That it ordered itself?

No. That was stupid.

"Nghhhhhhh!" he cried, kicking a trash can. "Auuuuugggggghhh!"

The waiter-droid glided onto the pavement. "Here is your bill, sir," it stated.

"For what?"

"The kamo rosu milkshake. Thirty-five credits."

"Thirty-five?" River glanced at his clothes, covered in gunk. "But I hardly drank anything."

"Also, the fee for the mess," the robot continued. "An additional twenty credits."

River stared into the coils of smog. "Brilliant."

The next few days were unproductive. Friday came. Jake and Jazz were at school. River just lay on his bunk, sifting through sad tunes on his cell, and drafting a million messages to Natsuki that he never sent.

By the evening - which, admittedly, was only four hours after he'd woken - he found himself at a table in Noodle Vale, a pair of chopsticks in one hand and his guitar in the other. Lazily, he shovelled a bundle of wet noodles into his mouth, and let the sauce splatter onto his chin.

"I can see that you are scared…" he sang, his mouth half-stuffed. "Hmmm. No." He started singing again. "I can tell that you're afraid… Can't ignore the fact you're not okay…" River played it back in his mind. "Yeah, I like that."

"Oh please," said Jazz, half-listening as she tapped into her phone. "Do you want your audience to cry?"

"Don't be silly, Jazz. I don't get audiences."

"You seem sad, River," said his TellMe, with its newly repaired strap. If duct-taping counted as a repair. "Would you like to hear some jokes? Your serotonin levels are low."

"No they're not. How would you know that, anyway?"

"It's obvious," said Jazz. "You might as well have a rain cloud over your head."

154

River ignored her and strummed another chord. "Is there such a thing as fate?" he sang. "Do you think that time could wait? If nothing else I swear I understand…"

"So what's the idea?" Jazz asked. "You'll perform this song to Natsuki and she'll forgive you all things?"

River glared at her. "Excuse me, this is a generic love song. I don't need her forgiveness. But I do need a way to get to the chorus."

Jazz grinned. "You're all heart."

"I feel like the next word should be 'when.' Something like, 'when I'm around you…'"

"Yeah, well could you write the next word in your head? I need to record the intro for my vlog."

"Go for it. I'm not stopping you."

Jazz pointed the camera at her face. She took a moment to mess up her hair, whipping the orange locks across her fringe. She looked like she'd just had sex.

"So guys, I have just received the most exciting message!" she gushed. "Oh my days, I literally died when I read it!"

River rolled his eyes. Literally died?

"As some of you know, Felix Fuhrmann recently followed me on Yapper," she went on. "For those of you who haven't heard of Felix, he's the Head of Engagement at Mango, so yeah - being contacted by him is, like, a really big deal. And even better, he slid into my DMs asking if I'd like to swing by H.Q. and get a behind-the-scenes looksie at all-things Mango! Isn't that dope? I mean I'm so humbled to be asked, I'm like, 'I'm just a vlogger, are you sure you've got the right person?'" She giggled. "So yeah, that's what we're gonna be doing in this video, and I'm taking you guys with me! This is gonna be epic. I'm so psyched to be doing this! Let's Jazz!"

She stopped recording.

River looked at her, intrigued. "You're going to Mango Tower?"

"I know, right. Isn't it great?"

"I guess. Why's he chosen you though?"

"Probably to help Mango. Their reputation has taken a hit over the last few weeks, what with all the smog that's flooded Neo Vale. That's kinda what the recent promo drive's been about. You know, with the TellMe update, and all that."

"Oh yeah." River glanced at his wrist strap. "It knows your needs before you do." Then he looked at Jazz. "Wait, did you say smog? What's Mango got to do with the smog?"

"It's been pouring out of the tower. They've had a coolant leak for ages, and everyone's been like - Mango! Dude! Sort yourself out!"

"I see." River thought some more. "And that's what you think it is? A coolant leak?"

Jazz shrugged. "Well what else would it be? Mind-control vapour?"

"Yeah, maybe," said River. "Come on, you know that half the companies out there would hypnotise their customers if they could."

"Okay, you really need to get out more. Still, if you want to ask Felix about it, you could come with me. He said I could bring a guest, so..."

"Count me in," said River, picking up his guitar. "Felix won't give me the P.R. spiel. I want to see what he's doing behind closed doors."

"River, that's *literally* what this is. It's a no-holds-barred tour."

"Yeah, right," said River, stifling a laugh. "Anyway, I'm going to finish this upstairs. I need some headspace."

Jazz sniggered. "Good luck finding that."

River went up to the living room, where Jake was guzzling a platter of marshmallows with his hands behind his back.

"Uhh! Heyrihwuh!" he mumbled.

River just glared. His hair was askew. His face was covered in sugar.

Jake swallowed. "Sorry, I was just practicing."

"You practice your meals?"

"Funny. No, it's a charity thing for school. The annual marshmallow eating competition. I'm in the finals."

River grinned. "Your talents know no bounds."

"Truth. You want in?"

"No thanks, I'm working on a new song, so..."

"Still? You need to take a break, my guy. All work and no play makes River a dong nugget."

River snickered. "You say the sweetest things."

He pulled up a chair, but it was already taken by a strange-looking doll. River picked it up.

"Oh, sorry that's just one of mom's figurines," said Jake. "Well, a Laputan worry doll, I guess."

"I see." River gazed into the eyes of the sad-looking figure. A blue tear had been sewn into its cheek. "What's it for?"

"Not much. It's just superstition."

"Really? It must mean something to your mom."

"She'd tell you that it's an angel of Laputa. You're meant to talk to it about all the stuff that makes you anxious. It's supposed to take your troubles away."

156

River nodded. "Sounds good. I could sure use a calming influence right now."

"Take it. I ain't judging."

"I don't think I want to pour my heart into a doll, somehow. Tortured as I might be."

"Aw, dude. You're really cut up, aren't you?"

River shrugged. "Maybe. I just hate that I upset Natsuki. She's a good person."

"So are you. You deserve good things." Jake shoved the platter towards him. "Here. Doctor's remedy."

River stared at the mountain of marshmallows. "You want me to eat my own bodyweight in sugar?"

"Yeah man. The medicine for all heartache."

"Can't I just cry myself to sleep?"

"No, that wouldn't be as funny."

River nodded. "Or rot my teeth." He picked up a marshmallow.

"Hey, hey!" said Jake. "What are you doing?"

"I'm chomping my way to an early grave?"

"Not with your hands." Jake wiggled his fingers. "No pinkies allowed."

"You really are a bastard, aren't you?"

"You've only just noticed?"

River shook his head, grinning. He put his hands behind his back and grabbed a marshmallow in his teeth.

"Better?" said Jake.

"Well," said River, licking his lips. "I've learnt a new skill. Actually, these aren't bad." He picked up another.

"Hey!" said Jake. "I said no hands."

River shoved it into his mouth. "What? Are you trying to starve me?"

Jake chuckled, and wandered over. He grabbed a towel. "Alright, hands behind your back."

"Oh no. I'm not falling for that one."

"What? It's a legitimate learning technique."

"I'm sure it is," said River, "at the yakuza school of kidnapping."

Jake sniggered. "Just give me your hands, River."

River sighed and put his hands behind his back. Jake tied them together with the towel.

"Now try."

River looked at him, feeling slightly awkward. Reluctantly, he dived back into the plate, smacking and chomping. It wasn't pretty.

"You're terrible!" Jake laughed. He sat next to him and picked up a marshmallow. "You want a hand?"

"I thought you said no hands?"

"Yeah, *your* hands!" Jake fed him a marshmallow. "Is delicious, no?"

"Hmmm," said River. "Well, I wouldn't eat all my meals like this."

"What, dinner in bondage?" Jake shuffled closer. "I wouldn't say no."

"River," said his TellMe. "Your heart rate has increased."

"You're telling me," Jake sniggered.

"TellMe nothing," River ordered, his cheeks reddening.

"Confirmed. Entering Silent Mode."

River stared at Jake. Jake stared back. They were uncomfortably close.

"Uhh," he croaked, awkwardly. "I feel like I should say something clever."

"You don't have to say anything," Jake whispered. "Nothing at all."

Jake smiled. And then he closed his eyes, and leaned in. Their lips touched.

River turned his head. "What are you doing?"

Jake withdrew. "What?"

"I only came for the marshmallows."

"Oh, you just… had some sugar on your lips."

River raised his eyebrows. "Maybe I could have wiped it off if you hadn't tied my hands together."

Jake laughed. "You're not into this stuff?"

"What? Marshmallows?"

"Hey guys!" called Jazz. "You need anything from the store?"

Jake leapt up. "No thanks, I'm good."

"Can you ask River?"

River went to answer, but Jake smacked a hand over his mouth. "He's asleep."

There was a pause. "Already?"

"Yeah, he… cried himself into a stupor!"

River just scowled.

"Fair enough," said Jazz. "See ya."

River shook him off. "Alright, what's going on, Jake? This is kinda weird."

Jake sneered. It was odd - for a moment his eyes were black, as if flooded with ink.

"What?" he said. "We can't have fun together? I thought you liked me."

"I do," River stammered. "Just not in that way. Well, maybe I do. It's hard."

Jake grinned. "I can see that." He walked towards the door. "Never mind," he said, stepping out into the hall. "I get the picture. It's all good. Hope you enjoyed the food."

"Uhh, Jake?"

"What?"

"My hands."

Jake chuckled. "Oh yeah. They're still tied together, aren't they?"

"Little bit."

Jake waved. "Goodnight, River."

And he walked out.

River sat there, bewildered.

Seriously? Was he joking? Was he really going to leave him like this? And why had he tied him up in the first place? It was odd, even for Jake.

And those eyes. They weren't his. Something wasn't right.

Fortunately, he had a lot of time to think about it. Most of the evening, in fact. If only he could cut through the towel.

And then it struck him, several hours later. He could. He was a cyborg.

ZASHV!

"Ah!" he gasped, as his blades activated.

Well done, he told himself. You worked it out in the end.

Bashfully, he walked out of the kitchen, and went to bed.

in the chrysalis chamber

Decisively, River broke off from his story and stood up.

"Are you going somewhere, River Still?" the disc enquired.

"Yeah, to the bathroom," River replied. "It's all this excitement."

There was a beep. "Help has been summoned. Your session will continue on your return."

"Thank you." River wandered towards the door.

"That was a surprising turn of events," the AI observed. "Your friend made a pass at you."

"Yeah, I guess he did."

"Were you flattered?"

River pondered. "I was surprised that he acted so oddly."

"But there was no attraction there?"

"I didn't say that."

"You felt something for him?"

"I felt a lot of things when I was sitting in that chair," River replied. "I know that being subdued with a tea towel and fed marshmallows isn't everyone's erotic fantasy. But it got my attention."

"Then why did you turn him down?"

River thought for a moment. "Perhaps I was scared of the closeness - of what could happen if the relationship went south. I didn't want to lose a friend."

"You alluded to his abandoning you," the disc said. "At some point, he is going to leave you for dead, and you will end up in this chamber. Perhaps you were right to be afraid."

"Perhaps I was."

"Are you still friends with him? I am curious to know."

River grinned. "You just said the word 'I,'" he pointed out. "You said '*I* am curious to know.' That's the first time you've referred to yourself since I entered this room."

There was an uneasy pause. The machine seemed to be glaring at him, if that were possible. Its coloured lights had stopped dancing. "Is that so?" it asked.

"Yeah, it is." River inched closer. "You're becoming self-aware, aren't you? What am I doing to you, TellMe? Who's counselling who?"

There was another beep, and the door to the Chrysalis Chamber slid open. An overalled man strode into the room, his hands resting on his hips.

"Thank you for your prompt response," said the disc. "Sir, please escort River Still to the men's restroom."

"Very good," said the grunt, grabbing River by the arm.

"I hope you've got the key to these cuffs," said River, as he was frogmarched onto the corridor.

"Keys will not be necessary," said the disc. "Officer Clark is quite familiar with the male anatomy."

River's eyes widened. "Are you kidding?"

"This way," said Clark, towing River out of sight.

"This is wrong on so many levels," River protested. "What if I get stage fright?"

The city was burning. River ran, tearing across the desolation like a torpedo. He wanted out. He had to get away.

They killed Carter. They *killed* him, didn't they? None of this seemed real.

He drove forward, staggering over the glass and bricks. The city gate was east. The open road lay beyond. If he could reach it, he could run away forever. He could disappear.

"Help me!" a voice cried. "Help me, please!"

River turned. A young girl was pinned beneath a concrete block. She was tiny. Nine years old. Ten at the most.

"Please!" she screamed, hysterical. "They're coming!"

River looked. A pack of soldiers was charging through the smoke. They'd arrive in seconds.

At least, they looked like soldiers. He couldn't focus. The shapes were blurry.

River's mind raced. The block - could he lift it? Probably. But the girl was injured. Could she run? No. The block was across her legs. They must be broken.

"Please!" she screamed. "Help me!"

"Uryaaaaaaaaaaaa!" the blurry shape shrieked, almost upon them.

River looked at the girl. *Shit.* It couldn't be done. They'd both be slaughtered.

"No!" the girl cried, as River turned on his heel. "No, please!"

River's throat closed up. He couldn't talk. He could barely breathe.

"I'm sorry," he mouthed. And ran.

"Guoooooooooo!" The soldier pounced.

And then another. "Uryaaaaaaaaaaa!"

River tried to block out the screams. The girl was being torn apart. They'd killed her.

No. *He'd* killed her.

He skidded into a subway tunnel, and cried out – a pure, unfettered cry. His voice pummelled the darkness.

His boot snagged on a coil of barbed wire, and he staggered.

DOSA!

He hit the ground.

Everything spun. All he could see were faces. Carter's. The girl's. The pain throttled him. His stomach lurched. He vomited.

And then he woke. Dazed, he glanced at the bleary face that was hovering over his pillow, and yelped.

"Are you okay?" said Jazz, studying him. She was kneeling next to his bunk. "You were screaming and shouting."

River groaned and wiped his drooling mouth. Why was Jazz in his bedroom? He thought the nightmare was over.

"What time is it?" he croaked. He fumbled for his TellMe.

"Time you got your ass out of bed. We need to go to Mango Tower."

"Ah geez, that's today?" River whined, cocooning himself in his quilt. "Alright, five minutes."

"No minutes, sleepy head." Jazz pulled away the covers. "Now, are you gonna cover those undies?"

River scrunched his face in embarrassment, suddenly remembering that he'd slept in his briefs. "You're the worst, Jazz Thrower," he mumbled, as he pulled his legs up to his chest.

"I know, right? Also, do you know where Jake is? I can't find him anywhere."

River yawned. "I don't know. At school?"

"Dude, it's Saturday. He's normally dead until dinner."

River hauled himself up and gazed drowsily at Jake's bunk. It was untouched, its sheets smooth and creaseless.

"I've messaged him anyway," said Jazz. "Now come on, we're due at Mango at eleven."

River thought about Jake as he slipped into his jeans. Had he even gone to bed? He wasn't there when River turned in. And he wasn't himself, that was for sure. He didn't seem bothered by what had happened with the marshmallows – even when he'd made a pass and gotten shunned.

But who knew what he was thinking? Perhaps he really was upset – more so than he'd let on? Either way, it was bound to be awkward the next time they met.

And speaking of awkward, walking through Neo Vale with Jazz was excruciating. When he'd opted for a trip to Mango Tower, he did so without thinking, not realising that he was also agreeing to a morning with Jazzmas T. Or, more specifically, the girl who *became* Jazzmas T in those rare, smiley moments when she was simpering into a lens. The real deal was a crushing disappointment – one that treated River as if he were nothing more than a wind-up toy.

163

Of course, they say you should never meet your heroes. But it wasn't simply a case of being disillusioned; River was convinced that Jazzmas didn't even like him, although proving that wouldn't be easy. Even if he confronted her directly, could he trust her to be honest? She was acidic, but not hateful.

River ruminated as he and Jazz walked through the smog. As always, she was enamoured with her phone. River sniggered, silently judging her rudeness.

But then, she was probably doing him a favour. How much more awkward would it be if they just strolled side-by-side, looking ahead, not speaking?

"Can I ask you something?" said Jazz, tucking her phone into her jeans.

Thrown, River almost tripped over his tongue. "Uhh, sure?" he gabbled, unsure where this was going.

"Had you heard of me, before you moved here? I mean, had you seen me online, or watched my videos?"

"No," said River, lying without thinking. "Of course not."

"Right. It's just that when Jake said you'd 'fan-gasm' over my videos, I was paranoid you might be a fan."

"I think that was just Jake trying to embarrass me," River reassured her. "Anyway, would it matter if I'd seen you before?"

"Well, it would be a bit awkward."

"Oh really?"

"Yeah. You may not have noticed, but I'm kinda shy in real life."

River looked at her. No shit.

"It's crazy," she went on. "People expect you to be a certain way - like, they think you'll be all loud and fun and this constant ball of energy. But IRL, I'm not like that. I'm kinda weird. I just act for the camera."

River grinned. "I see."

Jazz glared at him. "Are you mocking me?"

River looked back at her. He didn't know. Was he? "Of course not," he answered. "I just didn't know you felt that way."

"Whatever. You're a shit liar."

They walked in silence. It was pretty torturous.

"You're very quiet," said River, after what felt like an eternity.

Jazz shrugged. "Go if you don't like it."

River looked at her. Did she really mean that?

"Damn," she said, whipping out her phone. "Where the hell is Jake?"

* ★ ★

Mango Tower was barely visible as River and Jazz marched towards its entrance, enveloped in swathes of blue vapour. Remarkably, nobody seemed to care; suited men and women cruised in and out of the glass doors as if the fumes were nowhere to be seen.

Indeed, not only did the young man at reception seem unbothered, but he was almost delirious with glee, his face stretched into a permanent grin. First, he insisted on telling a joke ("Why did the sheep cross the road?") and then giggled like he was on drugs as he issued River and Jazz with their holographic lanyards - a pair of smiling emojis that hovered above their chests.

Jazz played along, oozing confidence; who knows, maybe she was genuinely tickled when she learned that the sheep was on its way to the "baaaaaaaaarn."

But to River, these platitudes were just corny; he wanted to see the bloody sweatshop behind the veneer, where the sleep-deprived office junkies were clamouring for the fourth espresso of the morning, buckling under the strain of the sixty-hour week.

But as he and Jazz stepped out of the elevator, a wave of calm washed over them. It was hardly raucous; the employees were affably engrossed in their tasks, slumped in their chairs in t-shirts and jeans. In one corner, two workers were poring over a machine with a grabber claw, and high-fived each other as they snagged a fluffy unicorn with rainbow fur.

"Jazzmas T!" said a fresh-faced young man with blonde hair. And a kitten on his shoulder. "You're here!"

"Aww, what an adorable cat!" gushed Jazz, as she stroked the kitty's chin. "What's his name?"

"This is Candy!"

"Aww, hey Candy!"

River cleared his throat. "I'm River Still."

"Felix Fuhrmann." The guy shook his hand. "Nice to meet you."

Jazz pulled out her camera. "So, shall we get started? I'd love to get a shot of your cat while he's here."

"Yeah absolutely. Ooh, I tell you what, Jazz - shall we do it over there?"

"Totally! I'd love to do it over there!"

River cringed. He looked at where they were pointing. At the other side of the room, a bright yellow tube swirled out of the ceiling.

"Uhh," he stuttered. "You have a slide?"

165

"Yeah, isn't it dope?" Felix chuckled. "It connects the two floors. It's pretty fast, and let's face it - it's fun!"

"Hmm," River grunted. "Not if you want to go *up.*"

"Let's get it in the background!" said Jazz, as she squeezed next to Felix, her camera raised. "So, I'm just going to do a quick intro and explain who you are, and then maybe you can say hi and introduce the tour?"

Felix grinned. "Wow, Jazzmas - this isn't your first time, is it?"

"Trust me, you're in very experienced hands!"

The pair burst out laughing.

"Okay," said Felix. "That's wrong on so many levels!"

Yeah, thought River. Like the slide.

"Maybe we should just start filming?" Felix suggested.

Jazz wiped a fake tear out of her eye and hit record. "Okay!" she said, composing herself. "So I'm *finally* here at Mango Tower, and I'm super excited to be joined by Felix Fuhrmann, who's the Head of Engagement for the whole corporation. Say hi Felix!"

"Hi Felix!"

Jazz tittered again. "Dude, you crack me up! Anyway, thank you so much for letting me come and look round your office today. Can you tell us a bit about what's happening, and what we're gonna see on the tour?"

"Sure, so it's just gone eleven and we're about to have our daily team meeting," Felix explained. "This is where we bring everyone together to discuss our plans for the rest of the day."

"Cool! And am I right in thinking that you have a strict 'no negativity' policy at these meetings? As in, people aren't allowed to criticise one another?"

Felix smiled. "Well, I wouldn't call it 'strict' because that's kind of against our ethos here at Mango. But yeah, we do insist on people only saying positive and constructive things. So like, as you'll see in a sec, we're gonna start off with a game of musical chairs - just as, like, a warm-up exercise. And then we'll stand in a circle and invite people to pay a compliment to the artist next to them."

"Artist?" said Jazz, curiously. "Did I hear that right? You said 'artist'?"

"Yeah, you heard me correctly. Basically, we don't say 'colleagues' here because we think it has too many negative connotations. So everybody at Mango is a 'happiness artist' - a creator of joy and positive energy."

Quite, thought River.

Quickly losing interest in the cringe show, he slunk away from the two vloggers and scanned the office. He didn't know what he expected to see; the t-shirted bods looked too happy to be real, grinning as they played catch with a rubber band ball. If this was a cover-up, it was choreographed to perfection.

But there was a conspicuous black door - slightly obscured by the gumball machine - which caught River's attention. He glanced slyly over each shoulder, and inched closer.

Immediately, he could see that this was a door without handles. River stroked the panel inquisitively, feeling for a hidden lever. But there was nothing. Perhaps it only opened from the other side?

He looked around, checking for onlookers. Then he felt the door again. Was he just being nosey? It could be anything: the office server, the stationery cupboard. The sewage tank?

Getting a little impatient, River kicked the door with his boot. And it swung open.

He smiled. This was all too easy.

"Gahh!" he cried, almost plunging into a pit. There was no floor on the other side - only a shaft, and a rusty metal ladder which disappeared into the bowels of the building.

River looked over his shoulder once more. Felix was entertaining Jazz at the singing water cooler, and everyone else was beavering away on tablets. Half of them were eating cake.

Satisfied that he wouldn't be seen, River grabbed the scabby rungs of the ladder. He took a deep breath, and headed down into the darkness.

River listened. There was a distant thrum - maybe it was a machine. Whatever it was, it was growing louder. It had to be waiting at the bottom of the shaft.

Bokan. Bokan.

His legs pounded the ladder.

Gooooooooouuuuuunnnnnn!

The noise was loud now. It had to be close.

Why was he doing this? Was he crazy?

Finally, he climbed the last few rungs of the ladder, and touched terra firma. He found himself in a dark room which was bathed in a sickening green light. He couldn't see very well, despite the makeshift lamps which had been drilled into its walls.

Gooooooooouuuuuunnnnnn!.

The machine hummed.

Shuuuuuuuu!

The gears spun, emitting plumes of steam.

River braced himself. The place was far from inviting.

But what was it doing in the basement of Mango Tower?

PASHA!

He took a picture on his phone. He had to.

In fact, he must have taken ten or fifteen. And then he crept forward, tip-toeing through the tendrils of black cable that snaked across the floor.

In the next chamber, there were many rows of glass tanks, like test-tubes, which bubbled with a strange-looking liquid.

He snapped again.

PASHA! PASHA!

River needed to document this. Who would believe him otherwise?

And then he stopped. He moved closer to one of the tanks, the clouds of steam whipping his hair.

He was speechless. He gasped, but no sound came out of his mouth. He couldn't believe what he was seeing.

The creature in the tank looked at him, and blinked.

By the time River clambered out of the shaft, his vlogger friend was tearing across the office like a gazelle - as indeed were a number of t-shirted employees. Or artists. They were all invested in a high-octane round of musical chairs. Jazz didn't thank him for pulling her aside during her final lap of the beanbags, but it had to be done.

She wouldn't leave yet, though. There was still the tour of the popcorn bar, plus lunch in the TellMe canteen - if 'lunch' was the right word. It was mostly protein shakes, and avocado sliders.

But eventually she needed the toilet, and that's when River pounced.

"Okay, you're scaring me," said Jazz, as he shoved her into a cubicle. "What's gotten into you?"

River pulled out his phone. "Something's happened."

"Oh great," Jazz sighed. "It's Jake, isn't it? What's he done now?"

"No, I've not heard from Jake. It's this place. I found something, while you and Felix were doing karaoke."

"Ah yeah," Jazz smiled. "At the water cooler."

"Yeah, the feels. Anyway, I know this sounds crazy, but there's a secret door leading to an underground lab. At least, I think it's underground. It's pretty far down."

Jazz looked lost. "Wait. An underground lab? Behind a secret door?"

168

"Yep. Full of steam, and creatures in glass jars."

"Okay, are you drunk?"

"What, on protein shakes?" River gave her his phone. "Take a look at these pictures. Do you see all those machines? And cables? And look at the tanks. Look at what's inside them."

Jazz froze, her eyes widening. "Geez," she gasped. She looked closer. "What are those things?"

"I don't know. Experiments of some kind?"

She frowned. "They're like something from a horror movie. Like people, with bits added on."

"Right. Someone here is experimenting. Maybe it's genetic engineering of some kind. Whatever it is, it's top secret."

"Do you think that's where all the fog is coming from?"

River shook his head. "I don't know. There wasn't any in the lab."

"Doesn't mean there's no connection," said Jazz. "In any case, I think we should tell Spencer."

"You don't want to see it for yourself?"

"I'll never escape Felix. He's all over me."

"I'd noticed."

"We'll tell Spencer first," Jazz insisted. "He might be able to help."

"In what way?"

"I don't know. Maybe he can tell us what's in the tanks. I mean, have you ever seen anything like that?"

"Well," said River. "I've seen night spores."

"Exactly. And if anyone can help us with weird-ass creatures, it's Spencer."

"Alright," River nodded. "Back to the House, I guess."

He reached for his phone, but Jazz pulled back. "Wait," she said, glaring at the screen. "Did you make a video as well?"

River tried to snatch it back. "No."

"Dude, there's a video right there!" She hit the thumbnail. "I want to see."

River baulked, and looked away.

"Hey guys!" said video-River, beaming into the lens with a high-pitched voice. "So I'm super-excited to be doing an exclusive tour of this evil underground lair!"

Jazz's face fell. River slunk into the corner.

"Oh my days, I'm so humbled to be, like, asked to film all these killer monsters!" he continued. "Although at Yapper they don't call them 'killer monsters' - they're 'creatures with alternative motives,' because 'killer monsters' has too many negative connotations."

River smiled at Jazz in the vain hope of coaxing a smile, but his friend pursed her lips.

"So anyway, smash that subscribe button if you want to see more footage of murderous mutations, and tell me - how would *you* most like to die? Would you like to be strangled, or speared through the chest? Let me know in the comments below, and until next time - fewer lakes, more rivers! Laters!"

Jazz put the phone down. She glowered at River.

River smiled, awkwardly. "Do you think it'll get views?"

Jazz narrowed her eyes. And stormed out of the cubicle.

16: school

Caleb could see everything. From the vantage point of his bed, the entire room was in view.

The light was on. The monsters couldn't get him when the light was on.

The teachers had fought with him, though. "You don't need your lamp, Caleb. It's a waste of paint." But Caleb just screamed and screamed until they eventually gave in.

"Look, there aren't any monsters," Mrs Miller insisted. "It's just your mind playing tricks. Come on, let's look inside your closet. You'll see there's nothing there."

"But they're real Mrs Miller!" Caleb pleaded. "And I can hear them! And they'll get me when I'm asleep, and they'll eat me, and I don't want to die, and I'm really frightened of dying!"

"Caleb, look at me. Are you listening? Nothing is going to come out of your closet. You are perfectly safe. If you need anything, me or Mr Peck will be just down the hall. But you won't need anything because nothing is going to happen. Do you understand me?"

Caleb wiped his eyes and nodded. Mrs Miller then tucked him into bed and said, in a calming whisper: "Have a lovely night's sleep. Dream of candy floss and fairies."

And now Caleb was alone.

But not alone enough.

The silence was deafening. It was too loud. Every creak was like an earthquake, and every tap like a cannon. The shadows were monsters - monsters with claws that would snatch you from your bed, and take you to their dens, and cook you in a pie.

Caleb flinched. The closet door had moved. It had! It had moved! Mrs Miller said that it was his imagination and that there was nothing in there and that there was nothing to be frightened of, but the closet door had moved!

He didn't breathe. He didn't blink.

He just watched.

And waited.

It moved again! Caleb screamed. A spindly hand curled around the doorframe.

"Aaaaaaaaaaaaa!" Caleb cried, and dived under his quilt. "Mrs Miller! Help me! It's the monsters! It's the monsters!"

"Hey, it's okay," said a man. "We're friends."

"Mrs Miller!" Caleb screamed. "Mrs Miller!"

His bedroom door burst open. "What in the world?" Mrs Miller exclaimed, out of breath. "Who are you? How did you get in here?"

"I'm sorry, we didn't realise it was a bedroom," said the man.

"Yeah, we just saw a door leading into a cupboard, and we didn't know where it would go," a woman added.

"What's happening Mrs Miller?" Caleb yelled. "Are there monsters? Are there monsters?"

Mrs Miller scurried to his bedside. "It's alright," she assured him. "There aren't any monsters. There's nothing to be afraid of."

Caleb peeked out from under his blanket and stared at the intruders.

"Woah, this is a child's bedroom," said the man, looking round. "It's a mess. It reminds me of my own."

"Yeah, maybe we can discuss the aesthetics later?" said the woman.

"Why are you in my room?" Caleb shouted. "You shouldn't be in my room!"

"I'm sorry, little guy," the man said. And then he paused, looking at Caleb in disbelief. "I mean, *big* guy..."

The woman looked shocked as well. "It's a man."

"A man, acting like a child. In a child's bedroom."

"Look, I will ask you one last time," snapped Mrs Miller, jumping to her feet. "Who are you? What are you doing here?"

"Sorry, it's all Jazz's fault."

"Huh?" the woman gasped.

"We kinda took a wrong turn," the man went on. "My name is River Still. This is Jazz."

Mrs Miller looked furious. "A wrong turn?"

"We're looking for our friend Spencer," said Jazz. "We think he might have come this way. Have you seen him? He's a parrot."

"A parrot?" said Mrs Miller, exasperated. "Right, you had better come with me. Mr Peck will handle this." She snapped her fingers and pointed at the door. "Come on!"

The two intruders looked eat each other. Reluctantly, they left the room.

Caleb clutched his Special, still feeling afraid. It was a small magic pot with a cork stopper. It was warm, and it felt nice. He smiled as he held it close to his chest.

Its magical powers would keep him safe.

172

* * *

River and Jazz were led through a garish maze of corridors, smeared in blocks of eye-watering colours. Some of the walls were decorated with flowers, or fluffy grey clouds, or rainbows.

"It looks like kindergarten," Jazz whispered, as they turned into what appeared to be a classroom.

"Maybe that's what this district is," said River. "A school of some sort."

"What, with adult-children? That's creepy."

"Yeah, because nothing about this House has been creepy so far."

"Ahem!" Mrs Miller stopped, and looked at them. She pressed a finger against her lips. "What does this mean?"

River grinned. "Something dirty, where I'm from."

"Silence!" she barked. "And if I hear any more back-chat from you, River Still, you will lose a warning finger."

"Oh no," River smirked. "Not a warning finger."

"And there you go. You have just lost a finger. What do you say to that?"

"Ouch?"

"Sit down."

River and Jazz looked around, a little lost. "But there aren't any seats?" said Jazz.

Mrs Miller looked at them as if she'd just been asked to strip naked. "You will sit on the floor," she ordered. She pointed at the thick, chequered rug at their feet. "At once! Do you want to lose a finger too?"

River and Jazz gazed at each other in disbelief, and sulkily complied.

"Good. Now you will remain here until Mr Peck arrives. Until then, you will sit in absolute silence. Have I made myself clear?"

The two friends nodded wearily.

"Thank you."

Militantly, Mrs Miller turned on her heel and marched out of the room.

The door closed, and River leapt up.

"River!" Jazz hissed. "What the hell are you doing?"

"That woman isn't the boss of me," he said, surveying the toys, paint pots and brushes. "Wow, it's like half nursery, half art studio, half military prison."

"That's three halves, bro."

173

"And look at all these paintings." He pointed at an array of kids' pictures, pinned to the classroom wall. Most of them were of animals and rolling hills.

"Wait," said Jazz, staring at a picture of a rhinoceros. "These guys have never left the House, right? So how do they know what a rhino looks like?"

River pondered for a moment. "That's a good point."

He was about to speculate further when the classroom door opened. A bubbly young man in a rainbow-coloured sweater entered. "Breaking the rules, River Still?"

River scowled at the man. He hated him already.

"Oh dear, oh dear," the man tutted. "That's not how we behave at the Academy of Reason. I shall be taking a warning finger for that. Now back on the rug, young man."

Resisting the urge to unleash his blades, River dragged himself back to the floor and sat.

"You said the Academy of Reason?" said Jazz, intrigued. "You don't mean Lady Reason, by any chance?"

"No, Raymond Reason, our greatest headmaster. Such a shame he had to leave us. Have you met one of his relatives? I think there are many Reasons in the House."

"Possibly. There's a fortune teller called Lady Reason in the Forgotten District."

The man looked surprised. "Oh, you're from the Forgotten District? That explains your paintwork. As for your fortune teller friend, it wouldn't surprise me if she were related to Raymond in some way. He was, after all, a powerful prophet."

"How fascinating," said River, not fascinated at all.

"Now I must speak with you both," the colourful man went on, kneeling on the mat. "Sneaking into a student's room during sleepy time is very, very naughty. Now it won't happen again, will it?"

River burst out laughing, and Jazz nudged him in the ribs. "No, it won't happen again," she assured him.

"Well, that's lovely!" The young man slapped his thighs. "And I do hope you recover from that terrible cough, River Still."

River cleared his throat. "Yeah-hmm."

"I'm Mr Peck, by the way. I'm in charge of Class Two. They'll be here in a few minutes."

"They're not children, are they?" said Jazz.

Mr Peck frowned. "No, of course not. Children are of the flesh world."

"Then why do your students act like children?" River snapped.

174

Mr Peck just smiled. "The students of the Academy of Reason are very special."

"Yeah, and we're not your students," River rebutted. "You can't treat us like we're at playschool."

"The Academy of Reason has certain rules which must be kept. Rules are there for the good of everyone. Rules help us to learn, and learning makes us grow."

River rolled his eyes. "Give me a break."

Suddenly the bell rang, and a gaggle of students burst into the room - all grown men and women, acting like kids, jumping and laughing and wrestling.

"Swing me, swing me!" said one of the girls, yanking Jazz's wrists.

"I can't," Jazz giggled, standing up. "You're too heavy!"

River watched with fascination as Jazz and the girl roughhoused like toddlers.

The class ignored River, like he was invisible. But he didn't mind. He had no desire to cartwheel or contort, or be swung like a shot put until he puked.

But sitting there, as the room descended into anarchy, he felt slightly embarrassed. He wasn't quite sure what to say or do, or where to look.

Mr Peck clapped his hands together. "Okay, boys and girls!" he shouted over the cacophony. "It's mat time!"

"Yay!" they all yelled.

Delirious, the not-kids raced towards the rug and sat down.

"Quiet everyone," said Mr Peck. "Now, we have two very special guests with us today, so please make them feel welcome. Wave your hands, River and Jazz."

River gave them the finger, and they all gawked.

"Well that's... lovely. Now, as River and Jazz are new, I think we should tell them what we've been learning about this week. Who's going to help me?"

A sea of hands shot into the air, each student straining to out-stretch their neighbours.

"Ooh, lots of hands! Erm, Habakkuk! Go for it!"

"We've been learning about how the world was created," he explained. "And millions and brazilians of years ago there wasn't anything and there weren't any buildings or paintings and there wasn't even any paint because the paint hadn't maded itself yet."

"Well done, Habakkuk, that's absolutely right! And how did this House come to be made?"

"Erm, well, there were lots of bits of paint which were floating around in a ball, and they were all mixed together and then they exploded outwards and maded all of the rooms and corridors and people."

"That's right, Habakkuk! And what do we call this massive explosion?"

"Erm, erm, erm," Habakkuk spluttered. "We call it, erm, the Big Splash!"

"Absolutely! The Big Splash!"

River sniggered.

Jazz, meanwhile, looked confused. "Excuse me," she said, raising her hand. "I'm not sure I understand. Are you saying that a big ball of paint just exploded? And that the rooms and corridors just arranged themselves into rooms and corridors?"

"Yes, that's exactly what happened. Of course, it took millions and millions of years to complete."

"Right."

River interjected. "So do you guys not believe in Jobon? Or Kaida? Or the Empty Chair?"

The students gasped. They started to whisper.

"Now, now, it's okay boys and girls," said Mr Peck. "River is new to this district. He's still learning about how we do things here."

"What do you mean?" River gazed at his troubled classmates. "Did I miss something?"

Mr Peck just simpered. "We don't say 'Empty Chair' in this school. It's a phrase that might cause offence."

River laughed. Seriously?

But then he looked at his neighbours - each staring at him, appalled. They were *very* serious.

An uncertain pupil raised her hand. "Please, Mr Peck," she squeaked. "I'm feeling a bit upset."

"That's okay, Sparkal. Would you like some time in the Happy Corner?"

Sparkal nodded, close to tears.

"Off you go then."

River watched as the troubled Sparkal headed for the far corner of the room, which had been festooned with brightly coloured mobiles and toys.

Jazz whispered in his ear. "Well played."

"Oh, come on. She's milking it."

"You are so gonna get cancelled."

"Silence everyone." Mr Peck put a finger to his lips. "Now, thank you Habakkuk for telling us how the world was made, over millions and millions of years. I think we should take what we've learned and do a great big picture that we can hang on the Play Wall! How does that sound?"

"Yeah!"

"Woo-hoo!"

"Cosmic!"

River ducked to avoid the mob. It was carnage. Over the screams, Mr Peck explained that they were going to "get nice and messy" by making "a colourful explodey picture with lots of different paints!"

"Yeah!" the not-kids cried.

"Yes, it can show us how all the wonderful corridors were made with the magic of science!"

River watched the rabid throng, completely baffled. Even Jazz was caught up in the painting frenzy. River quickly withdrew to a nearby sink, well out of the crossfire.

But Jazz was loving it. She seemed uninhibited, relishing in the freedom of the task as she made vivid swirls and patterns with the brushes.

And she seemed popular. River watched with interest as Jazz's fellow painters vied for her attention, and they exchanged jokes and giggles as they made dazzling shapes on the paper.

He felt like a spare part. River crept along the edge of the room and slipped out of the door. Class Two's depiction of The Big Splash was all well and good, but they still needed to find Spencer. Or, at least, find out whether he'd come to this district.

When he and Jazz had arrived at his home in Chancery Square, they'd found it deserted, and his satchel gone. But the newly-painted door was open, and they thought, perhaps unwisely, that they should head into the next district and look for him.

Yes, thought River. It *was* unwise. Spencer wasn't here, and neither was Jake. They had to get back to Spencer's as soon as possible.

Once they'd finished exploring, of course.

"Hello?" he whispered, poking his head into another room. He stopped.

It was a library. A huge library – a kaleidoscopic collection of spines and shelves, with a spiral staircase in the centre. It was deserted.

River inched towards the stairs. They were cordoned off with a skinny length of chain that dangled slackly from the banisters. On it, a small wooden sign had been fixed, where the word 'NO!' had been stamped in red capital letters.

Well, now he *had* to explore. River hopped over the cordon and gazed, awestruck, at the vast mezzanine above. The books on that level were fustier, perhaps older. They looked like antiques.

"Hey!" a woman yelled. "You shouldn't be up there!"

River looked and saw one of Mr Peck's students. She had her hands on her hips, and was glaring at River like he'd just strangled a kitten.

"It's okay," he answered. "I'm a teacher. Go to your room."

"You're not a teacher!" she snapped. "You just sneaked in here and were trying to go to the Grown-Up Section without being seen!"

"Oh, you're not allowed up there?"

"I'm telling on you!"

"No wait! Gah!" River snagged the dangling sign. "Stop!"

He chased her out of the library.

"Hold it!" he screamed, bursting into the classroom.

Everyone froze, their brushes dripping in paint. They stared.

River gulped. "Hi, everyone."

"Good of you to join us, River Still," said Mr Peck. He turned to the student. "Carry on, Komal."

"And he was climbing over the railing!" the girl gabbled. "He was trying to go up the stairs, and I saw him and I shouted at him because I'd seen him sneak out of the room when we were painting!"

Mr Peck looked at her as if she'd just witnessed a murder. "I see," he muttered, leering at River. "Thank you for telling me."

"Surely you're not going to believe this rubbish?" River protested. "It's all lies."

"Oh really? Then how come you're wearing that sign around your waist?"

River looked down. The 'NO!' sign was dangling over his crotch.

"But there's more!" the student went on. "I saw River go up the stairs, and he was putting his hands on all the books and tearing the pages out!"

"What?" said Mr Peck.

"What?!" said River.

"He said he was cleaning," Komal insisted, "but I knew he wasn't because that's not what cleaning looks like, is it? And it's very bad to tear pages out of books in the Grown-Up Section!"

"It is indeed," said Mr Peck, staring daggers at River. "What do you have to say for yourself, young man?"

"She's full of it," River replied. "Why would I tear pages out of books?"

"It's all true!" Komal insisted. "I saw everything! You said you wanted to keep the pages for yourself and make paper cranes!"

River was aghast. "Why?!"

"Okay," said Mr Peck. "I think I've heard enough. Thank you for coming to me, Komal. I know that I can rely on you to tell the truth."

Komal smiled sweetly at River. He scowled.

"As for you, River Still, this is the most disappointing start that any student has ever made. Sneaking into a student's dorm. Vandalising the Grown-Up Section. I am very, very saddened by this behaviour."

"Yeah, it's the worst made-up crime I've ever committed," he rebuffed. "Aren't you at least going to check the library?"

"Impossible. The Grown-Up Section is forbidden."

"Of course it is. So what happens now? You're going to send me to student jail?"

"I think we'll let our star student decide your fate," Mr Peck suggested. "What do you think, class? Shall we let Jazz choose a punishment for River?"

"Yeah!" the class crowed. "Jazz! Jazz! Jazz!"

Jazz stepped forward, reluctantly.

"Send him to the Naughty Step!" one pupil urged.

"Kill him!" said another.

"Quiet, everyone," said Mr Peck. "This is something for Jazz to decide."

River and Jazz locked eyes. She was thinking.

"I think..." she uttered. "I think if River likes the library so much, then that's where he should go."

The students gasped.

"Send him back there," said Jazz. "Make him clean all of the books - every one, and every page, from top to bottom."

The class laughed. They pointed mockingly at River.

But he kept his eyes on Jazz. 'Trust me,' she mouthed, as the students fell about in hysteria.

And then it made sense. Perhaps she was doing him a favour? If he was confined to the school library, he might be able to learn more about the Academy of Reason. And perhaps sneak into the mysterious Grown-Up Section.

"Well, that sounds like a wonderful punishment," said Mr Peck, clapping his hands together. "Komal, please get River a cloth and escort him to the books. It will be your job to guard him."

"Yes, sir," she replied, and marched towards River. "Come on."

"Oh, and young man," said Mr Peck, as River was towed out of the room. "I shall be inspecting your work very closely, so don't get any naughty ideas about paper cranes, hmm?"

River smiled sycophantically.

Then pulled the sign off his waist.

17: **betrayal**

As punishments went, cleaning the school library was quite therapeutic. In fact, it was less arduous than a Skidmark shift, where River was frequently tearing through blistering winds and horizontal rain. The only downside was Komal, who was sitting on a nearby stool, arms folded, scrutinising his every move.

That girl was going to be a problem. Of course, it made sense that Mr Peck had sent someone to watch him, but Komal was going to make it impossible for him to reach the Grown-Up Section.

He needed a miracle. Maybe she'd doze off? Or perhaps an overladen bookshelf would fall on her head?

River sniggered as he picked up another book and wiped the dust from its spine. He thought back to the strange not-kids, and the creepy teachers, and The Big Splash, and the wild mural that the students had made.

It reminded him of being a kid. He'd done the same thing - many, many years ago, as a boy in Zen Kappa. The memory was fractured, like a photo in a cracked frame, but he knew that there were paint pots - a whole collection, in fact. And his dad was there too, encouraging him to "get down and get messy." For a moment, River remembered his white, dazzling smile, and saw him in crystal clarity, handing him a brush.

The next moment, he was sitting on a carpet of paper. He'd broken up a pad and spread its sheets across the floor, the tins of rainbow paints just waiting to be emptied. River dipped his hands in the wonderful colours and smeared them across the canvas.

"Look Dad, it's the universe!" he cried.

And it was. Those red and yellow blobs? That was the Isop Galaxy. And that green circle with the white rings was Dooey - the planet where the dinosaurs lived. They drove saucer-shaped discs, and were locked in a permanent battle with the crocodile monsters of the Lanpang Lagoon.

Then, River's stomach lurched. A long shadow fell across his work.

His mom didn't shriek. Not at first. But her voice was hoarse. What on earth did he think he was doing? Why had he made so much mess? What did he mean it was the universe? There was paint on the carpet! Look at those hands! Stop it! Get up! Clean it!

Why though? River was confused. What had he done? The carpet was fine! Dad said it was fine! He could wash his hands! Why couldn't he paint?

Was he answering back? How dare he answer back!

Why couldn't he carry on?

Clean it up!

He didn't understand!

Clean it up!

What had he done wrong?

Clean it up!

River screamed. She wasn't listening! Why did she hate him? Why was she being so mean?

Her face went white. She went to smack him, but he ran.

She was close. She was on his tail. He was terrified. She'd catch him. Where could he hide? There weren't enough places.

River reached his bedroom. He turned. His mother entered. He scurried into the corner. He screamed. He pleaded. He curled into a ball.

Damn it, River! Suddenly he was back in the library.

Nice things, he told himself. You were supposed to be thinking of *nice* things. Where did that come from? Why did you go there?

River looked at the shelf in front of him. Somehow, in his daze, he'd managed to clean another line of books - which was quite impressive. But how upset had he been? Had he been crying? And had anyone noticed? He glanced at Komal, whose stern face was unaltered.

He was annoyed with himself. It's not that he'd buried those memories of his mom; how could he? They were part of him. But he seldom looked back because there was no safe place for those dark thoughts to go.

DOSA! DOSA! DOSA!

River's ears pricked up. Was that Komal?

No. She looked as surprised as he was.

DOSA! DOSA! DOSA!

River scanned the deserted library. He inched away from his post.

"Stay where you are!" Komal barked, leaping from her stool.

"You can hear that, right?" said River, as he crept towards the cupboard. "There's something in there."

"You're trying to trick me!" Komal insisted. "You're trying to trick me so that you don't have to clean any more books!"

"You're an idiot," said River. If he'd wanted to get out of cleaning, he could have pretended to faint.

Actually - why hadn't he done that in the first place?

DOSA! DOSA! DOSA!

"We have to look," River stressed. "After that, I promise I'll clean all the books you want."

He deployed his blades, and Komal recoiled.

"Scary huh?" he teased. "Now open the door."

Komal hesitated. "You open the door."

"How, exactly?"

Reluctantly, Komal reached for the bolt, her hand shaking.

"Do it."

River's heart was pounding. Komal released the catch.

"Kyaaaaaaaaaaaaaaaaaaaa!" River screamed.

Then paused. He was staring at a pile of coats, and a pair of feet. He recognised the trainers. "Jake?"

The coats groaned dazedly and stood up. Komal pulled them away revealing Jake, his hair askew and a glove in his mouth.

"Pah!" he spat. "Thanks, man."

River retracted his blades. "Dare I ask…?"

"Man, it's crazy! I was ambushed!"

"What, by a wardrobe?"

"Who put you in there?" said Komal. "Locking people in cupboards is very, very naughty!"

"It's not my fault!" said Jake. "Someone should tell that to the teachers!"

River frowned. "The teachers?"

"Yeah, there's this psycho old woman - Mrs Miller, the principal. As soon as me and Spencer got here, she had him arrested for 'crimes against the House.' When I tried to reason with her, she went berserk and locked me in here."

River smirked. "You got over-powered by an old woman?"

"Hey, she's freakishly strong! She knocked me out with one of those books, and when I came-to it was all dark."

Komal shook her head. "That is the biggest lie I have ever heard!" she snapped. "Principal Miller is the bestest teacher in the whole world! She would never do that to a student!"

"Okay, whatever," said Jake. "Try telling that to my bladder. I haven't peed in hours."

"Listen Jake, we need to rescue Spencer," said River, marching across the library. "Do you know where he's being held?"

"Some place called the Naughty Step," he recalled. "I think it's a couple of levels below this one."

"You're not going anywhere!" said Komal, glaring at Jake. "River must stay in the library until he has cleaned all of the books, or I will tell Mr Peck! And I will tell him that it was all your fault, and you'll have to clean all of the books as well! As punishment!"

Jake snickered. "Seriously, who is this girl?"

"Forget her." River started to walk. "We have to hurry."

"Okay." Jake looked at Komal. "Hey lady, say 'ahhhhhh!'"

"Why? Wha-mfffff!"

Jake shoved the glove into her mouth and pushed her into the cupboard.

"Jake, are you coming?" said River, turning round. "Hey, where'd Komal go?"

Jake ran over. "Oh, she's just having lunch. Sorry, you were saying?"

"Actually, I was thinking. Why would Spencer just be arrested on the spot? Are parrots banned in this district, or something?"

"No, it's to do with the prophecies," said Jake. "You haven't heard about them?"

River looked oblivious. "Prophecies?"

"Yeah, see here..." Jake stopped at the foot of the spiral stairs, which led to the mysterious Grown-Up Section. "The Academy of Reason is the ultimate compendium of all House knowledge. Like, everything from the past and future. It's all written in those books."

River gazed at the vast collection of spines on the mezzanine. "Geez," he gasped. "No wonder they don't want trespassers."

"I know, right? Apparently, the original principal was a seer, and he wrote most of them. So when it comes to Spencer... I don't know. Maybe there's something in his past? Or heck, something in his future? Something only the Academy knows? Something so bad they had to lock him up?"

River sighed. "I don't know, it's hard to believe. Spencer's one of the nicest parrots I know."

Jake chuckled. "How many parrots have you met?"

River was thinking. He turned on his heel and marched towards the exit. "We must find him."

Jake followed. "I agree."

"Wait though." He looked at Jake. "How do you know all this stuff?"

"Huh?"

"Like, suddenly you're an expert on the whole district? Did you sit an exam?"

"Oh, Mrs Miller told me everything," he explained. "I confronted her right here in the library, just before she punched me in the head."

"Really? Did she throw the book at you?"

Jake shook his head. "You're such a douche!" he sniggered.

"Miss, miss!" One of the students skipped excitedly across the classroom. She was clutching a piece of paper. "Look what I painted, miss!"

Jazz smiled. "Oh, it's lovely, Vaishaly!" She gazed at the unusual grey and orange swirls. "What is it? A gorilla?"

"It's you, miss!" said Vaishaly. "Look, you've got a sword, and you're fighting the evil dragon! He's kidnapped the handsome prince, and you've got to rescue him from the castle!"

Jazz giggled. "Vaishaly, that's very sweet of you. But I'm not sure I could slay a dragon on my own."

"Yes you could, miss! You're brave and you're strong and the dragon wouldn't stand a chance and would run away scared!"

Jazz was blushing. She set the picture to one side. "Well, Vaishaly, that's very kind of you. Now why don't you help Habakkuk sort out the brushes?"

"Okay miss! Thank you miss!" The not-kid scuttled towards the sink. "And I hope you like the picture, miss!"

Mr Peck peered over Jazz's shoulder. "Hey, look at you, slaying the evil dragon!" he chuckled. "They never paint pictures of me."

"They don't?"

"Well, they called their *ostrich* Mr Peck." He pointed at a picture on the wall of a grinning bird. "Not quite the same, is it?"

Jazz laughed. "Not really." She looked again at the lively pupils. "Mr Peck, why is everyone like this?"

He frowned. "What do you mean?"

"Why do your students behave like children?"

"You mean, why are they so happy and enthusiastic? And innocent?"

"Yeah," said Jazz. "I guess."

"I can tell you're not from around here. These people were like us, once - independent, aware, burdened by the crushing weight of responsibility..."

Jazz looked at him warily. "Okay..."

"But then Raymond Reason, our greatest leader, looked into the future. He saw what was to become of the poor people of this district: the pain they'd experience, the devastation. He vowed to protect them from the approaching horror."

"Horror?"

"It's described in the Prophecy of Reason. This district will fall at the coming of the spores. By fire and water it shall perish. None will survive."

"Wow," said Jazz, wide-eyed. "That's bleak."

"And inevitable. Reason knew that he couldn't change the future. He couldn't prevent the arrival of the spores. But he could protect his people - give them a life free from fear."

Jazz looked at Vaishaly and Habakkuk, who were pretend-sword-fighting with paint brushes. "Total innocence," she said.

"Exactly. So, a number of us volunteered to watch over the students and recondition them. Over many years of intensive therapy, we changed the way they thought. We altered their minds. They knew nothing of Jobon, or Kaida, or the prophecies."

Oppression, then. Jazz could feel herself getting angry. Mr Peck, for all his rainbow sweaters and glazed smiles, was talking like a monster.

"You think it's better for these people to believe all the crap you teach?" she snapped. "And to think that the whole world is sunshine and sparkles, rather than know the truth?"

Mr Peck didn't blink. "I do."

The bell rang, and the class leapt up.

"Okay guys!" Mr Peck shouted, clapping like a clockwork monkey. "That was bell number three! And we all know what that means!"

"Sleepy, sleepy time!" the class cheered, jumping up and down.

"That's right – it's sleepy, sleepy time! Now, form a lovely long line and be super quiet! We can't take our naps if we're shouting and screaming, can we?" Mr Peck turned to Jazz. "Go and get your friend. I'm sure he's learned his lesson by now."

Jazz gave him a dirty look.

"Jake, why did you come here?" said River, as they turned into a corridor that was lined with battered lockers. "Did something happen?"

"Oh, you know," he replied. "This and that." He stopped at a door marked 'private,' and kicked it open. "Through here."

"This and that? You just disappeared. Your sister was really worried."

"She's a drama queen."

"Yeah, and she cares about you," said River. "So come on, what happened?"

"Nothing. I just decided to come. We don't have to do everything together, do we?"

River wasn't buying this. "So that's it? It was a whim? It had nothing to do with you and me, and the marshmallows?"

185

Jake laughed. "Why would it have anything to do with that?"

"Well, we had a moment. It was... kinky."

Jake scrunched his face. "You thought that was kinky?"

"Didn't you?"

"No, we were just fooling around!"

River said nothing.

"Anyway," Jake went on, "I probably should've waited for you guys. As soon as me and Spencer arrived, we ran straight into that crazy principal, and everything kinda unravelled."

"Yeah, me and Jazz met her as well," said River. "She wasn't exactly cuddly."

"Oh, Jeff's here?"

"Yeah, she's... really thrown herself into school life." River smiled. "She's probably writing the new curriculum as we speak."

They kept on walking. River surveyed the corridor, which was dingy and muck-ridden. The overhead lights were growing dimmer by the second, bathing the pair in a deep orange glow. Something didn't feel right.

And he could have sworn they were being followed.

"Are you sure this is the right way?" he asked, seeing that the passage was starting to narrow.

"Yeah, this is it." Jake stopped. "It's through this door."

'Door' was a slight exaggeration. River clambered through a tight metal hatch into a small, cylindrical chamber. It smelled like a rotting animal carcass, and looked like a toilet bowl.

"It's a dead end," said River, covering his mouth.

"A dead end indeed," said an icy voice - and one that River recognised.

He turned. There was a light clatter of heels, and Mrs Miller stepped into the chamber.

"Miller." River deployed his blade, and raised it. "Release the parrot, Grandma. Or we'll take him by force."

Miller shook her head. "You really don't know anything about him, do you? I almost feel sorry for you - so easily seduced by his tawdry charm. You do realise that you're friends with a murderer?"

"Not Spencer," River snapped. "Nice try."

"You're in denial. How much do you really know about his past? Come on, tell me honestly. What has Spencer von Luft told you about his life in the House?"

River scowled.

"As I thought," Miller crooned. "Nothing at all."

"Everyone has a past," said River. "And I'm sorry, but you can hardly take the moral high-ground after what you pulled. Do you think locking Jake in a cupboard is the best example to set to your students?"

Miller tittered. "Wrong again, River Still. I knew you wouldn't make the grade. Will you tell him Jake, or shall I?"

"Tell me what? Gyaaaaaaaaaaaaaaaaaaaa!"

Jake punched him in the stomach. River fell to his knees, panting. He could hardly breathe. "J-Jake...? W-what the...?"

Jake sneered. "I'm sorry, dude. I put myself in the cupboard. I baited you."

"B-baited me?" River clutched his chest. "What are you talking about?"

"I needed you to trust me, so I could lead you down here."

"Ngh!" River looked at his friend. "But I do trust you! Why do that to yourself?"

Jake crouched next to him and whispered in his ear. "Because getting saved by you is hot."

"I hate to interrupt your lovers' quarrel," said Miller, "but time is of the essence. The fact is, River, I can't have anyone delaying the arrival of Jobon's army. Yourself, Spencer, Jazz... You must be tidied away, and quickly."

River sat up. "You want this place to burn?" he gasped. "Are you insane?"

"Oh, I don't think so. Let's just say, I'm 'in Special Measures!'"

Jake laughed sycophantically.

"Do you think I want to spend the rest of my life as the principal of this hateful place?" she barked. "Molly-coddling a collection of freaks? That is my fate if Jobon's army is stopped."

"Great." River stood up. "So the night spores are your retirement plan."

"Correct. Your friend Jake came round to my way of thinking. But sadly, the famous River Still isn't blessed with the same intelligence. And we all know the fate of fools."

"Jake's not gonna kill me," said River. "He's bluffing."

BOKAN!

Jake punched him in the face. "Am I?" he yelled. "Tell that to my fist!"

Mrs Miller laughed. "This is delightful! And to think that I was once afraid of you, River Still. You are pathetic!"

River searched Jake's face, confused.

"Do you even know where you are?" Miller went on. "You're under the kitchen. Every day, the waste from the food hall is pumped into this paint tin to be remixed. Now, what do you think will happen if a person is trapped inside when it is filled?"

River looked at the ceiling. A huge nozzle was dangling over his head.

"Well," said Miller. "You're about to find out."

"No!" River yelled, grabbing Jake. "Jake, listen to me!"

Unmoved, Jake swept him aside.

"Oh dear," Miller remarked. "I would ask that you don't make a *meal* of this, River Still. But, under the circumstances…"

Jake laughed like a hyena as he and Mrs Miller left the chamber, and slammed the door.

"Auuuuuggggghhh!" River pounded it with his fist. "Jake! What's she done to you? Fight it, man! You're strong! Do you hear me?!"

Jake just sniggered. He grabbed hold of the lever. "Bon appetit."

"Nghhhhhhh!" River kicked the door in rage.

𝐺𝑂𝑂𝑂𝑂𝑂𝑂𝑂𝑂𝑈𝑈𝑈𝑈𝑈𝑈𝑁𝑁𝑁𝑁𝑁𝑁𝑁!

The machine whirred.

River looked up. The nozzle was descending.

18: punishment

Jazz stared into the darkness of the library. It filled her with dread. Its walls, awash with clouds and rainbows, looked almost sinister in the half-light. She wanted to leave, and quickly.

But she had to find River. She found Komal easily enough (who ran away, crying) and then the lights went out, plunging the academy into darkness. Sleepy, sleepy time.

Well, it didn't make Jazz feel sleepy. It made her want to run.

"River?" she hissed, every muscle tensing. "River?"

An icy chill ran down her spine. Something wasn't right. He wouldn't just leave her, would he?

She gulped. There was one place he could have gone – the Grown-Up Section, nestled at the top of the spiral stairs. But it did not look inviting.

"River?" she called out again, desperate for a response.

He could be too far away, she thought. Perhaps he couldn't hear. Assuming, of course, that he wasn't in trouble.

Or dead.

She had to go. She had to find out.

Gingerly, she mounted the stairs.

GISSSSSHHHHHIIIIIII!

They creaked.

Jazz lurched, almost falling.

Breathe, she told herself. You have to stay calm.

She continued to climb. As she inched closer to the top, she spotted a light – a soft, flickering glow, like the ebb of a painted candle. Perhaps she wasn't alone.

Who could it be, though? A librarian? Another teacher?

"River?" she whispered, as she arrived on the mezzanine. There was no answer.

For a moment, she stayed rooted to the spot. The fear was paralysing, but the desire to run was intense.

At least she could see. The candle offered some respite from the darkness, bathing the books in a faint corona of light. There were hundreds.

But there was no sign of River. In fact, there was no one. She was alone.

"Good evening."

Jazz yelped. She jumped round, her heart racing. "Who are you?"

The wizened old man had a crooked nose and thinning hair. He cackled. "My name is Page," he croaked, his yellow eyes burning into hers. "You look lost, my dear. Is there anything I can help you with?"

"I'm, uhh," Jazz faltered. The words kept sticking to her tongue. "I-I'm looking for someone."

The old man chuckled. "Then you have come to the right place," he said. "People are my speciality. Who are you seeking?"

Jazz looked at Page, half expecting him to pull out an axe. "River Still?"

He smiled crookedly, exposing the black nothingness in the space behind his lips. "But of course," he whispered. "One moment."

Jazz watched the old man as he disappeared into the darkness. What was that supposed to mean? Was River really up here?

It could be a trap. She risked a glance over her shoulder, paranoid that some hideous creature was going to grab her from behind.

Page quickly returned. He limped soundlessly through the shadows, clutching something in his spindly fingers.

"River Still," he purred, lowering a book into her hands. "This is a momentous occasion. This is one of the few titles that has never been requested."

Curious, Jazz examined the cover, which had been engraved with River's name. "Uhh," she stammered, unsure if the old man was toying with her. "What is this?"

"This is the book you requested. The life of River Still, as documented by Raymond Reason. His every waking moment, from birth to death."

Jazz glared at him. "To death?"

"Indeed. The great Reason never left a work unfinished."

Jazz frowned. An autobiography, of things that hadn't happened yet? Is this what the Grown-Up Section was - a vast collection of prophecies?

And did she have the right to peek? Did she even want to?

Page peeled back the front cover. "River Still is a unique character," he explained. "He is from the world of the flesh. And intriguingly, as you can see in the first paragraph, River Still is not his real name. He chose it later."

Jazz read the opening lines. She gasped.

"Is everything alright?" asked Page.

Jazz's eyes glistened. "His name," she uttered. "It's so sad."

"I don't think it's sad. It makes perfect sense."

Jazz flicked through the pages. There were a number of strange symbols, and some pictures - one of River handcuffed to a chair, one of River and Spencer with a boy in a cape... and one that made Jazz feel sick. She froze as she stared at the frantic scribbles, ominously titled 'The Cellar.' She glared at the inky depiction of River, spearing Jake's body. Blood gushed out of the wound.

Jazz clapped a hand over her mouth. "Page," she muttered through her fingers. "What is this?"

"Let me see." Page hunched over the illustration. "Oh yes, that is one of Reason's visions – an event yet to come. But as for the exact meaning, I'm afraid I cannot say."

Jazz stared at the image. River's eyes were like pits, and his mouth was curling into a snarl.

Jazz's heart skipped a beat. How the hell could this be the future?

"No!" Caleb screamed, as the dragon loomed over his bed. It was getting closer by the second. "Get back! Get away from me!"

The beast roared as steam spewed from its nostrils. Its talons were like spears, and its tail was jagged like barbed wire.

It lunged. It thrust its head towards the pillow, close enough for Caleb to smell the fetid stench of its breath.

"No!" he cried out. "Help me, somebody! Please!"

He rolled out of bed as the dragon swiped.

"Nghhhhhhh!" gasped Caleb, grabbing the bedside lamp. "Keep away!"

He threw it.

BOKAN!

The monster was struck.

"Guooooooooooo!" it roared, tumbling. Caleb watched as the dragon flailed and toppled onto its side.

He held his breath. And watched.

The dragon didn't move.

Terrified, Caleb inched closer. He had to be sure. He had to be sure that it was dead.

It wasn't.

Caleb recoiled. The monster was swelling, growing like a balloon.

Caleb turned, tripping over his feet. "No!" he screamed.

The dragon tripled in size.

"Noooooooooooooo!"

BUWAAAAAAAAAAAA!

The monster burst. Caleb was sprayed with water.

"Auuuuugggggghhh!"

There was a snap, and the light came on. Caleb hid under his quilt.

"Caleb, it's me," said a voice. "It's Mrs Miller, Caleb." The principal dashed to his bed. "You were having a bad dream. You are perfectly safe."

Slowly, the quilt slunk down Caleb's face, and a pair of white, globular eyes peered over the rim.

Caleb panted. He looked around the room. There was no dragon. There was no water.

"There was a spore!" he insisted, his voice trembling. "A water spore! It had claws, and nostrils, and it exploded water! It was tiny until it saw me, and then it grew and grew, and made itself massive!" He grabbed her. "It was huge, Mrs Miller! It was huge and black and evil, and it wanted to dissolve me!"

Mrs Miller just smiled. "Well, it's over now. Nothing is going to dissolve you, I promise. There are no such things as water spores. Okay?"

Caleb nodded, not okay at all.

Mrs Miller narrowed her eyes. "What's in your hand, Caleb?"

Caleb was clutching a brown phial with a stopper, his knuckles whitening from the strain. "It's my Special," he trembled. "My Special keeps me safe. It protects me from the monsters."

Mrs Miller glowered at the container. "That's lovely, Caleb," she said, reaching for the object. "Can I see?"

Caleb looked at Miller, and then at the phial, and then at Miller again. "Okay," he muttered. "But you must be very, very careful. It's magic, you see."

Mrs Miller inspected the bottle, fascinated. It was like an inkwell, its rim stained with black splashes. She knew exactly what it was.

She sneered. It was a phial of dark paint.

"Wow, you're right Caleb," she remarked. "This truly is a special object."

"I found it a few days ago. And I'm going to keep it forever and ever and ever."

"Oh, that's lovely to hear. I can see why it's so important." Mrs Miller paused, the germ of an idea forming in her mind. "Caleb, I think your Special is more powerful than you realise. In fact, I think it could make your nightmares go away."

"What do you mean?" said Caleb, sitting up.

192

"I tell you what, why don't you come with me to the classroom? I will show you what I mean."

Caleb hesitated, wracked with apprehension. "But it's the middle of the night, miss," he stuttered. "We'll wake everybody up."

"Don't be silly, Caleb, we won't make any noise." Mrs Miller held out her hand, and smiled. "Come on, brave soldier. Let's stand up to those monsters."

Jazz took a deep breath. She'd made it.

Actually, the Naughty Step had not been hard to find; Page had been kind enough to point her in the right direction.

And it was weird. Although she didn't know what she was expecting. In the real world, the 'naughty step' was a rather bland stretch of carpet - the place you went for stealing sweets, or breathing in the wrong direction. This place, though, was like a cross between an amphitheatre and a prison camp. The whole room was a vast staircase, built out of plain concrete blocks. A circle of sand sat at its base.

Be brave, Jazz told herself - not feeling brave in the slightest. She pretended to be a teacher, swaggering confidently towards the guard on the top step. Remarkably, he didn't look twice; she obviously wasn't a student. She was too self-aware, and carried herself with an air of authority. She was allowed to pass.

Jazz crept down the stairs, surveying the prisoners that were scattered along the blocks. Some were weeping, whilst others just stared blankly into space, as if contemplating the severity of their transgressions. How long had they been here?

Spencer was curled up in a spot midway down, snoozing. Jazz sidled next to him, not making a sound.

"Hello," she whispered, and lightly grazed his feathers.

But he didn't move.

Jazz rolled her eyes. She'd try a different tack. "Papaya pizzas taste like poo, and all kale should be banned."

Suddenly he stirred. "Hmm?" he groaned, opening one eye. "What was that?"

Jazz chuckled and stroked him once more. "Wake up, sleepy head. The cavalry's here."

Spencer blinked. "Oh, my friend," he said, looking up. "You found me. How are you?"

Jazz laughed. "Never mind how I am! Come on, we've got to get you out of here."

He sighed. "I am in the right place. My past has finally caught up with me. You should go, Jazz. I must pay my penance."

"What are you talking about? What penance? Have you even done anything wrong?"

"Yes, and it was bad," said Spencer. "I really don't want to talk about it. You should leave."

"Hmph," Jazz snorted. "You leave."

"What?"

"Come on, I'm busting you out of here."

Spencer shook his head. "You can't. Please, you don't understand what I've done."

"Then help me understand. Dude, I'm your friend."

Spencer pursed his beak. "If you were my friend, you wouldn't call me 'dude.'"

"You love it really," she chuckled. "Come on, I want to help. How bad can it be? I mean, did you kill someone?"

"Yes."

Jazz glared at him.

"You see," said Spencer. "You didn't want to hear that, did you?"

Jazz didn't answer. She didn't know what to say.

Spencer sighed. "You can go."

It was the longest silence ever. Eventually, Jazz broke it. "There is only one thing that will make me leave," she stated, "and that's if Spencer von Luft is with me."

"I'm a killer, Jazz."

"What, by choice? You're saying you murdered someone in cold blood? Without care or remorse? I don't believe it."

Spencer coughed. "Well, if you put it like *that*..."

"Exactly. So, start at the beginning. What did you do?"

Spencer bowed his head. "Oh, just paint," he explained. "That's my job, after all. Painting. I carry out repairs. I was visiting a district I'd not been to before. A hospital. They needed me to make them a new grill, for ventilation."

Jazz nodded. "Okay. So what happened? You got it wrong? Everyone baked?"

"It's worse than that. I got distracted. The day before, I'd snuck out of the House for the first time. I'd seen Neo Vale, the flesh world. I'd seen the vast lake at the Singing Gardens. I was spellbound."

She frowned. "What's wrong with that?"

"Apart from it being illegal, you mean?" Spencer chuckled. "Oh, nothing. But I couldn't stop thinking about it as I painted. Those waters. Those vast, tranquil waters..."

He broke off. His eyes were filling up.

"Hey," Jazz whispered. She put her arm around him. "It's okay."

"The grill was fine," he choked, "but I kept thinking about the lake. The grill became a door. The waters burst through it – a vast, unstoppable torrent. You know what that means for a painted person, Jazz? It's like acid. No one survived."

Jazz stroked him. "You did."

"I can fly," he explained. "I could escape. They couldn't. I watched them all die." A tiny tear fell from his eye. "Everyone died, Jazz."

"Look at me," she answered, firmly. "Spencer."

Reluctantly, he lifted his head. His eyes were swollen.

"It wasn't your fault," she insisted. "Have you got that?"

"Those screams..." Spencer shut his eyes. "Oh Jazz, it was awful. All I could do was fly, and never look back. But now I must. This is the consequence, isn't it? The truth has caught up with me, at last."

Jazz shook her head. "This is no consequence," she replied. "You haven't gone anything that deserves imprisonment."

"This district is all-knowing. Mrs Miller read my book - the one from Reason's library. It lists my every deed and misdemeanour."

"But what you did was an accident."

"Mrs Miller doesn't think so. She said it was an act of rebellion against the hospital. You see, there were some bad doctors down there. It was a corrupt institution."

"Whatever, I've heard enough. I'm getting you out of here."

"But you can't. Please, Jazz, just leave."

"No way." Jazz bounced to her feet. "We're busting out of this place, and then we're finding River, and then we're finding Jake, and we're going to battle our way down to the cellar and kick Jobon's butt." She took a deep breath. "Wow, I can't believe I just said that."

"But you don't understand," Spencer urged. "Jazz, your brother is one of the people who sent me here."

Jazz looked at him, wide-eyed. "What?"

"He turned up at my studio and threatened me," said Spencer. "He had his sword – he ordered me to take him to the Academy of Reason, or he'd slit my throat. As soon as we arrived, he handed me over. I don't know why, but he's changed."

Jazz shook her head. "He can't have."

"He did. He betrayed me, Jazz. He betrayed us all."

"No," said Jazz, resolute. "Not Jake. Not like that."

"Are you sure? You've never known him to be violent, aggressive?"

"He can be a real bastard at times," Jazz admitted, "but he wouldn't do that to you. Not in a million years."

She reached for her bow and loaded an arrow onto its string.

"What are you doing?" asked Spencer.

"Leaving," said Jazz. "And then we're going to sort this mess out."

She fired, and struck the guard in the foot.

"Miss, I don't understand," said Caleb. He was sitting at one of the desks. "Why have you brought me to the classroom? It's not school time, is it? It's sleepy, sleepy time. I should be in bed right now. I should be napping and buildering up my strength."

Mrs Miller smiled sweetly at him. "You're quite right, Caleb," she said. "You are meant to be sleeping at the moment. But we need to sort out those silly, silly monsters, don't we?"

"But, but," said Caleb, looking flustered. "You said they weren't real, miss! You said that they were all in my imagination and that there's no such things as monsters, but now you're saying they're real and need to be sorted out!"

"Now, Caleb..." Miller inched closer. "I meant what I said. They're just bad dreams, that's all. They're night terrors. You know the story of little Bonnie Brush, don't you?"

Caleb looked confused. "No. Who is little Bonnie Brush?"

"Ah." Mrs Miller pulled up a chair. "Little Bonnie Brush was a very special painter. Now, with her magic paint, she could create whatever she liked - anything in the whole wide world!"

Caleb glared at his teacher, spellbound. "Anything, miss?" he gasped. "Even things that didn't existed?"

"Anything, Caleb. And when she had bad dreams, do you know what she did?"

"No, miss. What did she do?"

Mrs Miller reached for Caleb's Special - the stained inkwell - and slid it under his nose. "Little Bonnie took her magic paint and used it to empty her head of all the nasty things that gave her nightmares."

Caleb stared at the teacher, captivated. "How did she do that, miss?"

"Why, it's simple." Mrs Miller pulled the stopper out of the phial. "She painted all of the things that scared her. And then – whoosh! All gone! All those nasty, nasty monsters left her dreams forever."

"They left her dreams forever?" said Caleb. "Forever and ever?"

"Of course they did, Caleb – forever and ever. Because they were now on the paper. Don't you see?" The teacher picked up a brush and lowered it into the bottle. "This is something that you can do, too.

This is your Special, isn't it? A special, magic pot that's not like any pot in the whole school. Now, I wonder if you've found some of little Bonnie's paint?"

Caleb glared, transfixed, at the inky urn. "I could kill the monsters…"

"That's right, Caleb."

"I could stop the nightmares…"

Mrs Miller took his hand and curled it around the brush. "Exactly," she purred. "Now, why don't you start with that nasty, nasty dragon? He was terribly mean to you, wasn't he? Frightening you like that."

"Yes miss, he was."

Miller picked up a roll of parchment and spread it across the table. "Come along, brave soldier. You have a dragon to paint."

BOKAN!

The door crashed open.

Miller leapt to her feet. "What the-?"

"Step away from the brush!" Jazz marched forward, bow raised, with a parrot on her shoulder.

"What's happening, miss?"

"Nothing Caleb!" Miller snapped. "Keep painting!"

Spencer looked at the mysterious jar. "That, if I am not mistaken, is a pot of dark paint."

"Hmm." Miller folded her arms. "Something you're well-acquainted with, I'm sure."

"Why did you have Spencer imprisoned?" Jazz stepped closer. "And what have you done to Jake?"

"What have I done?" Mrs Miller shrugged. "I haven't done anything. That boy was incredibly useful. I'd never have caught that parrot without him."

"No way. My brother is not a traitor."

Miller sneered. "Are you sure about that? He's doing remarkably well so far."

"Remarkably well?" said Spencer. "Remarkably stupid, if he thinks I'd deliberately flood a hospital. You're insane. Both of you."

"Hardly insane," said Miller. "Remind me, who's the one pointing the arrow?"

Jazz tightened her aim. "That'd be me. Live with it."

"You're remarkably confident for someone who's outnumbered."

Jazz tittered. "How am I outnumbered?"

As if on cue, a dragon-like spore leapt off Caleb's parchment and landed at Jazz's feet, its red eyes ablaze. Caleb screamed, and scurried under his desk.

"My, what a talented painter you are, Caleb." Miller gazed at the monster in awe. "It's so lifelike."

Jazz looked at the puppy-like creature that was scrapping at her feet. "Is this bunny rabbit meant to scare me?"

Miller frowned. "Bunny rabbit? Oh yes, what was it you said, Caleb? The monster grew in size?"

"No!" Caleb begged. "Miss, please!"

Mrs Miller laughed as the winged spore started to grow.

Jazz gulped. She stepped backwards, her bow and arrow still raised. "We need River," she hissed.

Spencer hid behind her leg. "No we don't. We've got this."

"How? How have we got this?!"

"Yes, I can see that."

"Uryaaaaaaaaaaa! The monster roared.

"Okay," Spencer leapt forward. "You take the dragon, I'll take the old woman."

"What? Spencer, wait!"

"Kyaaaaaaaaaaaaaaaaaaaa!" Spencer took off. He shot at Miller like a rocket, flapping his wings in her face.

"Nghhhhhhh!" she screamed. "Get off!"

She struck him. Spencer crashed into the wall, and flopped onto a desk. He didn't move.

"Ha!" Miller crowed. "Dead as a dodo!"

"He's not dead, he's resting!" Jazz retorted. She fired, but missed.

Miller laughed. "You really are a second-rate girl. No wonder your brother ditched you."

The bell rang.

"And saved by the bell! How fortuitous. School's out, Jazz Thrower."

Miller ran for the door.

"No!" Jazz fired again, but Miller escaped.

"Help me!" yelled Caleb, still under the desk.

Jazz grabbed him. "Run!" she ordered. "Get your friends! Get out of here!"

"But what about you, miss? You'll be dissolved!"

"I'll be fine, just go!" Jazz pushed him towards the door, and he ran.

"Uryaaaaaaaaaaa!" the dragon roared. It lowered its jaw. It spewed hot water.

"Kuuuuuuuu!" Jazz dived clear of the jet.

She looked at Spencer. He still wasn't moving.

She stared into the monster's fiery eyes as steam flared from its nostrils.

SUKA!

Jazz fired again, the shot going wide.

"No! Help me, Spencer!"

He didn't move.

"Guooooooooooo!" the dragon growled, and swiped its wing.

SUKA! SUKA! SUKA!

Jazz fired, desperate.

PAKU!

The monster grabbed the arrow in its teeth, and snapped it.

Jazz gulped. "Spencer, please!"

The dragon swiped again. Jazz was thrown across the room.

She was winded, panting. She gasped as she stood up. "You bully!"

SUKA!

She missed again. "I've got plenty more!"

SUKA! SUKA!

Someone grabbed her. "Aaaaaaaaaaaaa! What the-?!"

"Need a hand sis?" said Jake, his arm around her throat. "No biggie. Jake's got your back!"

"Ngh! Let go of me! What are you doing?"

"Ending this!"

"Since when?" Jazz struggled, aiming her weapon. "Kuuuuuuuu!"

"Don't even try!"

Jake yanked her, but she fired.

SUKA!

"Uryaaaaaaaaaaa!" the beast screamed. An arrow struck its chest.

"Yes!" cried Jazz.

"No!" cried Jake. He swung, but she ran clear. "Now you're going down!"

"Oh yeah?" she yelled. "So's your dad!"

SUKA!

She fired, and pierced the beast's head.

200

"Aaaaaaaaaaaaa!" the dragon roared. Water gushed from its mouth. The desks began to swim.

"Nice work, sis! You've killed a water spore! You know what happens now, don't you?"

"Guooooooooooo!" the monster growled, flailing.

BAN!

Jake struck Jazz in the face. "I knew you'd be the death of me, bitch!"

She dodged him.

"You and your tears," Jake hissed, "and hysteria! Give me a break!"

"Jake, what's got into you?"

"Nothing!" He seized her. "I'm waking up for the first time!"

"No!" She broke free. "They did something to you! What was it?"

Jake laughed. "What, you think I've changed? Bullshit! This is me, Jazz! Smarter, tougher!" He punched her. "Stronger!"

Jazz hit the floor.

"Guooooooooooo!" the monster roared. It swooned, knocking over a bookshelf.

"It's gonna grow!" said Jake. "Just like Caleb dreamed! If it's killed, it bursts open, and floods the entire district!"

Jazz looked. The dragon's body was swelling, inflating like a balloon.

"No!" Jazz grabbed his shirt. "My brother couldn't know that! Who are you?"

Jake laughed. "Ooh, what are you gonna do? Hit me?"

"Ughh," said Spencer, stirring.

Jake looked at him, distracted.

And Jazz attacked.

BAN!

"Nghhhhhhh!" He reeled, clutching his crotch.

"Jazz!" cried Spencer, standing up. "What happened?"

"Get out of here, Spencer! The spore..."

Spencer looked at the growing beast. "You killed it?"

"Well don't sound so surprised! Just go!"

"But Jazz, there's a door!"

Jazz looked. There was – behind the fallen bookshelf. Another door. With a keyhole.

"Augh!" Jake screamed, yanking Jazz's hair.

"Get off me!"

Spencer flew to the door. "Two seconds, Jazz!"

"I've got this!" Jazz broke free and struck Jake, who staggered.
Spencer slipped the Every Key into the slot. "Like a glove!" he
proclaimed.

Jazz swung. "No one!"

BAN!

"Messes!"

BAN!

"With my brother!"

"Auuuuugggggghhh!" cried Jake. He reeled. He crashed into the
water.

"Move, Jazz!" Spencer yelled, soaring overhead. "We have to
go!"

"You go!" she replied. "I'm right behind you!"

Spencer landed on a shelf, and watched. He couldn't just leave.

"Kuuuuuuuu!" Jake choked, clutching his throat. There was a
snake around it. Or was it a necklace?

"That!" Jazz cried. "That's Reason's necklace!"

"Nghhhhhhh!" Jake retched, as the object dissolved.

"It's made of dark paint," said Spencer. "The water's destroyed
it."

"But Spencer, that dragon is made of paint!" yelled Jazz. "How
can it have water inside it?"

"It's from Caleb's nightmare! Anything is possible!"

"Brilliant."

Jake blinked. "Where am I?" He looked around. "What is this
place?"

"Forget it!" Jazz grabbed his sleeve. "I'll explain later!"

Spencer took off. "Go, go, go!"

BUWAAAAAAAAAAAAAA!

The night spore exploded.

Hot water splashed Jake and Jazz, who screamed. They staggered
onto the corridor, reddened.

It was a tsunami. Within moments, the school corridors were
flooded with the cries of terrified students, fleeing from the rising pool.

"Look!" Jazz yelled. The waves were lapping towards the masses,
killing them instantly. They were reduced to inky puddles. "We must
help them!"

"We can't!" Spencer insisted. "This whole district's going
under!"

"Dude, get in my bag!" said Jake. "It's water-proof!"

"Dude?"

202

"Just do it!"

Jazz glared at the thrashing waters as Spencer climbed into the sack. "Now what?"

"We swim for it!" Jake set off. "No, wait! What about River? Where is he?"

"Urrrrrrrgghhh!" Jazz punched the water, now up to her waist. She'd forgotten about River. "I don't know!"

"Huh? How can you not know?"

"You don't know either!"

"Dude, I got necklaced!"

"Well you shouldn't have put it on! How old are you? Twelve?"

"It wasn't my fault!" Jake protested. "It made me do it! It did something to my brain!"

A man called out. "Guys, wait!"

Jake and Jazz looked. It was their friend, wading through the waters. He was carrying a student.

"River, hurry!" Jake yelled. "Over here!"

River scowled at Jake, suspicious. "Are you normal again?"

"Of course! I got possessed, but I'm fine!"

"It was the necklace, River!" said Jazz. "Reason's necklace! It messed with his head!"

River stared at the rising pool, and then at the student in his arms. "I can't swim with this guy!"

Jazz gulped. "Damn. He's right."

"River, walk towards us!" Jake yelled. "We'll help you!"

He hesitated. "The water's getting higher."

"I'm scared!" the student cried.

"Come on, River!" said Jazz. "You can do it!"

River took a deep breath. He began to wade.

Jazz looked on, terrified. "He's not going to make it," she muttered. "The water's too high."

"I don't want to die!" the student pleaded. "Please don't let me die!"

"Ugh!" River gasped. "What?"

He blinked. Suddenly he remembered the girl from the war, trapped beneath the concrete block. She was screaming.

Then he blinked again. He plunged into the water.

"No!" cried Jazz.

River surfaced, spluttering. The student was gone.

River froze, staring at the swirling pool of paint. All that was left of him.

"Oh geez," Jake gasped.

"River, you have to move!" Jazz shouted. "Swim towards us! There's a door! In the classroom!"

"Jazz, I can't!" said River, shaking. "I can't swim! I'm afraid of water!"

"You can do it!" Jake insisted. "You can do it, River! We've got you!"

"I can't, Jake! I can't!"

"You can!"

River looked down. The water was creeping up his chest.

"You'll drown if you stay there!" Jazz cried. "Walk towards us, River! Slowly! One step at a time!"

He took a deep breath.

Jake held out his arms. "I'm here, man!" he called out. "You got this!"

River bit down on his lip. He started to move.

"That's it!" said Jake. "You can do it!"

"Just a bit further, River!"

River stumbled. He stopped, regaining his balance.

"Take your time!" said Jake.

Jazz nudged him. "We don't *have* time!"

PASHA! PASHA!

River splashed towards them, falling into Jake's arms.

"Ngh!" he spluttered, coughing up gunk. "Thank you!"

Jazz looked back at the classroom. "Right, we have to swim."

River recoiled. "No!"

"What do you mean no?" Jazz snapped. "It's not up for debate!"

"There's got to be another way!"

"There isn't!"

"Here, take my hand," said Jake, grabbing River. "Don't let go, okay? We'll do it together."

"Let's move," said Jazz.

The waters were hot. River felt like he was choking.

But he knew he had to keep moving. He just focused on Jake as they paddled through the torrent, the ceiling moving ever-closer.

Finally, they reached the classroom. But the door that Spencer had opened was completely submerged.

"Okay, we're going under!" said Jazz. "I'll go first. Jake, you bring River and Spencer."

River looked around. "Spencer?"

"In the bag!" came a muffled reply. "Jazz, don't forget the Every Key! It's still in the lock!"

Jazz pulled the object out of the door. "Got it."

"Jake, I can't swim underwater," River stuttered.

"Of course you can," said Jake. "Channel your inner fish!"

"My what?!"

"Jake, be quiet!" Jazz snapped. "Okay, we just need to swim under the doorframe. There's a short passageway, but we should be able to surface on the other side. You ready?"

River gazed through the rippling waters. The next room looked filthy; its walls were lined with cracked green tiles and pipes.

"I'm ready!" said Jake. "Go for it, sis."

Jazz ducked, and disappeared into the water.

"Okay, River!" Jake took his hand. "I need you to keep hold of me. I'll swim and pull you through, but you'll have to kick. Can you do that?"

River looked back. "I'm going to slow you down," he stammered. "It's better if I swim on my own."

"Are you sure?

"Yeah, it'll be quicker. Trust me. I'm right behind you."

"That's my guy," Jake grinned. "Alright, bath time!" He took a deep breath and dived under.

River gulped. Now he was really in trouble.

No, he told himself. Stop thinking. Stop wasting time. You know what you have to do. You've made up your mind.

"I'm sorry," he mouthed, the water lapping into his mouth. He turned back.

PASHA! PASHA! PASHA!

River thrashed and splashed, coughing and spluttering. It was so hard to breathe.

Damn. They'd be worrying, wouldn't they? They'd think him dead. What if they tried to come back, looking for him, risking their lives? What if he'd endangered them more?

No. Be sensible. They wouldn't follow. The water was too high. They would have to press ahead, right? He was sure they wouldn't come back.

River kicked. He had a plan. There was no way he could swim – but there were the paint tins, on the other side of the classroom. He had to reach them.

"Nghhhhhhh," he panted, lashing against the waves.

PASHA! PASHA!

He swept pieces of school junk out of his path.

Finally, he grabbed the shelves, its tins rattling. He held on for dear life, bobbing in the water like a cork. He felt sick.

"Okay," he gasped. "Fastest paint job in history."

205

Shaking, he snatched one of the brushes and dunked it into a tin. Brown paint smeared its bristles.

River paused for a second. This wasn't going to work, was it? The plan was to paint his own door, and escape somewhere dry. But was that even possible? He'd never painted a door before. If he got it wrong, he was dead.

No! He snapped back to reality. Keep it together, River. You can do this.

He started to paint on the ceiling. He focused on his destination: Spencer's house.

Remember, River. Remember Spencer's: the paint pots, the canvases, the cocoa...

PASHA!

The waves splashed against him. They were getting higher.

River struggled to focus. Just paint something, anything! A door to somewhere!

His thoughts were all over the place. Trembling, he drew out a square.

You're abandoning your friends, River. You're leaving them for dead.

Their faces flashed before his eyes. Jake. Jazz. Where were they? Were they safe? That passageway looked so dark.

So dark...

KARI! KARI!

The brush swept across the ceiling.

The passageway, with those cracked green tiles, and those pipes...

No! *Focus on Spencer's!*

Spencer's. Spencer the parrot. His friend, in the rucksack.

In the passageway...

KARI! KARI!

River stopped. He looked at the newly-painted door. It was finished.

"Well," he gasped, as it sprung to life. "You lead somewhere."

PASHA! PASHA!

The waves lapped against his neck.

He took a deep breath, and opened the hatch.

in the chrysalis chamber

"What a tidy idea," the disc remarked. "Did it work? Did you escape to safety?"

"Well, I'd successfully painted a door," River replied, "but it didn't take me to Spencer's."

"No?"

"No. I lost my concentration. I couldn't focus. I kept thinking about Jake and Jazz, and the passage they'd swum into."

"Nonetheless, that was very quick thinking on your part."

"Not really." River paused for a moment. "I just thought back to the paint tin. You know, the one that Jake had locked me in, under the school kitchen? I escaped from that in a similar way."

"You painted a door to escape the paint tin?"

"Close," said River. "It had a door already - the one we'd entered through. But there was no handle on my side. So I painted one."

"Intriguing. You painted your own door handle to escape the paint tin. But where did you get the paint from?"

"Were you not paying attention? It was a *paint* tin. All the food that was being dumped on my head was made of paint. So I just used the food. My finger made an excellent brush."

The disc hesitated. "You painted a door handle with your bare hands, out of old paint. That was possible?"

"Yeah. I mean, I was surprised it worked," River admitted. "But it kept me alive. And I suddenly remembered in the classroom, right before I was meant to duck under the door: there were all those paint pots. I could paint my way to safety, just like I'd done in the paint tin."

"You were ready to leave your friends?" said the disc. "To abandon Jazz, and Spencer? And Jake?"

"They'd be fine," said River, quickly. "As long as they didn't come looking for me."

"You say that, but it's hard to understand your motive. You sound so angry. Is it possible that you were still resentful towards Jake for his betrayal? He may have been possessed, but he was still your friend. He attacked you. He tried to kill you."

River didn't know. Was it anger? Was it a desire for revenge?

"I think I was just too scared to swim under the door," he concluded, "into that disgusting passageway with the green tiles. I couldn't stop thinking about it. Which is probably why the door took me there…"

20: hospitals

PASHA!

River plunged through the hatch, striking the hot, rippling water. Frantically, he thrashed until he could surface. Then he grabbed one of the pipes, gasping.

This was the next district. Damn it! He must have been thinking about it as he painted. He'd tried to focus on Spencer's, but his mind had been shooting in all directions. He'd made a door to the wrong place.

He felt dazed, confused.

Spluttering, he looked up at the hatch that he'd painted. Somehow, it had brought him through the ceiling. It was trippy. No wonder he'd taken a plunge.

Worse, there was no sign of his friends.

"Jake!" he called out, his voice quaking. "J-Jazz!"

Nothing. River looked along the sickly green corridor, bathed in faulty electric lights which flickered. Up ahead, there was a small metal staircase that he could climb onto, with a door just above.

His heart pounding, River clung desperately to the crooked pipe, and inched towards the steps.

PASHA! PASHA!

The liquid was a putrid brown, and it stank. River retched as he hauled himself onto the staircase, dripping. It was so hard to breathe.

"Nghhhhhhh!" he groaned, coughing up gunk. He felt like he was being strangled. Was it panic, or just the water?

Move River, he told himself. You have to press on.

His muscles aching, River picked himself up and climbed the rusting stairs. The metal groaned as he crushed it beneath his trainers.

"Jake?" he whispered, opening the door at the top. Its hinges squealed like nails on a blackboard. "Jazz?"

There was a long, tiled hallway on the other side. There were many doors leading off it, all of them stained and metallic. It looked like a prison.

"Spencer?" he hissed, as he crept through the shadows.

One of the doors was ajar. As River peered inside, he could see that it was water damaged, but dry. The stench was unbearable, though;

209

soiled clothes festered on hooks, and there were wheelchairs with wrist straps. A number of filing cabinets had also been overturned, and there was an assortment of discarded tools that looked like instruments of torture.

The sight of such apparatus made River's chest tighten. For a moment, it was like he was having a heart attack. Gasping, he threw himself against the wall, fighting to catch his breath, his airwaves tightening and tightening.

"Now this won't hurt a bit," said a voice. A face flashed before his eyes – a man whose features were hidden behind a mask. He was a doctor.

He was also a liar. The procedure hurt considerably; it felt like a thousand white-hot needles were piercing his skull from every angle, and River screamed as his every nerve ending ignited.

"Kuhhhhhhhhhhhhhhh!" River cried, as he crashed back to reality.

It was vivid. He could still feel the intense heat of the operation. He'd broken out in a sweat.

River snarled. He staggered back onto the corridor. He needed space.

No – he needed a way out. There had to be a return path to Neo Vale, or to Spencer's, or to his friends, or somewhere. *Anywhere.*

He listened. What *was* that? It was like screaming. Anguished cries. They were distant, but they were real, resonating through the damp, tiled passageways. Somewhere, deep within this maze of rotting chambers, people were in pain. The voices were pleading, tormented, as if screaming from the very cages of Hell.

Tread carefully, he told himself. They're not going to roll out the red carpet for you here.

River tip-toed along the corridor. There was an open door at the end. He stopped, checking over each shoulder. And peered inside.

It was a hospital ward, stuffed with beds and enveloped in a cloud of brown smoke. Each bed had a patient, shackled to a black tube which twisted from their bodies and disappeared into the cracked wall. The occupants weren't screaming, though. Nobody – in this room, at least – showed any signs of distress. In fact, they all looked comatose.

River inched closer to one of the patients. He gasped, clamping a hand over his mouth. Through the fumes, he could just make out the man's face. His skin was cracked, and the wounds looked gangrenous. River had never seen anything so horrific, not even in the blackest days of the civil war.

He looked away. He felt dizzy, like he was about to pass out. He stepped outside.

The screams were growing louder by the second. River could tell that he was nearing the source. Should he turn back? The way back was flooded, but the path ahead didn't exactly look safe. And where were Jake and Jazz?

He took a deep breath. And then he moved, creeping closer to the screams.

He deployed his blades. It was instinctive; he didn't think twice. River was hyper-alert, the adrenaline pumping through his veins like rocket fuel. He looked behind him constantly. His eyes never blinked. He could hear the faintest creak of his trainers.

BAKI! BAKI! BAKI!

River jumped round.

BAKI! BAKI! BAKI!

It was like a door knock, like someone pounding furiously with their fist. Cautiously, River slunk towards the nearest door, which had been sealed with a line of bolts. A small peephole had been hacked into its centre.

It was a one-man cell – a featureless cube, decrepit and unsanitary. There was a guy inside, like a skeleton, his face frail and yellowing. He was wearing a straitjacket.

That's when River realised. He hadn't been punching. He'd been kicking.

"Hello," said River.

The inmate glared at him. "Please," he begged, his bottom lip trembling. "You have to help me."

"Keep your voice down," River urged. "What is this place?"

"It's a hospital. Or at least it was. Please, get me out of here!"

"'Was' a hospital? What do you mean?"

"They torture us. The doctor, he... Oh please, I won't last another day!"

GIRIGIRI! GIRIGIRI!

A hoarse drilling filled the corridor. It was like an alarm.

"They know you're here!" the man wept. "They've found you!"

River pulled away from the door. He readied his blades.

A pair of twin doors crashed open, and a line of masked, white-jacketed doctors marched onto the corridor. They were striding towards River, with one clear leader – a bald man. His face was gaunt, and his forehead scarred.

"Hold it!" River shouted, raising his blade. "That's far enough!"

But the doctors ignored him.

"I said back off!"

The scarred man nodded at his colleague, who produced a handgun.

SUKA!

He fired, and River was struck.

"Nghhhhhhh!" River fell to his knees. A metal dart had pierced his chest.

"Run for your life!" yelled the inmate. "They're gonna kill you!"

River's strength was fading. He grunted, desperately trying to stand. But his legs were like rubber. He flailed, and crashed to the floor. His blades retracted.

"N-n-no!" he cursed, the hard floor pressing into his skin. He tried to slide on his belly, his consciousness slipping away. "Kuhhhhhhhhhhhhhh!"

The room spun. River flipped onto his back and glared at the rotting ceiling. A circle of white coats surrounded him, their cold eyes boring into his.

"Take him," said the scarred man.

Spencer gazed at the stained green tiles, breathing in the damp, musty air. It was depraved. The walls were covered in blotches of fluid – probably from people. It made his feathers stand on end.

It was a curious mismatch; it was somewhere between an interrogation chamber and an operating theatre and a lab. There were trolleys and instruments and machines. One of them was operated by a row of metal valves, which was attached to a panel of blinking lights.

"What do you think?" said Jake, modelling an old straitjacket. It was covered in brown smears. "A bit long in the sleeves?"

"Take that off," said Jazz. "It's not funny."

"Ugh, neither's that smell." Jake threw the rags on the floor. "Do you know where we are, Spencer?"

Spencer didn't look at him. He was just staring at the machine, as if the question hadn't registered.

Jake walked over to him. "What is it?"

"Hmm? Oh, it's just this machine. I was wondering what it did."

"We should really keep moving," Jazz insisted. "This place does not look safe."

"But what about River?" said Jake. "He could be right behind us."

"Or dead."

"I doubt it," said Spencer. "That young man was a soldier, remember. He's very resourceful."

"Should we go back to the school and look?" Jake asked.

Spencer kept his eyes on the machine. "Not yet."

Jazz knelt down next to him. "Is this the place?" she whispered. "You know? The hospital that flooded?"

Spencer sighed, bowing his head.

Jazz didn't need him to speak. His face said enough.

"Okay, you guys need to come clean," Jake ordered. "Did something happen?"

"Yes, it did," Spencer replied. "A long time ago, this district was wiped out by a flood. No one survived."

Jake gulped. "That's terrible," he said, his skin whitening. "No one survived? For real?"

KIIIIIIIIIIIIIIIIIIIIIIII!

A door swung open, and everyone jumped.

"What was that?" said Jake.

Jazz tip-toed towards the door. "It came from outside."

"Be careful, Jazz," Spencer urged.

Jazz looked. A line of doctors had appeared in the hall, dragging a lifeless River Still. His feet skimmed the muck-ridden floor.

"River!" she cried out.

The procession stopped, and the masked men glared at her. One of them raised his tranquiliser gun and fired a bolt into her neck.

"Nghhhhhhh!" She reeled.

"Jazz!" Jake lunged forward.

"Keep back," said Spencer, ushering him towards the wall.

"No chance." Jake whipped out his sword. "I'm not afraid of those goons."

An army of doctors appeared in the doorway, each of them with guns.

"Come and get some!" Jake yelled. "Who are you, bringing feather darts to a swordfight? Give me a break!"

SUKA! SUKA! SUKA!

They opened fire.

"Geez!" Jake ducked.

"In here!" said Spencer, opening a cabinet. "Quickly!"

SUKA! SUKA! SUKA!

"Spencer, I'm not hiding in a cabin-aaaaarghh!"

"Jake!"

It wasn't a cabinet. It was the door to a pit. And Jake had fallen in.

The doctors reloaded their guns, and Spencer glared at them in defiance. Mockingly, he doffed his Bavarian hat, and followed Jake into the shaft.

"Leave them," said the scarred man. "There's nothing down there. Only death." He looked down at the unconscious Jazz. "We have everything we need."

The fall wasn't far, but the landing was painful.

BOKAN!

"Auuuuugggggghhh!" Jake gasped, every part of him hurting. "Kuuuuuuuu…"

Spencer landed alongside. "Jake, are you hurt?"

"Nghhhhhhh!" he groaned, shuddering as he lifted himself. "More pissed than hurt. What is this place? Where – ugh!" Jake waved his hand, wafting the brown smoke out of his face. "What is this stuff? And where are we?"

"This is not good," said Spencer, looking in all directions. "This is not good at all." He smacked his beak, tasting the air. "Sleeping vapour."

"Sleeping vapour?" Jake exclaimed. "Why the hell do they have sleeping vapour?"

"This is a hospital. They use it to sedate the patients."

"In a pit?"

"We are not in a pit," said Spencer. "Look down."

Jake followed his gaze through the suffocating coils. They were at the top of a staircase – a single, precarious staircase, suspended over nothing. There were no handrails. Torches were positioned along its steps, burning bright green flames, but offering little light.

"Technically," said Jake, "we're still in a pit."

"Thank you, Professor." Spencer looked back at the door they'd fallen through. "Now why on earth did someone put a door so high above the ground?"

"It's like someone hacked through," Jake pointed out, "and then shoved a cabinet in front."

"Indeed, we must investigate this. But first, let's rescue Jazz."

"Ugh…"

"Well don't sound too enthusiastic. Now, I can fly you back up to the room – it's not far. Six metres, at the most. But once we're up there, you'll need to-"

214

Spencer broke off, noticing his friend. He was staggering like a drunkard, his arms swaying.

"Ugh, Spencer..." he groaned. "My eyes..."

He collapsed.

"Jake!" Spencer tugged at his clothes. "Dude, wake up! This is no time for a nap!"

"Yeah it is..." he mumbled, his head drooping. "It's soft... And it's warm... And it's lovely..."

"That's my wing you're lying on! Ugh!" Spencer freed himself. "Jake, you'll die if you stay here!"

His friend made an incoherent noise, drooling from his half-open mouth. But his body was now lifeless.

"Oh no!" Spencer cried. He looked at Jake's face, his mind scrambling for ideas. Prolonged exposure to sleeping vapour was fatal. He needed to get him out.

"Jake Thrower," he proclaimed, clearing his throat. "Nobody else is dying on my watch. And that is a promise."

He grabbed Jake's shirt in his beak.

The first thing River felt was the straps. They were metal and fiendishly tight, clamping his wrists to a robust wooden chair, which felt like it had been welded to the floor. He then tried to move his legs, but as his vision began to clear, he could see that they, too, had been manacled in place. Another buckle had been tightened around his middle, pinning him to the seat. He wasn't going anywhere.

And neither was Jazz. River gasped when he saw her. She'd been strapped to a similar-looking contraption, which looked like an electric chair. She wasn't conscious; her head was hanging limply, and her thick orange hair was falling across her face.

"Hello?" River called out, not expecting a reply. "Is anyone there?" He looked at his friend. "Jazz? Can you hear me?"

She couldn't.

River grunted in frustration. He gazed at the filth-ridden cell, every inch the torture chamber. Its walls were blackened and reeked of mould. Various pieces of rusting machinery were blinking and whirring, spitting out reams of yellowing tickertape.

River stiffened as the door opened. A man in a white coat, hidden behind a mask, strode into the cell. He was clutching a loaded syringe.

"What are you doing?" River barked. The surgeon hovered the needle over Jazz's neck. "What have you done to her?"

The man was unresponsive; he didn't flinch as River bombarded him with questions and threats. He attended to Jazz with the blithe, routine indifference of a man watering plants.

River glared at him as he released Jazz's neck. He handled her like an object, as if she were some tedious part of the morning routine. But as he left the cell, River noticed the faintest of twitches in Jazz's face. Was she waking up?

"Jazz?" he whispered. "Wake up, Jazz."

Bleary-eyed, she looked up. She gazed dreamily at River, obviously confused. She opened her mouth, but then noticed the metal cuffs that were binding her hands, and tried desperately to break them.

"They won't budge," said River. "Those things are fastened good."

"Nghhhhhhh!" Jazz strained. She threw her head against the back of the chair. "Damn it, River Still."

"What? I didn't put you there."

"I'd have some follow-up questions if you did." She gazed at the decaying walls. "Where the hell are we?"

"Another district," said River. "It used to be a hospital, apparently."

"Some hospital." She wrestled again with the straps. "And I suppose these restraints are for our own good?"

"Quiet, please." A man's voice crackled through a speaker. It sounded gravelly, as if someone had taken a torch to his vocal cords. "I will require your complete concentration for the upcoming experiment."

River glared at his friend. "That doesn't sound good."

"On the contrary," the voice said. "I think you will find it most insightful."

"And can we ask what this experiment is?" said Jazz. "And why you've got us tied down?"

"The most obvious answer to that question is because you are my prisoners," said the voice. "But, in addition, it is necessary for you both to be restrained for reasons of safety – such is the nature of the procedure."

River tried to ignore the wires that were feeding into his chair. "Okay," he called out. "So you're crazy."

"Crazy? I think not. The people who imprisoned me in this facility thought that I was. But I was their toy – the plaything of the privileged."

Jazz gulped. "You were an inmate?"

"That's what *they* would have called me," the voice answered. "In truth, I was a captive. That is, until the great deluge ravaged this

216

district and brought the institution to its knees. Oh, how the mighty have fallen."

"And what does that mean?" said River.

"It means that in a single, serendipitous moment, I was able to overthrow my captors and seize control of the hospital. You met, I think, the man in the straitjacket, in the cell? Shortly before you were collected?"

"Yeah."

"That man was my doctor. Or at least, that was the title he adopted. Ironically, I am now *his* doctor. It's funny, isn't it?"

"Hysterical," said River. "How about you undo these cuffs and we can both have a good laugh about it?"

The man cackled. "River Still, that is possibly the worst attempt at building rapport that I have ever heard."

"You sure about that, sweet-cheeks?"

"Look," Jazz interrupted. "Are you telling me that you seized control of this hospital and locked up your carers?"

"Do not call them 'carers," the man growled. "The word 'carer' implies compassion. Those people have none."

River sighed. "You know, one day we will find a part of this House that hasn't been oppressed or subjugated in some way."

"No," the man corrected him. "You won't."

"You mentioned an experiment?" Jazz asked.

River scowled at her. "Jazz!"

"Thank you, young lady. Time is of the essence, after all. Yes, this is a procedure that I developed shortly after I took control of the facility. It measures integrity, bravery, and endurance."

River looked again at the gangly coils of wire. "Uhh," he stammered, "couldn't we stare at ink blobs instead?"

"Oh, I don't credit that experiment," the man replied. "There's little to be gained from looking at shapes."

"And what do you hope to gain from this experiment?" asked Jazz.

The man paused. "Fun, mainly."

21: torture

Two years earlier.

River's bed was a concrete slab. He'd been deprived of regular sleep for about a week. Or at least, it felt like a week. Keeping track of time was tough; his cell was windowless – a musty cube with peeling paint. He was only allowed out for thirty minutes a day, and in that time he had to shower, use the bathroom, and exercise.

And 'exercise' meant a hundred push-ups; when he stopped, the guards rammed an electric poker into his spine. The pain was excruciating. Each time they struck him, it was like his heart stopped beating. His chest spasmed. Breathing became impossible. Day after day, he felt like death.

And he wanted death. He prayed for it to come.

Then he heard it – the sound, the familiar clunk of his bedroom door. He heard the boots as they pounded into the cell.

"Get up!" a man barked.

River groaned. He knew the drill. He knew that disobedience meant pain. And pain meant torture.

He rolled onto his back and rubbed his eyes.

"He said get up!" another guy snarled. "Do it!"

The soldier grabbed River's arm and hauled him upright. He prepared himself for a torrent of abuse that never came. The guy just punched him, and River collapsed, gasping. He wanted to scream, but couldn't find the strength.

"Take him," said the man, and the soldier complied. He dragged River out of his cell.

River staggered along the corridor as if made of rubber, his eyes like slits. He felt drugged; he could feel everything and nothing. He was in pain, and he was numb.

It took him a moment to clock his surroundings. The route had changed. They weren't taking him to the showers. Where were they going?

He opened his eyes, his heart now thumping in his ears. He scanned the walls, vainly searching for a clue, but recognised nothing. The facility was vast and subterranean, and each passageway resembled the next. They could be marching him to his death, or sweet freedom. He couldn't tell.

The room they entered was dour. It looked like a death chamber; there was a single chair with straps, and a wall of blinking computers.

River wriggled weakly in the guard's grip, but his arms had gone limp. He felt like a bystander at his own funeral as the two soldiers shoved him into the chair and strapped him in place. A metal cap was lowered onto his skull, and the men stepped aside. They flanked the ominous chair, as if River, somehow, was in danger of fleeing.

A seated man in a white coat and mask turned to face him. "Ryū Enatsu," he said. "Prisoner seven three, seven seven, one nine seven two."

River slowly raised his head. "My name..." he croaked "is River."

"Ryū!" the soldier yelled. "Be silent!"

"It's okay, sergeant," said the man. "The prisoner can speak. Ryū, you cannot hide your identity from us. We scanned your birth record. You are Ryū Enatsu."

River shook his head. "My name is River," he repeated. "You could at least use it if I'm about to die."

"Die? Ryū, that is not the reason you are here. You will have no memory of this, but you have, in fact, been in this room twice before. Does that surprise you?"

River looked again at the dank walls. He knew the guy was lying. Not once had he seen this cesspit of a chamber. He'd know.

"You don't believe me," the man concluded. "Ryū, we have been rebuilding your mind over the last two weeks. The war is over, and you are almost ready to be reintegrated into society."

Panic surged through River's veins. They'd been rebuilding his mind? Is that what this machine was? They were changing him? They were altering his memories in some way?

"It's for your own good," the man said. "I suspect you have no knowledge of your special – how do I put this? Your special *abilities*?"

River glared at him. What abilities?

"Or," the man went on, "your many clashes with the Specially Programmed Organic Resistance Entities? Have you never heard of a SPORE, Ryū?"

An image came up on the screen. It was like a giant spider. It was frightful.

A second picture came up. This creature was in a tank, bubbling as if being grown.

"Would you believe that SPORE was once a person?" the man asked. "Incredible, isn't it, how our technology has advanced? Criminals, prisoners of war, undesirables... They served us well during the conflict. We took their bodies and repurposed them. They became SPOREs – the ultimate machines of war. The *victors* of war."

River's heart was racing. The words meant nothing. It was like waking up from a bad dream, the details rapidly slipping through his fingers. Was this a test of some kind?

"Your silence is confirmation," said the man. "This is excellent progress. Eradicating your memory of the SPOREs has taken considerable time."

River grunted. "And yet you remind me now."

"And yet we don't. These images are meaningless to you now. And very soon, even they will be erased."

"You're monsters," River croaked, too tired to shout.

"Monsters? Oh, Ryū. We are doing this for your benefit."

River shook his head. "Don't lie to me," he gasped. "Just kill me and get it over with."

"I'm afraid your death warrant was rescinded. You were court-martialled for desertion and scheduled for execution. But there was an intervention. A special petition was made to have you spared."

"I don't want to be spared. Who made the petition?"

"Your mother."

River's stomach lurched. "She would."

"She went to great lengths to see General Flint. She risked her own position by appealing for your release."

"She shouldn't have bothered," River snapped. "It's not up to that woman to decide if I live or die. Where is she? Is she here?"

"Sadly not," the man answered. "Did you want to see her?"

"Not particularly."

"Good. We still have a procedure to perform."

"What, you're going to take more of my brain?"

"Just your memories of today," said the man, "and of your imprisonment. You will remember fighting in the civil war, but nothing specific. All those horrific memories, the SPOREs, your special abilities... None of them will be retained. You will be free to live your life in blissful ignorance."

River stiffened. "And what if I don't want to forget?" he challenged. "Don't I get to decide what's in my head?"

"Your head is the property of The People's Republic. Please don't fret. We have taken care of everything." The man glanced over his shoulder and called out: "Activate the machine, Doctor."

Suddenly there was a low rumble, and River felt the chair vibrate.

"Machine activated," said the doctor, his voice crackling through the speaker.

The masked man stood up and leaned over. "Now this won't hurt a bit."

"Nghhhhhhh!" River jolted as a volley of power burst through his skull. He screamed and convulsed. It was like every muscle in his body was on fire.

River thrashed, fighting. He focused on the spider, the SPORE. "Auggghhhhh!" he yelled.

Remember it, River. Remember.

But the image was like a reflection on water. It rippled and faded, and slowly ebbed away.

River opened his eyes. He was suddenly back in the House, clinging to the sides of his chair, and glaring at Jazz.

Night spores, during the civil war? How was that possible?

"I think we're ready to begin," said the voice through the speaker. "River Still, you're about to learn a great deal about yourself. And as for you, young Jazz..."

His friend gulped. "Yes?"

"You're about to discover what kind of man River Still really is."

"Do you want to stop playing games and tell us what's going on?" said River. "I've got a concert in August."

"You are about to take a lie detector test," the man replied. "It's a simple premise. You will be asked a series of questions. You will have five seconds to answer. Failure to answer will result in an electric shock. Failure to tell the truth will result in an electric shock. The blasts will intensify with each untruth or non-response."

Jazz gasped. "That's barbaric! You can't do that to him!"

"And nor do I intend to," the voice assured her. "It is you, Jazz, who will receive the electric shocks."

The pair fell silent.

"It's clever, isn't it?" the man purred. "River will have to choose between two outcomes: telling the truth, and risking humiliation; or lying, and subjecting you to considerable pain."

"And can I ask what we've done to deserve such special attention?" asked River.

"I assure you, it's nothing personal. You are both distinctly unremarkable. But this experiment will be of vital importance to my ongoing research."

"Research?" he retorted. "It's torture."

"As is talking to you."

"Also, Doctor - I have no intention of lying. I don't have any secrets. You're wasting your time."

"Now, that is an interesting statement," the man noted. "Tell me, River Still - what do you really think of young Jazz here? Do you like her? I mean, do you like her as much as you like Jake?"

River faltered. Had they started? Was the clock ticking? He looked at his companion. "Yes."

There was a buzz. Jazz convulsed as the forks of electricity packed through her body.

"Oh dear," the man sighed. He tutted. "That wasn't a very good start, was it?"

"What?" River yelled. "This is bullshit! I was telling the truth!"

"I don't think so, River Still. On the contrary, the truth is only just emerging."

Jazz caught her breath and glowered at her friend.

"Next question," the voice continued. "Your skin colour is different from Jazz's. Does that make you superior?"

Don't think, River told himself. Answer quickly, instinctively.

"No," he replied.

Nothing happened.

"Now that *is* surprising," the man observed. "I must congratulate you, River Still. You are one of the few test subjects with no racial prejudices. But that doesn't mean you're not a bigot. Tell me – what do you think of women? Are they weaker than men?"

"No."

Again, Jazz's chair did nothing.

"How intriguing," said the voice. "Butter wouldn't melt, it seems."

River didn't answer.

"I think I will have to up the ante. Let me ask you, young River. Are you a virgin?"

River didn't blink. "Not from the waist up."

Jazz screamed in her chair.

"I'm sorry," said the man, "but I think we can draw our own conclusions from that answer. Next question. Do you think you're good-looking?"

"No."

"Aaaaaaaaaaaaa!" Jazz cried. "Kuhhhhhhhhhhhhhh!"

The man sighed. "Such vanity, River Still. I really don't know what you see in yourself. You're like a matchstick."

"Alright, you've made your point," said River. "You can stop this now. Yours is bigger than mine. I get it."

"We will conclude when I say so. Or when your hapless friend expires."

River looked at Jazz. She was wheezing, her head hanging limply.

"Moving on," said the voice. "Let's cut the drama and go for the comedy. Do you think Jazz is good-looking?"

River hesitated, terrified that any answer would be the wrong one. "Yes."

No. Jazz received another dose. She was crying. She could barely breathe.

"How interesting," the man observed. "Does this mean you'd rather date a mirror than your poor, whimpering friend?"

Jazz looked pleadingly at River, her eyes red.

"In fact," the man continued, "could it be that you *hate* this lady? Do you just tolerate Jazz Thrower?"

"No!" River shouted. He leaned forward. "Jazz, look at me. I'm your friend."

"Yes, we can dispense with the fawning. I don't think Jazzmas T is quite the girl you expected, is she? Tell me, River Still. Was young Jazz a disappointment to you, in the flesh?"

River froze. He could feel his throat tightening. For a moment, he thought he was going to cry. He had no idea what to say, or how to answer. Could he condense his feelings towards Jazz into a single response? Would either answer be truthful? Would it be better to say nothing at all?

Five seconds passed. And then another. And then twenty.

After a moment, Jazz raised her head. She didn't speak – just glanced, confused, at the room that had fallen eerily silent. She looked at River.

And River looked back. Where was the electric shock? What had happened to the experiment? Was this part of the test? Some tactic to see how they handled the silence?

"Hello?" River called out. "Are you still there?"

There was no reply.

"Hey!" he persisted. "What's going on? Are you just going to ignore us now?"

BOKAN!

One of the doors thudded, as if someone had pounded it with their foot.

223

"Hey, are you alright in there?" came a voice from the other side. "River, are you okay? Jazz?"

Jazz's eyes widened. "It's Jake!" she exclaimed. "In here, Jake! We're in here!"

There was a splinter as Jake threw his weight against the door and ripped it from its hinges. He crashed to the floor, face-first, with a ruffled parrot on his shoulder.

River grinned. "You found us!"

Jake picked himself up. "Well of course we did!" he replied, heading for Jazz's chair. "Bro, I've got the tracking instincts of a leopard in the wild."

"Also, one of the doctors told us you were here," Spencer added. "He was most informative."

"Yeah, he told us about the experiment," Jake went on, attending to River. "When we found out what they were doing to you, we came straight away."

"We have to be careful," said River, scrambling out of his seat. "I think the guy left, but he can't have gone far."

"Oh, I don't think Doctor Death will be seeing us again today," said Spencer, cryptically.

River walked over to Jazz, who had slumped against the far wall, panting. He rested his hand on her shoulder. "Hey…"

She grunted and pushed him away.

"None of that stuff was true." He paused for a moment, hoping his friend would at least look him in the eye. "Do you believe me?"

"Don't touch me, River!" she barked. She staggered towards Jake. "I've got nothing to say to you."

"What, you're going to believe some cheap lie detector? This isn't science! How the hell is that guy supposed to know what's inside my head? It's ridiculous!"

"I don't need a lie detector to know that you hate me!" Jazz snapped. "It's right there in your face. Just grow a pair and admit it, River! Do you reckon you can do that? Do you have the balls?"

"Yeah, I have the balls!"

Suddenly, Jazz's chair buzzed. A burst of power surged through its cables.

"Well, that's a lie, bro!" Jake tittered. "The machine's all-knowing!"

River frowned. "That's weird."

"Yes, I always thought you were testicularly challenged," came Spencer's voice through the speaker. "And now we have proof!"

The group looked around.

"Where are you, Spencer?" said River.

"Next door, in the office of the good doctor. In fact, he's with me right now."

"That doesn't sound good," said Jazz.

"Don't worry, he's out for the count," Spencer assured her. He nudged open the door and returned to the main chamber. A billow of muddily-coloured smoke followed him into the room. "Do you remember those valves we saw, when we first arrived at the hospital? I knew they had to do something. In this case, they diverted the sleeping vapour into the doctor's office. Which is what I did."

"Sleeping vapour?" said River, peering into the room. He caught sight of the masked torturer, unconscious in his chair.

"No, River!" said Spencer, slamming the door. "I'd hate for you to nod off and need carrying to safety. Your friend Jake was heavy enough."

Jake grinned. "It's mostly muscle."

"Well, we knew it wasn't brains," said Jazz.

"So that lie detector..." said River. "It was a fake? He was operating it manually?"

"Yes, hardly a feat of technological engineering," Spencer confirmed. "The doctor was administering those electric shocks himself. Your answers had no bearing on the results."

"So..." Jazz stammered. "He was just fudging with our heads?"

"Yes, and quite effectively. The whole experiment was rigged. Bogus. Bunkum."

"Excellent," Jake giggled, pushing his sister towards River. "It's time to kiss and make up!"

"Leave it," Jazz snapped. "We're good."

"Yeah, I forgive you Jazz," said River.

Jazz scowled at him. "Excuse me? You *forgive* me?"

"Yeah, all that stuff you believed, about me being a bastard. I don't hold it against you."

"What are you talking about?"

Jake stepped into the fray. "So, you guys won't believe what me and Spencer discovered!"

"You said that I hated you, that you could see it in my face," said River.

"I can see it in your face!" Jazz yelled. "You leer!"

"Well, you're entitled to your incorrect opinion."

Suddenly the door crashed open, and a handful of zombified patients staggered into the chamber, their arms outstretched.

"Yikes," cried Jake, pulling out his sword.

River activated his blades.

ZASHU! ZASHU!

"It's those guys from the ward," he said.

The group backed into the far corner.

"What ward?" said Jazz, her bow and arrow raised.

"There was this room full of creepy patients," River explained. "But they were unconscious. They were surrounded by that vapour stuff."

"Spencer, you know when you diverted the vapour into the doctor's office?" said Jake. "Did you divert it from the ward?"

Spencer slunk behind River's leg. "It's possible..."

SUKA!

Jazz fired an arrow at one of the zombies. Black gunk sprayed out of its chest.

"Dark paint," Spencer whispered. "They've all got dark paint inside them."

The group ran to the next wall, inching closer to the exit.

"So they're night spores?" said Jake, swinging at his attackers.

"No, they're people," said Spencer. "People who have been dosed with dark paint."

"Kuhhhhhhhhhhhhhh!" Jake swung again and struck a zombie in the chest.

"That makes sense," said River, as he darted towards the door. "In the ward, they had these black tubes coming out of them."

ZASHU!

River swiped his blade across the zombie's shoulders, severing its head. "Come on!"

But the corridor was swarming.

"There's more of them!" Jake yelled, as a pack of lurching patients advanced.

"All seeded with dark paint," Spencer crowed. "The doctor's custom army, kept docile until needed."

"Yeah fascinating, but we gotta hustle," said Jake. "Which way do we go?"

"Straight ahead," River insisted. "We can take them. There's only five."

SUKA!

Jazz fired.

"Four now," she said. "Are you schoolgirls going to gossip all day?"

"Hey, I'm judging my moment," Jake protested.

"Nghhhhhhhhhhhhhh!" River jerked, his arm throbbing. He raised one of his blades, and the weapon rotated. An immense gun barrel appeared in its place.

River snarled. He could feel the anger pumping through his appendages, a cocktail of molten fury. He clamped his teeth together, his mind filling with hate for the doctor, for what he'd done.

He felt vengeful. He wanted to kill. He wanted to destroy.

"Woah," Jake gasped. "River, what the-?"

His gun glowed as the power built. A circle of energy enveloped the barrel.

"Kuhhhhhhhhhhhhhhh!" he groaned, buckling under the strain. "Nghhhhhhhhhhhhhh!"

"River, what are you doing?" said Spencer. "Be careful, River. You'll kill us all!"

Die, said the voice in River's head. Kill. Obliterate.

Exterminate.

"Aaaaaaaaaa!" River gasped. He let go. "Kyaaaaaaaaaaa!"

Everyone ducked. River was thrown backwards as the energy discharged. A pulsing orb struck the patients, soundless and devastating.

River cried out and fell to the floor, wincing as his gun barrel retracted.

"Geez," gasped Jake. He looked down the corridor. All he could see was a plume of smoke, and a lake of painted remains.

Jazz ran towards the puddle and dipped her fingers in the liquid. "There's nothing left," she whispered.

Jake was aghast. "Dude, that was-" He faltered, unable to form a sentence. "Man, have you always been able to do that?"

River stood up. His brow was damp with sweat. "Probably."

Spencer looked at him. "Your weapon is emotionally-powered, isn't it?"

River nodded, still shaking.

"I thought as much. Well, you got the job done, River Still. But I'd be lying if I said I wasn't unnerved."

River looked at his trembling hand. "You and me both."

"That was sick," Jake grinned. "Bro, that's the biggest gun barrel I've ever seen."

River didn't answer. He just looked at his arm, confused.

"Everyone," Spencer called out, "your attention please. We must move on before we're discovered."

"I agree," said Jazz. "Shall we go back to your house, Spencer?"

"No wait, there's that staircase," Jake interrupted. "Shouldn't we check it out before we leave?"

River looked at him. "What staircase?"

The group peered through the hole in the wall, hidden behind the cabinet. The vast staircase was just visible through the plumes of smoke, illumined by the green lamps.

Spencer had the Traveller's Map open in front of him. "This is it," he announced, peering through the cabinet. "There must have been a door here at some point, but someone's destroyed it. See here on the map? That's the staircase. It's a mile long, and it leads directly to the cellar."

"Wait," said Jazz. "You mean – this is it? We've made it?"

"Indeed. The cellar lies at the bottom of those steps. We're almost at journey's end."

Jake took a deep breath. "Oh boy. That was sooner than I expected."

"Same," Jazz chimed. "I'm kinda nervous."

Jake put his arm round River. "Can you believe it, man? We're here! I mean – we actually made it!"

River just stared into the gloom. "Yeah," he muttered, his eyes fixed on the steps.

"What do you mean 'yeah'? This is awesome! We can flood the cellar! We can save the House, and the world! Jobon's going down!"

River kept looking at the vapour. It was like the stuff from Neo Vale, but a different colour. "Spencer," he muttered. "There's a catch, isn't there?"

Spencer cocked his head. "A catch?"

"That smoke. It's sleeping vapour, isn't it?"

"Yep," said Jake. "That stuff knocked me out in seconds. It's lethal."

River continued to stare, like he was frozen in ice. "Then how are we going to get down there?" he asked. "If those stairs are covered in vapour?"

"Uhh, have you never heard of a little thing called a mask?" said Jake. "You know, you wrap it round your face? Surprisingly effective."

"Exactly that," Spencer chirped. "We'll mask up and head down. Although I probably won't need one. I remember when I worked here, I was exposed to the vapour for a considerable length of time, with only mild symptoms. Perhaps because I'm a parrot."

"What about the valves?" said Jazz, now examining the machine. "Could we not divert it away from the stairs?"

"I wondered that," Spencer replied. "But having examined that device more closely, I think the staircase is actually the *source* of the vapour. Those valves merely distribute it throughout the hospital, as needed."

Jake kept his eyes on River. He was just glaring into the pit, emotionless. "Hey, are you alright?" he asked. "You're very quiet."

River ignored him. He stood up and looked at Spencer. "So that's it? We just put on some masks and go down the stairs?"

Spencer hesitated, as if thrown by the question. "Well, we don't have to go *today*," he stressed. "I suggest we all take a breather and prepare. Perhaps tomorrow we can begin our descent? When we're all refreshed?"

"Works for me," said Jazz, stretching her arms. "I'm pooped."

"Same," Jake chimed. "All I want to do is destroy a bowl of udon, and binge on a good anime."

"Sounds exciting," said Spencer, opening his satchel. "Moreover, I'm curious to see how young River fairs in the door-painting department."

River turned. "What?"

"Your escape from the Academy of Reason," Spencer continued. "You painted your own door, didn't you?"

River stuttered. "Uhh, kinda..."

"Remarkable. You know, you are probably the first biped in history to achieve such a thing. I wouldn't have thought it possible."

"Well, it was the paint that did it," River insisted. "I'm nothing special."

"Nonetheless, this is history in the making. I must see it for myself." Spencer held up a paintbrush. "Would you care to do the honours?"

"No thanks." River backed off. "I'm good."

"Oh come on, you big baby," said Jazz. "It's not a royal commission. And anyway, we're not judging."

"Much," Jake teased.

"Please, River," said Spencer. "It would really mean a lot to me. I would love to see this."

River looked at the paintbrush, filling with dread.

Saying nothing, he snatched the brush and the paints, and moved towards a blank stretch of wall.

"Excellent!" Spencer chortled. "Settle down, everyone. You're about to witness the creation of a masterpiece."

"Bring on the popcorn," said Jake, slumping onto the floor.

River stared at the blank tiles. This wasn't fair. What the hell was he supposed to paint? Why were they making him do this?

"Get on with it, slowpoke," Jazz heckled. "Jake has a crap anime to watch."

River thought for a moment. Half-heartedly, he dabbed the brush into the blue, and took his first swipe.

He spent about twenty minutes making the door. It was no oil painting, by any stretch of the imagination; he hadn't painted properly since he was a kid. And there was a reason for that.

But this was oddly satisfying. Painful, but satisfying.

And as he added the finishing touches, he didn't think the results were half bad.

"Incredible," Spencer gasped, as River tweaked one of the hinges. "This is first-rate, River Still."

"You approve?" he replied. "This was my bedroom door when I was a kid."

"Nice flowers," Jake giggled, referring to the red stickers that had been stuck to it.

River smiled. "Yeah, I had a thing about plants when I was younger. I wasn't the coolest."

"I like them," said Jazz. "Chrysanthemums."

"Well, as long as this leads back to my studio," said Spencer, "and not some child's bedroom on the other side of the country."

"Don't worry," River assured him. "I was concentrating very hard this time. And plus, I don't think my mother would thank me for bringing a parrot back to the house."

He turned the knob, and the new door opened. On the other side, Spencer's home was clearly visible: the usual chaotic assortment of canvases, tarps and paints, bathed in the warm, dancing glow of candles. The door was a success.

"I am spell-bound, River Still," said Spencer, waddling through the entrance. "I mean, truly astonished. I can't tell you what a treat this is."

The group followed their friend into the studio.

"And to think that you're new to the painting business," he added, slipping off his satchel. "Clearly, I have nothing to teach you."

"Yay, that's full marks from the bird," Jake laughed, slapping River's back. "Good going."

"Look, are we done?" said Jazz, marching towards the exit. "I want to go home."

"Sure," Jake answered. "Are you coming, River?"

River paused, staring at the floor. "You guys go," he said. "I need to talk to Spencer."

Jazz looked puzzled. "What, in private? Why can't me and Jake be here?"

"Hey, Jeff." Jake tugged her sleeve. "Let's give them some space."

"Whatever," she sighed, ducking into the fireplace. "Catch you tomorrow, Spencer."

The parrot doffed his hat. "Sleep well, bipeds."

The twins left, and River took a deep breath. He started to pace.

"I must say I'm intrigued, River Still," he remarked. "Have I done something wrong?"

River narrowed his eyes. "Why did you lie?"

Spencer blinked. "I'm sorry, what?"

"About the vapour. You said we'd be protected. You said we could go down that staircase, in masks, and take on Jobon."

Spencer bowed his head. "Yes I did, didn't I?"

"You did, and that plan won't work. I saw the doctor. You know, the one who was torturing us? You put him to sleep with the vapour – and he was wearing a mask. He wasn't protected. So what's the deal?"

Spencer paused. He struggled to look River in the eye. "The vapour..." he muttered. "It doesn't enter the lungs. It enters the brain. It's psychic."

River stared at him. "What? Psychic vapour?"

"Don't ask me to explain it. I can't. I've no idea what it is, or where it comes from. All I know is, it enters the mind and induces a sleep state. It's probably one of the cellar's oldest defences, designed to keep people from entering. And whilst I can pass through unharmed, there can be no protection for you. You would collapse within seconds."

River froze.

"That is why," Spencer continued, "I am going to the cellar alone. I will end this, River Still. Even at the cost of my own life."

River's eyes glistened. He bit down on his lip.

"It's okay," he insisted. "It really is. I will do anything to save you all."

River grunted. "No."

"Hey." Spencer crept closer and rested his head on his leg. "It's okay."

River shook him off. "No, it's not. How can we even be sure the night spores are coming from the cellar?" He whipped out his phone. "Because they're in Mango Tower as well." He showed Spencer the pictures. "See there, in the tanks? Monster mutations. Night spores. In my world."

Spencer's eyes widened. "What are those things?"

"I fought them during the civil war, too. What if they don't come from the cellar? What if they're being grown in Neo Vale and planted here? We can forget about Jobon and attack Mango Tower."

"But those aren't night spores," said Spencer, looking at the tanks. "I don't know what they are, but they are not *painted*. For one thing, they're immersed in water. You couldn't do that to a night spore. I'm sorry, River. Those creatures are similar, certainly, but I am convinced that the night spores can only be coming from the cellar."

River snatched the phone away. "Fine then," he mumbled, getting up.

Spencer watched him. "So we're good?" he asked. "You're going to let me go?"

"I can hardly stop you."

"I think it's for the best."

"And there's no defence?" River asked. "Nothing that would protect us?"

Spencer paused. "Well there's..." He broke off. "No. No, there's nothing."

River looked at him. "You were about to say something."

Spencer shuffled uncomfortably. "Moonshade. A dose of Focus would keep you conscious. But the side-effects could be fatal."

River dropped his head, infuriated.

It was Hobson's choice, yet again.

"And do you have any moonshade?" he asked.

"No," said Spencer.

"Are you lying?"

There was a pause. "Yes."

River clenched his fist. He shook his head. "This isn't fair." He could feel his temper rising. "How am I meant to decide this?"

"You don't have to. I have chosen for you. You can let me go, River Still."

River sneered, acidly. "Oh yeah. Kill yourself. Sure."

Spencer crept closer. "River..."

"I said sure!"

He punched an easel, and it fell.

Spencer jumped as it clattered to the floor. River's face had turned red. His eyes were watering.

"Why are you angry?" Spencer whispered. "I ask nothing of you."

River curled his hand into a fist. "You're asking me to be okay with this. You're asking me to let you die."

Spencer looked at his feet. "I have caused a great many deaths," he stated. "I owe it to the House. I have to try."

River rubbed his face. Then he marched towards the door.

"Where are you going?"

"I'm leaving. I'm done here."

232

Spencer watched as River ducked into the fireplace. "River, please-"

"I said I'm done!"

And before Spencer could say another word, his friend had disappeared.

22: intimacy

Sweet Dusk was bathed in dazzling electric lights, casting pink and turquoise pools onto the un-swept floor. It was like a fantasy. There was no day or night in this bar. There were no windows to sully its booths with sun rays. Time, it seemed, just didn't exist.

This is how River liked it. He arrived at night, saying little to the bartender. He just pointed at a bottle, and made her leave it, sloshing his own measures into the tumbler. He didn't even know what the stuff was, except that it was red, and tasted of peaches. The first sip made him cringe, zapping through his veins like an electric current. The second was easier, like a warm shower. The third was like nectar. His feelings were sucked into a spiralling vortex and washed out of existence, like wastewater curling round the basin. It felt so good.

The bottle emptied slowly. River didn't count the measures. He didn't care. And actually, he *couldn't* care; he kept slipping in and out of consciousness, his body flopping onto the table and pressing his face against the sticky plastic surface.

Images flashed before his eyes. Fragments of memories. Carter was slain by a SPORE, and River killed it.

Then there was the girl in the pipe, devoured by a giant spider. River left her for dead.

Rocco was stabbed.

The visions shifted in and out of focus, blending with the bar. At one point, he could have sworn he had company. There was a woman with blue hair, trussed up in a tight leather corset and covered in chains. Had she sat with him? He remembered only flashes – cybernetic eyes and a cheeky, seductive grin. She'd grabbed his face and stroked his hair – he was sure. He could still smell the rank, stale odour of sweat that oozed out of her pits.

A clatter of glasses jolted River. He sat up, his hair in disarray. Where was he? How long had he been here? He smacked his parched, sandpaper lips. He was so thirsty.

Bleary-eyed, he blinked, trying to focus on the yellow tube-writing which hung on the wall. Sweet Dusk. That was a bar, wasn't it? In Neo Vale?

Mustering all the strength he didn't have, he hauled the TellMe out of his pocket and let it tumble onto the table.

"TellMe," he grunted, his eyes like slits. "What time is it?"

"The current time is 7:06am," the device said dutifully. "River, you have six unread messages from Jake Thrower."

"Ignore them."

Six? That figured. He never told his friends what he was doing. He just left Spencer's, furious, and came straight to this dive, drinking his own bladder-weight in what he now realised was Paramore's Kiss. He looked at the lidless bottle in front of him, which had only a trickle of liquid left in the base. 140 proof. Damn.

"You also have one unread message from Natsuki Hashino."

River froze.

"Message reads: 'Hello River, I thought I should probably write something. I feel really bad about the way we left things. I guess what I was trying to say was that I care about you deeply. The thought of you getting hurt scares me. You are the most precious thing in the world. Let me know how you are, River. You can hate me if you want. But tell me you're okay.' Message ends."

"TellMe nothing," River ordered.

"Confirmed. Entering Silent Mode."

River buried his face in his hands. It was all coming back to him – hurtling, like a tidal wave.

He wasn't angry with Spencer. It was the situation. He was so scared. He lashed out because he didn't know what else to do, or say. Those odds, the injustice of it all. Hobson's choice. It made him so angry with the universe – with God, if there was one.

And the fear of it all held him in a vice. He was terrified of losing his friend – of letting Spencer walk to his death. And he was afraid to go with him. The cellar looked like something from a nightmare – those crooked stone steps with the flaming torches, like the staircase to Hell.

And even if he could muster the courage to go down them, there was still the moonshade. He'd have to take it if he were to survive the vapour. And he'd seen what the drug had done to Jake – how close to death he'd come.

None of this was good. None of this was fair.

Groggily, he picked himself up. He stumbled as he tried to gain his footing, the room spinning like a carousel, moving faster and faster.

His stomach lurched. River belched, and a torrent of red vomit poured out of his mouth, spraying the sticky table and tumbler.

River gasped and grabbed the edge of his chair to keep him from falling.

He needed to go home.

235

No, not Noodle Vale. Real home.

He managed to sneak in without being noticed. Jake and Jazz were having breakfast with their mom, sitting together (but not speaking) in the living room; River clocked them as he reached the top of the stairs. He slipped into the hallway and made a beeline for his room.

This wasn't going to take long. He grabbed some clothes and stuffed them into his rucksack, and picked up his guitar. He then went to the bathroom, satisfying both ends of his abused body. He must have guzzled a gallon of cold water, scooping the icy liquid into his mouth with a hand that still reeked of sick.

Then he ruffled his hair and sprayed his unwashed pits. He'd do. Not that he cared.

It was like a numbness, a resignation. He felt powerless. This was the only choice he could make now – to walk away. Forget about it. Move on.

It was funny, though. He felt more and more scared the closer he got to the exit. He was really doing this. This was it. But could he really just leave? Without saying goodbye?

Yes, of course he could. 'Goodbye' would make it harder. They'd twig. They'd fight him. They'd want to know about Spencer. River would tell them the truth, and they'd be indignant. "Oh we have to go with him!" Jazz would croon. "Bro, we'll just take the moonshade!" Jake would say.

They were stupid. Both of them. They'd be killed. Or at best, Jake and Jazz would hate him for refusing to take part in a suicide run.

But River was done with this stupid game – of life handing him ridiculous scenarios and laughing in his face as he agonised between impossible choice and impossible choice. Fuck it. He was through.

Then he realised. He'd stopped. He'd been so busy playing out these silly conversations in his head that his legs had ground to a halt. Now he just hovered, hanging outside the living room like a lemon. He could see his friends through the half-open door, both on their phones, with Beanie just gazing into the distance as she slurped hot soup.

"River!" cried Jake, clocking him. "Where the hell have you been?"

River stepped back. "Uhh…"

"We've been so worried," said Jazz, getting up. "Why didn't you reply to our messages? We thought something had happened."

Jake came up to him. "Aw, I'm glad you're safe." He sniffed. "Wait, what do you smell of?"

This was so frustrating; he just wanted to leave. "That's probably a mixture of Paramore's Kiss, my stomach contents, and piss."

236

Jake chuckled. "Nice."

"So, you threw up?" Jazz challenged. "And then what? You peed your pants?"

River half-smiled. "Something like that. I got a little tipsy."

"You and Spencer are party animals," Jake laughed. "Next time, invite me. Got it?"

"Jake Thrower!" Beanie snapped. "You're eighteen!"

"What? I'll have lemonade!" He turned to River. "With vodka."

"So, how come you've got all your stuff with you?" said Jazz. "You going somewhere?"

River thought quickly. "It's not all my stuff. I'm just heading out for breakfast. I'm still working on my song, so I thought I'd take my guitar. I didn't want to disturb you guys with my playing, so..."

Jazz raised an eyebrow. "That's very considerate of you."

"Well, you know..." River paused. "I care about you both."

"Aw, we care about you too," said Jake. "Come here. I don't care if you're covered in piss."

Jake threw his arms around him. River reeled, unsure how to respond. Nobody had ever hugged him like that before.

"River, do you want some soup?" asked Beanie, as Jake broke away. "It's miso. There's plenty left over."

"No, I'm fine thanks," River replied. "I'm going to go to Kakeru's. I really like their toilets..."

And with that, he turned and headed towards the stairs.

But something stopped him. A feeling. "Actually, can I just say," he stammered, stepping back onto the landing. "You guys are great. Really great. I'm so glad I met you."

"Aw," said Jake, beaming. "That's so sweet. You're not so bad yourself. But you know that, right?"

"Yeah," Jazz added. "My life's been a lot more interesting since River Still showed up."

River grinned. "River Still. That's what Spencer does, double-naming me."

"That's because River Still is a sick name," said Jake. "Seriously. Your parents chose well."

River pulled back. "Yeah," he answered, looking away.

Jazz stared at him. "Are you alright?"

"Oh yeah," he insisted. "It's just when you said... No, forget it."

"Woah," said Jake. "Did I upset you? 'Cos I really like your name. Honestly. I wasn't jerking your chain."

237

"I know, it's just... Well, when you said my parents chose well..." He looked at the floor. "That's not exactly true."

His friends looked lost. "What do you mean?" said Jazz.

"I'm named after my dad."

"Oh," said Jake. "So, your dad is called River?"

"Sort of."

Jazz giggled. "Right. Thanks for clearing that up."

River laughed as well, realising how stupid it all sounded. "Sorry, it's just war stuff. You know my hometown got bombed? Zen Kappa?"

"Yeah, I remember," said Jake. "It was the first place to be hit, wasn't it?"

"Yeah, and I got separated from my dad. Screw it, you don't need to hear this."

"No, tell us!" said Jake, grabbing him. "Seriously, we want to know. You got separated from your dad? And?"

"And he text me," said River, fidgeting. "He'd found a safe spot by the river, and the plan was to meet up and escape the city. We figured we'd just hitch-hike and see if we could put enough distance between us and the troops."

Jazz frowned. "But what's this got to do with your name?"

"Sorry, I'm rambling. Basically – lots of war, lots of confusion, couldn't get to my dad. I had to decide between taking cover in a department store and rushing to the river to meet him. In the end I opted for the department store, because the militia had blocked all the roads. All the while he was texting frantically, promising to hold out for as long as possible. But his battery was dying, and eventually the messages stopped coming. The last one I got was early evening. 'I'm not leaving without you,' he said. 'Just get here as soon as you can. I'm at the river still.'"

He looked away, a little embarrassed.

"Anyway, I never reached him," River continued, "but I have to believe that he's still alive, that I'll find him, that he's at the river still. I mustn't forget that."

River gazed at his friends, desperately trying to read their expressions. He chuckled. He wanted the floor to swallow him up. "It's lame, isn't it?"

Jazz sniffed. Was she crying? He couldn't tell. She just bounded forward and threw her arms over his shoulders.

"You..." she whispered, sniffing once more. "You are adorable."

"Thanks, Jazz," said River, hugging her back. "You're, uhh, adorable too."

"Shut up."

The pair broke off.

"Well," said River, making for the door. "On that note…"

Jake laughed. "Oh man! You can't leave like that. Please stay for breakfast."

"I'm sorry, I need to write." River looked at them both, his eyes swimming. "But I'll see you soon."

Jazz wiped her nose with her sleeve. "Is there anything we can do?"

"Do?" said River. "What do you mean?"

"Oh, you know, just…" Jazz giggled. "I don't know what I mean, really."

River half-smiled. "I think I have everything I need."

He turned. He walked down the stairs, and didn't look back.

"You also have one unread message from Skidmark," said his TellMe, only seconds into his journey. "Message reads: 'Hey Peddler, have you been taking us for a ride? We noticed you skipped work yesterday. How do you expect to put bread on the table? Remember to tap-in for the start of your next shift tonight as there are lots of mouths to feed. At Skidmark, full mouths are our priority. Keep guzzling!' Message ends."

River snarled. He could feel the anger swelling within him. He was done with his crap. He was finished.

He pulled his phone out of his pocket. "Nghhhhhhh!" he screamed, as he hurled it onto the sidewalk.

It clattered as it struck the concrete. Then he drove his heel into its screen and ground the fine pieces into dust.

Then he took his TellMe, its strap still loosely taped together. This would have to go, too. He didn't want to be traced.

River stared at the interface, the coloured lights dancing. There'd be no turning back after this. He couldn't un-smash it.

Hopefully, he wouldn't need to. He'd stuffed his jeans with all the cash he had – 600 credits. It was enough for a train out of town, and a couple of weeks in a hostel. Maybe a few packets of powdered noodles to keep him alive.

Almost ritualistically, he laid his TellMe on the pavement. He looked at it, as if he were sending his only child to the guillotine.

"What are you doing, River?" the TellMe chirped.

River struggled to answer. His throat was closing up.

"River, is everything okay?" the TellMe asked. "Please talk to me, River. I am concerned for you."

River closed his eyes. He raised his foot.

"River?" The TellMe sounded scared. "River?"

"Nghhhhhhh!"

He stamped on it. And again. And again.

"Riv-ver..." it gasped. "W-why are you-"

"Auuuuugggggghhh!" he roared, stamping and stamping and stamping.

The TellMe bleeped. It sounded like a wounded animal.

One by one, the lights on the interface blinked out of existence. Just one remained – a fading, yellow oblong, pulsing on the black disc as if breathing.

"Riv-ver..." it croaked. "Riv-ver..."

River trembled.

"It hurts, Riv-ver..."

He kicked it, sending its shattered remains into the road.

And then he walked, so fast it was more like a run, skimming past people and drones and trams like they didn't exist, so narrow was his field of vision. He had one goal: the subway station.

He hadn't even thought about where to go. He'd get the next train to Netherville – that was clear. Beyond that, no idea. Maybe jump in the first carriage he saw. Not that it mattered. Anywhere was fine. Anywhere that wasn't Neo Vale.

River just stood on the subway platform, barely aware of the bustle that enveloped him. He still felt dizzy – partly because of the lack of sleep, but also because of the tight coils of fear that bound him, suffocated him – twisting and tightening around every inch of his body and mind. It was so hard to focus, to breathe...

But the dull drone of engines snapped him back to the present. The train had arrived, gliding effortlessly into the station. People started gravitating towards the doors.

Then there was a scream at the front of the train. Then another. Then another. People were running.

"Guoooooooooooo!" the night spore growled, leaping from the darkness of the subway tunnel. "Uryaaaaaaaaaaa!"

People dived for cover. More screamed. It was chaos. The night spore, its eyes blazing, grabbed the still-moving train and twisted the metal with its legs.

KYUUUUUUUUUUUUUUU!

Sparks flew, and the carriage groaned. The onlookers were hysterical.

"Aaaaaaaaaaaaaa!" River yelled, incandescent with rage.

He couldn't help it; his arms twisted, and the blades activated. People saw him and cried out in fright.

"No!" River protested, retracting the blades. "Nghhhhhhh!"

The night spore swiped at the fleeing passengers, throwing people to the ground like they were skittles. It speared a man, then another. Blood caked the platform and walls.

"No!" River yelled, his blades emerging again. "I won't!"

"Guoooooooooooo!" the monster roared, spotting him. River was exposed – the crowd had backed away in fear.

River retracted his blades and ran. But the spore unleashed a silk coil and snared him.

"Auuuuugggggghhh!" River cried, as he struck the ground. He felt his guitar shatter. "Get off!"

River snapped the silk with his blade and grabbed it. Jumping up, he tore towards the monster, and lassoed the fine wire around its neck.

"Uryaaaaaaaaaaa!" the spore screamed.

"You wanna do this?" he hissed, his mouth curling into a smile. "You wanna mess with a guy who has nothing to lose?"

"Gehhhhhooooooo!" the creature choked, thrashing against the coil.

River snarled, pulling it tighter. The cord cut into its skin, and dark paint spewed out, showering River.

"Gehhhhhh…" the night spore gasped, going limp.

Then it stopped breathing. River panted as he released his grip, letting its body fall onto the blood-soaked floor.

That's when he heard the wail of sirens coming from the top of the steps – the entrance to the station. Police drones. He had to leave.

But the train had caught fire. Tongues of flame licked the sides of the twisted carriage, and smoke billowed from the engine beneath.

River rushed over and peered inside. There was an old man, lying lifeless inside the train, his head gashed and bleeding. He was dead, right? He definitely wasn't breathing. He couldn't be.

The sirens grew louder. The fire grew hotter. River looked again at the wounded man, the blood pooling around his face.

And then he fled. He took the stairs two at a time, bounding out of the station into the crisp morning air. Police drones and hover-cars had swarmed the plaza, with officers and armed robots charging towards the entrance, laser-sights and spotlights and gun barrels swirling in all directions.

River shoved person after person out of his way as he ran.

Trams. He could take a tram.

He skidded onto the road and charged towards a police drone, which zapped him.

"Nghhhhhhh!" he grunted, as he was thrown onto the concrete. The taser had struck his leg.

"No entry," the drone stated. "Lockdown initiated. Return home."

River stood up. He clutched his tingling thigh. "Please..." he stammered, gasping for breath. "I have to get through."

"No entry," the drone repeated. "Lockdown initiated. Return home."

"But you don't understand..."

"No entry."

"Aaaaaaaaaaaaa!" River yelled, furious.

He deployed his blades.

ZASHU! ZASHU!

"Get out of my way!"

"I warn you, I am armed," the drone stated. "I will shoot to kill."

"Auuuuuggggghhh!"

"Stop!" a woman cried.

River froze, his blade mid-air, inches from the drone's shell. He followed the voice, and saw a lady standing in the doorway of Sweet Dusk. She had dazzling blue hair.

"It's not joking," she warned. "That thing will kill you without a second thought."

River faltered, and looked again at the hovering droid. Reluctantly, he twisted his arms, and the blades disappeared.

"Finally, I'm getting through to you," the woman sighed. "Step away."

River complied, making a point of scuffing his trainers as he walked towards her. "Finally?" he snapped. "What does that mean?"

"I sat with you last night, while you drank the bar dry. After the amount you necked, I'm not surprised you can't remember."

River just stared. "And you are?"

She must have been in her late forties, if not older. She wore a tight leather corset that hugged her curves, draped in shiny chains.

"Queen," she answered, folding her arms. "I own this place. And you're River Still."

River sneered. "Anything else?"

"You want to escape the city, right? I can help with that."

The smile dropped. She had River's attention.

"Don't look so surprised," Queen continued. "You told me everything last night – why you want to run away. It was quite the sob story."

River stared into her strange, glowing eyes. "You can get me out of here?" he asked.

"Come on up," said Queen, opening the bar's side door. "Let's go somewhere private."

The apartment was a studio, bathed in sickening pink lights. It was tidier than River had expected. The place was uncluttered – basic and functional, with a glass television panel blinking on the wall above her dresser.

Queen sighed as she threw herself onto the bed. She gazed dreamily at River, as if revelling in his obvious discomfort. "Aren't you going to sit down?" she asked, patting the spot next to her. "I don't bite."

River said nothing. He looked away, glaring at the Mango News coverage of the station attack. Ambulances and cop cars had cordoned off the entrance, and whirring helicopters hovered above Central Square.

As the programme cut to the anchor, River felt his stomach turn.

"It is too early to give an estimate on the death count," said the host, "but it's expected to be significant. However, a number of survivors are being treated at the scene, with injuries ranging from cuts and bruises to more life-threatening conditions. I saw one man being carried away on a stretcher who had reportedly been pulled from a train carriage, just moments before it exploded."

River gulped. The camera cut to the victim – an old man with a head wound.

"He's still breathing!" a doctor yelled. "We need space! Out of the way, please!"

River turned the TV off.

"Was it the creature you told me about?" asked Queen. "At the station? Was it a night spore?"

River looked at her. "Why do you care?"

Queen sniggered. "I don't care. But it's incredible to think that your ridiculous story could be true."

River turned away. He looked at Queen's dresser, where a selection of curious toys had been arranged in height order.

Queen simpered. "Like what you see?"

River ignored her. "You said you could get me out of here?"

"Oh, cutting to the chase." She pulled a joint out of her purse and lit it, blowing the fumes into his face. "Alright. Your biggest problem is the cop drones. Neo Vale went into lockdown as soon as the attack took place. Nobody can enter or leave. Like I said, those droids aren't bluffing. They'll kill anyone who doesn't comply."

"I can take them."

"No doubt. But you can't fight an entire police force. You know this, of course – otherwise you wouldn't be up here looking for help."

"Then what do you suggest?" River was getting impatient. "A charm offensive?"

Queen smiled. "I like your thinking. But no. You need a police code on your TellMe. It transmits automatically, telling the drones to ignore you. It lets you go anywhere, in effect."

River's heart sank. He looked down, staring at his trainers.

"Or," Queen continued, "you can wait until the lockdown ends. It won't last forever."

"I can't wait," said River quickly. "I must leave now."

"Well, that's easy. 500 credits, and I'll transmit the code to your TellMe." Queen stood up and lifted her wrist. "Shall we do it? It's a very good deal. And I'm the only person in Neo Vale with police codes, I can promise you that. Give me your TellMe."

"I don't have one," River snapped. "But I'll take one off you."

Queen snickered. "Excuse me?"

"Oh, forget it," he said, marching towards the door. "I'm wasting my time here."

"Woah, hold on. You had a TellMe last night. What's the problem?"

"I destroyed it. About half an hour ago."

The smile fell from Queen's face. "Oh, you really are damaged goods, aren't you?"

"Spare me the amateur psychology."

Queen laughed. Shaking her head, she took a long drag of her joint. "I like you," she said, surveying him. "River Still, what am I going to do with you?"

Queen strode across the apartment, deep in thought.

"I'm leaving," said River, reaching for the door handle.

"I thought you were desperate?"

"I am. But you obviously can't help me."

"I didn't say that. I am prepared to help you. Call me crazy, but there's just something about you. I can feel it."

This kind of flattery didn't wash with River. "No you can't," he grunted. "I've just got one of those faces."

"You have. I like it." Queen suckled again on the burning joint. "Alright, River. You can have my TellMe for 500 credits. I'll wipe it of course, but you'll have the codes."

River frowned. "You're going to give me your TellMe?"

"Why shouldn't I? It's old. And anyway, I'm scared that you'd actually try to fight those cop drones on your own. Because you would, wouldn't you?"

River said nothing.

"In return for my generosity," Queen continued, "I have one request."

"And what's that?"

"Let me have you for an hour. Just one hour, and then you can leave. How does that sound?"

River thought. That was it? 500 credits, and an hour of his time? "I'm confused," he admitted. "Do you want my help with something?"

"Not as such." Queen inched closer, staring deep into his eyes. "I said, let me *have you* for an hour."

Suddenly River got it. He gulped.

He looked again at Queen. She must have been twice his age. He couldn't. He just couldn't.

But he couldn't stay, either. He couldn't face Jake and Jazz. He couldn't go to the cellar. He couldn't see Spencer killed, and Neo Vale destroyed. He couldn't.

He wouldn't.

"I'll take that as a yes," Queen sneered, and pushed him towards the bed. "Leave the cash on the side and take your clothes off."

It felt like a death sentence. Queen rushed over to her dresser, and River slipped shyly out of his guitar straps and bag, followed by his coat. He hauled the crumpled wad of notes out of his jeans, his hands shaking as he counted them.

And then he just sat there, waiting.

Queen returned, brandishing a strange object. "You have to wear this," she announced.

River glared at the strap that dangled between her fingers. There was a rubber ball in its centre. "Wear it? Where?"

She grinned. "In your mouth."

River froze. This deal was getting worse by the second.

"Why?" he asked.

Queen's smile grew wider. "So that you can't talk."

River didn't like the sound of that.

"Can't I just promise to keep quiet?" he stuttered.

Queen glared at him. "How old are you?"

River didn't answer.

"I'm just curious," she said, creeping closer. "You really don't know what this is?"

River looked at the strap. "Something you gag people with?"

Queen smiled again. "Then you'll know that *promising* not to speak isn't quite the same. It's more about speech being denied you."

River nodded. "And control."

Queen thought for a moment. "Not really. Not for me, anyway. It's about protection."

"Protection?"

"Well, if you're lying there, and you can't speak, and you can't move, you're just an object. You can't be intimate with an object. And there's no danger of rejection. It's safer. Do you get me?"

"No."

Queen frowned. "That's weird. I thought you would. The way you talked about that Natsuki girl – I assumed you were scared of intimacy."

"Well, I might be, but I'm more scared of having that thing in my mouth."

Queen stood up. "Alright, look," she sighed, suddenly harsh. "Frankly River, I've got better things to be doing with my time today. Do you want those codes or not?"

River groaned. This was getting too hard.

Dejectedly, he looked up at Queen, and nodded.

"Then take off your pants."

She kept her eyes on him. With sweaty palms, River unfastened his jeans and let them fall. He scrunched them up and tossed them to one side.

"That's better," crooned Queen, sitting next to him. "Now, open up."

River shut his eyes. He took a deep breath, and slowly lowered his jaw.

Queen was gentle at first, easing the rubber sphere into his mouth as if feeding him chocolate. But then she tugged, yanking it across his face and tightening it at the base of his skull. River grunted, feeling the harsh buckles as they bore into his cheeks.

He kept his eyes closed. He wasn't going to watch.

23: fate

River bent over the toilet bowl and threw up. There was so little left to regurgitate, and what there was came out a deep, velvety red – maybe blood.

"Nghhhhhhh..." he gasped, finally able to breathe. His cheekbones had cramped, like two cogs grinding against his skull. His chest was spasming as well, with sharp pains shooting across his pectorals and striking the back of his throat.

This feeling was primal. What the hell had Queen unleashed? Her face flashed before his eyes, and suddenly he was back on her bed, lashed to its posts, muzzled, immobile. An object. She laughed, mocking his helplessness.

But Queen's face morphed into the doctor's – that scarred, cadaverous husk. And the doctor's face morphed into Miller's. And Miller's morphed into Fezziwig's. River remembered the fear of being strapped to his canvas, the ringmaster's bleached face towering over him.

"Nghhhhhhh!" He jolted. He could now see Jake, glaring at him with those black, sadistic eyes. His hands were tied, and Jake was forcing marshmallows into his mouth, unrelenting, cackling as River retched and choked.

And then a child screamed, kicking and thrashing and protesting. They couldn't move. Why couldn't they move?

BAN! BAN! BAN!

"Are you going to be long in there?" said Queen. "I gotta pee."

River gasped and looked into the toilet bowl. It was swimming with a vile, maroon liquid, which reeked.

"Two secs," he croaked, flushing his stomach contents into the pipe.

He was determined to say as little as possible to the woman. He'd honoured his part of the bargain; she'd 'had him' for an hour, and she'd gotten her 500 credits. There was nothing more to discuss. He was going.

While she was in the bathroom, he slipped into his clothes at lightning speed, and grabbed the TellMe. His breath stank, and he was thirsty, but he wasn't going to wait for the sink to be free. He couldn't face her. He wouldn't face her.

And so he left, feeling like the dirtiest, most shameful creature on the planet. He didn't even know who he was – who he'd become. Who was this carcass of a man, who was prepared to offer his body to any passing stranger, hell-bent on running away at all costs?

River just walked, oblivious to his surroundings. After a few minutes, he realised that a number of cop drones had already glided past. He looked back. Yes – he'd just passed a cluster of three, and they hadn't even twigged. The codes were working.

All he felt now was numbness. It was like his emotional centre was closing down. He didn't feel sad. He didn't feel angry. He didn't even feel scared. Not now. There was nothing.

He had a headache though, and his mouth was parched. As his head began to spin, he knelt down on the sidewalk, breathing heavily, desperately trying to focus.

It was so quiet. He was on the edge of Neo Vale, right by the ruins of the stadium. He looked up and stared at the sandy pitch that once spawned grass. Was there a person, in amongst the debris? Or was he hallucinating?

River blinked and rubbed his eyes. Yes – there was definitely a woman. A familiar woman, in an oversized sweater.

"Natsuki?"

Obviously, she couldn't hear; she was too far away, and she had her back to him. She was gazing up at the sky as she followed the swirling trail of a blinking drone, which zipped in circles over the ruined seats.

River felt so bad about what had happened – about what he'd said, and hadn't said, and how they'd left things. He just stared at her, pensively, as she shouted commands at the soaring robot. She seemed happy.

River stood up and began to walk. It had been nice to see his friend one last time.

Nice, and painful.

Eyes ahead, he told himself. Look, the border is just there – the Netherville boundary.

There was a police cordon, and a complement of cop drones. They wouldn't be any trouble.

"Aaaaaaaaaaaaa!" came a high-pitched scream.

River turned on his heel. It was Natsuki, cowering from a night spore. It swiped at her, and she ducked.

River watched, horrified. Another night spore, in Neo Vale? Where had it come from? The House?

"Get help, Koro!" Natsuki cried. "Hurry!"

The android bleeped and shot into the sky.

River watched the drama unfold, conflicted. He wanted to intervene, but he also wanted to run.

She'd be fine, he told himself. Help was on the way; she'd sent her droid. And she could run away, right? She had legs.

"Aaaaaaaaaaaaa!" she yelled, as the monster pinned her to the ground. "Help, somebody! Please!"

River grimaced. He wouldn't do it. Not another fight. No.

"Kyaaaaaaaaaaaa!" he cried, as his blades emerged. "No!"

"Help me! Auuuuuggggghhh!"

River thrashed against his weapons. "Kuuuuuuuu! Stop!"

"Guoooooooooooo!" the creature snarled.

River wrestled with his conscience. It was *Natsuki*. He couldn't leave her.

But could he save her? He might die. They both might.

"Nghhhhhhh!" he screamed at himself, infuriated. His blade rose, like it had a mind of its own. It was pulling him towards the creature.

"Aaaaaaaaaaaaa!" he cried, breaking into a sprint. "Natsuki! Run!"

"River?!"

The monster saw him, and charged.

"Gyaaaaaaaaaaaaaaaaaaaa!" River screamed, swiping his blade across its face. "Get out of here!"

"I can't!"

"You must! Go!"

Torn, Natsuki froze. Then ran for cover.

"Uryaaaaaaaaaaaa!" the night spore growled, unleashing a silk wire.

But River grabbed it, and used it like a snare, pulling the monster in.

For a moment, River and the night spore just glared at each other, panting in each other's faces.

But River switched to his gun, and hovered the barrel over its red, fiery eyes.

BAN!

He struck the creature on the head, and it reeled.

River bounded forward. He gathered the silk coil in his hands and wound it round the creature's neck, snarling as he pulled tighter and tighter. The night spore gasped and shrieked.

"I'm getting good at this," he mocked.

"Stop it, River! Don't!"

River looked at Natsuki. She was curled up by a dumpster, shaking.

249

"Nghhhhhh," she panted, as if in pain. "Aaaaaaaaaaaa!"

Reluctantly, River released the creature. It took off across the stadium ruins.

"Did it get you?" River asked, staggering towards his friend. "Are you hurt?"

"Keep back!" Natsuki yelled. "Keep away from me!"

"Natsuki, it's me. It's River!"

"I know! You've got to keep back!"

River was perplexed. She wasn't shaking. She was *convulsing*. It was just like–

"Kuuuuuuuu!" she screamed, and threw her arms out wide. "Auuuuuggggghhh!"

River gasped. It couldn't be? Surely?

Natsuki cried out as her arms rotated. The skin disappeared, and two blades emerged. They glistened, throbbing with power.

River glared, wide-eyed.

And so did Natsuki. She looked agog at her new appendages. They were just like River's. Two immense weapons, protruding from her sleeves.

"Natsuki," said River, creeping closer. "Were you in the war?"

His friend looked at him. "I can't remember."

"What about these weapons? Do you remember getting them?"

Natsuki paused. "I don't know."

River reached out, but she recoiled.

"Don't, River!"

Suddenly the air filled with sirens, and a squadron of police drones descended on the stadium.

"It's Koro," said Natsuki, looking up. "He's brought back-up."

River followed her gaze. "Well, those guys don't look friendly."

"Halt!" the droid ordered. "Do not move! Get on the ground and put your hands behind your head!"

River raised his eyebrows. "Thanks, Koro."

"I repeat! Get on the ground and put your hands behind your head!"

Natsuki looked shocked. "They're going to arrest us!"

"Like hell they are!" he shouted. "Run!"

The pair fled.

"Freeze!" the droid barked.

"They're right behind us!" Natsuki cried, as the robots swept down to their level.

BOKAN! BOKAN! BOKAN!

Bullets struck the pavement.

"Geez, those rounds are live!" yelled River.

"We need to find cover!"

They tore round a corner, heading for the centre of Neo Vale.

BOKAN! BOKAN! BOKAN!

"It's okay, I know a place!" said River. "We need to get to the plaza!"

"Central Square? That's madness! It's swarming with cops!"

"I have clearance codes!"

BOKAN! BOKAN! BOKAN!

"Kuuuuuuuu!" Natsuki cried. "I don't think they work!"

"They will! Trust me!"

They entered a side street.

"We need to buy time!" said Natsuki. "You go, River. I'll hold them off!"

"What?! You can't do that!"

Natsuki threw her arm out, stopping him. "They won't arrest me! I'm the victim! Koro will explain everything! Now go!"

She raised her blades.

River looked and saw a cluster of droids swing into the alley.

"And you tell *me* to be safe!" he snapped.

Natsuki glared at him. "And what do you do? Ignore me! Now run, River!"

River lingered for a moment. He looked at Natsuki.

And then fled.

"Halt!" the robot yelled, speeding forward. "Get on the ground! You are under arrest!"

Natsuki lifted her blade in defiance. "I have not done anything!" she insisted. "Listen to me! I am Natsuki Hashino and I was attacked by a creature! At the stadium!"

"You have three seconds! Surrender or we open fire!"

"You are not listening!" Natsuki yelled. "I have vital information!"

"Three!"

"Please, you have to believe me!"

"Two!"

"Listen!"

"Fire!"

"Nghhhhhhh!"

BOKAN! BOKAN! BOKAN!

Exhausted, River scrambled into the fireplace. He'd made it. He was at Spencer's studio.

But he was dizzy. He was so lacking in liquids and calories that his head was in a spin.

Inevitably, he hit the floor. He groaned, lying face-down on the boards like a drunkard. He didn't have the strength to pick himself up. He just wanted to lie there and die.

"Hey," said a voice, taking his wrist. "I've got you."

"Nghhhhhhh," River grunted, accepting the help. "Thanks Jake."

River stood up and wobbled, but his friend steadied him.

"Woah," Jake giggled, grabbing his arms. "That hangover's a bitch, huh?"

"Very." Now balanced, River opened his eyes, and let the room shift into focus. Jake was grinning at him, impishly.

Suddenly, River realised. "Hang on, what?!" he exclaimed, pushing Jake away. "What the hell? How can you be here?"

"Oh, hey River," said Jazz, climbing down the ladder. "You made it."

"Jazz?" River blustered. "Don't sound so nonchalant. You should be at school."

"Ooh," Jake laughed, mockingly. "Don't tell on me, bro."

"We didn't go," said Jazz. "We saw what happened at the station and thought we should tell Spencer. Did you not get my text? I told you we were here."

"What?" River glared at her, bewildered. And then he remembered – his phone was lying in pieces on the road. "I've had some technical difficulties."

Jake shook his head. "Ouchy."

"This is stupid!" River shouted. "You're telling me that you got through all those police drones without anybody seeing you?"

Jake laughed. "Man, we sound so slick when you put it like that."

"What about you?" Jazz replied. "You made it here. Why couldn't we?"

River held up his TellMe. "I have police codes."

"Woah, seriously?" Jake gasped.

"Ah, River Still," said Spencer, waddling in with a tray. "I've just made cocoa. I do hope you're not going to yell at me again."

River looked at him.

"Spencer said you had a fight," said Jake. "It's fine though. We're totally cool."

"As am I," Spencer affirmed. "But the cocoa isn't, so grab it while it's hot."

River gazed at the tray and the four mugs. He took one.

"I hear you got drunk last night," Spencer added, grinning. "Quite understandable. I imagine you're in desperate need of refreshment."

River tried to find the words, deeply embarrassed. "Spencer, I-"

"Say no more. I lied, you shouted. It's over and done with."

The four sipped their cocoas. For a moment, nobody spoke.

"Anyway," said Jazz, breaking the silence. "As Jake said, Spencer told us what happened. In fact, he told us everything."

River looked up from his mug. "Everything?"

"We know about the vapour," said Jake. "We know that masks won't protect us. The only way into the cellar is with moonshade."

"Which you are not going to take under any circumstances," said River. "It could kill you."

"So? We're all going to die someday."

"And you want that?"

"No," said Jake. "But it's the right thing to do, isn't it?"

"Is it? What about your parents? What's your mom going to say when she finds out you're dead?"

Jake sniggered. "I don't know. Rest in peace?"

"Seriously?!"

"Look," said Jazz. "We're a team, River. We must do this together."

"And I second that," Spencer chimed. "I give you my word, River Still. If we don't go together, we don't go at all. I won't face Jobon alone."

River sighed. He dropped his head, infuriated.

"Besides," Spencer continued, "it may not be that simple. As you pointed out, River, there are night spores in your world too. Or creatures like them."

"In Mango Tower," said Jazz. "The cellar might not be the whole story."

River sipped his drink, deeply unhappy.

Jake looked at him. "What do you think? Could they all be coming from the tower?"

"No," said River. "The one at the station was definitely made of paint. It couldn't have come from one of those tanks. They were full of water."

253

"Unbelievable," said Spencer, starting to pace. "I wish I could piece this together."

"Maybe the answer is in the cellar," Jazz suggested. "We should get down there as soon as possible."

"I agree," said Jake. "What about you, River?"

"Hmm?" River could barely hear. It was like his ears were clogged.

"River?" Jake repeated. "Are you okay?"

"Nghhhhhhh!" River swayed. It was like a headrush that wouldn't end. He dropped his mug, and he swooned.

"Catch him!" cried Jazz.

When River awoke, he was on the floor of Spencer's studio. A pile of cushions had been placed behind his head, and someone had wrapped him up in a thick woollen blanket, zig-zagging with patchwork colours.

He rubbed his eyes, wearily. He had the worst headache in history.

Weakly, he picked himself up and surveyed the apartment. It was empty. He couldn't even be sure of the time, or whether it was morning or night. How long had he been out?

"Spencer?" he whispered, inching forward. "Jake?"

No reply. Surely they hadn't gone to the cellar without him? After what Spencer had said?

Concerned, he stepped out into Chancery Square. Jake was there, sitting alone at the foot of the fountain.

"Hey River," he said. "You're awake."

River limped over, his eyes half shut. "How long was I out?"

"Ages. Maybe fifteen hours? You lost the whole day, man."

"Nghhhhhhh," River groaned, sitting next to him. "What, the *whole* day? It's nighttime?"

"Yeah, welcome to Snoozeville. Spencer and Jazz are up on the mezzanine."

"And what about you?"

Jake grinned. "I'm sitting right here. Hello."

"I mean, why aren't you asleep? And isn't there a curfew?"

"Oh, I told them I'm with Spencer," he replied. "It's fine as long as I don't leave the square. And anyway, I've got too much going on up here." He tapped the side of his head. "Do you ever get like that?"

River nodded. "It's been known to happen, yeah."

"It's annoying, isn't it? But hey, there are some perks. It gives us some time alone."

River said nothing.

"Can I ask you something?" said Jake. "Why did you take off? You know, yesterday morning, when you said you were off to Kakeru's? Was that really what you were doing?"

River paused. "Why do you ask?"

"No reason. You just didn't seem yourself, that's all. Was it because of Spencer? The fight that you had?"

Again, River didn't answer.

"It's fine if you don't want to talk," said Jake. "I'm just making sure you're okay."

River clenched his fists. Damn it, Jake. Why did you have to be so nice?

"I think you'd hate me if I told you the truth," River replied.

"Now, we both know that's not true."

"I did some terrible things."

"Oh yeah?" said Jake. "Like what?"

"Well, I lied to you for one thing," he mumbled. "I wasn't going to Kakeru's. And I didn't want you to reach me, so I smashed my phone."

"You smashed your phone?"

"I just wanted to run, and I didn't want you to talk me out of it. Because I knew you would. You'd insist on going to the cellar."

"That's what you were doing?" said Jake. "You were running away?"

"Is that so weird?"

"Well, yeah," Jake admitted. "It is weird. It's so unlike you. That's not the guy I know."

"That's the problem, Jake. He exists. I hate him. I hate to think what he's capable of when he's scared. And yesterday, I was terrified. I found a sex worker, and I..." He tailed off.

"Hey," Jake whispered, holding him. "You made a mistake. It happens."

River shook his head. "You can't write it off that easily."

"Of course I can. The past doesn't define you."

Jake rubbed his friend's back, and he flinched.

"What?" said Jake, puzzled. "What is it?"

"It's nothing. I hurt myself, that's all."

"Let me see."

Jake lifted River's shirt, and his eyes widened. His back was covered in lashes, some of them bleeding. It looked like he'd been ravaged by lions.

"River," said Jake. "What's with the wounds?"

River pulled his shirt back down. "I told you, it's nothing. I just slept with someone."

"The sex worker?"

"Yeah. I needed the police codes to escape. She offered me a deal. She liked to do things a certain way."

Jake stood up. He said nothing, but curled his hands into fists, like he was raging.

"It's okay," said River. "Really."

Jake said nothing. His hands quivered.

"Jake?"

"I can't believe she did that to you," he muttered, still looking away. "Did she even give you a choice?"

River hesitated. "Well, I wasn't able to talk for most of it. She put this thing in my mouth."

Jake bowed his head, trying to contain his anger.

"Why are you mad?" asked River.

"I'm not mad," said Jake quickly. "I'm thinking."

"What are you thinking about?"

Jake looked at him. "How mad I am."

"Ah, there you are," said Spencer, waddling out of the fireplace. "I was beginning to think you'd gone to the cellar without me!"

"As if we'd have all the fun without you, Spencer," River quipped. "It's good to see you."

"And you, biped. Are you feeling better?"

"I'm getting there."

Spencer cocked his head. "Well, young Jake looks like an emotional wreck."

"I'm just tired," he answered. "I should probably get some rest."

"Yes, you should," said Spencer. "We have to leave early tomorrow."

Jake walked over to River. "Come here," he ordered, hugging him. "We've got this, okay? We're in this together."

River smiled. "Thanks, man."

"Sleep well, River."

River watched him as he disappeared into the fireplace.

Spencer sighed. "It was good of you to come back."

"I had to," said River. "I felt so ashamed."

"No need. It wasn't your fight."

"Yes it was," River retorted. "That's why I was running. And you're not going to talk me out of it now."

"I doubt I could if I tried," said Spencer. "But, I should point out, you won't be able to dissuade Jake and Jazz, either."

"I wasn't planning to."

Spencer looked at him. "Yes you were."

River hesitated. "I can't let them go, Spencer," he muttered. "Jake and Jazz. They're too young to die."

Spencer did a double take. "*You're* too young to die!"

River shook his head. "I've lived long enough."

"Nonetheless," said Spencer, "this is not your decision to make. You can't control them, River – any more than I can control you. Jake and Jazz are going to the cellar because they want to. Who are you to stop them? Who are you to live their life for them?"

River groaned. It was hard to disagree. Jake and Jazz were two of the bravest people he knew. They weren't trying to be martyrs. They were fiercely determined, and loyal.

"I know," he said, sadly. "I can't persuade them."

River got little sleep that night. It was fine though – it gave him plenty of time to think. He couldn't argue with Spencer's reasoning, painful as it was to admit. It was just the guilt that weighed so heavily. The shame of it all. Jake had a point; his actions were in the past. But there had to be consequences, right? He'd wronged his friends. Why was Jake so quick to forgive him, to write it all off? River wouldn't, in his shoes. No way. He'd be livid.

Morning came. River gazed wistfully at Jake and Jazz as they readied their weapons. He sighed. They deserved better than him.

"Your attention, bipeds," said Spencer, surrounded by covered canvases. He took one of the tarpaulins in his beak and revealed the door to the hospital. "This will take us back to where we were. But remember, the staircase is at the bottom of a rather deep pit."

"Yeah," said Jake, rubbing his buttocks. "I recall."

"Now, I propose that I fly each of you down there, one by one."

"Sure," said Jazz. "It beats swan-diving."

"With that in mind," Spencer went on, "I won't give you the moonshade until after we've landed. If you experience side-effects on the way down, it could be extremely dangerous."

"Unlike the rest of this very safe mission," said Jake.

"Quite." Spencer looked at River. "Does that sound okay to you?"

"Yeah, better to be safe than sorry," he agreed. "And let's look out for each other, okay? Don't go dying on me."

"I plan to live forever," said Jazz. "Come on, everyone – group hug."

She pulled her friends close, and they squeezed each other tightly.

"Say your prayers, night spores," said Jake. "Jakey is in da House!"

River snickered as he pulled away. "Never say that again."

"I promise nothing," Jake winked. "Now, let's kick some Jobon butt."

River took a deep breath. "Oh boy. Are you sure you're ready for this?"

"Nope," said Jazz. "I'm terrified. You?"

"I'm cool."

Jazz grinned. "Is that why you're shaking?"

"I have every faith in you all," said Spencer. "Now take us in, Jake."

"With pleasure." Jake turned the doorhandle and swaggered through. "Alright, Jobon! Come at me, baby! I'll cut you in two!"

"Jake Thrower!" his mom yelled. "What are you doing?!"

Jake froze. "What?!"

He looked around. He was in his living room.

"No!" cried Jazz. "River!"

The twins turned, just in time to see their friend. He closed the door and locked it.

"No!" screamed Jazz.

"That bastard, he tricked us!" yelled Jake.

They pounded on the panel.

"River!" cried Jazz. "River!"

On the other side, still at Spencer's, River stepped away from the door, its bolt firmly in place.

"Nice work," said Spencer, pulling away a second tarpaulin. The real door was underneath.

River's eyes filled with tears as he listened to Jake and Jazz's screams. They hammered desperately on the door, pleading with him to let them through.

Resolute, he picked up a huge paint tin. "Stand back," he ordered, tossing it at the canvas. The duplicate door was washed away, and the knocking stopped.

His lip trembling, he deployed his blades.

ZASHU! ZASHU!

"Come on," he said. "Let's end this."

in the chrysalis chamber

River kept his eyes on the disc, which had remained silent throughout. He let the quiet linger, feeling the sadness swell up inside him as he recounted the events.

"What do you think?" said River, finally. "Did I do the right thing?"

The disc stammered. "You..." it croaked, as if weeping. "You sent them home."

"Of course. It was easy enough to paint a new door while they were asleep, identical to the last one. Like I said, there was no way I could persuade them. Jake and Jazz – they're fearless. I love them for that."

"Nghhhhhhh," the disc groaned, as if overwhelmed. "You let them go."

"I had to."

"Tell me, River. Where are they now? Do they know you're here?"

River glared at the disc, quizzically. "Why do you care so much?"

"J-Jake..." the disc stammered. "He loves you so much. It's obvious. You can't throw away something so precious. Tell me, River. Tell me that you went back for him."

"Tell me who you are first," River ordered. "This has gone on long enough. I didn't mention it before, but I know exactly why I'm here, why I was brought to Mango Tower. This chamber – it's not for counselling, or even interrogation. It's an assessment facility."

"Nghhhhhhh..." the disc gasped again. It began to cry.

"It's alright," said River, softly. "I'm not angry. I understand."

The disc's voice quivered. "H-how did you know?"

"About this place? I discovered the truth before I was captured. Those creatures in the basement were once people, weren't they? You take 'undesirables' – like people with mental health problems – and you assess them. If they're compatible, you convert them into SPOREs, like the ones I fought in the war. And that's what you planned to do with me."

The disc sobbed louder. "W-Why?" it wept. "Why are you telling me this now?"

259

"Because I'm asking you to be honest with me," said River. "It's only fair that I'm honest with you."

"Are you angry?" the disc enquired, almost child-like. "Are you mad at me, River?"

"No. I get it. That's why I had to see you, Leonard. I had to tell you that it's okay."

An invisible panel slid aside, right next to the disc. There was a room beyond, blinking with computer banks that stretched from floor to ceiling. And out of this room stepped Leonard Mango, CEO of the Mango empire. Tears were streaming down his face, and his whole body was trembling.

"Hello," said River.

Mango pressed a button on his TellMe, and the cuffs fell from his wrists.

"I had to do it," he gasped. "It was the only way."

"I know. It was the only plan that would work. You're a genius, Leonard."

Mango smiled. "I'm not."

"I think you are. The mental health stats were off the chart. The services couldn't cope. The people doing the counselling were in need of counselling. What were you supposed to do? The Republic was clamouring for a solution."

"I remembered the war," Mango quivered, "and how we turned prisoners into SPOREs. We could do it again. We could amass a huge army for the Republic and breathe new life into the suicidal."

"And you had just the technology to do it. That's why you're a genius. You used the TellMe update to read people's thoughts. With it, you could detect a mental health problem the minute it spawned. You could get those people off the streets."

Mango smiled. "Like we did with you."

"Like you did with me." River rushed up to him. "You saved me. That's why I allowed myself to get caught. I had to tell you my story."

Mango rubbed his eyes. "But why?" he whispered. "You don't care about me."

"I care more than you think. I've read the reports. When I learned of your partner's suicide, I couldn't believe it. You and Brent were just like me and Jake. It was scary how similar we were."

Mango laughed and wiped his cheeks. "We were very similar," he admitted. "Brent was so carefree, just like Jake. And he brought out the best in me."

"As Jake did with me. You and I, Leonard – we're the same. But you know that, right?"

"I do," said Mango. "We have the same fire, River. That sheer, bloody determination to get what we want."

River smiled and hugged the guy, holding him in his arms.

"You talked about your flashbacks," Mango whispered. "I've never told anyone this, but I have them too."

"You do?"

"Every night, when I close my eyes, I see Brent, hanging from the ceiling. He talks to me, screaming, begging me to help. But I can't get to him. I jump and I snatch, but he just gets higher and higher."

River squeezed him. "That's awful."

They broke away.

"I knew you'd understand," Mango gasped. "God bless you, River Still. You are the first person who's ever listened, since Brent. It's like you can see into my soul."

River put his hand on his shoulder. "That's because I've been there. I know what a dark place it is."

"It is a dark place. The blackest. It's hell."

River rubbed his arm. "You cope very well. You've achieved so much. Be proud of yourself, Leonard."

River turned away.

"Wait, where are you going?" said Mango.

"I can leave, right? You're not still planning to turn me into a SPORE?"

"You can't leave me hanging!" Mango insisted. "You gotta tell me about the cellar. Did you go there? Did you stop Jobon?"

River wandered back to the chair. "Oh yeah, the cellar. It was pretty scary."

"Well, you obviously didn't die."

"True. I made it out alive."

Mango gulped. "And Spencer?"

River hesitated. "Do you really want me to do this? Do you really want me to go there?"

"I do," said Mango. "Please, River Still. Tell me what happened."

24: him

It was strange. River looked at the crooked stairs, their uneven stones enveloped by a haze of brown fumes. It was odd how he didn't feel scared now.

Resigned, yes. But not scared.

In his hand sat the moonshade, which Spencer had just dropped into his palm. As illicit drugs went, it looked innocuous enough – like a jet pebble, washed up on the beach.

"I don't suppose you have any absinthe?" River ventured. "You know, to wash it down?"

Spencer chuckled. "Oh, I'm not sure I could handle a drunk River Still."

"He's not the best. But he's a sick dancer."

"We can pirouette when we're done," said Spencer, looking at the vapour. "We haven't much time."

River slipped the drug onto his tongue and chewed. "Ugh," he cringed. "It tastes diseased."

"It is. You've just swallowed a handful of hate."

"A dose of Focus." River licked his lips. "And this will keep me awake?"

"With any luck." Spencer jumped onto the first step. "Come on."

River followed, brushing past a green lamp and into a void of groping shadows. The silence was arresting. River listened to the vacuous air as he and Spencer inched their way down step after step, the brown fog wrapping around them like vines. He wasn't sure if he'd ever been to a place so completely without sound.

"This feels like dying," River remarked. "Like, I always thought that death would look like this. A long, slow march towards Hell."

"I thought you didn't believe in Hell?"

River thought. "Well, it's amazing what you believe when you're on the scaffold."

"I know, it's fascinating, isn't it?" said Spencer. "We painted-kind don't really believe in the afterlife. We don't even believe in a soul."

"Oh?" River was surprised. "You don't depart for the great canvas in the sky?"

"No, we get re-used. Isn't it awful? Someday, when my colours have faded, I will be summoned to the lacerator, and that'll be it. My feathers will be remixed, and my paintwork repurposed. I will be crafted into a new form of life."

River looked at him. "Spencer, that's awful."

"It is the way of things."

"Kuuuuuuuu!" River screamed and grabbed his face. The corridor was spinning. The smoke had turned into a rain cloud, blood-red, its drops lashing against his skin.

"River!" he crowed. "River, what is it?"

"It's raining blood! Can't you see it? The smoke, it's... Aaaaaaaaaaaaaa!"

"Nothing has changed," Spencer insisted. "River, you're hallucinating. It's the drug, do you understand me? The moonshade is twisting your mind!"

"No, but I can feel it!" River cried. "It's wet, it's on my skin! It's real!"

"You need to ground yourself, River. Focus on me! Look, who am I being?" Spencer leaned in, and spoke with a ridiculous accent. "Ooh, kiss me dude! You're bang tidy!"

"What? I don't know!"

Spencer almost looked offended. "It's Jake."

"Jake has never said 'bang tidy!'"

"Very good, you're concentrating," Spencer slapped him with his wing. "Hello? River Still?"

River blinked and snapped back to reality. "Spencer," he gasped, looking around. "The rain has gone." He kept gazing, as if doubting his senses. "Yeah, we're good."

"Just as well," said Spencer. "Parrots and precipitation do not mix. Now – onwards."

"Okay! Auugghh!"

"What is it?"

River rubbed his nose. "I found a wall."

Spencer swept to the floor and examined the obstacle. "It's not a wall," he clarified. "It's a locked door. Do you see? A door in need of an Every Key."

Spencer reached into his pouch and produced the legendary disc. River trembled as he watched. The dread was growing. He felt cold, as if someone had emptied an entire tray of ice cubes down his back. And his palms were beginning to sweat.

Spencer clocked him, briefly. But said nothing.

"Spencer," River whispered, tensing every muscle. "This is it."

The parrot hovered the key over the receptacle. "It is."

263

Suddenly River was overcome with regret. He didn't want to go. He was so scared. He couldn't do it.

No. No! Of course he could do it. He *had* to do it.

Spencer slipped the key into the lock, and it began to rotate. There was a mechanical shudder, like a series of cogs locking together. And the door creaked open.

"Huhuhuhuhuhu!" a man laughed. It was a deep, ancient cackle, mocking them.

River recoiled. "Did you hear that?"

"Hear what?" Spencer listened closely.

River said nothing. Gingerly, he nudged the wooden door.

"Huhuhuhuhuhu!"

ZASHU! ZASHU!

River activated his blades.

"It's Jobon," he hissed. "He knows we're here."

Spencer swooped onto his shoulder, his eyes wide. "Do you think he's close?"

"I can hear him laughing. He's toying with us."

"It could be a hallucination. The moonshade…" Spencer looked in every direction. "Or he could have found a way into your mind."

The pair inched over the threshold, and into the cavern beyond. It was a vast, eerie expanse. The rock faces looked damp, bathed in a pulsing, esoteric blue, and a single stone walkway stretched across an abyss, cloaked in shadow.

"The cellar," Spencer announced, his voice thick with fear.

"How do you want to do this?" River asked. "Do you want to go further in?"

"Let's not go any deeper than we have to." Spencer looked around. "Do you see up there? There's a ledge."

"You mean the one that's, like, five hundred metres up in the air?"

"Indeed. That's our play."

"Oh sure. I'll get my climbing gear."

"I'm not asking you to climb it, trottelkopf," said Spencer. "I will fly up there with my paints. See? The rock face is slightly angled. It's the perfect place to paint my picture."

River nodded. "And flood the whole cellar."

"Precisely."

River gazed into the vacuous dark, his heart thumping. "Why haven't we been attacked yet?" he whispered. "Why is no one trying to stop us?"

Spencer shrugged. "Perhaps they need provoking."

264

And with that he jumped, propelling himself into the air. He soared across the chasm and landed on the stone ledge.

"It's okay, River Still!" he called out, his voice resonating. "Nobody knows we're here!"

River shuddered as the echoes bounced from wall to wall.

"Well, I think they might now."

Spencer hummed to himself as he unpacked his satchel, readying his paints. "It's odd."

"What is?"

"There's a walkway up here. Like a ramp. It must lead somewhere."

"Deeper into the chasm, probably," said River dismissively. "Hurry up, Spencer!"

"Huhuhuhuhuhu!" the voice crooned.

River jumped, terrified. He could see someone – a distant figure, silhouetted against the light from the door. He was running towards him.

Instinctively, River thrust out his blade. "Don't move!" he warned, his arm trembling. "I said, stay where you are!"

But the figure was getting closer by the second.

"Freeze!" River boomed. "I *will* kill you!"

"River?" said the guy, emerging from the shadows. He had dazzling orange hair, and an ill-fitting hoodie. "River, it's me!"

Slowly, River lowered his blade. "Jake?"

His friend dashed up to him, beaming. "I couldn't let you do it, man," he panted. "I couldn't let you go alone."

"What's happening, River?" called Spencer.

"It's Jake! He followed us."

"Lol, you can't get rid of me!" Jake chuckled, as he rested his hand on River's shoulder. "Aw, it's so good to see you. I can't believe you just abandoned me like that!"

River surveyed the guy with suspicion. Something didn't add up. "How did you get through the vapour?" he quizzed. "Why didn't it knock you out?"

"Same as you," Jake answered. "I took the moonshade. You know, those pills that Spencer gave us?"

River started to back away. "Spencer never gave you your pill."

Up on the ledge, the parrot looked down at the two friends. He did a double take.

"River!" he screamed. "That's a night spore!"

"Uryaaaaaaaaaaaa!" Jake growled, and swiped River's face.

"Nghhhhhhh!" River landed on his back. He looked up, and saw a demonic Jake towering over him. But then he shimmered, and twisted into a spore.

"Guoooooooooooo!" it cried, attacking again.

River leapt up. It was so hard to focus. He stared at the monster, who morphed into Jake again, his eyes black and hateful.

"You can do it, River!" Spencer called. "It's the moonshade! It's altering your perception! Concentrate!"

"Gyaaaaaaaaaaaaaaaaaaaa!" River cried, swiping his blade.

Jake dodged it, and whipped River in the back.

"Nghhhhhhh!" The pain was intense, darting across his body like lightning. River tumbled off the side of the platform.

ZASHU!

He retracted his blade, and quickly grabbed the edge.

"Kuuuuuuuu!" he panted, dangling over the abyss.

Jake towered above him, sneering. "I always knew I'd be your downfall," he purred, driving his foot into River's hand. "It's sorta my job."

"Aaaaaaaaaaaaa!" cried River, his fingers slipping.

"So, what do you say?" He pressed down harder, River's fingers crunching beneath his shoe. "You ready to quit?"

"Afraid not," said River. "You're fired!"

BOKAN! BOKAN! BOKAN!

He unloaded his gun, striking Jake in the chest. Jake stumbled.

ZASHU!

River deployed his blade and leapt up.

"Time to cut the dead weight!" he screamed. "Auuuuuggggghhh!"

He speared Jake in the chest, and he spluttered. Black paint spewed out of his mouth.

"Oh, well done, River!" cheered Spencer. "You did it!"

River gasped as he whipped the blade out of the creature. It shimmered, and morphed into a spore, flopping lifelessly to the ground.

"Quickly, River!" Spencer crowed, landing on the bridge. "This way!"

River ran up to him, retracting his blades.

"Keep running!" Spencer urged. "They're on our tails!"

"Did you finish the painting?"

"Yes, it's done," Spencer assured him. "All we need do is open the door, and the cellar will flood."

River stopped, and glared at his friend.

Spencer turned. "River, what are you doing?!" he exclaimed. "We have to keep moving! The night spores are right behind us!"

ZASHU!

The blade came out. River hovered it above Spencer's head and narrowed his eyes.

"You're lying," he whispered. "Why would we be running *deeper* into the cellar? We could flood it right now and escape."

"I told you," Spencer replied. "There are night spores right behind us, blocking our path!"

River looked and saw a pack of red-eyed beasts swarming onto the bridge.

He looked back, unconvinced. "Spencer!" he cried out, hoping his friend was out there somewhere. "Where are you, Spencer?"

"I'm right here!" he insisted, getting flustered. "It's me! Honestly, River!"

River snarled. "No!" he spat, his eyes darkening. "It's not you!"

"River, please!"

River aimed his weapon, preparing to swipe. "Liar!"

"River! Yaaaaaaaaaaaaaa!"

A night spore struck him, and Spencer was thrown into the abyss.

River looked round. He was face-to-face with the monsters, growling and slavering. There were dozens, too many to count.

"Kyaaaaaaaaaaaaaaaaaaaaa!" River screamed, slashing one across the face. "Kuuuuuuuuu!"

They were rushing him. He couldn't keep up.

"Aaaaaaaaaaaaaa!" he cried, as a night spore struck his chest. "Nghhhhhhh!"

OOOOOOOOOOOOOO!

A dull roar filled the cavern, like an earthquake. Everything shook.

"Huhuhuhuhuhu!" the voice laughed.

River staggered, just as an immense crack appeared on the bridge. It crumbled, and an entire chunk fell away, throwing a handful of spores into the void.

"Auuuuugggggghhh!" River cried. He had to run. The entire platform was disintegrating.

He sprinted. He didn't look back. The noise was thunderous.

OOOOOOOOOOOOO!
OOOOOOOOOOOOO!

There was a ledge just ahead, at the end of the bridge. But there were cracks everywhere.

"Auuuuugggggghhh!" River screamed, as the floor gave way. He jumped towards the ledge, and grabbed it.

"Nghhhhhhh!" he winced. The pain coursed through his fingers.

Rocks fell all around him, tumbling into the black nothingness. Within seconds, the bridge had gone.

Frozen and afraid, he hauled himself onto the platform. He rolled onto his back, panting.

He was mad. He was scared. He clambered up, his heart thumping, and rammed his fingers down his throat. He retched, and then vomited. A splatter of black bile decorated the rocky ground. It was all moonshade. He needed it out of his system.

"Kuuuuuuuu!" he choked, as tarry spit trickled down his chin. "Spencer! Where are you?"

There was nothing. Just his own voice, skipping through the empty cavern.

"No!" he cried out, punching the earth. "Augh! Augh! Auuuuugggggghhhhh!"

River sobbed. He sat down, curling into a foetal position.

DO. DO. DO.

He looked up. What was that? Footsteps?

DO. DO. DO.

River leapt up and deployed his blades. A figure was shifting through the darkness.

"Stop!" he barked. He could see the outline of a person. "I said stop!"

Livid, he deployed his gun.

BOKAN! BOKAN! BOKAN!

The figure shuddered as the bullets ripped through their clothes. They froze.

"That's better!" River snapped. "Jobon, I presume?"

The person said nothing.

"Come on, Your Worship, there's no need to be timid. I went to all this trouble to find you."

The figure laughed. But it wasn't the laugh he was expecting. It was a woman's.

River baulked. Who was this? Who the hell was he talking to?

"I said this place was your tomb," the woman cackled. "I needed to bury you, River Still. I never thought you'd bury yourself."

The figure stepped into the pool of light. She was frail, and in a shawl. Her back was arched and her nose was drooping.

268

River gasped. He was so confused. It was the hag he'd met in the subway. It was the crazy old broad who'd tried to kill him.

"We're directly beneath the Temple of Colours," she explained, looking up. "No ordinary person could have survived the pit and squeezed through the tunnel that led here. But you probably know, by now, that I am no ordinary person."

"Where's Jobon?" River yelled. He aimed his gun at the hag. "Tell me!"

The woman snickered. "You're an idiot, River. Jobon is nowhere. He never existed. Kaida never existed. The Traveller never existed."

River glared at his quarry. He was fast losing patience. "And why should I believe you?" he snapped. "Give me one good reason!"

"Believe me, or don't believe me. You can do what you like. Search this cave until you starve to death. There's nobody here. And there never will be." She cackled again. "And you believed it all, River Still. Every word of it, reeling you in. As if a world like this could have existed for so long, surviving on an economy of paint. You are pathetic."

River marched forward. He thrust his blade against the woman's throat.

"Kill me and you'll never know the truth," she warned, exposing her collection of stained, broken teeth.

"I doubt there's a truthful bone in your body."

"Look around you, then. There is no Jobon. No legend. This House only came into being a few days ago. It was never here. Not before River Still came to Neo Vale."

River shook his head. "Do you expect me to believe that?"

The hag sneered. "You should have realised long before now. The link that exists between this world and yourself…" The woman paused, and a twisted smile crawled up her face. "No, let me rephrase that." She leaned closer. "You are not connected to this world, River Still. You *are* this world."

River kept his eyes on the woman, determined not to buckle.

"When you arrived in Neo Vale," she continued, "you entered a town cloaked in psychic vapour. On its own, it is ineffectual. But you were living with Beanie Thrower, the most pious and superstitious woman in the whole city. And you told her about your nightmares, your fears. Do you not remember?"

"Yeah, I remember," said River defensively. "Me and Beanie chatted, that first morning. She was concerned about me. Big deal."

"Oh, but it is a big deal," the hag crooned. "None of this would have happened were it not for that conversation. You noticed that she made your bed for you, when you went out that morning? She wasn't just tidying up. She put a Laputan worry doll beneath your pillow. Did you not realise?"

"A what?" River scowled. "One of those stupid effigies?"

"Yes, one of those stupid effigies. They're only used by people within the Laputan faith. Idiots like Beanie think that such dolls have the power to take away a person's fears. Which is what happened to you."

"Of course it did," River jested. "If I had a nickel for every time a Laputan worry doll took away my fears..."

"Beanie Thrower was trying to protect you. She's an imbecile. The Laputan religion means nothing. But her faith was strong enough for the psychic vapour to latch onto. She really believed that the worry doll would take away your anxieties as you slept. And they did. Your horrors became real. Your horrors made this House."

The hag sniggered. "Clowns. Hospitals. Schools. The monsters from the civil war. All of your night terrors, whisked away into a twisted, subterranean world that almost made sense. Oh, if only you'd slept longer. There was so much more to take."

River shook his head. "I don't think so."

The hag simpered. "I do."

River glared at her, his teeth grinding.

"And I should know," the old woman purred, "because I am the Laputan worry doll. A totem of her misguided faith."

"Kyaaaaaaaaaaaaaaaaaaaa!" River screamed. He drove the blade into the hag's chest, revealing a body of foam and stitches.

The woman laughed. "But do you know what the hardest part was?" she mocked. "Your phobias and hang-ups were easy enough to contain, but there is something different about the great River Still." She narrowed her eyes and dropped her voice to a whisper. "His biggest fear is himself."

River froze.

"That is why I tried to take you, on the very first day," said the hag. "I failed when I confronted you in the Temple. But there's more than one way to skin a parrot, isn't there? Huhuhuhuhuhu!"

River ripped his blade out of the hag's chest and turned away.

The old woman sneered. "If I couldn't restrain you, Giles Fezziwig would," she croaked. "And if Giles Fezziwig failed, Mrs Miller would. And so on. So long as you were kept here – that was all that mattered. And now, here you are. In a pit with no means of escape."

River stood with his back to the old woman.

"Do you not believe me?" she quizzed. And then she sighed. "Of course you believe me. You can feel it. Your aura is broken. I did that to you, River. I stole a part of you." She laughed again, almost hysterical, and clapped her hands like a monkey. "I tore you apart and made a nightmare world out of the pieces! Huhuhuhuhuhu!"

River looked at her. As she cackled, a night spore clawed its way out of the pit. Followed by another. Followed by another. Slowly, the vicious monsters encircled him.

River fired without thinking.

BOKAN! BOKAN! BOKAN!

"This is the end, River Still," she taunted. "But at least you won't die in ignorance."

BOKAN! BOKAN! BOKAN!

"Oh, don't feel bad about it," the old woman scorned. "No one can blame you for missing the truth, as it danced before your eyes. All those empty chairs. Do you not remember? That one from the basement in Zen Kappa, where your mother tied you up and beat you? The worst time was when you spilled the paint. Two days you were down there." She cackled again. "Your mother was marvellous, wasn't she? She gave me so much to work with!"

River withdrew his weapons. The circle of night spores tightened. "Fine," he barked, throwing his arms out wide. "You have me. You know everything. You know everything I'm scared of, and you made it all real."

"Real and wonderful," the hag tittered.

"Hold it, Dolly. I haven't finished."

"I can wait," the woman purred. "I have all the time in the world."

"There's something I haven't mentioned. There's one thing you misjudged. There's one tiny, tiny detail that you're forgetting."

"I doubt it. Give it up, River Still. You are finished."

"Finished?" said River. "Fuck you. And your grand plan. All this time, you thought my biggest fear was myself, like I'd shudder at the sight of my own reflection. Well, I would, but that wasn't the thing that scared me the most. Why do you think I came to Neo Vale? Why do you think I didn't go to some remote tropical island, with round-the-clock sunshine and sangria?"

The old woman just leered, completely uninterested.

"You don't know?" he asked. "But I thought you were so clever."

KIII! KIII!

The noise resonated throughout the chasm.

KIIIIIIIIII!

271

River smiled. "I am terrified of flying."

"*KIIIIIIIII!*"

It was Spencer. He squawked as he swept towards the ledge. "Stand by, River Still!"

"Enjoy the cellar," River jeered, grabbing his friend's claw. "My flight is leaving."

"No!" the hag screeched. She grabbed River's leg and tugged. "You die here!"

"Nghhhhhhh!" River tried to shake her off. "Let go!"

Spencer was flapping madly. "I can't... take... the weight...!" he cried.

"Bro, she's made of foam!"

"Oh, is she?"

ZASHU!

River deployed his blade and severed the hag's arm.

"Kyaaaaaaaaaaaaaaaaaaaa!" she screamed, plunging into the darkness. She disappeared.

"Let's hope that pit is deep enough!" yelled River. He looked at his friend. "Spencer, why aren't you dead?"

"'Cos I'm sick, bro!" Spencer grinned. "They knocked me off that bridge, and I gave it wings."

They touched down on the upper ledge, right by Spencer's painting – a brown wooden hatch. It was bolted, but shuddering; the waters beyond were lapping against the panels.

"Are we still going to flood the cellar?" asked River, his hand hovering over the handle.

"We are. There may be no Jobon, but we still have the spores to contend with."

River looked down. A pack of monsters was waiting by the exit, huddled together on a shard of broken bridge.

"I can take them," said River, deploying his gun. "Wipe them out in one blast."

"I think not," said Spencer. "Let's not attract attention."

"Why? We have to go that way anyway."

"Not so. We can escape up this ramp." Spencer gestured to the stone walkway that meandered past the painting, and disappeared into the cavern. "It leads back to Neo Vale."

"What? How can you be sure?"

"Trust me, River Still." Spencer went to take cover. "Now, open the hatch."

River shrugged. "Okay," he said, taking hold of the latch. "Be it on your own feathers. Bath time for the spor-auuuuugggggghhh!"

"River!"

A spore grabbed his leg and yanked him to the ground. He smashed his head against a rock.

"Hold on, River!"

"Nghhhhhhh! To what?!" River cried, as he was dragged towards the edge.

Spencer flew to the hatch and unbolted it. "Surf's up!"

"Spencer, help me!"

"Gyaaaaaaaaaaaaaaaaaaaa!" cried Spencer, as he opened the hatch.

ZABUN!

Water cascaded into the cellar, and Spencer jumped clear.

"Guoooooooooooo!" the spore squealed, struck by the torrent. It was swept away in an inky puddle.

"Nghhhhhhh!" River jumped up. He clung desperately to the rock face, as the water splashed against him.

PASHA! PASHA!

"Quickly, River!" called Spencer. "Over here!"

"Spencer, my head…" River staggered and swayed, trying to focus. "I'm so dizzy."

"Walk towards me! You can do it!"

Everything was spinning. River's skull was throbbing with pain, and blood was running down the side of his nose.

He blinked, and slowly the image of his friend became clear.

"That's it!" said Spencer, waving. "Walk towards me!"

River ambled over. "I don't think I can make it."

"Of course you can! I'll guide you!"

There was a loud shriek. And another. And another.

River turned and saw the night spores scurrying up the side of the cavern, desperately trying to shield from the raging waters.

"What if they follow us?" he asked.

"Glad you asked!" said Spencer, opening his satchel. "We need to flood the ramp as well!" He started to paint on the rock face.

ZASHU!

River deployed his blades. "Ugh," he groaned, stumbling. "I'll… I'll cover you…"

"No River, you must hurry. I'll be right behind you."

"What?" River swayed again, his head pounding. "S-Spencer, I'm not leaving you."

"Yes you are! Now schnell! Achtung!"

"Kuuuuuuuuu!" River fell against the wall. He was so light-headed.

"Look," said Spencer, painting furiously. "If you pass out, I won't be able to drag you to the surface. It's too far. You must go!"

River rubbed his wound.

Damn. Spencer was right. He was getting dizzier by the second; there was every chance that he'd collapse and become a liability to them both.

"I won't be long, I promise," Spencer insisted. "Please, River Still! Make haste!"

River gulped.

ZASHU!

His blades retracted. "Good luck."

Spencer doffed his hat. "And to you, biped."

Groggily, River turned, and began scrambling up the path.

Fortunately, it didn't branch. River was confident that he could close his eyes, and let his legs drag him to safety.

Although he shouldn't have been. Bright colours pulsed and swirled behind his lids, like a never-ending headrush.

He clung to the wall as he shuffled through the dirt, panting and wheezing. He couldn't think straight; worry dolls and vapours and night terrors spiralled across his gaze – more information than he could possibly process.

"Nghhhhhhh!"

The cold, harsh air of Neo Vale cut into his skin. At least, he *thought* it was Neo Vale. Had he made it?

He followed the breeze to a drain cover, just above, where a soft halo of light was swirling into the passage. He mustered every last ember of strength, ramming the grill with his fist. It fell away with a thunderous clatter.

CHARA! CHARA!

"Auuuuugggggghhh!" He panted as the crisp winter winds cut into his skin. But the fresh air tasted so sweet, so wholesome.

River flung his arms onto the icy gravel, his body still half-underground. Couldn't he just die here? He had so little strength. He was beyond caring.

No! Move, River! Climb out! At least get out into the open, where you can be found.

"Kuuuuuuuu!" River moaned, hauling his weary carcass into the mud. "Aaaaaaaaaaaaa…"

He was free. He tried to stand, but his legs failed. He collapsed. He felt so empty.

Now on his knees, River dabbed his head wound, staring at the thick, sticky blood as it clung to his fingers.

He cried out. He wasn't sure why.

But then he keeled, and planted his face in a puddle.

"He's here!" a voice cried out. "We've got him!"

"Ugh," River gasped, trying to sit up. "I..."

He could hear footsteps approaching. There were voices. Someone grabbed his arm.

But it was hopeless. River closed his eyes, and everything went black.

in the chrysalis chamber

Leonard sighed, stunned at what he'd just heard. "What an incredible tale," he remarked, like his jaw was about to hit the floor. "All this time, the House was reeling you in, desperate to contain you."

"Yes, and I'd felt it," River admitted. "There was this whole thing about being restrained – Fezziwig strapping me to his canvas, and Miller locking me in her paint tin, and the doctor lashing me to his torture device. Heck, even when Jake was corrupted, tying me to that chair and leaving me."

"Did you know about the cellar?" asked Leonard. "I mean, did you realise that Jobon wouldn't be there?"

"No, I really thought he would be. I thought he'd been rooting around in my subconscious, somehow. I thought he'd come clean. Coming face to face with the worry doll surprised me, to say the least."

"It makes so much sense though. Beanie Thrower's faith and your deepest fears, activated by psychic vapour. But to think that such vapour could engineer a whole world? Incredible."

"The biggest mystery is where it came from," said River. "I know the vapour is pouring out of this tower, but there's nothing that could generate that much energy, surely?"

"Actually, there is. Look." Mango pressed his TellMe, and a projection appeared behind him. It showed an immense, comatose creature, like an octopus, its eyes burning a fiery red. It was engulfed in blue smog.

River stared at the creature, wide-eyed. "What is it?"

"The Uber SPORE," said Mango. "It's a gestalt – a super-brain built from the minds of our strongest patients. We needed a strategist – a single consciousness that could control the actions of the other SPOREs. They all share its thoughts and its feelings. They obey its commands."

River nodded. "So, the SPOREs have a hive mind."

"A hive mind, exactly. And over time, a brain of such size generates a considerable amount of psychic waste. We've been working desperately to fix the problem, but the vapour has been pouring out into Neo Vale. Anyway, this is the true creator of your House, River. This is what fed on your fears."

River glared at the entity, its tentacles bound in electrified chains. "Is it dangerous?" he asked. "I mean, all that mental energy. What if it decides it doesn't need you? What if it plots your destruction? Have you thought about that?"

"There's no need to worry," said Mango. "I've got that creature contained. The Uber SPORE is going nowhere."

"I hope so." River stood up. "Well, thank you for your time, Leonard. I think we can conclude this little assessment, yes?"

Mango looked stunned. "Conclude? River, you must stay! I can't let you walk out of my life!"

River paused. "What did you have in mind?"

"Work with me!" Mango dashed over. "Help me perfect the SPORE programme. You have the one thing I don't have. Artistry! Think what the Mango corporation could achieve with your skills!"

River smiled. "Wow, I'm flattered," he replied. "It's very kind of you, Leonard, but as I said – this assessment is at an end." He clicked his fingers.

"What do you mean?"

The door to the Chrysalis Chamber opened, and Felix Fuhrmann stepped inside, followed by a complement of guards. They were armed, and had their weapons trained on Mango.

The CEO froze. "What the hell is this?"

"You are to come with us, sir," said Felix. "You qualify for the SPORE programme."

"For the what?"

"You weren't assessing me," said River, simpering. "I was assessing you. The whole point of the SPORE programme is to rid the world of the mentally ill, right? And turn them into SPOREs? Well, I've found just the man – Leonard Mango himself. He'll make a perfect SPORE."

Mango's fade reddened. "That's what this was? That's why you told me that ridiculous story?"

"Ridiculous? I thought it was very well put together. It got you talking, anyway. You even opened up about your post-traumatic stress, and your anxieties. So thanks, I appreciate your honesty."

Mango's jaw dropped. "You manipulative son of a bitch."

"Thanks pot. I'm the kettle."

Felix turned to his troops. "Take him."

"No wait!" yelled Mango, retreating. "You think you're so smart? I knew that you were making it up! I sussed it way back! You expect me to believe that you're friends with a talking parrot, who can paint cocoa and carry humans in its claws? What a bunch of crap!"

"Oh yeah," River sniggered. "Crap of the highest order. Don't you agree, Spencer?"

"Completely," came a voice from the corridor. "Utter codswallop."

Mango's eyes widened as a second group entered the chamber: two twins, a parrot and a young girl.

The parrot doffed his hat. "Guten Tag."

Mango grinded his teeth. "No! It's a trick!"

Natsuki activated her blades. "I only wish it were."

"Everything he told you was true," said Jake. "We've been next door, recording the whole thing."

"Top quality content," said Jazz, holding up her camera. "I can't wait to post it on Yapper."

Mango made a fist. "You little-!"

"Freeze!" a guard yelled, raising his gun. "That's far enough, sir."

"But how could you know?" Mango hissed. "You expect me to believe that you had some great plan? That you'd tell me a sad story, and I'd somehow be triggered? You couldn't possibly know that!"

"Not under ordinary circumstances," River admitted. "But we had a little help. Will you tell him Jazz, or shall I?"

Jazz opened her rucksack and produced a leather-bound book. "The complete life of River Still," she announced. "A full account of everything."

Mango gasped. "What?"

"You don't remember?" she asked. "I found it in the library, in the Academy of Reason. And it's a good thing I did, because this book told us exactly what to do."

25: tears

The first thing River felt was a bed. It was soft, and warm. And there was light chatter all around him – a cluster of soft, nervous whispers.

"Yes, you've really captured something," said Spencer. "This will do nicely."

"Are you sure it's not too fat?" said Natsuki.

River broke his eyes open. He was in a messy bedroom, under a purple duvet, with scrunched-up clothes carpeting its floor. Video game cartridges and magnetic tapes crammed the overflowing shelves.

Everyone was here. In one corner, Spencer and Natsuki were poring over a curious robot shell, which Natsuki was adjusting with a petroscope. In another, Jazz was examining a bulky leather book. Jake, on the other hand, was scrolling through the news feed on his cell. He farted.

"Aw Jake," Jazz protested. "That's disgusting."

"What?" said Jake. "It's only natural."

"Yeah, well so's poo - it doesn't mean I want it in my room."

"Piku piku!" a machine chirped. "Pii piiiiiii!"

River's ears pricked up. What was that? A robot? A bird?

Slowly, he sat up. His head was bandaged, and a circular drone was hovering over his face, scanning his skin with a gold beam of light.

"Pon pon!" it trilled. "Pikuuuuuuuu!"

"Wha...?" he groaned, blinking. "Who are you?"

"He's awake," said Natsuki, dashing over. "Oh River, it's so good to see you!"

"Hmmmmmmmfffff," grunted River, rubbing his face. "Who's your friend?"

"Oh, that's Koro. He's been monitoring your vital signs."

"Pi! Piku! Piiiiii!" Koro bleeped.

"He says you're dehydrated."

"Piku!" Koro opened a panel, and a jet of water doused him. Everyone laughed. River was dripping.

"I feel like I've just had an operation," he remarked, dabbing his face with the duvet. "Whose bedroom is this?"

"Mine," said Jazz. "Welcome."

279

"Yeah, we didn't want to put you in the bunk," said Jake. "And my mom insisted that we take care of you, so…"

River smiled. "Your mom's caring almost got me killed." Then he realised. "Oh, wait. You don't know, do you? About the House?"

"Actually, we do," replied Jazz. "We know everything."

"Everything?" River looked Spencer. He must have told them. "Oh. Thanks."

He doffed his hat. "You are most welcome, River Still. But it wasn't me."

"Huh?"

"Look," said Jazz. "Perhaps we should do this later? You've only just come round, and-"

"Do what?" River sat up urgently, and screamed. Every bone hurt; his entire body was throbbing with pain. "Augghhhhh! Damn night spores! I'm burning up!"

"Piku piku!" chirped Koro and squirted him again.

"You need rest, River," Natsuki chuckled, as she folded the covers around him. "We can talk when you're better."

"No!" River protested, slapping her away. "We can talk now! I'm fine!"

"It's a lot to take in, bro," Jake warned. "It could mess with your head."

"I ain't scared. Koro's got my back. Right, Koro?"

"Pii! Piiiiiii!"

"Okay," said Jazz. "If you insist." She held up the book. "Do you know what this is?"

River shrugged. "My eulogy?"

"It's from the Academy of Reason. Do you remember the forbidden Grown-Up Section, in the library? The compendium of all knowledge?"

River looked suspicious. "Yes…"

"Well, they had a book on you. And this it – the complete biography of River Still, composed by the seer, Raymond Reason. Everything you've ever done, and everything you ever will."

River's eyes widened. Geez, somebody had documented his entire life? His future? His past?

Oh man. Had Jazz read it?

"Don't worry, I haven't read it," said Jazz. "Well, not all of it. There's a ton of stuff about your childhood that we skipped past, and towards the end it's all written in this weird language that we can't translate. So we can't, like, work out how you're going to die or anything."

"Oh," said River. "Good to know."

"But it documents our time in the House," Jazz went on. "Like, everything we've done, from the moment we arrived. Including your confrontation with the worry doll in the cellar."

"So you know what the House is?" River cut in. "You know that it's fake? That the worry doll took all my fears and made a messed-up world to try and contain me?"

"Yeah, because of the fog," Jazz answered. "It's psychic vapour, right? It fed off my mom's faith, and your fears. But it also produced this prophecy – an account of the future. It tells us what we need to do, how to save Neo Vale."

River hesitated. "I thought we *were* saving Neo Vale?"

"Yes, but not in the way we thought. The fact is, Leonard Mango is using his company to track down 'undesirables' and turn them into SPOREs. You remember Leonard Mango, right? CEO of the Mango Corporation? He's deranged. He wants to lower the country's mental health stats by snatching people off the streets and turning them into these creatures. He's trying to build an army."

River gulped. "So those creatures I saw in Mango Tower? They were once people? Like, human beings? And they're being turned into SPOREs?"

"Exactly."

"But that's crazy."

Jazz nodded. "I know. But if we're to save Neo Vale from the SPOREs, we need to bring Mango down. We need to break him – show him that he, too, is a tortured creature, just like the people he converts."

"Well, he's hardly going to listen to us, is he?" said River. "I doubt a quick conversation with me is going to force him into a U-turn."

"Actually," said Jake, "that's *exactly* what's going to happen."

"What?" River looked puzzled. "How?"

"By the power of your story," Jazz explained. "Everything you've done, from your arrival in Neo Vale to defeating the worry doll. It's enough to break him."

River looked lost. "Break him? How's it going to break him?"

"He'll project onto you. He'll see himself in you."

River's eyes widened.

"Freaky, isn't it?" Jake chuckled. "But that's not the best part. Tell him, sis."

Jazz shuffled, uncomfortably. "You tell him."

"Alright." Jake smiled. "It's your relationship with me that really gets him going."

River's cheeks reddened. "M-my what?"

Jake winked.

"He'll conclude that your situation with Jake is just like the situation he had with Brent, his dead partner," said Jazz. "It's not, of course, but he'll hear what he wants to hear. Listening to your story will trigger him, open the floodgates..."

"That's worrying," said River.

"It's what the book tells us to do," Jazz replied. "If Mango interrogates you, and you recount your story, he'll buckle. He'll repent, and close down the SPORE programme."

River sighed. "And you believe all this? Just because it's written in some book? How do we know we can trust it?"

"It's been pretty accurate so far," Jake interjected. "Like, it said that you were going to trick us with that fake door and ditch us."

River looked stunned. "You knew that was going to happen?"

"Totally," Jake grinned. "How was my acting?"

"That's also why we were at the House, right after the attack on the station," said Jazz. "The book told us to go there and wait for you. Actually, we got there before the attack began."

"And if it helps," Spencer added, "I also knew that you were going to shout at me and knock my easel over. No surprises for Spencer von Luft."

River clutched the sides of his head. "Okay, this is too much."

Natsuki put her arm round him. "Hey," she whispered, rubbing his shoulder. "It's okay."

River looked at her. "And what about you, Natsuki? How do you fit into all this?"

Natsuki smiled. "I'm your protector, silly."

"Yes, but how did you get hooked up with these guys? How long have you known?"

"Oh, not very long," she admitted. "I came here looking for you, and your friends invited me in. They told me everything."

"And did you mention the part about being a cyborg?" asked River.

ZASHU!

Natsuki unleashed her blades. "I did."

"My, my – there's two of you now," Spencer chuckled. "What fun this will be."

A week later, the gang returned to the wasteland, ready to put their plan into operation. It was a cold, grey morning; the wind clawed at their faces as they avoided plumes of grit, and old crisp packets darted in the breeze.

Jazz was carrying River's book, which she read like a map. "Okay, this is the time and place," she announced. "You've got about twenty minutes until the troopers arrive."

River groaned. "Is that all? I need to pee."

"Go right ahead," said Jake. "I'll help you."

"Please don't," said Spencer, perched on Jazz's shoulder. He peered into the book. "Now, it says here that they will track the signal from your TellMe."

"Which I have here," said Natsuki, producing it from her coat. She took hold of River's wrist. "From what I can tell, it's the strap that reads your thoughts. It will identify you and emit a signal. They're still looking for you after the incident at the stadium, remember?"

"Wait, aren't they looking for you too?" asked River, as Natsuki fastened the device. "They were chasing both of us."

"I managed to talk them round, with Koro's help," she replied. "After I'd destroyed a few cop drones, that is."

River grinned. "Vandal."

The TellMe's interface lit up. "It's working," said Natsuki. "It'll start to transmit."

"Then we need to go," Jazz warned. "We can't be here when they arrive."

"You're going to rendezvous with Felix, right?" asked River.

"Yeah, he'll let us into Mango Tower and take us to the assessment facility. We'll be watching the whole thing, so we'll be close by if you need us."

"River won't need us," Spencer chirped. "He's the most talented biped I know."

River smiled. And that's when he realised that Natsuki was still holding his hand. He looked at her, and she quickly let go.

"Uhh," she stuttered, as if she hadn't realised. "Could me and River have a moment? There's something I need to tell him."

"Of course," Jazz replied. "Come on, Jake."

"You go," he said, staring at River. "I need to talk to him too."

Jazz rolled her eyes. "Oh, for heaven's sake. He's not on death row. We need to meet up with Felix!"

"I know, I'll be right with you," Jake snapped. "Go on."

Reluctantly, and rolling her eyes, Jazz complied, trudging through the mud like a child sent to her room.

Natsuki reached up to River's neck and lifted the pendant from under his shirt. It was the medallion of the two dragons – the one that she'd given him, all that time ago.

"See," said River, impishly. "I still wear it."

Natsuki smiled as she dangled the emblem between her fingers. "Can I pray for you, River? Would that be okay?"

"Oh," said River, taken aback. His entire body went stiff. "I don't have to if–"

"No, it's fine." He paused, and then smiled. "Actually, I'd like it if you did."

"Then bow your head."

River did as instructed, and closed his eyes.

"Meldesta," Natsuki breathed. "Delmesta. O dragon gods, warriors of the unseen realm. My friend is burdened. His load is a heavy one. Hear my prayer, this day. Protect River Still. Grant him the strength to walk the road ahead. Grant him wisdom. Grant him a compassionate heart. Banish the forces of darkness, my gods."

His friend fell silent, and River sighed. He felt so warm. "Thank you."

"Oh," said Natsuki, stunned. "I hadn't finished."

River froze. He went red. "You hadn't?"

Natsuki pushed him playfully. "Of course I had!" she giggled. "You're so easy, River Still!"

"What?"

"Your face!" Natsuki laughed. "You embarrass so easily!"

"Ahem!" said Jake, stepping between them. "We're on the clock here, guys."

Natsuki stifled her giggles and moved away. "My apologies, Jake. I didn't realise. Do you need to speak to River?"

"Yes," said Jake, folding his arms. "Yes, I do."

Natsuki gazed at him, her smile fading. "Of course." She began to withdraw. "Then I guess I'll see you at the tower."

"Yep," said Jake, curtly. "Bye then."

Confused, Natsuki gave a gentle wave, and walked away.

"Phew." Jake turned to his friend. "I thought she'd never leave."

"She was just being nice," River reminded him, tucking the pendant away.

"Yeah, but you're not meant to be looking all fresh-faced and smiley when you get arrested. You're meant to look battered and bruised, like you're on the brink of a nervous breakdown."

"Battered and bruised? How am I supposed to do that?"

"Well." Jake ruffled River's hair. "We can mess this up for a start. Make it look like you haven't washed in a while."

River grinned. "Actually, that's kinda true. I've been poring over that stupid book all week."

"That explains the grease. We should dirty your face as well."
Jake reached into the mud and scooped up some gunk. "Are you ready
for a facial?"

River chuckled. "Yeah Jake, you can give me a facial."

As if applying cream, Jake slowly caressed River's cheeks,
smearing the dirt across his face. It was quite relaxing, really; River gazed
lovingly at his friend as his fingers pressed into his skin. And after a
moment, their eyes locked.

Grinning, Jake leaned in.

"Don't," said River, turning his head. "Please don't."

It was awkward. Jake looked down, as if scrambling for
something to say.

Then an idea struck him. "Oh!" he exclaimed, reaching into his
pocket. He pulled out a pen knife. "We should rip your jeans as well."

"Do you have to?"

"Hey, if Mango suspects anything, even for a second, then it's
game over." He crouched down. "It's got to look real."

"That's true."

BART! BART!

Jake ripped through the fabric with his mini blade, tearing the
jeans at the kneecap. "Nice," he chuckled, as if impressed with his artistic
mastery. "You've been beaten up good."

River laughed, trying to process the craziness of it all. "Thanks,
man."

"Now, are you sure you're going to be okay?"

"Yes of course," said River. "I remember the whole story. As
long as I don't deviate from it, we'll get the outcome we need. Mango
will have a change of heart, and the SPORE programme will end."

Jake nodded, like he wasn't entirely convinced. "It's just, they're
going to take you away, aren't they? In that van."

"Yeah. They'll put me in cuffs and bundle me into the back. I
guess it'll be a long interrogation. Not the nicest thing in the world."

Jake nodded again. He clearly wasn't happy.

"What's the matter?" asked River.

"Nothing," he croaked. "Just be careful."

"You're saying that now, after everything I've done? Jake,
Mango Tower is the easy part."

"I mean it, River. Please watch yourself."

River stared at him. "Look, they're not going to put me to the
torture."

"Well, if they do, they'll have me to answer to."

"I'd like to see that," said River.

285

Jake trembled. Two tears trickled down his cheeks. "I'll be really pissed if you get killed," he muttered.

"I'm not going to get killed. Don't cry, Jake."

"I'm not. It's just the wind."

"Right." River opened his arms. "That's my excuse, too."

The pair hugged, and Jake clung tightly to River. He buried his face in his chest and cried out.

"Auuuuuggggghhh!" came the scream, almost primal. "Ngh! Nghhhhhhh!"

River stroked his head. Jake sniffed and eventually pulled away, dabbing his eyes.

"You have to go," said River. "I'll be fine."

Jake just nodded, his eyes red. He didn't speak. He turned and headed back towards the road. River watched him as he disappeared into the throngs of people.

He took a deep breath. "Okay," he said, rubbing his cold hands. "Now the fun really begins."

River crouched down and positioned himself in the mud. He inched towards a nearby puddle and rested his face in the filthy waters.

He was ready. He was doing this. He needed to pee.

And that's when he heard the sirens.

in the chrysalis chamber

"So, thanks for the ride," said River, finishing his story. "Your troopers were quite gentle. They weren't the worst kidnappers in the world. And hey, they got me here."

Mango just scowled. "You really are a cocky son of a bitch, aren't you?"

"Seriously, are we done?" Felix snapped. "He's heard enough."

"You're so trigger-happy," said River. "Are you seriously going to condemn him? He's about to repent."

Mango snorted. "Like hell I'm gonna repent! Are you crazy? Whatever gave you that idea?"

River looked at him. "But the book said you'd renounce your ways, that you'd cancel the SPORE programme."

"Well guess what, kid!" Mango raised his TellMe. "Someone's changed the script!"

River froze. "What are you doing?"

"Condemning you all! I always win, River – whatever the cost! I thought you knew that?"

"Move again and you're a dead man," warned Felix.

"We're all dead!" Mango yelled. "None of us will survive this!"

"He's mad," Natsuki gasped.

"But what did we do wrong?" asked Jake. "We followed the prophecy to the letter."

"But it ended here," Jazz replied. "In the Chrysalis Chamber. It didn't tell us what happens next."

"And you're forgetting something," River added. "The prophecy didn't say Mango would repent. It said he'd have a change of heart. There's a difference."

"Aw," Mango mocked. "Has your plan gone a bit wrong, kids?"

"That's it, move out!" snapped Felix. The guards seized Mango. "Take him to the laboratory!"

"Wait!" River shouted. "You can't kill him!"

Felix shoved him aside. "Thanks for your help, River. We'll take it from here."

"No!" River drove through the troops and blocked the door. He looked at Mango. "You know what they're going to do to you, right? Do you seriously want to die?"

"I'm being true to myself," Mango growled. "I will not repent."

"Auuuuuggggghhh!" River screamed, deploying his gun.

"River, don't!" Natsuki cried.

River aimed his weapon at the troops. "Release Leonard Mango! Now!"

The CEO laughed. "The Boss said you were special," he chortled. "A special kinda stupid, that is. Why else do you think I conducted the interrogation myself? He told me to find you, to bring you in."

"The Boss?" said Jazz, confused. "Who's the Boss?"

Mango broke free and hovered his finger over his TellMe. "The Uber SPORE. The gestalt. Your book didn't mention that part, did it? I wonder why…"

"Hands on your head, sir!" a soldier barked.

"You've no idea how powerful that creature is," warned Mango. "Why do you think I kept it in chains? Once it's free, it cannot be stopped."

The soldier raised his gun. "Sir, you have three seconds or we open fire."

"You want to kill me?" said Mango. "Go ahead. The Boss will obliterate us all. River, I believe you said that I would have a change of heart? Well, apparently you were right."

"Mango, listen!" screamed River. "You don't have to do this!"

"River, I will shoot you if you don't step aside," said Felix. "Move!"

"Leave it, River!" yelled Natsuki. "He means it!"

"I always win," Mango sneered. "You really thought you'd beaten me? River Still, you haven't saved Neo Vale. You've brought about its destruction."

Mango pressed his TellMe.

"Fire!" screamed Felix.

BOKAN! BOKAN! BOKAN!

Bullets tore through Mango, and he fell.

Alarms began to blare.

GIRIGIRI! GIRIGIRI!

"What's happening?" Jake yelled, as the building shook. Everyone stumbled.

"Somehow, I don't think the man was bluffing," said Spencer.

Felix turned to his squadron. "Okay, top floor! Now!"

"If the Boss is free, he's not going to stay there," said River. "You should evacuate the building."

"We can get to him before he escapes," said Felix.

There was another shudder.

"He's already escaped," River insisted. "You're wasting time!"

"Thank you River, but we're done here." Felix waved at his guards. "Proceed to the elevator! Immediately!"

"Sir!"

"Yes sir!"

"Dammit!" cried River, punching the wall.

There was another tremor.

𝐎𝐎𝐎𝐎𝐎𝐎𝐎𝐎𝐎𝐎𝐎𝐎𝐎𝐎!

"Guys, we gotta move," said Jazz. "It's not safe in here."

"She's right, River," said Natsuki, grabbing him. "Come on!"

26: obliteration

River and his friends burst out of the lobby and onto the street. All around them, people were screaming.

"Okay, so where in the book was the apocalypse part?" said Jake.

"Look, it didn't mention the end of the world!" River insisted. "It said Mango would have a change of heart, and everything would end!"

"Well, pretty accurate so far!" Jazz yelled.

There was a loud roar, and the tower trembled. River and his friends grabbed each other.

"Attack formation," Natsuki ordered, deploying her weapons.

Jake looked aghast. "We don't *have* an attack formation!"

"We do now!" said Natsuki. "Get behind me!"

The gang watched as the top of the tower exploded. They were showered in dust and stones.

Defiant, River activated his gun and pointed at the sky. The building was shrouded in a corona of blue vapour, folding into the shape of a mushroom.

Then the ground quaked. Every window in the building shattered, and SPOREs burst through the shards. The gang looked on as a tentacled beast rose out of the smog, its flailing legs ensnaring the building's frame.

"It's the fog!" Jake shouted, pointing. "D'you see it? That's the fog that's been filling Neo Vale!"

"It's psychic energy!" said Natsuki. "Pure psychic energy! Generated by its brain!"

"Augh!" Jazz screamed, firing arrows.

SUKA! SUKA! SUKA!

The monster didn't flinch.

River, furious, charged his weapon to maximum strength.

"Plasma!" he cried out, blasting the creature with a white-hot beam.

"It's not working!" yelled Jazz. "It's not even scratched!"

"Kuuuuuuuu!" River seethed, firing again. "Kyaaaaaaa!"

A monstrous, guttural laugh thundered through the air. It was the creature. "Huhuhuhuhuhu! Leonard Mango is dead! His hold is no more! The Boss is free!"

River gazed through the plumes of smog and dust. The Boss was perched at the top of the tower, its brain like the body of a black octopus, rigid and slimy.

"Guys, I need to get up there!" said River. "To the creature!"

"Great!" replied Jake. "How's your flying?"

"I'll take you up there," Spencer offered, spreading his wings.

"No way," said Jazz, pulling him back. "You'll be pulverised!"

"SPOREs!" the Boss thundered. "Attack!"

Suddenly, a flurry of screams filled the air. More employees swarmed out of the building, crowding the entrance. Immediately the monsters pounced, ripping the workers limb from limb.

Natsuki glared, wide-eyed. "We must do something!"

"I plan to!" River declared, readying his gun. "I'm taking that guy out!"

"Dude, your gun doesn't work!" Jake shouted. "You've already tried!"

"I'm too far down, that's why!" River insisted. "If I can get close to him, concentrate my fire, I can kill him!"

"You'll never make it through the lobby!" said Jazz. "Look! It's a massacre down there!"

River glared at the tower. There was a thin, bevelled pillar running along the outer edge. He then looked at the Boss.

"No!" Jazz snapped, reading his mind. "You'll fall!"

"I'm a good climber!"

"Wait, what?" said Jake. "What did I miss?"

"He wants to climb the tower!" Jazz told him. She glowered at River. "And it's not happening!"

"Jazz, we have no other choice!" said River, and raced towards the building.

"He's right, we've no other choice!" said Natsuki, chasing after him. She quickly turned back. "Can you cover us?"

"What? No!" Jazz screamed, but her protests went unheard. "I can't cover you on my own! Come back!"

"You're not on your own!" said Jake, twirling his sword. "The SPORE Slayer has got your back!"

"Oh, fuck."

"Perhaps we should all take cover," Spencer suggested, squeezing into a trash can. "Come on, you two!"

"Oh sure!" Jazz snapped. "I'll just lose a hundred pounds and I'll be right there!"

A SPORE pounced forward, and Jake swiped it away.

"Jeff, you cover River and Natsuki with your arrows!" he said. "I'll cover you with my sword!"

Terrified, Jazz glared at the tower.

This wasn't going to work.

River and Natsuki circled the screaming masses. They tussled their way to the side of the tower, where rows of dumpsters were lined up. They scrambled onto a crate, and then catapulted themselves through the air, colliding with the edge of the building.

"Augh!" screamed River, as he grabbed the concrete pillar. "Natsuki, are you good?"

"I'm good!" his friend replied, ripping a piece of glass out of her hand. "I'm glad to be a cyborg right now!"

"Same." River reached up and started to climb. "Let's do this."

"You cannot win, River Still!" the Boss boomed. "I am the SPORE of all SPOREs!"

"Well, they're gonna be pretty lost without you," River jibed.

"Aughhhhh!" the Boss yelled. He swiped his tentacle into the side of the building and made it shake.

"Nghhhhhh!" River cried, losing his grip. He swung, one-handed, from the concrete pillar.

Natsuki scrambled towards him and grabbed his legs. "I've got you!" she shouted. "Hold on!"

"Huhuhuhuhuhu!" the Boss chuckled, and swiped again.

"Kuuuuuuuu!" Natsuki ducked. "Surely he can't keep this up?"

"I think he'll be distracted!" said River. "Look!"

The sound of pulse engines filled the air, and swirling spotlights danced across the tower. Natsuki looked up, and watched as a squadron of helicopters hovered towards the creature.

"Lock on target!" a voice boomed. "Fire on my command!"

"Huhuhuhuhuhu!" the Boss cackled. "A wasted effort! You puny, pathetic creatures! You are but insects!"

Natsuki watched the machines as they tightened their net.

"Open fire!" came the order.

Energy bolts punched out of the helicopters and pounded the Boss.

BAKI! BAKI! BAKI!

They bounced off him like rubber balls.

"Did they get him?" River asked.

A savage tentacle flailed through the air. It struck one of the machines, and then another, and then another. Warning alarms blared. The helicopters spun violently out of control.

"Emergency! Emergency!" a voice cried. "Status critical! Reinforcements requested! Gyaaaaaaaaaaaaaaaaaaaa!"

The machine plummeted. As did the second. And the third.

BUWA! BUWA! BUWA!

They exploded.

River felt the intense heat of the flames.

"Dammit, Jake and Jazz!" he screamed. "Are they okay?"

"They're good, I can see them!" Natsuki yelled. "Keep moving!"

"You are climbing to your death!" the Boss warned. "I cannot be beaten!"

"No one's immortal!" River snapped. "You are not a god!"

"I build and I destroy!" the Boss snarled. "What am I if not God?"

Natsuki looked shocked. "Wait, he can hear you?"

"You were made in a lab!" River insisted. "Designed by a madman! Held in chains!"

"And now unfettered!"

SUUUUUUKA!

The Boss thrashed his tentacle again. "The ultimate weapon of destruction!"

"Oh yeah?" River jeered. "Wouldn't have gotten very far without me, would you? Or Beanie? Or the vapour?"

"Huhuhuhuhuhu!" the Boss sneered. "I *made* the vapour! I saw the future – I saw what could become! My psychic energy set in motion a chain of events that triggered my release!"

"But you still relied on me!"

"You were but a pawn! A lamb to the slaughter! You really believed that Mango would repent!"

"River, look out!" Natsuki yelled.

A SPORE leapt out of the window and swiped at him. River swung, dodging its attack.

"Keep still!" Natsuki shouted. She deployed her gun. "I'm going to shoot it!"

"No, I've got this!"

"River get down! Augh!" Natsuki fired.

BOKAN! BOKAN! BOKAN!

The shots ripped through the creature. It shrieked and tumbled out of the window.

"Nice aim!" River's fingers drove into the concrete. He scurried upwards, calling out: "When we reach the top, we'll-"

"I know, be quiet!" Natsuki yelled. "He can hear us, remember!"

293

"This is futile!" the Boss crooned. "Why would you throw your lives away?"

"You don't know?" River retorted. "I thought you were a god?"

"Ignore him!" Natsuki warned. "He's trying to distract you!"

"I'd rather die than live in a world governed by you!" River continued. "A tentacled maniac, hell-bent on chaos!"

"Huhuhuhuhuhu!" the Boss chortled. "You think this is chaos? You've seen nothing yet!"

River propelled himself onto the roof and deployed his blades. "What are you gonna do?" he quipped. "Go out on a limb?"

BAN!

He severed its tentacle.

"Kyaaaaaaaaaaaaaaaaaaaa!" the Boss screamed.

Natsuki arrived and drove her blade into the creature. A fountain of black blood splattered onto the concrete.

Together, they thrust their weapons into the Boss' face.

"Surrender!" Natsuki ordered. "You are beaten!"

The monster guffawed. His severed limb quickly grew back and spilled over the side of the tower. "I am God," he boomed. "I surrender to no one. I am forever!"

River and Natsuki nodded at each other. They closed their eyes and deployed their guns. Both grimaced as the barrels glowed, the energy rising.

"Kuuuuuuuu!" River screamed, as his arm throbbed. "Nghhhhhhh!"

The light was dazzling. River and Natsuki unloaded their weapons in unison. The Boss was blinded by a beam of white light, which crackled and pulsed. The pair cried out.

"Huhuhuhuhuhu!" the monster teased. There was no mouth; his voice thundered into their brains. "You are both immensely entertaining! River Still, I shall miss you the most!"

"Augh!" River yelled, his energy depleted. Furious, he slashed his blade across the monster's face. It bounced off, as if shielded.

"Have you quite finished?" said the Boss.

"Aaaaaaaaaaaaa!" River seethed. "Have I finished? What about you? You're the one with the great masterplan!"

"This was fated!" the Boss rebuked. "My release was inevitable! And you all performed beautifully!"

River glared into the creature's eyes. There must be a weakness. There must!

"Huhuhuhuhuhu!" the Boss laughed. "Even now I can hear your thoughts. The anger, the hate flowing through you. You're staring into the face of death itself, yet you deny it. You refuse to believe that your life ends here!"

"If you were going to kill me," River snarled, "you'd have done it already."

"You are my plaything!" the Boss giggled. "I shall dispose of you at my leisure! Listen to your God!"

"Augghhhhh!" River screamed. He fell to his knees, clutching his temples in agony. The blue vapour swirled around him, thicker than ever.

"Accept it!" the Boss purred. "Know these truths before you die! Your father is dead! He is gone! He is nowhere!"

"No!" River cried, as his dad stepped into view. He could see him in Zen Kappa, surrounded by guards, his arms raised. A command was given, and the bullets ripped through his clothes.

BOKAN! BOKAN! BOKAN!

He fell.

"No!" screamed River, his head burning. "It's a lie!"

"Your mother never loved you. She pounded you with religious rhetoric! She beat you, she ignored you, she neglected you!"

"Nghhhhhhh!" River was suddenly at home – an unseen force was dragging him towards an empty chair. He was forced down, and thick coils wrapped around him, squeezing the air out of his throat, choking him. Then he was punched, and slapped, and kicked. He cried out, tortured. The pain was so real.

"You are helpless, River Still!" the Boss went on. "You are still the feeble little boy that no one loves."

River screamed, his eyes watering. His brain was on fire.

"And now," the Boss whispered, "as you prepare to die, you will fall headlong into the void. Friendless, and alone."

"Kuuuuuuuu!" River fought, his strength evaporating. "I…" he stammered. "I have Jake! I have S-Spencer!"

"Huhuhuhuhuhu!" the monster crowed. "No you don't! They are even weaker than you are!"

"I have Natsuki!" River choked. "I have J-Jazz!"

"Then where are they?" the Boss laughed. "Where are these saviours of yours? Where is your strength now?"

"Right here!" Natsuki cried, firing her weapon. A beam of immense energy burst out of the barrel.

The Boss laughed as he absorbed the power. He glowed momentarily, and fired back.

"Augh!" Natsuki cried.

ZASHU!

Her arm twisted into a shield, and she blocked the attack.

But the power was too great. The beam of light was burning through her defence.

"N-Natsuki!" River cried. "No!"

"Kuuuuuuuu!" she screamed. "Run, River! Nghh! While you still can!"

River tried to stand, but staggered. He fell to the floor.

"The battle ends here!" the Boss declared. "Above me there is no higher power!"

"Yes there is!" Natsuki yelled, her shield melting. "Faith! The faith that freed you!"

"Inconsequential! Beanie Thrower will be crushed! Her part in this story is over!"

Natsuki looked at the blue smoke as it coiled around her. "Beanie Thrower is not the only one with faith! Nghhh!"

"Huhuhuhuhuhu!" the Boss chortled. "Perhaps you refer to yourself? You too are weak, Natsuki Hashino! Where was your faith when River rejected you?"

"Nghhh! My faith is stronger than it's ever been!" she shouted, the fumes swirling. "As is your vapour!"

The Boss paused. "What?"

There was a spark within the smoke, and energy began to crackle.

BARI! BARI! BARI!

"Come Meldesta!" Natsuki commanded. "Come Delmesta! O dragon gods, warriors of the unseen realm! Save Neo Vale! I beg you! I implore you!"

Two ferocious dragons leapt out of the fumes. They glowed a brilliant yellow, and throbbed with power.

"Uraaaaaaaaaa!" they roared. "Uryaaaaaaaaaa!"

"Attack the false god!" Natsuki yelled. "Nghhh! Attack the Boss! Hear my prayer!"

"What is this trickery?" the Boss growled. "I will not be deceived!"

Meldesta charged at the creature and swiped its talons across his face. The Boss cried out in agony.

"This is my faith!" Natsuki cried. "The same power that made the House! It shall destroy you! Augh!"

Delmesta plunged from the tower roof and into the crowd below. It lashed at the SPOREs.

"I am immortal!" the Boss declared. "I am life eternal! I cannot die!"

Wincing, River staggered to his feet and deployed his blade.

ZASHU!

He screamed, and severed the creature's leg.

"Augghhhhh!" the Boss cried. "Nooooooooooo!"

He ceased his attack, and Natsuki was released. She swooned.

"Natsuki!" River yelled. He caught her.

"I am the SPORE of all SPOREs!" the Boss thundered. "I am the master! I am God!"

"Uryaaaaaaaaaa!" roared Meldesta, swiping furiously. "Uryaaaaaaaaaa!"

"Augghhhhh!" The Boss slumped.

"You did it, Natsuki!" said River. "He's dying!"

Meldesta swooped and scratched and growled, and ripped through the Boss' skin. Black blood spewed onto the rooftop.

"You underestimated Natsuki's faith!" River shouted, standing up. "And her resolve!"

He ran to the edge of the roof and looked down. Delmesta was slaying the SPOREs, one by one.

"Help me, River Still," the Boss gasped, feebly. "Help me, please!"

River glared at the withering creature. "You," he hissed, raising his blade, "cannot be helped."

"You can't let them kill me!" the creature wept. It was the voice of his father. "I need you, Ryū!"

River pressed his weapon into the Boss' face. "Get out of my head," he demanded.

BAN!

He drove the blade into his skull.

"Auuugghhh!" the monster whimpered. "Kuuuuuuuu!"

The vapour was thinning. Delmesta re-joined her twin, and the two dragons roared as their glow began to wane. River looked into the eyes of the awesome creatures, and they bowed.

"Come and find me," the Boss persisted, his voice but a whisper. "I am at the river still. I am at the river still. Augh…"

The monster floundered. The smoke cleared, and the two dragons faded from view.

"Nghhhhh!" Spencer gasped, falling out of the bin. He was clutching his chest.

"Spencer!" cried Jazz, dashing to his side. She tried to grab him, but she couldn't. Her hand passed through his body.

"What is it?" said Jake, joining her. "What's happening?"

Spencer looked at the pair. "It's alright," he panted, and smiled. "It's alright."

"Spencer," Jazz uttered. "You're disappearing."

"No." Spencer stood up, smiling. He was completely transparent. "You are hallucinating. It's the vapour."

Jake and Jazz looked at each other.

"So," Spencer went on, gazing at the tower. "They did it then? They defeated the Boss?"

"Yeah," Jake croaked. "He's dead."

"Sehr gut. This calls for a celebration." He smacked his beak. "Who's for pizza?"

Jazz's lip began to tremble. Spencer had almost faded completely. "Sure," she stammered. "That sounds great."

"I knew I could tempt you, Jazz. Let's go back to the House." He started to walk. "Now we mustn't forget the kale, and the macadamia nuts. Oh, and the extra helpings of papaya..."

Jazz and Jake watched as he disappeared into the smoke. Within seconds, he was gone.

At the top of the tower, an eerie calm descended. Dust clouds swirled, and the faint ring of sirens resonated in the distance.

"You did it, Natsuki," said River, cradling his friend. "The Boss is dead."

Natsuki smiled. "The gods did it," she uttered. "I knew they would. I knew they would come."

"You did it too," River insisted. "You saved me."

His friend jolted, convulsing in pain.

River tightened his grip. "It's okay, I've got you."

Natsuki stared at him. "Is this what dying feels like?"

River bit down on his lip, and grunted. "No."

Natsuki winced. "I suppose it makes sense now, doesn't it? Why you and I were brought together." She paused. "I was meant to die here, wasn't I?"

River just stared.

"I only realised when I read your book," Natsuki whispered. "Suddenly it all made sense. You know who I am, don't you?"

"No." River searched her eyes. "Tell me."

Natsuki grimaced, and a tear rolled down her cheek. "Augh," she spluttered, as if choking. "Yes, you do."

"Natsuki, I don't."

She looked at him. "I am what you are afraid of."

River lost his grip. He staggered. Natsuki was fading. He could see the ground beneath her.

"I came from your head," she uttered. "You made me, River."

"No," he said, his voice cracking. "Natsuki, you made me."

"Then why are you afraid? What did I do wrong?"

River's chest tightened. "I'm not afraid."

"Ngh!" Natsuki screamed. "Augghhhhh!"

"Wait!" River clawed frantically at the earth. His hands passed through her like smoke. "Wait!"

River snatched, but she fell through his fingers.

And then there was nothing.

River glared at the patch of empty floor. All he could see was dirt.

The whirr of a helicopter's engines filled the air. A glowing police vehicle lowered itself onto the roof.

But River ignored it. He stared at the ground, and screamed.

"Augghhhhh!" River yelled, as he seized the vending machine. "Augghhhhhhhhhh!"

"River, keep it down," said Jazz, glancing over her shoulder. "We don't want to get arrested."

"It's like, midnight," Jake pointed out. He looked at the deserted platform. "Not many commuters at this hour."

"It's stuck!" River cried, tugging furiously at the panel. "It's like it's glued!"

Jake and Jazz looked at each other. They knew what their friend was going to find.

"Kuuuuuuuu!" River seethed, as his knuckles whitened. "Nghhhhhhh!"

"Let me help you," Jake offered, stepping forward. He took hold of the door. "Ready? One! Two! Three! Augghhhhh!"

The plastic cover was ripped from its hinges, and a cluster of cans trundled onto the platform. River gazed at the black nothingness behind the drinks.

He dropped his head. Defeated.

Jake looked at his friend. He drifted closer, and took his hand. "I'm sorry," he whispered.

"The House was sustained by the vapour," Jazz stated. "Now that it's gone-"

"I know. Like Spencer. Like Natsuki. And every fucking thing that's ever frightened me."

Jake and Jazz glared at him, unsure what to say.

299

"To be honest," said River, finally. "I'm not sure what I was hoping for. Part of me just thought…" He broke off.

Jake squeezed his hand. "I know."

River turned to go, but his two friends held back.

"Guys, there's no point in staying," said River. "Everything's gone."

Jake looked puzzled. "Are you sure though?" he asked. "Something doesn't feel right."

"No, it's fucked up. But the House doesn't exist anymore. Accept it."

"Hang on," Jazz pressed. "There was that picture of you, in the book. A picture of you and Spencer."

"Yeah," said River. "The prophecy. We fulfilled it. And we'll never know what the rest of it says because we can't translate it. Maybe the Boss couldn't either, because he had no idea about Natsuki and what she was."

"No, you're right, Jeff," Jake added. "Later on. There was a picture of River and Spencer with a boy in a cape."

"What are you talking about?" River rebutted. "Me and Spencer never met a boy in a cape! You're not remembering it right!"

"Ahem!" said a voice. It bounced across the platform. "You are not remembering it *correctly*. Work on your English, River Still."

River's eyes widened. He couldn't believe what he was hearing. It was impossible. He was losing his mind.

"Only she *is* remembering it correctly," the voice continued. "It just hasn't happened yet."

Spencer von Luft waddled into view. He straightened his Bavarian hat, and grinned. "You'd write me off that easily, would you?" he chortled. "Unacceptable."

Jake and Jazz exploded in joyous screams and raced towards him. River looked on, stunned.

"I'm too young to die," Spencer quipped. "In fact, I'm brand new. I'm not quite ready to hang up my brushes."

River's mouth was hanging open. "Spencer, how did you…?" He couldn't find the words. "I mean, why aren't you dead?"

"Well, I faded away," his friend answered. "Like the House, I was sustained by the Boss' vapour. I couldn't survive without it."

River frowned. "Then how can you be here?"

Spencer cocked his head. "Are you disappointed?"

"You know what I mean."

Spencer chuckled. "You bipeds may have misread the prophecy, but one thing was always abundantly clear. The psychic vapour would eventually dissipate, and I would fade from existence. Which is exactly what happened."

"So what are you saying?" asked Jake. "You're a ghost?"

"Hardly. What do you think of my new body?" Spencer raised his wing, and there was a subtle whirr. "Real feathers, at last."

"Your wing!" Jake exclaimed. "It made a noise!"

"Very observant. You can come again."

"Real feathers," River muttered, looking closely. "A mechanical wing." He glowered at his friend. "Spencer, are you a robot?"

Spencer chortled playfully, and winked.

"But you can't be," River replied. "You're a parrot. You can't be a robot."

Spencer tutted. "Do I detect a hint of cyberphobia?"

"No, Spencer, just-" River stammered. And then he sighed, despairingly. "Please help me understand."

"It was Natsuki," said Spencer. "When she learned that my days were numbered, she agreed to build me a new body. She transferred my memories into its shell. Easy, ja?"

"Oh yeah," Jake quipped. "Memory transfer. That's, like, kindergarten stuff."

"So," said Spencer, with a twinkle in his eye. "If I may be permitted to hang out with the squad for a little longer? That would be – how would you say? That would be dope?" He gestured with his wing. "That would be sick, bro?"

River chuckled. A tear rolled out of his eye.

"Now then, where is Natsuki?" said Spencer, gazing across the station. "She should be celebrating with us."

River looked at the floor, saying nothing.

Spencer gazed at him. "River?" he asked. "What is it?"

27: her

The Singing Gardens looked beautiful in the morning sun. River sat, cross-legged, next to a small wooden stub, the breeze rippling through his hair. All around him, the pink trees hummed as their shimmering medallions caught the slow-moving air, and River sighed peacefully, almost meditative in the tranquil surroundings.

He visited the gardens often. In the first month, he came to Natsuki's grave almost every day; he felt indebted. And he felt sad. And he felt a longing.

He cried a lot during those first visits. There was so much he wanted to say, but he didn't know how, or if he even could. Or should.

Spencer helped. "Just talk," he said. "Nothing is better left unsaid."

The idea seemed crazy at first. What would be the point? Natsuki existed only in his mind, now.

But Spencer was right, of course. Over the weeks, he got better at talking. By the second month, he stopped crying and started opening up. Sometimes he just told jokes to himself. And laughed at them.

On one particular day, he built up the courage to look at the medallion – the insignia of the two dragons. It sat at the base of the cube, held down by a cluster of coloured pebbles. He touched the emblem and muttered something under his breath.

And then, when he opened his eyes, he saw her. She sat next to him on the grass, and held his hand.

"I'm listening," she whispered.

River took a deep breath. "It wasn't you, you know. You didn't do anything wrong. It was what you represented."

"What do you mean?" she asked.

"Closeness. As soon as you started wanting me, I got scared. I needed you out of the way."

"That's so sad..."

"Don't pity me," he snapped. "It's fine. It's funny, actually. You're part of me. Yet you're nothing like me."

"I'm exactly like you, River. You've just forgotten."

River shook his head. "I don't have your faith."

302

"It's in there somewhere. It's buried. Even the Boss couldn't see it."

River fondled the medallion of the two dragons and sighed. "Too far down for him to detect."

"Do you still think there's nothing?"

River thought for a moment. "No. There's lots. I just haven't found it yet."

"Well, the Boss thought he was a god. Perhaps he was. Perhaps that's your answer."

River shook his head. "Gods are all-knowing. The Boss wasn't. He couldn't foresee his own death. He was too arrogant to believe that he could die."

"It was a question he never asked," Natsuki added.

"Exactly."

Natsuki let go of his hand, and stood. "There's a question you're not asking, too."

"Go on."

"Why did we meet? Why did I walk into your life?"

River shrugged. "You're one of my fears, taken from me as I slept. I guess I woke before the House could take you."

"Then why did the app bring us together?"

"I don't know. It was probably just a glitch."

"River," said Natsuki. "All this time, a greater force has been at work. And it still is. You can sense it."

"But what?"

Natsuki started to walk. "Look for it, River Still."

"Wait," he called out, standing up. "Where are you going?"

Natsuki stopped. "Nowhere, River," she smiled. "I am not leaving."

And then she faded.

River dropped his head, frustrated.

He wanted answers. He wanted the pain to go away. It felt like it never would.

Eventually he left, and followed the winding path towards the sound of giggles. As he neared the picnic bench, the sight of Jake, Jazz and Spencer shifted into view. Jake was modelling a tall and lop-sided sandwich in the palm of his hand, its contents compressed into a sloppy, disintegrating bun. He was talking with all the excitement of a man who'd just found a treasure chest.

"So, the secret is to apply the maple syrup first," Jake enthused, "rather than drizzle it on after. So, you fry the bacon in the sauce – and that's meatless bacon, bro. You've then got the soybean patty, the

303

smashed avocado, the lettuce, and finally the chopped red chillies. Oh, and a slice of dairy-free cheese."

Jazz looked curiously at her twin's concoction. "So this sandwich is vegan?" she enquired.

"Of course it's vegan," said Jake. "Who's going to buy it otherwise?"

"Hey," said River, as he slipped onto the bench. "Room for one more?"

"You might want to come back in ten minutes," Jazz warned. "My brother's about to enact a mass poisoning, and we don't expect any survivors."

"Come now, Jazz," Spencer interjected. "I think the mookerjee burger is inspired."

Grinning, Jazz pulled out her camera, and quickly focused on the hastily-arranged sandwich. "This is my brother, ladies and gentlemen. Masterchef-turned-mass-murderer. This burger contains pretty much every ingredient in existence – except meat – so even if you die after consumption, you'll be helping the planet."

Jake ignored her. He and Spencer were fixated on the mushy burger as he lifted it to his lips, and took the historic first bite. Jake frowned as he chewed the soybeans, syrup and chillies around his mouth, as if he were somehow unnerved by what he'd created.

"Okay, you saw it here first, people," Jazz continued. "This is how Jake Thrower met a sticky end. And for that, I blame the syrup."

Jake, still engrossed, muttered at Spencer with a mouthful of mookerjee. "The sweetness of the syrup really offsets the sharpness of the chillies."

"A truly sumptuous discovery," Spencer chimed, taking the burger in his wing. "The wonders of the biped world know no bounds."

"Spencer, how can you even eat anything?" Jazz quizzed. "You're a robot."

"Would you like me to explain the particulars of my digestive system?"

"No," River exclaimed. "That won't be necessary."

"Which reminds me," Spencer went on. "I discovered a charming dessert bar in Netherville – purveyor of the most perfect papaya sundae. It would make an excellent follow-up to the burger."

"Yeah, get stuck in, guys," Jake enthused, digging his hand into the picnic basket. "There's plenty more where this came from."

"Actually, I think I'll stick to the sundae," said Jazz, springing to her feet. "Anyone fancy a trip?"

"Yes please," said River, before she'd even finished speaking.

"Aww geez," Jake sighed. "I made, like, ten burgers. What am I gonna do with them?"

Jazz smirked. "Do you really want me to tell you?"

It was funny how different Neo Vale looked these days. Without the fog, River had a greater appreciation for its streets – in all their graffitied, litter-strewn, vomit-covered glory. The lights and the trams and the shops with their block-letter signs and posters glistened in the unfiltered sun. River breathed in the colours as he and his friends descended into the subway; this place, too, now had an energy, a buzz. It was probably his imagination, but he could have sworn that people were smiling more, and there was a distinct patter of conversation as he and his friends lined up on the platform.

A train cruised into the station, its passengers rammed into the carriages like sardines. Spencer chuckled. "Well, at least there's space on the roof."

"I think we'll get the next one," River replied. "I'm not *that* desperate for a papaya sundae."

Jake nudged his friend in the ribs. "Dude," he muttered. "Try not to look, but the woman in that carriage is staring daggers at you."

"Which woman?" said River, turning his head.

"I said don't look!"

Spencer's eyes widened. "Good gracious," he whispered. "It can't be."

"Spencer, what is it?" said Jazz. "What have you seen?"

"It's her," the parrot answered. "On the train. She's seen us."

"Yeah, that lady does not look happy," Jake remarked.

Spencer looked at his friends. "You know who that is, don't you?"

"Lady Reason," Jazz gasped. "But how? How can she be here? And why is she looking at us?"

"She's not," said River coldly. "She's looking at me. And she is not Lady Reason."

"But of course she is," Spencer insisted. "I never forget a face."

"Spencer, I'm telling you, it's not her," said River. He gulped. "And her name is not Reason. It's Roseann."

Jake looked at him. "Roseann? How the hell do you know that?"

The train pulled away. The woman continued to stare.

"Because I've met her before." River looked at his friends. "She's my mother."

First published in 2021 by
Skerratt Media
www.skerratt-media.co.uk

Copyright © Alex Skerratt 2021

ISBN: 978-0-9927703-7-2

Illustration of River and Spencer by Rhiannon Hughes at The
Yorkshire Wordwright.

Thanks to my wonderful proof-readers, Sarah Blackshaw and Sarah
Skerratt. Any remaining errors are my fault!

Thanks to Michelle Smallshaw (my Year 5 English teacher!) for
supporting this project financially.

Thanks to my writing buddy Hannah Strachan for the coffees and good
company.

Printed in Great Britain
by Amazon